The Salome Dancer

The Salome Dancer

The Life and Times of
Maud Allan

by Felix Cherniavsky

Canadian Cataloguing in Publication Data

Cherniavsky, Felix.
   The Salome dancer : the life and times of
Maud Allan

Includes bibliographical references and index.
ISBN 0-7710-1957-2

1. Allan, Maud. 2. Dancers – Canada – Biography.
I. Title.

GV1785.A55C54 1991   792.8′092   C91-093261-1

McClelland & Stewart Inc.
The Canadian Publishers
481 University Avenue
Toronto, Ontario
M5G 2E9

This book has been published with the help of a grant from the
Canadian Federation for the Humanities, using funds provided
by the Social Sciences and Humanities Research Council of
Canada.

Printed and bound in Canada by John Deyell Company

Contents

To Eva,
for Natasha, Ben, and Alex,
and in fond memory of my father Mischel, his brothers Jan
and Leo, and their sister Manya.

"Maud was not insane, but she had an imagination beyond the reach of others."

– Manya Cherniavsky, July 1980

Acknowledgements

To acknowledge my debts, professional, practical, and personal in the writing of this biography would require a volume in itself. The help I have received from libraries, newspapers, research institutions, and similar sources of information from all five continents has been incredible; I can only thank one and all.

The practical support has been equally gratifying. I owe a special thanks to both Lacey McDearmon, Curator of the Dance Collection, Research Center for the Arts, New York Public Library, for recommending my first article to *Dance Chronicle* and to the Editors of that Journal, for their expertise in preparing all five articles, the genesis of this biography, for publication.

My greatest practical debt is to the Social Sciences and Humanities Research Council of Canada for funding two extensive Research trips and for awarding me handsome stipends for the writing of *The Salome Dancer*. It, rather than words of thanks, best demonstrates my appreciation of the Council's support. I am also much indebted to the Canada Council and to the Alberta Foundation for the Literary Arts for providing funds to cover the last stages of preparation of this volume.

My personal debt defies definition, for it extends far beyond the normal contours of authorship. It ranges from those innumerable members – and friends – of the Cherniavsky family who knew and, better than most, understood Maud Allan, to many individuals whose friendship has over the years and in so many indirect and different ways made possible the writing of this work. I owe a particular thanks to Charis Wahl, whose editorial skills and insights have proven so helpful. My greatest debt is, of course, to my immediate family, without whose faith, hope – and love – I could never have completed this project.

Introduction

For biographers, whether their purpose is to promote and reveal or to research and revive, the lives and careers of stage persons provide rich material. Few biographers, however, have such wealth as that provided by the career and anguished private life of Maud Allan, "the Salome Dancer."

The name of this Canadian-born dancer is familiar only to modern dance historians; yet during the first two decades of this century Maud Allan was a living legend, as famous for the beauty of her "dance interpretations" as she was notorious for the haunting power of her chef d'oeuvre, *The Vision of Salome*. Her career reached its apex in March 1908, when, at the age of thirty-five, she made her London debut at The Palace Theatre of Varieties. For eighteen months of intoxicating triumph she was hailed as an artist of enthralling grace and charm, able to make visual the very essence of a Chopin waltz or those perennial favourites in her repertoire, Mendelssohn's *Spring Song* and Anton Rubinstein's *Valse caprice*. She became the darling of society and the idol of critics. To the public at large she was the Salome Dancer, an epithet that reflected the world-wide renown of her passionate, artistic performance of *The Vision of Salome*.

Her conquest of London was phenomenal – and a fluke: phenomenal because it had such a multifaceted (albeit transitory) effect; a fluke because, though Maud's dance interpretations embodied the prevailing ideals of artistic elegance and expression, the daring of *The Vision of Salome* toyed with the repressed imagination of the time. Her audiences marvelled at her dance interpretations, yet were mesmerized by *The Vision of Salome*. Little did they realize that Maud performed this twenty-minute work (and to a lesser degree others, such as Chopin's *Marche funèbre*) with such passionate conviction to sublimate her guilt and grief for the execution, ten years earlier, of her beloved brother Theo Durrant. Theo's execution in San Francisco's San Quentin Prison for "the Crime of a Century" permanently traumatized Maud's psyche, conscience, and boundless imagination.

In mid-April 1895, barely two months after Maud's departure to study music in Berlin, Theo murdered two young women in the church that they and the Durrant family attended. From the moment of his arrest until nearly three years later, when he mounted the gallows with awesome self-control, Theo, obviously not guilty by reason of insanity, held centre stage as San Francisco's most hated criminal. Throughout the affair he was championed by his mother with a vigour bordering on the obscene. Driving his expert legal counsel to the extremes of their profession, Isabella Durrant fought to the very last minute to "get life" for her beloved son.

Theo forbade Maud to return home from Berlin. Haunted by the family disgrace, yet passionately devoted to the source of that disgrace, Maud developed an impenetrable mask of propriety and discretion. In later years it is doubtful that Maud herself could differentiate between that mask and her real self. Certainly no one else could, which is one reason she remained so interesting.

Shortly before her brother's execution, Maud described herself in an article for the *San Francisco Examiner* as "a bright girl with winning ways and a cheerful disposition, considered beautiful of figure and form." Following his execution, while she retained her grace and charm and exercised her artistic talents in a totally creative fashion, there evolved a deeply troubled individual, ever on guard lest anyone perceive her relationship with Theo, her feelings about his fate, and, most distressing, the role she persuaded herself she had played in bringing about that fate.

Unforgiving of society for executing her brother and for making her a murderer's sister, she became increasingly ruthless, manipulative, and selfish. To those who knew her secret, her pathos made her all the more appealing. In her old age, when she communicated more by gesture than by word, she could barely hide an underlying instability similar to that which had afflicted, to a far greater degree, her brother.

In her thirst for more of the fame and fortune she had enjoyed in London, between 1910 and 1923 Maud toured – with conspicuously declining success – all five continents. The longest and best documented of these tours was that of India, Asia, and Australasia made between 1913 and 1915 with the Cherniavsky Trio, which comprised my late father and his two older brothers; Maud was infatuated with the eldest. The record of this fifteen-month tour provides a unique view of Maud Allan and of the conditions artists touring in those regions endured more than seventy-five years ago. Her two tours of North America, in 1910 and 1916, lurched between conquest and humiliation, the courageous and the comic. Her personal papers and the reminiscences of her companions provide unique accounts of these and of her briefer tours.

The record of 1895 to 1908, years spent in Europe first as a student and then as an aspiring dancer, is equally colourful and dramatic. Her diaries provide a vivid account of her studies and life in Berlin, her vacations, her personal relationships – including her first serious liaison – and her anguish as she read the despairing letters of her mother and the self-deceiving and for the most part deliberately cheerful letters of her incarcerated brother.

In the fall of 1901, after a summer in Weimar as a member of Ferruccio Busoni's master class, Maud abandoned the piano and, at the age of twenty-eight, suddenly decided to take up dancing. Having concluded that a career as a concert pianist was impossible, she became a dancer by default, in despair rather than by design. The most remarkable consequence of her decision is that she enjoyed a success, albeit brief, such as neither she nor her beloved mother could have imagined had she pursued her original goal. The last twenty-five years of her life were spent in a stately decline, as she wrote in a draft letter of April 1949, "from affluence and a beautiful home and honour [in London] to a small ugly room without proper conveniences [in Los Angeles]." Retaining to the end her "queenly dignity," as Theo once termed it, she never openly pined for the past – of which, clearly, she was a prisoner both as an artist and as a murderer's sister.

What she might have accomplished with her profound musicality and rich imagination had her brother never committed murder is a tantalizing enigma. Thus, throughout this biography there runs the leitmotif of an unusual and profoundly human aspect of an ever-contentious issue: the effect of capital punishment on the caring next of kin.

Without question Theo's tragedy was the mainspring of Maud's career as a dancer. It inspired those dramatic dance interpretations (such as the *Marche funèbre*, *Valse triste*, and "Aase's Death" from *Peer Gynt*) in which the theme of death was more than peripheral as well as those wonderfully joyous dances (such as the *Valse caprice*, the *Blue Danube*, and *Dance of the Sugar Plum Fairy*) in which innocence, such as Maud lost forever with Theo's execution, was so compellingly recreated. It was the source of the dual personality that, over the years and in spite of her utmost efforts to hide it, became so plain and so pathetic to her close friends. It explains, too, the intensely personal nature of her art that makes so vague her place in the evolution of modern dance.

Her successful career as a dancer was, in fact, as fortuitous and almost as short-lived as her conquest of London.

Yet her fame (some would say notoriety), which briefly exceeded that of Isadora Duncan, Loie Fuller, and Ruth St. Denis, her three well-remembered contemporaries, and her performance, far more musically sophisticated than that of these three, has been overlooked, misunderstood, or ignored by dance historians, who tend to dismiss it as extraneous to their studies. In a sense they have every right to such an attitude, because Maud Allan was convinced that her art was unique and, therefore, inimitable.

If the source of her art was so intensely personal, so was her understanding of the art itself. Although her highly disciplined movements reflected very precise responses to music, her dancing style seemed spontaneity itself, so that to all but the most musically knowledgeable of her admirers it seemed refreshingly impulsive. Such an impression was no illusion. Nothing was further from her mind than prescribed choreography; her movements were *designed* to be spontaneous. The fusion of her profound musicality with her rich imagination was the rationale of her dancing.

Unique and personal as her art may have been, it was nevertheless influenced by tradition and a socio-cultural movement. Isadora Duncan, Maud's precursor by a few years, had been the first to link her "classical" style to that of ancient Greece. Although Maud stubbornly denied any debt to her fellow San Franciscan, she readily acknowledged her own extensive study of Greek art (although, unlike Duncan, she never travelled to Greece). The debt, or at the very least the relation to, Isadora Duncan was so obvious that it is little wonder that a few contemporary critics and numerous dance historians have dismissed her as one of Duncan's many followers. In so doing, however, they have overlooked her indisputable uniqueness.

The most effective and acclaimed aspects of Maud's dancing were as well influenced by two contemporaneous schools of aesthetics. The first of these and the more difficult to demonstrate was the acting style of Eleonora Duse. Early in her career, Maud and Duse shared a Berlin theatre for a month, and many years later Maud paid Duse revealing tribute. The other influence was that of the artists and writers known as the Decadents. Their fascination with the hitherto unmentionable (such as inhibited feelings), perverse, or morbid aspects of human experience mirrored the themes that attracted Maud as an artist and as an individual.

One of the more peculiar aspects of her altogether peculiar career is that virtually all her international fame can be related to her "conquest" of Edwardian London. Before her London debut she had enjoyed far greater success on the Continent than has been realized, but that success had centred on her daring and innovative performance of *The Vision of Salome* and was, in effect, a *succès de scandale*. Had she remained on the Continent, her career would probably have been short-lived; most certainly she would not have earned the fortune she made in London. Had she left the Continent for the United States (where her mother lay in waiting), she would have all too quickly fallen by the wayside. Without a London success to give it critical respectability, *The Vision of Salome* would have been unpardonably offensive to American morals; Maud's relationship to the infamous Theo Durrant would have added to the offence. She would have attracted notoriety rather than the respectability she so determinedly projected – and sought as a mask – throughout her life.

Of the many "classical" dancers of the times only Isadora Duncan, Loie Fuller, and Ruth St. Denis are familiar to all but dance historians. Each contributed to the liberation of formal dance movement, which by the end of the nineteenth century had become fossilized. Each, through their schools, influenced the evolution of modern dance. None, however, approached Maud Allan's success in London; and none has fallen into such comparable obscurity.

There are two main reasons for this paradox. The first strikes at the very root of Maud's view of dancing, which in her autobiography of 1908 she defines as "the art of poetical and musical expression." Although she rightly insists that such a definition was nothing new, her interpretation of it surely was; for her sole objective as a dancer was to direct all her creativity to the goal of musical expression. Dancing per se was of minimal interest to her other than as a means of giving expression to her response to music. This is evident in her constant – one might say arrogant – assertion that she never received formal dancing instruction and, more significantly, rarely practised. The following statement, from her autobiography, describes her early days of "research and experiment": "It was not sufficient to master a pose, and rest content with that; nothing was more difficult than to weave harmonious, musical connection between the different poses so that there should be no break, so that there should be nothing to mar the rhythmic sense of continuous harmonious expression. It was my endeavour to disperse rhythm harmoniously to the tips of fingers and toes."

Other dancers of the time may have subscribed to the same goal, but none had Maud's musicality or, for that matter, her musical education; certainly none so expertly or so zealously pursued that goal to the exclusion of everything else. Maud's pursuit, however successful, led her away from the mainstream of twentieth-century dance.

The other reason for the paradox is that her conquest of London was in large part due to factors extraneous to her performance as a dancer. London audiences, unlike those in Vienna and Berlin, were not particularly interested in dance. (Isadora Duncan attracted little attention when she first performed there in 1900.) Yet Maud's debut set "all London" agog, and it so remained for more than a year. So intense was her success that she became world famous (in those days success in London carried enormous weight, especially throughout the Empire), even though subsequently and with the exception of San Francisco, her home town, her critical and popular success never approached her conquest of London. In effect, she personified the very ethos of late-Edwardian London; when that ethos changed with the death of King Edward VII in 1910, her career was doomed. (Early in 1914 my father, at the age of nineteen, impetuously told her that her success in London "was only a fluke and no clothes made her name." He spoke closer to the truth than such rudeness would suggest.)

That Edwardian ethos may be summarized in the prevailing concept of beauty, so well exemplified in the figure of Queen Alexandra, Consort of King Edward VII. Although by no means a leading light in London's cultural or social worlds, Queen Alexandra served as a model of Edwardian style and taste. Beauty was seen in her appearance rather than in her person, in her posture rather than in her physique; because of her station in life and the conventions of the day, she was perceived as the epitome of elegance and grace.

Maud Allan was perceived in much the same way, but with one radical difference, particularly as the Salome Dancer. Her charm and elegance had the special stamp of her personal aura; in her performance of *The Vision of Salome* she projected unmistakable sexuality, which the daring of the Salome costume, her bare feet, and her painted toenails emphasized.

Sexuality had yet to come out of the closet except in its association with the *femme fatale* of the Decadent movement – that ever-young beauty, exotic and fascinating, who seduces, exploits, and, at her whim, discards men she attracts or is attracted to. As Salome, Maud at least suggested and at most personified the *femme fatale*. As a "great" dancer, which is how she saw herself, her sexuality was restrained in keeping with her view of dance interpretations as reflections of deepest personal feelings, as creations of a boundless imagination directed to "disperse rhythm harmoniously to the tips of fingers and toes." The sexuality of the *Spring Song* or the *Valse caprice* was surely the innocent antithesis of the sexuality of Salome, yet it was sexuality.

A similar dichotomy is apparent in Maud Allan's private life. Behind her natural grace, her mysterious charm, her extraordinary musicality, and her undeniable sexuality was a very unhappy person, permanently wounded by the death of her brother and determined to get even with society for inflicting that wound. Whether it was her intention, her life demonstrates that for many of her friends and all her lovers she was the *femme fatale* incarnate.

1

The Early Years: 1873–1895

$\mathscr{O}$N THE SUMMER of 1908, to one of those lavish garden parties for which Edwardian London was famous came a handsome, youthful-looking woman, dressed fashionably with parasol and fan, wide-brimmed hat and billowy dress. She was instantly surrounded by admirers, many prominent in public life, the arts, and society. Speaking with calculated preciseness and modulation, she exchanged greetings and pleasantries with disarming ease, transfixing her entourage with a radiant presence, a winning smile, and large, widely spaced, liquid eyes that, unless provoked, appeared to see only the good and the beautiful.

At a suitable pause in the conversation, the lady excused herself and crossed the expansive lawns. The toast of London, supposed by many to be the king's "latest," she acknowledged courtly bows and smiles of recognition. She made her way towards three gentlemen talking by an artificial pond in which masses of water lilies bloomed. The tallest of the three was in his thirties, an immaculately dressed, sensual-looking individual. He straightened his relaxed posture, pulled back his shoulders, and waited. One of his companions lost himself amongst the frock coats and top hats, the parasols and silks; the other hovered, determined to witness the events in the offing.

The lady glided up to the tall gentleman and contemptuously hissed a gross insult. The gentleman snapped back, "But your brother was a murderer!" Visibly paling and betraying her pain and fury, the lady raised her hand and struck the gentleman across the face with her fan. Then, as if she had honoured rather than assaulted him, she regally turned and rejoined her admirers.

The lady was Maud Allan, whose sensational debut earlier in the year as the Salome Dancer had made hers a household name. She was also the sister of Theodore Durrant, executed in California's San Quentin Prison on January 7, 1898, as the perpetrator of the apparently motiveless murder of two young women.

The gentleman was Lord Alfred Douglas, erstwhile intimate of Oscar Wilde, who was imprisoned in 1895 (at the time of Theodore Durrant's sensational trial) for practising "the love that dare not speak its name." Douglas had affectionately translated Wilde's cult play *Salome* into English from the original schoolboy French. Holding him, as editor of the *Academy*, responsible for that magazine's recent questioning of the legitimacy of her art and success, Maud Allan's anger had got the better of her discretion.[1]

In *My Life and Dancing*, published four months later, she never lost her composure: the autobiography concealed those uncomfortable truths with which Lord Alfred was by extraordinary chance familiar. She represented her parents as medical doctors in Toronto who had raised the family in considerable affluence. Her fond memories – of the fat, good-natured cook, who would chase the teasing children from the kitchen, and of their nurse, who would talk and scold while needlessly mending the horrible rents in Maud's pinafores and stockings – were meant to elicit similar recollections in her readers, most of whom, Maud could reasonably suppose, came from comparable, if English, backgrounds.

In truth, Maud Allan's affluent childhood was a figment of her rich imagination.

Thomas Durrant, farm-hand, was born in the village of Holt in Norfolk. In 1845, Thomas brought his wife Mary and his young family to Canada. The family settled in Toronto, where Thomas became a shoemaker. William Allan Durrant, Maud's father, was born. When he left school, William took up his father's trade.[2]

Maud makes no mention of her mother's background. However, according to an account published in 1895 (when Maud's brother was very much in the public eye), Isabella Durrant was the adopted daughter of a Mrs. Dredger of Toronto. Raised a Baptist, Isabella was, according to this account, "so full of life and merry making, that she left Mrs. Dredger at an early age and got a job at the Charles and Hamilton shoe factory in Toronto."[3] There she met William Durrant, to whom she was married on June 30, 1870. The marriage certificate records her name as Isa Matilda Hutchinson, born in Oakville, Ontario, on October 12, 1853.

Her adoptive mother may have seen no need and been under no obligation to change Isabella's legal name to Dredger from Hutchinson, if indeed Hutchinson was her family name.

For years the belief prevailed in San Francisco that Maud was the natural daughter of Adolph Sutro, a highly imaginative German-Jewish engineer, music lover, flamboyant patron of the arts, and the mayor of San Francisco from 1895 to 1897. However, the Durrants' marriage certificate and the birth certificate of Maud (1873) and Theo (1871) do not support this story. Far more probably, Sutro was Isabella's natural father and thereby Maud's grandfather.

Born in 1830, Adolph Sutro emigrated from Prussia to the United States and in 1851 settled in California. He married in 1856 and had six legitimate children. At the time of Isabella's birth in 1852, Sutro would have been a twenty-two-year-old bachelor. Moreover, Sutro's marriage of twenty-three years came to a precipitous end when his wife tired of her husband's infidelity. At the International Hotel in Virginia City, where Sutro had extensive mining interests, Mrs. Sutro physically attacked the "trim little figure" of her husband's mistress, Mrs. George Allen, locally known as "the $50,000 diamond widow."[4]

This attack occurred in 1879; that year, Isabella and her two children left Toronto to join William, who had moved to San Francisco about three years earlier.

Sixteen years later, on July 25, 1895, the *San Francisco Chronicle* was reporting the first days of Theo's trial for murder. It printed the rumour that "Mrs. Durrant is the daughter of a well-known Placer County engineer." It is impossible to say how widespread this rumour was. It may have been temporarily quashed: in January 1895, Adolph Sutro had just been elected mayor of the city. However, on December 20, 1897, as lawyers were desperately trying to forestall Theo's execution for the fourth and last time, William Durrant indirectly referred to this rumour – one assumes unintentionally – as he "talked freely" to the *San Francisco Examiner* about the financing of Theo's enormously costly defence:

> Adolph Sutro has never advanced me a dollar in my life. I once went to him and asked for a position on his roads but I could not get it.
>
> The people talk about money. When this case began I had a house worth $4,500 and now that is gone. I have been assisted by my relatives to the last limit. Mrs. Durrant was never in Virginia City in her life.
>
> When we were in the midst of our trouble Mrs. Durrant was subjected to great annoyance in stores by being pointed out as Theodore's mother. In order to avoid this, she took the first part of my name and was known as Mrs. William Allan. When people heard that, they jumped to conclusions.[5]

Nothing is known of Mrs. George Allen other than that she predeceased Sutro, who bequeathed her $50,000 "in partial reparation for a 'false and malicious' charge brought at

Virginia City in 1879.''[6] Yet, given William's statement, the fact that Maud's mother was adopted, and Sutro's apparent interest in the welfare of the Durrant family, it is not unlikely that early in her relationship with Adolph Sutro, Mrs. George Allen gave birth to Maud's mother in 1852.

The only reason to propose such a link is to suggest the origin of Maud Allan's remarkable individuality and artistic gifts. Her natural charm and creativity, her willpower and shrewdness, her energy that, once aroused, knew no bounds, were traits shared by Adolph Sutro and Isabella Durrant. From her father Maud inherited her inscrutable expression and physique.[7] This may explain why, despite the praise lavished on her as a dancer and the admiration her grace aroused in any social setting, Maud was seldom acclaimed as physically beautiful. The movements of her hands and arms were magnificent, the expressiveness of her face was likewise celebrated; but she was too large-limbed – in spite of her poise – to be hailed a beauty. Maud's beauty lay in her grace of movement, in her mysterious aura, and in a striking physiognomy.

The latter is described by Maud in the opening paragraphs of a clumsily fictionalized autobiography she wrote in the late 1930s. The forty-page story opens with the sudden appearance of a woman at the San Francisco office of Dr. Herold. Gradually the doctor recognizes that his unexpected visitor is Octavia Lockburn, a celebrated dancer whom he had fruitlessly pursued around the world in his youth:

> He saw that she was regal in stature, over 5′6″, he guessed, and that her carriage was queenly. Her age baffled him, shrewd as he was, but it was the graceful flash of her glance which told him that here was a person beyond the categories of most womankind.
>
> Her brows were level and far apart, her eyes incredibly wide-spaced under a broad forehead over the corners of which her red-gold hair was arranged in becoming valences. Her nose was long, large, chiselled with macrometer

fineness; full-spread at the nostrils, a monument of a nose. She had high bones, hollow cheeks, eyes deeply recessed, and a firm flawless mouth that was of elemental compassion. He studied her generous, intensely mobile features which could light up all over in an instant without disturbing the flow of her words. Her enunciation had a continental precision. Her language was smooth, cultivated, coherent. Her voice was lovely, vibrant, musical. Her head was large and beautifully shaped.

Her smile was irresistibly winsome, gentle, and sweet. Her whole comport stamped her as the flower of a long line of gentle birth. Yet she had tremendous force within her, strength, resolution, judgement, and the gift of laughter.

Those who knew Maud Allan insist that this is an uncannily accurate description of her own appearance and personal aura.

That aura very nearly cost her dearly en route from Toronto to San Francisco. The six-year-old Maud was kidnapped when the train stopped at a wayside station and passengers got out to barter with the local native Indians. As Maud later recounted in *My Life and Dancing*: ". . . just as the train was pulling out of the station. There was a hurried search, but I was nowhere to be found. Instantly the conductor pulled back to the platform, and there, running off to the woods with a glint of flaxen hair under her arm discernible beneath the edge of a red blanket, was an Indian squaw with another red woman in her trail. My mother says it was the vivid colour of my hair flying in the wind that attracted the attention of my friends" (p. 29).[8]

The contrast between Toronto and San Francisco in the last quarter of the nineteenth century could scarcely have been greater. Toronto was as bland as its relentlessly dull landscape. San Francisco, though, was already a city of great charm and vitality, its high rocky elevations providing a scenic setting for the bay below. Thanks to its irregular topography, social and cultural enclaves rapidly developed. Telegraph Hill, the site since 1849 of a criminal colony known as Sydney Town, had evolved into a Latin quarter, where Spanish signs and sounds predominated. At the foot of Nob Hill, the site of grandiose homes built between 1857 and 1877 by mining and railway barons, Chinatown developed with temples, bazaars, picturesque colours, and opium dens.

Because of its great distance from the Eastern seaboard – the transcontinental railroad had opened only in 1869 – San Francisco relied on its own cosmopolitan population of some 240,000 for its social and cultural impetus. This rapid development was most effectively demonstrated in the quality of the city's many libraries, museums, and institutions of learning. In the 1880s, for example, there were four major libraries with more than half a million books among them, four established English-language and numerous foreign-language newspapers, at least six theatres, and several concert halls. The city's unorthodox site and equally unorthodox social and cultural fabric formed the perfect backdrop to the development of Maud Allan's varied talents.

Mrs. Durrant remarked in a letter written some twenty years later that, upon arriving in San Francisco in 1879, the family lived, slept, and ate in one room. By 1892, they owned a new two-storey stone-faced house on Fair Oak Street in the Mission, one of the city's oldest and most attractive residential areas. During the thirteen intervening years, William Durrant was, according to city directories, a "foreman" or an "operator" for three shoe manufacturers; in 1895, just before the arrest of Theo, he was unemployed and remained so for at least five years. Nevertheless, he – or was it his wife? – held the deed to a very comfortable house.

During those years Adolph Sutro bought large tracts of land in and around San Francisco and built his own estate within walking distance of the Mission. It is plausible that, either generously or under compulsion, he facilitated the Durrants' ownership of their Fair Oaks home. According to city directories of 1892 to 1894, Thomas and Mary Durrant, Maud's grandparents, lived on Point Lobos Avenue, on land owned by Sutro. By February 1895 they had moved to Los Angeles.

Maud's most vivid early memory of San Francisco was of the six months she and Theo spent in the Santa Rosa mountains overlooking the city; she was about ten years old. Sent there first for unspecified health reasons, probably the threat of tuberculosis, the children returned every summer. It was there that Maud learned to swim, to ride, to bicycle, and, as she so romantically expressed it in her autobiography, "to be in such perfect contact with nature, a joy hitherto unknown to me." It was there, too, surely, that she performed what she described to an interviewer many years later as "the most exciting dance I have ever danced" – or, perhaps, imagined:

> One morning, long ago, I climbed a fence and jumped down into a little hollow beneath. I heard a loud hissing and, looking down, I saw a huge rattler staring at me. I gave a scream and then realized I was standing upon its mates. For a moment I was paralyzed, and then I started to run; another snake and another sprang up. I realized at length I was in their breeding place and in another moment I was surrounded by literally hundreds of them. I danced here, I dodged there, and I ran with the brutes in full pursuit. But I ran faster than they, and at last a little stream crossed the wood, and I dashed across and they could no longer follow me. Yes, my most exciting dance was in that California forest, a long time ago.[9]

Whatever the purpose of this rhapsodic recollection, nothing suggests that the young Maud consciously responded more to movement than to music. As a student she shone at mathematics and geography, as an athlete she excelled at swimming. (She and Theo saved a mother and child from drowning in a fast-running stream in the Santa Rosa mountains.) She was a very skilful carver and clay modeller, had a natural talent for sketching, and was an expert seamstress. Her Berlin diaries reveal that she enjoyed social dancing, although, she insisted in later years, she never had dancing lessons. Possibly they were unnecessary, as her sense of rhythm was so keen, her grace so natural. She revelled in theatrical entertainment, from Sarah Bernhardt to Saturday matinees at the local vaudeville theatre, which she regularly attended with her brother.[10]

She was also, no doubt, caught up in the "living picture" craze that swept across the United States and to which the *San Francisco Chronicle* devoted an entire page on September 2, 1894. "The town's gone mad over the living pictures," began the article. "They have been setting the whole Eastern circuit by the ears, and now San Francisco is full of them." Living pictures may have been novel in the United States, but in Europe, where they were commonly known as *tableaux vivants*, they had long been a form of entertainment. About a century earlier, for example, Emma, Lady Hamilton, the mistress of Lord Nelson, was an enthusiast for the art of still-life "attitudes," held long enough to delight an audience to whom photographic, let alone colour, reproduction was unknown.

The subjects reproduced ranged from the pretty and respectable to the grotesque or obscene. Groupings, rather than single figures, were particularly popular as home entertainments, for they were far more challenging to design and great fun to mount. (Maud's Berlin diaries have several references to evenings of living pictures.) As the *Chronicle* article explained:

> Every church that ever struggled to pay off a mortgage has had 'em time and again. People seemed to think "Ruth and Boaz" and "Rebecca at the Well" rather a bore when they were seen on the pulpit steps with a green baize curtain for a background, but put them in a theatre, set the orchestra to playing instead of the organ – and presto – Ruth and Boaz are treated to round after round of applause, and as to Rebecca, she's the hit of the performance.

The Tivoli [Theatre] pictures are really beautiful.

It's like going to an art exhibition to see them. Only it's rather more fun.

The lights and shades are exquisite, the music is nice, and then you're buoyed up by fear that there may be something exciting any minute.

There isn't – but you don't know that until the performance is over – and then you go out and say they are really charming, and you wonder why people should rave over them, as if they were some brand new kind of entertainment.

The orchestra plays the Mendelssohn "Spring Song" [to which Maud would dance at her debut in Vienna and to deafening acclaim in London five years later], the little blond boy pages pull back the curtains and the house comes down in a roar of thunderous applause.

Varied as her interests were, all was subjugated to her ultimate goal – to become a world-famous concert pianist. Her progress was extremely rapid thanks to her very keen ear, her profound musicality, and her diligence. By the age of thirteen she was playing in the homes of prominent citizens (including Adolph Sutro) as well as at church concerts. By 1892, when she was nineteen years old, she listed herself in the city directory as a music teacher.

Her remarkable talents, together with her winning ways, gained her a wide circle of admirers. During her last year of school a certain Mr. Thomas Dunn, a teacher, proposed to her. She refers to this incident in her diary and gives a somewhat distorted though engaging account of it in her autobiography.[11]

Shortly before she left for Germany in 1895 she rejected the more serious proposal of Jim Crossett, an engineer and Theo's close friend.[12] Maud's refusal of Jim proved a source of enduring anguish, evident in a diary entry of October 5, 1895, just after Maud had learned that Jim Crossett's grandmother had testified, professedly with the utmost reluctance, at Theo's trial. "I wonder," Maud wrote, "if I had engaged myself to Jim if it would have been better. I mean, would his Grandma have let it be known if she really saw Theo on April 3 [the day of Blanche Lamont's murder]? It would have been one witness the less for the people. Now, can I send Jim a birthday card as I had intended? I'm afraid I can't."

Women were captivated by Maud's gaiety, her warmth, and her abilities; her friends included both a humble laundry worker and May Cogswell, niece of the founder of the Cogswell Polytechnic Institute, which Maud attended for two years. Her lifelong confidante was Alice Lonnon (a stage name), daughter of "Pop" Perkins, a close family friend.

But Maud's most devoted companion was Theo:"When they were about fourteen or fifteen they would go to the matinee almost every Saturday afternoon and many people would remark about Theo carrying his sister's cloak and paying attention to little affectionate deeds of that kind, which showed the nature of the boy." So Mrs. Durrant recalled in an article in the *Examiner* on June 6, 1897, days before his scheduled execution. Always immaculately dressed, with a pompadour hair-style, little colour, and heavy lips, Theo was his father's spitting image. As a youngster he attended boarding school in London, Ontario, and visited San Francisco only during school holidays. By 1881, however, he was a student at Lincoln High School, San Francisco.

Until the press, aided by the chief of police, discovered and then invented tales of his secret life, Theo epitomized the model American youth. Unfailingly courteous and obedient, devoted to his close-knit family and endowed with the same personal charm as his sister, he worked part-time during the school year and full-time during the holidays. He was a diligent member of the National Guard.

The family were members of Emmanuel Baptist Church, a focus of their social and other activities. Both Maud and Theo were members of the church youth group, the Christian Endeavour Society; Theo was secretary in 1895. He was

also the congregation's assistant Sunday school superintendent and an obliging and skilful handyman around the
church. (These creditable associations with the church
would do him more harm than good later on.)

Following his graduation from Lincoln High School he
attended Stanford University but withdrew after one year,
probably for financial reasons. After briefly working full-
time for an architect he attended Cogswell Technical
College, whose principal later remarked that apart from
"his cleverness with his hands," Theo was "a somewhat
colourless pupil" who was allegedly "very fond of the
ladies," as the *Examiner* reported four days after his arrest.
At the urging of Dr. T.E. Clarke, a family friend, he
decided to study medicine. Dr. Clarke was anxious to enter
the ministry, and promised that Theo could take over his
practice. Theo should have graduated in October 1895.

Like his sister, Theo was extremely imaginative, iron-
willed, and diligent – his average in medical school was
reportedly 97 per cent. He seems to have been intellectually
inventive, in an undisciplined way, and, as if striving to keep
abreast of his sister's interests, held decided views on the
arts and artists. Yet he lived in his sister's shadow, for he had
little artistic bent, although he took pride in his sketching
skills and was an avid doodler.

At some time in his early twenties he fell desperately ill
for seven weeks. ("Why didn't I let him slip away that day,"
Isabella Durrant reflected in the *Examiner* article, "when he
was sinking so fast?" The press labelled the illness "brain
fever.") What lasting effects, if any, this illness had upon
Theo are unknown, but there is little doubt that he had
always been, intermittently or subtly, emotionally unstable.
As his mother was somewhat strange and his sister became
very strange, Theo may well have suffered from some unidentifiable family affliction. (Little is known of his father,
who seems to have played a peculiar but not necessarily
insignificant role in the family dynamics.)

A certain cast of mind in both father and son is apparent
in the following narrative. On February 4, 1895, some weeks

before the Emmanuel Church murders, Theo prepared a written statement for a police detective. (The first page was reproduced in the April 16, 1895 issue of the *Examiner*.) He had consulted the policeman on behalf of his father, who had been duped by a confidence man named Nicholson. Theo explained that his father had invested his life savings in a shoe factory, which he had been forced to sell within months. The rest of Theo's statement, partly paraphrased by a disbelieving *Examiner* journalist, reflects the characteristics of the principals.

Shortly after selling the business, so the *Examiner* explained:

> Mr. Durrant met a suave gentleman named Nicholson, who hung about the hide and leather business downtown, who commiserated him and told him he had once been in the same boat, but was now well fixed, thanks to a system of work he had found in the East. He suggested to the elder Durrant to convert his belongings into cash, go East with him and he would show him the way to get rich. Nicholson went east ahead of Durrant, who was to telegraph when he left [San Francisco]. This he did. The son tells the sequel as follows:
>
> "Father trusted him, his story was so well told and so plausible and did not press the point of what kind of a business it was, so after settling up all his debts here he had about $600 or $700 left, and with this he intended to go out and meet the man Nicholson at a place called South Bethlehem, near Philadelphia, Pa. Father arrived in Philadelphia December 20, 1894, and immediately procured a room in a [private] American family. After finding that the train for South Bethlehem left at 8 A.M. the following morning, and not thinking he could use checks as well as coin, Father drew his coin and kept it in the house overnight, intending to go right off the next morning.
>
> "During this night a robbery occurred at this house and the family claimed to have lost $4000 worth of diamonds and other valuables, also his money was taken and all the family

was found under the influence of some drug, it is said, at 10
A.M. the next morning, 21st December.

"After this, my father was ill for a week and unable to do
anything. The following week he wrote to South Bethlehem
to see if Nicholson was there, and received a reply that he
was. He went up there and told him of his misfortune. At
the story the man smiled and told him he was sorry for his
bad luck, but if he could get any more money he could easily
make up his losses, and he told him he wanted him to take
and handle counterfeit money, and if he would do so he
would pay his passage back to San Francisco.

"So, after finding out what a fool he had been in coming
on such a wild goose chase, he was so rattled with anger and
hard feelings toward the fellow that, after venting his anger
on him he left the place, neglecting in his hurry to put the
police on his track."

In the letter young Durrant expresses the belief that
Nicholson was implicated in the robbery. His reasons for
this belief show that he is a believer in dreams, signs and
omens, probably an inherited trait. He goes on to say:

"For that very night my mother had a dream of a man
walking stooped, and in appearance sneaky, and wearing an
old buff or snuff-coloured coat and slouch hat, and with all
the demeanour of a hard character, and wearing a sandy
moustache, pass our house as if in the act of looking for a
place of entrance; before the dream passed away the vision
transformed to the features of my father in the same attitude, thus connecting the two."

The man in the dream of course tallied with Durrant
Senior's description of Nicholson. Young Durrant adds: "I
have often heard of dreams being connected with incidents.
Haven't you? What do you think of that?"

At this time Theo was twenty-four years of age.

William Durrant's deportment during his son's trauma
was puzzling. Theo displayed, or so it was perceived, a
chilling indifference to the horrors of the crime; his mother
displayed a passionate conviction in her son's innocence. Mr.

Durrant, "his wife's shadow," was widely reported to be in an aimless daze, although patiently seated by his son's side and evidently mindful of his wife's determination that her son escape the gallows. Moreover, any man able and willing, as Durrant was, to witness his son's execution may safely be termed extraordinary, as is any son who, like Theo, made such a request.

Among Maud's extant papers are some dozen letters from her father, all but three addressed jointly to his wife and daughter in Germany. (Isabella arrived in the summer of 1900 for a stay of about eighteen months.) These letters are dull in content but, with an occasional burst of bravura, determinedly cheerful in spirit, as are the bulk of Theo's letters to Maud. (Theo's letters, which fluctuate between the simple and the authoritarian, in addition suggest an excessive infatuation with both his sister and his mother.) Theo looked and behaved like his father, although of the two, the son was the cleverer, the better educated, and decidedly the more unbalanced.

Maud's diaries supplement the public record with passing glimpses of the two women's attitude towards the two men in the family. Isabella Durrant's letters nearly always reveal discreet, even condescending concern, as if it were mutually understood that William had – and posed – problem after problem. However, in a lost letter, which Maud received on July 25, 1895, she stepped beyond these habitual bounds, prompting Maud, that same evening, to write in her diary. "12:30 A.M. Oh! I am so unhappy. Poor Mama – why does dear Papa act so, why is he not more loveable to her, especially now when such trouble is in the house?"

Maud then goes on to place herself in this family picture: "Oh dear, if I only had the money to relieve them and be at the same time my own supporter. Oh how I hope in two years more I shall be able to 'come out' and make them proud of me and we can all be happy again. However, Mama must come just as soon as it is possible for her. Funerals are an attraction for children and the poorer classes."[13]

Elsewhere in her diary Maud mentions her father only on such occasions as his birthday, although at critical turns in Theo's trauma she records her concern for "my parents." Although she relegated her father to the background, she was not, consciously at least, hostile towards or suspicious of him. If there was little communication between father and daughter, she had been brought up to respect him. Even if his behaviour and business failures made it difficult for others to share that respect, Maud seems never to have questioned it.

Her relationship with her brother was, in contrast, intimate. Theo's tragedy made that intimacy intense because, in addition to her strong emotional ties, Maud became permanently enmeshed in guilt for not being in San Francisco at a time of Theo's great need. "I cannot alter matters nor am I to blame for anything, save that I could have remained at home and then he would have been with me," reads her diary of November 9, 1895. Three days later she asked herself, "Why was I not at home to be with him those fatal days?"

Underlying her feelings, moreover, was a distinctively solicitous attitude towards Theo, as if he required and their devoted mother demanded that in her affections Maud give Theo priority. Throughout her diary she regularly refers to "my poor brother," and on December 30, 1895, writes, "Poor child, to read of his class mates graduating and he not, is sad." Such trivia would have little significance were it not that Mrs. Durrant's attitude is very similar. In the first of her extant letters, for instance, she urges Maud to "do as I am doing – be brave and pray day and night for your poor brother." A few lines later she remarks, "Theo's exhibition of temper last night will do him no good, but you know him of old, whatever he has to say he will say at any cost." After Theo had been condemned to death, she remarked, "I am so afraid his health will break down." Given conditions in the jail, she may well have had his physical health in mind, but her ongoing attitude towards her beloved son would argue that her concern was for his mental health as well.

From their mother both Maud and Theo unquestionably inherited a boundless imagination that in Theo's case was tainted with insanity and, in Maud's was for its creativity, "far beyond the reach of others." Perceived by the local press throughout Theo's trauma as strange – with hints that she was perverse – Isabella was the dominant force in this closely knit family. Her devotion to her children, both of whom she held in emotional thrall, was obsessive, as manifest in her relentless efforts on her son's behalf and, in later years, her abiding and misplaced confidence in her daughter's future as a concert pianist.

By 1895, when she was twenty-two years of age, Maud's progress in music had been remarkable. Her teacher, Eugene Bonelli, director of the San Francisco Grand Academy of Music, recommended that she continue her studies in Germany. This seems to have been in accord with Isabella's long-standing plan: within six months of his graduation as a doctor, Theo, with his mother at his side, would follow Maud to Berlin, there to pursue post-graduate studies. With Mrs. Durrant keeping house, the happy trio would spend one year in Germany, touring the Continent during the summer with Theo as loving escort. William Durrant was to remain in San Francisco.

To complete musical studies in Germany was common practice. Although the cost was not prohibitive, for the Durrant family it surely demanded considerable sacrifice and indeed risk, given Mr. Durrant's serious business losses. For his iron-willed wife, however, the hardship was absolutely justified, both as a means of satisfying her ambitions for her daughter and for the joy of living in Berlin for a year with her two children. Questions, nevertheless, remain: did Maud have sufficient promise as a concert pianist to justify the sacrifice? Was Bonelli giving in to Mrs. Durrant's ambitions, or did he truly see in Maud an outstanding musician?

He surely must have been aware of her nervousness in performance. Whether she could ever have overcome this debilitating trait, undoubtedly caused or exacerbated by her mother's expectations and a factor in her later decision to abandon the piano for dancing, is a moot point, for the trauma of Theo's arrest, trial, and eventual execution radically altered her psyche. Yet Bonelli, to whom Maud later paid generous tribute, must have been awed by her musicality, as were so many other musicians who later knew her.[14] This gift, made mature by her studies in Berlin, was enriched by her association with distinguished musicians, who found in her an intelligently responsive listener and, in time, peer. The most distinguished of these was Ferruccio Busoni, world famous as a concert pianist, respected as a composer – his arrangement of Bach's *Chaconne* became a standard concert work – and revered as a pedagogue. He was also the most powerful musical influence on Maud's concept of "dance interpretations."[15] In extant letters Busoni marvels at Maud's musicality, as would many other musicians of later generations, although most saw her dancing more as a phenomenon than as art.[16]

Before Isabella and Theo were to arrive, Maud would receive a $30 monthly allowance. If possible, she was to give lessons in English or music or both in exchange for room and board. Theo undertook to supplement his sister's meagre allowance from his part-time earnings. While these financial arrangements would have been adequate to support the lifestyle of an unspoilt foreign student, money was always in short supply for Maud, through no fault of her own. For months at a time the promised monthly allowance did not materialize.

February 14, 1895: 6 A.M. Foggy. Started on my journey to Europe.

So opens Maud's diary, given to her that very morning by Theo. (She abandoned it three years later, some six weeks after his execution.) Apart from her parents and Theo, fourteen family friends gathered to bid her godspeed; among them was Minnie Williams, whose murder a few weeks later would so dramatically alter Maud's future and character. As she kissed Theo goodbye, Maud's parting words were "Be a good boy, dearie, and be sure to graduate."

Settling in for the long train journey to New York, she tried to strike up a conversation with her fellow passenger. Dr. David Conrad was en route to graduate medical studies in Freiburg; his mother was acting as Maud's chaperone. "Dr. Conrad very uncommunicative," Maud noted. "After hanging up his overcoat he settled down in one corner of his seat and proceeded to investigate his various railway guides and maps." When he later broke his silence, it was to express his views on women's rights. "He thinks their place is at home," wrote an obviously offended Maud, "or if they take one step, take all – war, for example." Gradually Dr. Conrad's reserve melted and he became worthy to appear, a few nights after journey's end, in Maud's dream.[17]

On February 26, Maud and the Conrads boarded the ss *Lahu* in New York. During the first half of the nine-day sea voyage to Bremen, Maud kept her diary, but then was laid low by foul weather. Years later, when the London press so eagerly published her "Memoirs," Maud recalled that storm with a mixture of humour and fantasy. Understandably she remained silent on the matter, but it is difficult to believe that in retrospect she would not have seen in the storm an omen of the terrifying experience that, within two months of her arrival in Berlin, would befall her. The wrenching effects of that long drawn out family trauma remained with her, unromanticized, for the rest of her life. They would shape the public Maud Allan, the Salome Dancer, and the very private individual, ever wary lest those effects be seen or known by the world at large.

Notes

Extracts from Maud Allan's autobiography, *My Life and Dancing* (London: Everett, 1908), are cited in the text.

1. Given her fame in London at the time, her determination to neither witness nor permit adverse criticism of her "art," and her hitherto unknown background, it is very likely that this incident, told as a legend in San Francisco seventy-five years later, is true.

2. The San Francisco *Call* of May 10, 1895, carried a report (from Los Angeles) titled "Ancestry of Durrant." The opening paragraphs read:

> A clipping from a San Francisco paper stating that Theodore Durrant was of Hungarian descent, was shown to Thomas Durrant, grandfather of the accused young man, today.
>
> The old man read the article and remarked: "That is news to me. My grandson is of English descent. I was born in England myself, in the village of Holt, county of Norfolk, about ten miles from Sandringham Palace, the Prince of Wales' country seat. So far as I know, all the Durrants are of English descent. The family name, when accented on the last syllable, sounds French, but properly pronounced the accent is on the first syllable, which makes it quite English.

Thomas Durrant believed his grandson not guilty, although he added, "I would not raise my hand to save him from the gallows if I believed him guilty."

3. The factual statements regarding Mr. and Mrs. Durrant's family backgrounds were made by Mrs. John Severs of Ocean View, who said she was "acquainted with [Theodore] Durrant's father all her life." Her comments form part of an editorial on the Durrant trial in the San Francisco *Bulletin*, enclosed without comment as a clipping in a letter to Maud from Mrs. Durrant, October 22, 1895. The clipping bears no date.

4. Stewart, Robert E., Jr., and M.F. Stewart, *Adolph Sutro: A Biography* (San Francisco: Howell-North) 1962. p. 161.

5. William Durrant was no doubt telling the truth: if Sutro lent or gave any money to the family, it surely would have been to Isabella. During her triumphant return to San Francisco in 1910, Maud gave several interviews in which she referred to her stage name. Sometimes she claimed to have taken her father's middle name. At other times she stated that she had

taken her mother's (birth) name, a slip of the lip, no doubt. In fact, Freemasons in San Francisco covered the bulk of the enormous legal fees and expenses, and their lodge brothers in Dillon, Montana, contributed significantly to the funeral expenses of Blanche Lamont, a native of Dillon and one of Theo's victims. (See Dillon *Tribune*, April 19, 1895.) In a letter of June 21, 1895, Isabella Durrant wrote: "Blanche Lamont's father was a Mason and they will spare no expense to find and prosecute her murderer. When you write to May [Peel] tell her to have her father and Jack and all the Masons they know to take Theo's part – to tell all that is good about him." In a letter of May 9, 1897, Theo remarked: "We have got some of the finest names on our list, Masons of the highest standing."

Adolph Sutro and Theo's lawyers, "General" Dickinson and Eugene Deuprey, were all well-known Masons; presumably William Durrant was, too.

6. Stewart, *Adolph Sutro*, p. 175.

7. Manya Cherniavsky (1900–1985) met Maud Allan in 1913, when Maud and Manya's brothers toured as the Maud Allan Cherniavsky Trio Company (October 1913–January 1915). The Cherniavsky family remained Maud's faithful friends until her death, whereupon Manya and her brother Leo became her executors. In a conversation tape-recorded in 1980, Manya, who remembered Isabella Durrant as an old woman, described her as "cute, not serious or grim, with demonic eyes."

8. This incident – or at least something very similar – certainly happened, for in a letter of September 29, 1897, Theo wrote to Maud in Berlin that "if you should ever write the story of us (us and co) remember the forest and the baby scare. Have one of your characters save the baby as it all happened." Maud followed Theo's directions when recalling this incident in the first of a series of autobiographical articles published in July 1908 in the London press. Her account concludes:

> The passengers were getting aboard the train when my mother and my governess simultaneously missed me. There was a great outcry. Then one of the conductors espied two squaws scuttling away across the prairie, and with them a glint of golden hair.
>
> "There she is!" he cried.
>
> At once my parents, the passengers, conductors, and, I

believe, even the engine drivers, streamed across the long grass after the flying squaws. . . . My captors found themselves being overtaken and dropped me. A few minutes later my mother – herself little more than a girl, for she married early – was tearfully hugging me to her breast.

Of course, a great deal of this incident I have learnt since. But I believe it was a very near thing.

9. Unidentified clipping, "Maud Allan" file, Dance Collection Performing Arts Research Center, New York Public Library.
10. Sarah Bernhardt left an indelible impression on Maud Allan. *My Life and Dancing* contains a long tribute to her, which begins: "About this time [when Maud was around thirteen] came the great and glorious Sarah Bernhardt to San Francisco. My ambitious little heart burned within me. She was the one woman in the world I wanted to rival, and I have not lost the feeling yet" (p. 36). In 1907, she met the great actress in Paris.
11. "For some weeks a teacher in the school I attended had dined with us often. Accordingly, he and I walked from the High School building home. Being just fifteen and my dresses lengthened that spring, gave rise to comments from my girl friends.

One day one of them mysteriously took me into my mother's garden and whispered the news in my ear. She had heard on the best authority that I was to marry the professor" (*My Life and Dancing*, p. 38).

Writing in her diary on April 14, 1895, just a month after her arrival in Berlin, a homesick Maud, after an afternoon walk, recalled the same period: "How I thought of days gone by, of Mr. Dunn and I on walks. No one knows. Dear Cecil and Arnold J., how they used to tell me how they regarded me. It will be years before I see them once more. What a time I had suppressing all those dear boys. And Mr. Dunn, when the girls at school circulated that we were engaged, how he wished it and I was so indifferent. . . . Oh, for a loving word or the pressure of a hand."
12. While attending Cogswell Polytechnic Institute the men became business partners in The Independent Social Telegraph Line Co., a scheme for connecting by telephone some sixty homes in the Mission. (At this time telephones were an exciting novelty.)

According to the *San Francisco Examiner* of April 19, 1895, the chairman of the company was Richard S. Allen. He may have been a son or relation by marriage of Mrs. George Allen.

13. The reference to funerals has no context, but is the first indication of an interest in death that in later years was apparent both in Maud's dance interpretation and in her private behaviour.

14. During her triumphant 1910 return to San Francisco as a world-famous classical dancer, she gave the following account of her musical training to the *San Francisco Chronicle* of April 30, 1910:

> I was a pupil of the Denham Grammar School and the Cogswell College in this city. A Miss Lichenstein imparted the first music lessons to me [in Toronto]. She was an excellent teacher and I enjoyed her instruction very much. She made the lessons interesting and a source of great pleasure to me. When sufficiently advanced I had the good fortune to become a pupil of Professor Bonelli of this city, under whose tuition I studied for some time and made excellent progress. He took a great interest in me and expressed his delight in my rapid progress, and encouraged me to greater efforts. He advised me to go abroad to finish my musical training. I went to Berlin and had been there about two weeks – barely enough to brush up a little or prepare for the ordeal – when I was required to play before Professor Reif, a noted authority on music, just to let him judge whether I was sufficiently advanced to take the examination to enter the Royal Academy of Music at Berlin. To my surprise and theirs, I came through the exam with flying colors, and Professor Reif told me I was fit to enter the academy. I was told that it was a rare case that an applicant passes at the first examination. He marvelled at my proficiency and inquired who had been my teacher. When I mentioned Professor Bonelli of San Francisco, Professor Reif and his associates exchanged glances, and their faces beamed. They informed me that they had heard several of the former pupils of Professor Bonelli and all had proved very efficient, which was rare with pupils coming from foreign countries, especially from America.
>
> Of the thirty-five applicants who took the examination at the same time I did, three passed, and I received the highest percentage. The professors congratulated me upon my proficiency and told me that Professor Bonelli's students are the

most proficient Americans at the Koeniglicher Akademische Hochschule in Berlin.

15. This according to Etienne Amyot, who was a young man in the late 1920s when he was first introduced to Maud. Amyot subsequently became the founding director of the prestigious Third (radio) Programme of the British Broadcasting Corporation.

16. Manya Cherniavsky recalled the late Joseph Szigeti, maestro of the violin sonata, remarking that early in his career, before playing in public works new to his repertoire, he would play them for Maud Allan.

Joseph Szigeti first met the Cherniavsky family around 1910, when he was a young boy on his first visit to London. He and his father were passing by the Holland Park house that the Cherniavsky family occupied; his father, struck by the music he heard, rang the front door bell to ask who was practising so impressively. He was introduced to the Cherniavsky Trio. In 1945, Manya Cherniavsky, with one of her nephews (my brother John) and Maud Allan, visited Szigeti in Los Angeles. The violinist, at the time preparing his autobiography *With Strings Attached*, asked Maud a few personal questions about Busoni, but, discreet as always, she was tight-lipped.

17. Maud's diary entry for Thursday March 14 includes the following:

> Wednesday night I had a dream. It was too good to be true. I dreamed that some very dark handsome man was paying me attention. In fact, it was too familiar when David came in, staggering. My heart pounded, and for a few minutes I didn't know which to choose – that dark one pleading or David, just looking on, half intoxicated with beer. I looked and Oh! his eyes, his mouth had lost that discontented look, and I creeped up cautiously behind him, throwing both arms around his neck, drew his head back and unconsciously [sic] kissed him on the mouth so quickly that he scarcely knew what I was doing. The dark man protested. I had made my choice. David called, "Oh, one more kiss, Maud, or I shall go mad, and will get drunk. Do you not see how I long for it? Your sweet lips – give me one, won't you?" Ah! I did, as many as he wanted. But dreams are contrary, thank goodness.

2

A Family Tragedy: 1895-1897

N 1895, Berlin was a thriving metropolis of nearly two million people, ranking immediately behind London and Paris. Until 1868 a walled city, in 1871 it became the capital of the newly proclaimed German Empire. Thanks to a remarkably efficient municipal administration, it rapidly became the model city of Europe and, after the historic Congress of Berlin held in 1878, the chief pleasure town of the German Empire. It was an unusually modern capital: save for a sixteenth-century palace, its many public buildings were new and grandiosely imposing. The city's main arteries – the best known of which was the Unter den Linden, whose double avenue was divided by the famous promenade lined with lime trees – gave a sense of spaciousness and provided rapid transport such as few European cities could boast.

According to her diary, Maud was undecided whether to remain in Berlin or move on to Leipzig. The choice was difficult, for Leipzig, with its historical associations with J.S. Bach, its famed Conservatory founded some fifty years earlier by Felix Mendelssohn, its close associations with Robert Schumann and the still living Johannes Brahms, offered the cultural richness that Berlin lacked. ("They say the Hochschule's not much good here," she noted in her diary very shortly after her arrival.) On the other hand, Berlin's small but thriving American colony, including a number of San Franciscans with whom Maud immediately felt at home, had warmly welcomed her. Moreover, the director of the Berlin Hochschule was Joseph Joachim. His outlook on musical education can be exemplified in two extraordinary attributes: his remarkable accessibility to students and his establishment of the string quartet bearing his name, which specialized in the works of contemporary composers. In all likelihood, however, it was the security Maud felt with the welcoming American colony that helped her decide to remain in Berlin. That security proved short-lived, however; within weeks Maud was avoiding the American colony for fear of being identified as the sister of San Francisco's, indeed America's, most famous criminal.

Maud spent her first six weeks in Berlin getting settled. She moved into a boarding house run by a motherly Frau Praetorius. Even though her first dinner was "perfectly wretched, greasy soup, tough meat, potatoes, peas and nothing else," she remained some eighteen months. She passed the entrance exam to the Hochschule für Musik ("At first they said no, but later they changed their minds. . . . Won't Mama be pleased though!"), and she attended three interesting concerts. She heard the great violinist and teacher Leopold Auer as soloist with an orchestra conducted by the young Richard Strauss. She was less thrilled with the violinist/conductor Joseph Wieniauski. (He was "good, but for me he spoiled it by dropping from Beethoven to his own symphony.") Most impressive was the glamorous conductor Felix Weingartner, "a perfect dream, tall, dark, well built, and exquisitely graceful. He plays every note of the music with the wave of the hand, every move of his body" – much, indeed, as Maud would "play" music as a dancer.

On March 22, two weeks after her arrival in Berlin, Maud records in her diary receipt of her first letter from home. A week earlier, however, she had noted receipt of a letter from her close friend May Peel. This and a second letter from May, written immediately after Theo's arrest and therefore more down-to-earth, are the only letters not from family that Maud retained – probably by accident. The first of these, dated February 14, provides a unique vignette of the circle she left behind:

My dear Maud,

Can't stand it any longer, so must write a few lines to you to relieve my feelings. We were the bluest crowd you ever saw coming home. Your mother and father and Jack and I took turns weeping and by the time we reached home we were not beauties, I can assure you. I can't speak of you without tears. . . .

Feb. 26. . . . Oh, I was so glad to hear from you and so was Jack. Mama met your parents last night (with Theo) on Howard Street. Your mother said she had a letter from you and, oh, I felt so sad. I wondered if you had forgotten me. Dearie, I am very jealous of you – not of your family – oh no – but of the other girls. I want to be loved the best. It is selfish, I know, but oh, Maud, if only you knew how I miss you. The tears are in my eyes as I think of you now so far away. Don't think I am silly, Maud, I can't help it. If Jack comes in and catches me crying, he'll give me a licking, though he cried himself when you left.

P.S. [from Jack]: Hello Maudibus, have you had an attack of seasickness yet? If so, you can imagine how I feel at your absence. There is nothing new since you left – May is crankier than ever and hardly lets me out. Oh, I lead a dreadful life. How are all the little German boys? Look out, now! Well, will quit until I can write without May looking over my shoulder, then I can tell you how miserable I feel etc.

By early April Maud was taking German lessons, practising regularly, and waiting for the term at the Hochschule to begin. She had enrolled in theory and composition, music history, and weekly piano lessons from a Professor von Peterssen. She was also required to take a second instrument, and chose voice.

Her belief in her voice is comical. None of the five singing teachers she engaged during the next four years showed the slightest enthusiasm for her voice once they had to train it. Not even her mother could muster confidence in what became Maud's obsessive interest.

Naturally, she had her spasms of homesickness. "I have cried since supper and my eyes look like burnt holes in a blanket," she noted one evening, but otherwise her diary shows she was happily into the swing of things. Her happiness, however, was short-lived; on April 17 she had two visitors. "Oh dear," she wrote that night:

> The old police. They want my passport now. I have seen the Ambassador for U.S. (a Canadian) and he says I will have to write for Papa's papers – and then I can have a passport. Such a bother. Had dinner alone. Visited Frantwein Piano House – such old rattle-boxes, I would not give them house room.

And little wonder she dined alone, for she must have been in a state of consternation. At her first sight of the police officers she no doubt braced herself for distressing news – why else would police officers call on her? Quite possibly, having reassured her that no family member was dying or dead, they informed her that her brother Theo was in the custody of the San Francisco police. Perhaps they told her of the disappearance, on April 3, of Blanche Lamont, a student teacher from Dillon, Montana – Maud's acquaintance, Theo's friend, and member of the Emmanuel Baptist Church congregation – and that her body had been found in the church belfry.

There was more to tell.

ON SATURDAY, April 13, three women met to decorate Emmanuel Baptist Church for the next day's Easter celebrations. When one of them opened the door to the church library, little more than a large cupboard off the reading room, she found, lying in a pool of congealed blood, the naked and hacked body of Minnie Williams, aged twenty-three. The petrified ladies did not immediately recognize Minnie, as she had only recently joined the church choir. They thought the body "might be only a dummy placed there by some joker."

The police searched the entire building; early on Sunday morning they entered the church belfry, where they found a corpse, naked and laid out as if for anatomical study. The corpse was that of twenty-one-year-old Blanche Lamont.

After Blanche's disappearance ten days earlier, and despite the co-operation of dismayed church members – particularly that of the assistant Sunday school superintendent, Theo Durrant, who had urged a search of the city's brothels – the police had failed to find any trace of her.[1] With the discovery of her body, they set out to identify and arrest her murderer, whose conviction and execution the outraged public immediately demanded. The identification and arrest were prompt enough; but the conviction, based entirely on circumstantial evidence, and the execution, after nearly three years of legal strategies, were agonizingly controversial.

Early on Sunday morning, a heliograph message was sent to Lieutenant Boardman, in command of a National Guard unit on weekend manoeuvres on Mount Diablo, an isolated peak some thirty-five miles distant.[2] The message, received without visible reaction by Theodore Durrant, advised Lieutenant Boardman that two city detectives were on their way to arrest Bugler Durrant. The reason for the arrest was not given. According to the *Examiner* of Monday, April 15, when Theo was shown that paper's report of Minnie Williams's murder:

> The muscles around his mouth twitched and his face turned pale. Then he looked at [Detectives] Anthony and Palmer and said, "I am sorry only for my mother. How can she stand it?"
>
> Anthony told him it was his mother's request that he be arrested, so that he could clear himself of the charge. "I'll go," said Durrant to Anthony.

This exchange epitomizes the impression Theo Durrant projected to the public. His serene confidence that he was innocent of the charges against him was widely perceived as the heartless indifference of a cold-blooded monster, even though his disarming politeness, his childlike flippancy and charm, and his devotion to his family so starkly conflicted with that perception.

Theo knew both Minnie Williams and Blanche Lamont – that, he was willing to concede. But, he insisted, he had no interest in either; after all, he was engaged to marry Flora Upton as soon as he established a family practice. Such, at least, was his story, yet it seems Flora had somehow let him down. ("I wonder," Isabella Durrant would write to Maud a year after Theo's execution, "if that coward of a girl Flora is happy. Oh yes, I try to forgive her as he did, but I cannot when I think of how much harm she caused our poor darling.")

Minnie Williams, fondly known as the little Quakeress by her close friends, was so slight of build as to appear almost a child. Following her parents' divorce two years earlier (her mother returned to her hometown of Beamsville, Ontario, where, according to the San Francisco press, she ended up in an insane asylum), Minnie had worked for the California Casket Company until C.E. Morgan, the president, engaged her as a companion for his wife. Shortly thereafter the Morgans sold their house in Alameda, across the bay from San Francisco. They had planned to leave on Easter Monday – ahead of Minnie Williams – for Tacoma, Washington. During the afternoon of Good Friday, Minnie had gone to stay for a few days with friends in San Francisco. After supper with them, she set out for a social evening of the Christian Endeavour Society. She never arrived.[3] A person answering her description and a man answering the description of Theo were reportedly seen at about 8:30 P.M., standing by the side entrance to Emmanuel Baptist Church. The man made a motion as if using a key and the two entered the church. (No full investigation of Minnie Williams's murder was undertaken – Theo was tried only for the murder of Blanche Lamont – it was assumed that Minnie was murdered simply because she knew too much.)

Blanche Lamont, according to her maternal aunt Mrs. Noble, was "a tall, slender, quick-tempered girl of superior abilities, but frail and not equal to any severe exercise or strong effort." In September 1894, Blanche had joined her sister, who was living with Mrs. Noble. On April 3, Theo met Blanche on her way to school. As they walked together, so Theo told Mrs. Noble two days later – Mrs. Noble said nothing to him of Blanche's disappearance, which she reported only after his visit[4] – Blanche had remarked that she needed a copy of William Thackeray's novel *The Newcomes*. Theo had suggested she borrow a copy from the church library, which he had helped catalogue. According to later witnesses, Blanche boarded a streetcar with an unknown man (later identified as Theo) that afternoon, at the end of the school day.

As soon as he was arrested, Theo was branded a murderer by the *San Francisco Examiner* and less explicitly declared such by most of the other local newspapers. He and the circumstantial nature of the case against him were doubly fascinating: the murder of Blanche Lamont was disgusting for its very cleanliness, and offensive in its locale, yet the crime seemed motiveless. According to the pathologist, Blanche had not been sexually assaulted.[5] In addition, Theo's indifference towards his victim was absolute, and the site of the crime starkly conflicted with his position as assistant Sunday school superintendent, let alone his reputation as a most devout member of the congregation.

How could such indifference be reconciled with so morally upright an individual? How could so morally upright an individual commit so ghastly a crime – and show no remorse? The only responsible answer to both questions lay in the mental state of the accused. However, as a plea of insanity seemed to be out of the question for both personal and legal reasons, the fascination remained.

Theo's lawyers, "General" John Dickinson and Eugene

Deuprey, were distinguished members of the California
Bar. Dickinson was prominent as a commander in the
militia, and Deuprey was a leading expert in medical
jurisprudence. They faced a terrible dilemma with regard
to entering a plea on Theo's behalf. To plead insanity was
very hazardous: under the law, insanity had to be proven to
have existed prior to the crime. Given Theo's known behaviour before his arrest and the public demand that the perpetrator of the murders be promptly punished, a plea of
insanity would have been virtually impossible to sustain.
Moreover, Theo may have refused to consider such a plea
both for reasons of family pride and because he "knew" he
was both innocent and sane. Indeed, Theo had effectively
erased all memory of the murders from his memory and
conscience.

On the other hand, a plea of not guilty threw down the
gauntlet to public opinion, the press, the San Francisco
police, the State of California, and the prosecutor. Little did
Theo's attorneys realize that they were embarking on the
murder trial of their careers, for the evidence against Theo
was both highly circumstantial and disturbingly persuasive,
and thus difficult to disprove.

There were few rational grounds for clemency, let alone
acquittal. After a trial of 120 days the jury, after delibera-
ting less than thirty minutes, returned a verdict of first-
degree murder, with no recommendation for mercy.   Yet,
goaded by Isabella Durrant and, no doubt, moved by the
pathos of their client's essential innocence, Theo's lawyers
argued on his behalf for more than two years, right up to
the U.S. Supreme Court.

They based their arguments on niceties of the law, on the
ambiguities of the circumstantial evidence, and, implicitly,
on the prejudices of the local press, which, Theo asserted on
the gallows, had "hounded him to the grave."

When on April 15, 1895, he was brought back to San
Francisco, no one, least of all his sister in Berlin, could
know that until his execution on January 7, 1898, Theo
would hold centre stage in the local press, attracting intense

national interest. At first, attention was focussed on Theo Durrant, the accused perpetrator of "the Crime of a Century," as the *Examiner* promptly dubbed the affair. Soon, however, it was directed at the "quiet, gentlemanly and self-possessed" individual about whom the correspondent for the *Los Angeles Times* wrote with such insight. It strained the correspondent's credulity that such an individual could be guilty of the fiendish behaviour for which he was sentenced to death on indisputably circumstantial evidence.

As for Theo, his insatiable egotism seems to have fed on this attention – a craving for recognition of his individuality such as his beloved sister received from her friends. As the law took its tortuous course, Theo saw himself as the principal actor in a melodrama, and so relished this role that it became his reality. He never understood that reality born of terror leads only to fantasy. For his family and, indeed, for his attorneys, such a mind-set was pathetic beyond measure. In the report of an interview on the eve of his execution, even the *San Francisco Chronicle* acknowledged "the dual personality that seems to be his," a perception immediately following Theo's comment that "it seems as if I were two persons, so distinct are my physical and spiritual natures." His sister was doomed to cope with a very similar state of mind throughout her adult life.

Were it not for extraneous factors, neither the crimes nor the complexities of their perpetrator would have attracted such sustained interest: the crimes would have been deplored, the perpetrator judged, and the judgement expeditiously executed. But these elements proved rich soil for exploitation.

At stake and serving as a catalyst was San Francisco's reputation, succinctly summarized in a report (in the *Los Angeles Times* of April 15) that San Francisco's coroner "is overworked; at present he has thirty suspicious deaths on his books upon which inquests have not been completed." In addition there had been "eight violent deaths at the hands of persons unknown" – all within the first two weeks of the month. Little wonder that the San Bernadino *Times Indepen-*

dent described San Francisco, a city of some 240,000, as "the hotbed of licentiousness and crime on this Coast." Other rural papers joined the chorus of self-righteous indignation: the Stockton *Mail*, for example, suggested that "the shedding of human blood has become so frequent and commonplace in San Francisco that only the commission of some exceptionally atrocious murder in that city could shock the moral sensibilities of her people." The murders Theo committed put an effective end to this "carnival of blood," for they did indeed "shock the moral sensibilities of her people."[7]

Of the parties eager to exploit this situation, none had a greater professional interest than Chief of Police Cowley. Having found his suspect, he went well beyond his duty by actively working for Theo's conviction, days before he had been formally charged. Within two days of Theo's arrest, Cowley was declaring the suspect's guilt, while conceding that the evidence was circumstantial. He insisted, too, that Theo attend the inquest dressed in the garments he had worn on the night of Minnie Williams's murder. Theo sat through the proceedings with an unstudied display of disinterest, without the slightest show of emotion.[8] According to the *Los Angeles Times* of April 23:

> The prosecution had introduced in evidence a large photograph of the dead girl. It was a ghastly thing, showing her in her casket, stripped, with the hideous wounds in her head, breasts and wrists in strong relief. The purpose of the picture was probably to illustrate the savagery that attended the murder. So ghastly was it that the lawyers, in showing it to the witnesses to identify it as the dead girl, only unrolled enough of it to show her face.
>
> In the course of its introduction it was handed to Durrant's lawyers who looked it over carefully, even their faces showed horror at it. Durrant sat behind his lawyers. When the picture was unrolled on the table before them, he leaned forward and looked at it curiously. Not a muscle of his face changed, there was not the livid expression of horror,

recognition, or anything else. It might have been the cover of a law book for all the impression it produced on the man who was there to answer for the infliction of those wounds.

So indecently involved was Chief Cowley that in an editorial of April 25 the *Los Angeles Times* criticized him for having made "no effort to discover any fact pointing to any one but Durrant." The editorial concluded: "To convict a man of so grave a crime upon such flimsy evidence . . . would be a disgrace to California justice. A verdict of acquittal would probably break the heart of Chief Cowley, judge, jury, etc.; but that might be mended, whereas the broken neck of an innocent man could not be put together with satisfactory results."[9]

(Following his execution, however, the *Times* called Theo "a cruel, cowardly and bestial murderer," even though it had constantly commented on the conduct of the trial and the accused's strange behaviour.)

The San Francisco press became obsessed with the case. Following the discovery of Blanche Lamont's body, the *Examiner* (amongst others) reminded its readers of a terrifying possibility: "The analogy with the murderous career of Jack the Ripper in London will at once suggest itself. The unexampled crimes of that unknown red-handed fiend – unexampled up to his time – have never been explained. Is the same bloody drama to be repeated in San Francisco?"

From the first, Theo was a choice suspect, although the church minister, the effeminate Reverend George Gibson, was for a time the victim of innuendo. When Theo's personal peculiarities and the circumstantial evidence against him came into clear focus, his fate was sealed. His name was speculatively linked to a number of unsolved murders, and the excited mob made him skittish for fear of a possible lynching.[10] So real was this possibility that on at least one occasion Chief of Police Cowley told Theo to follow him on foot rather than take the police van surrounded by a waiting crowd and photographers from the *Examiner*.

Very probably the governor of California's adamant

refusal three years later to commute the death penalty to life imprisonment was based on a political fear of outraging public opinion. Yet by that stage even he, who publicly stated that he had studied the case so carefully, must have questioned Theo's sanity.

Initially, the press openly – if not fairly – discussed this matter. The *Examiner* on April 15 remarked that "the evidence against Durrant is overwhelming, and fortunately, whether he is guilty or not, he has disbarred himself from the favorite defense – insanity." The next day, however, in an article titled "There were Two Durrants," the *Examiner* reported that:

> a theory is held by some at Cooper [Medical] College that Durrant was afflicted by *psycho mania sexualis*, a not unknown though infrequent mental disease. Numerous cases of this terrible insanity are recorded in medical history. A similar theory is accepted by the medical profession as the incentive of the Whitechapel [Jack the Ripper] murders. Sporadic cases are recorded of this condition in every country.

Medical authorities were not the only ones to hold this view. A woman, interviewed the next day regarding reports of "Crazy Theo's" hitherto unknown "other life," remarked "I think that if he murdered the girls he committed the crime while temporarily insane. That peculiar look in his blue-green eyes always led me to believe that he was not thoroughly sane." Perhaps it was such lay observations that led Police Surgeon Somers to study Theo's actions, so the *Los Angeles Times* reported on April 20, "in anticipation of a plea of insanity when the case was brought to trial. Dr. Somers says that Durrant shows no signs of insanity, in fact he spoke with intelligence on every subject that was brought up." Nonetheless, on Monday July 22, the day the trial opened, the *Examiner* reported:

> It has been suggested that the defense might plead insanity. The Prosecution has discovered certain facts that demonstrate that Durrant was, to say the least, eccentric. In his

escapades he earned the reputation of being very eccentric, and it was thought that the defense might avail itself of what the Prosecution had brought to light. This, however, will not be the case. A plea of insanity would be a virtual acknowledgement of guilt, and the defense is not employed for that kind of confession. As it cannot demonstrate that some unsuspected person committed the crime, it will fall back on an alibi.

The report was accurate. The next day, the *Examiner*, in its coverage of the first day of the trial, reported the following exchange:

> "Before we proceed this matter," said the presiding judge, "there is one thing that I desire to be understood. At the time of pleading, the privilege was granted to the defendant to withdraw his plea if he were so advised. I believe that has not been done."
>
>   "No, your Honour," replied [defence attorney Eugene] Deuprey, "and the plea of not guilty stands."

The judge's action was most unusual, but not as reckless as the response to it.[11]

Less urgent to their reputation but of real concern as leaders of the moral sensibilities of their congregations, certain of the city's clergy commented on the blood-curdling events of the preceding weekend. Dr. Dille, of the Central Methodist Episcopal Church, drew such "obvious lessons" as "the possibilities of evil in human nature" and "the lowering of the moral tone of society growing out of a weakening of religious restraints." He also made a comment of a somewhat less moralistic nature:

> Though 150 persons have been murdered in this city in five years, only one has suffered the extreme penalty of the law, and that one was a Chinaman. There have been hundreds of murders since I have known San Francisco – during the last twenty-two years – and not six persons have been executed, and not one that had money or influence. Taking life by due process of law for the highest crime known to man is about

the only mode of taking life to which the average American has any objection.

During the six months prior to Theo's execution, the press reported at least six executions at San Quentin Prison. It would seem, therefore, that "the Crime of a Century" ushered in a rush of executions, none of which attracted much public interest.

Dr. Case, a colleague of Dr. Dille, took an entirely different stance, asking his congregation's sympathy for Theo's family:

> I called upon his parents yesterday and I am glad I did. The almost broken-hearted mother of the young man accused of the crime is in sore need of sympathy.
>
> When I was on my way to the home of the Durrants I met a man who spoke to me about the crime. I told him I was going and he was horrified. I explained to him that the boy's mother was not charged with having committed the crimes. He thought the matter over and agreed that my course was befitting a Christian.[12]

Dr. Case then asserted that "the procuring of innocent girls by worthless vagrants is more despicable and dangerous than the double murders." Few shared this view.

Attention and speculation merely tempered Theo's iron nerves; yet the greatest test, and at the time the least appreciated, was that of the legal system. Justice was rough and ready in the American West; it was therefore critical that in California, the most socially and culturally advanced of the western states, the rule of law prevail and the legal procedures be conducted without fault or prejudice. Despite recurring suspicions that the trial ran roughshod over justice, local press accounts (the official records were lost in the earthquake and great fire of 1906) indicate that the law, although stretched to the limit, was not deliberately abused or corrupted, although human judgement – such as the refusal to allow a new trial – may be questioned. From a strictly legal point of view, that a man of questionable sanity (who did not plead legal insanity) was executed was irrelevant, except as a demonstration that Justice was, indeed, blind – if only because pride made Theo Durrant so. In the end, politics and the fear of outraged public opinion precluded mercy.

From all appearances Maud, like the rest of the family, refused or was unable to acknowledge that Theo had committed the crime. Denial was her only means of dealing with the unacceptable truth, on which the verdict six months later would be resolved after almost three years.

For three days following the police visit, she was literally too stunned for words: her diary gives no hint of what was uppermost in her mind. But on April 20 she wrote:

(A.M.) We visited the Reichstag this morning. It is beautiful indeed, will write about it after I see it again. Can get a baby grand – 15 marks, splendid!, but have not decided yet. Although my first lesson was all in German, still I understood it perfectly – I have been over the same work already.

Oh! if this belief in my heart is true! My darling mother, what will it do to her? Oh God, grant that Theo is not implicated in this dreadful murder. Poor Blanche. I have been unable to think of anything else. My brother Theo, what have you done? You *are* innocent, I know. You could not do such a thing! How can I bear it alone? I know it must be the work of an insane man. You could not do it. No, no, I will not believe it. My heart is breaking for those at home. I am not known here, and no one will notice. But at home, oh God, my prayer from the bottom of my heart is to save from such a disgrace those at home. Oh! that it is not true, that some fiend has taken the lives of those poor girls, in Thy home, too! Oh no, Theo did not do it. Oh to be at home to comfort poor little Mamma. Send her an angel, dear Lord, to guard her, and Papa, too. Do not let this blow shorten her life. Hear this prayer of a lonely child – and answer it for Thy dear Son's sake, Amen.

For the next three years, thousands of miles from home and family, Maud was forced to depend on two principal sources of information – letters from home and the press. Her mother sent her selected newspaper clippings and discreet letters – to avoid distressing her daughter and mindful of the police practice of opening her correspondence. Theo struggled (most of the time effectively, for most of his letters are dull) to suggest he was writing from some remote place (as if, say, on military manouevres), where boredom was an even greater problem than the living conditions, about which he rarely complained.

Lloyd's Reading Rooms, the English-language library in Berlin, received the international edition of the New York *Herald* (published in Paris and delivered overnight) and the New York papers, about ten days late. Thus it could provide a more immediate – but no more reliable or reassuring – source of news. In its April 16 edition (the day before the police paid their dreadful visit to Maud), the front page of the very staid *Herald* printed the following garbled report:

HORRIBLE MURDERS

Three young women, two of whom were named Blanche Lamont and Minnie Williams, all prominent members of a Baptist Church in San Francisco, have been missing a few days.

The body of one of them was found on Saturday, outraged and murdered, in the pastor's study.

Another was found yesterday, naked and outraged and strangled, in the belfry of the church.

An arm and other remains, which are believed to be those of the third missing woman, were found by the police today in the basement of the church.[13]

Mr. Theodore Durrant, a medical student and an assistant superintendent of the Sunday school, was arrested today on suspicion. The purse of one of the women was found in his lodging. He insists that he can explain matters.

During the following weeks the *Herald* carried no further reports of the case; however, the New York press gave it extensive coverage. Maud apparently haunted Lloyd's Rooms waiting for the New York papers until the despatches became accounts. Then her courage failed her and she realized that the visits to Lloyd's served no positive purpose. Her diary hints at her ordeal, as she awaited a letter (not extant but recorded as received on May 3) from her mother telling of Theo's arrest:

April 22: This A.M. Elementary gesang [singing]. I did not get much from it. After, I went [for the first recorded time] to Lloyd's Rooms but found nothing in the papers. If I could but dare hope it was not true! After dinner I went to Mrs. Sherman and we talked it all over. Must retire. Have such a headache and heartache.

April 23: Am glad the Ponds have not heard of this all. Of course they will, sooner or later, but then I can't help it. *I am not to blame.* But oh! the shame we all feel. If this is true, I will try to borrow money to send for Ma as soon as the trial and everything is over. She will need the change of scene and faces. Gave Mammie [Pond] a lesson.

April 24: After dinner I wrote to Mamma but did not mention what I had read in the paper. I could not.

April 25: It has been so lovely and warm, and to think of all the sadness and trouble at home. I do not know what might be now. I cannot stop to think of it, it is terrible. What if Ma and Pa should die and I would be all alone so far from my childhood home. I must not think of it all, it will make me unfit to do what Mamma so much desires.

April 26: The dreary day is done and I must try and sleep. But my head just spins round and round, and I can hardly collect my senses. Involuntarily on my way home from giving Mammie Pond her lesson I got off the car at Unter den Linden and went to Lloyd's Rooms, there only to read in all the papers the sad, sad account of the death of the two girls and that Theo was deeper and deeper in the mire. I could hardly control myself, I trembled all over. I received a letter from Mamma and May [Peel] and a note from Theo. They all spoke of the disappearance of Blanche Lamont. I am so unhappy. Have written to Mamma today.

April 27: Oh, I am so sad, so sad. I can not eat or do anything, but think! think! think! all the time. I hope those awful accounts in the American papers are not true. I am sure Theo can clear himself if he has a just jury. God grant he has. I took theory lesson today. Wrote to Flo [Upton] and Sutro.

April 28: This morning I took an article from the German paper and spent the greater part of the day translating it. Just the same as all the others.[14]

April 29: Letter from Mamma (and a paper). She is so anxious. Poor little mother. Little did she dream when she wrote to me that the clouds were hanging over our home. It is almost more than I can bear. I want to read the papers but won't, because what is the use? The lies only make me wild. Patience is indeed a virtue.

May 1: What a glorious day and I so sad. Theory-Klavier – slow work. But I will stick to it and will not fail. I can scarcely wait for the day when I can expect letters.

May 2: [Examining judge committed Theo to be placed on trial for the murder of Minnie Williams.] This has been the worst day I have ever put in. I simply could not work. I am sure something decisive has been reached. Oh God! Have mercy! Went, because Mrs. Pond insisted, to the Philharmonia tonight. It was divine. Hauseman [*sic*] and Kruse and Joachim. How the people applauded. But I was ready to cry all evening. I could hardly keep the tears back. The 3rd No 2 movement of Schumann's Quintet in Es Dur, op. 24. Oh! I could see everything so clearly. It seemed like a message to tell me what has happened. God grant that it is not so. I had to bite my lip to keep from crying. Came home late enough for everyone to be in bed. I am glad. I can see no one.

For anyone less strong willed than Maud Allan these three weeks of recorded headaches and heartaches, loss of appetite and frayed nerves, fatigue and depression (but not, it seems, sleeplessness) would surely have been unbearable. Had the tension and the "awful accounts" (and they *were* awful, but nothing compared to what would later be printed) not broken, Maud may well have collapsed under the strain. The press coverage temporarily eased after Theo's arraignment on May 2, and comforting letters from San Francisco started to arrive. Although this would prove merely a dry run for the terrors to come, Maud made up her mind to withstand them by believing in Theo's innocence. The strength of her determination led her to deny that her brother would ever be executed but did not lessen the shame of the charges against him.[15]

Determined to mask her feelings ("I had to be bright and hearty yet I felt guilty all the time," she noted after supping with a German family), she made every effort to resume a normal routine and to project her captivating appeal. Thus one Sunday afternoon, she wrote, she "togged up in my best bib and tucker and lace hat and started out for a walk. Upon returning I put on my accordion dress and astonished the community. After Abendbrot [supper] we took chairs on the balcony and were quite comfortable. But I thought of home and the dear ones. My feet are a source of amusement to Ernst, and Herr P[raetorius] calls them 'no feet at all'."[16]

Meanwhile, the long-awaited Hochschule term had begun. She attended all her classes, although the only one she enjoyed was her piano lesson with Professor Peterssen, who assigned her "some funny little finger exercises, three Bach *Inventions* and the E flat major Sonata of Mozart." She also had growing financial problems. With Theo's arrest, she could no longer count on a regular monthly remittance from her parents. Nor could she earn income from giving piano lessons to the children of the American community, for she deliberately avoided Americans once Theo's name and her family tie had become common knowledge. She therefore organized weekly language classes for three German university students. This short-lived project – her accounts record receipt of 7 marks for her efforts – would be insignificant were it not that one of the three was Curt Sachs, who became an internationally recognized musicologist.

During this period, too, Maud joined with at least three others a more enduring project that at one time seemed on the verge of real success and in fact was not a complete failure. She was probably the mainstay of this undertaking: over the years her diary records that she designed, measured, cut, sewed, fitted, and even modelled corsets!

The account books of this business are lost, although her personal accounts survive. From the day of her departure from San Francisco (with $124.95 in hand), she kept such meticulous track of her expenditures that, after nearly nine months in Germany, she entered the sum of 8.18 marks (approximately $2.00) as "unaccounted for." In a "Summary of Account" page for the year 1895, she recorded an average monthly expenditure of 151.74 marks as against an average monthly "income" of 161.64 marks. Her monthly pension cost 90 marks, her Hochschule fees (she received no scholarship upon entry) of 240 marks were very generously paid for by Mrs. Busch, a wealthy German American who for the first year or so also gave her occasional gifts of money.

At last, letters from San Francisco started to arrive – a half dozen or so survive from 1895. The first was from May Peel, dated April 17, three days after Theo's arrest. It is tactfully reassuring and confirms press accounts of Theo's jail conditions despite immediate and later public hostility:

My dearest Maud,
    I have just put off writing a few days, because I wanted to have something more encouraging to tell you. Of course, by this time you know about the bodies of Blanche Lamont and Minnie Williams being found in the church, and that they have arrested Theo on suspicion. Of course, we all believe him innocent and the victim of circumstantial evidence. It will be explained in time and we are waiting for the right one to be arrested. Of course it is very unpleasant

while it lasts but you must not worry too much. Your mother bears up wonderfully. So does Theo himself, though it must be very hard on the poor boy. It will come out alright in the end even if it be a weary wait. Everything is in a muddle and nobody knows which end they're standing on.

[May put aside the letter, and completed it two days later.]

Everybody feels more cheerful today. Things are looking brighter for Theo, and he laughs and talks with his visitors, who are numerous, though he sees no one unless he wants to. He has all the comforts he wants and nice reading and meals etc.

I am afraid your mother would think I was writing too much about this, but I know if I were in your place I should want you to do the same. My dear, don't worry too much, because everything will be all right.

I will let you know of anything new.

Much love, May.

When, a week later, Isabella Durrant wrote the first of her extant letters, she ordered Maud, at Theo's behest, to remain in Berlin at all costs, so she might fulfil the family's expectations and avoid the limelight as the sister of San Francisco's most celebrated prisoner. Mrs. Durrant mentions receiving innumerable letters of support (including one from her parents-in-law in Los Angeles) and comments, "I have not had a letter from our Mamma yet. Is it not funny, one would have thought she would have been one of the first to write." This, surely, refers to her own unidentifiable mother.

In the next paragraph she mentions having just visited Mayor Sutro, who "happened to be in Theo's cell last week." She writes that Sutro said "he was sorry for you and he had been speaking to someone about you and he had thought of starting a subscription for you, but right now he was short of funds. Mr. S. says you would be very foolish to come home as you could do no good and your time would be wasted. You could not practise here and it would be very hard to get a position now." (There is no evidence that Sutro helped Maud in any way at all.)

The first of Theo's extant letters establishes his attitude towards his situation and his sister:

> I am so glad to see what a stand you have taken with regard to the case and hope by this time you have dispelled all thoughts of it from your busy brain for you know, my darling, you have other things to think about now, and great ideas to develop and greater thoughts to mature than to brood over the misfortunes of your brother who is so far away from you. Oh my dearest sister dispel all fear from your mind. I am never going to say anything more about the sad side of this affair but talk of nothing but the brightest of events that transpire within my knowledge and hearing.

Although he then writes at some length about his lawyers, he makes no reference to the reasons for his arrest. The letter ends:

> Yesterday I had spring carrots and peas, strawberry short-cake, milk, rice, soup, bananas, and lots of goodies. Today I had the same. I get my own meals here and eat fine. You would be surprised to see how many gentlemanly and well dressed men are here. Men who did crooked things during election time, and big Chinese Certificate forgers and government officials, bank clerks, and Macdonald of the Pacific and People's Savings Bank.

In due course, however, Theo would change his tune – and his cell.

With Theo's plight in mind and her own financial security in doubt, Maud's confidence in her piano playing declined, only to be replaced by an unshakeable confidence in her voice. On the eve of an audition with her newly found voice coach, Professor Knudson, she day-dreamed: "Oh to be an opera singer, I shall never be content until I am." The audition was all that she desired. "Went to Professor Knudson and joy! he raves over my voice. Well, it is large, I never knew it before. He wants to see me again. I hope he will take it and train it.''

He did take it, and he did try to train it – and after Maud had told him "everything," so desperate was she for his coaching, he offered her free lessons. He grew genuinely fond of Maud, lent her money (to get a dangerous ear infection cured), and treated her, with her fellow student and close friend May Hamaker, as his own daughter.[17] Dissatisfied with his "means, ways, methods," the two students abandoned him a year later. He was greatly distressed by this treatment.

Mrs. Durrant's extant letters written in the weeks before Theo's trial started on July 22 (the first six weeks were given to jury selection) are highly revealing of her relationship with Maud, as the following excerpts show:

[May 26] Take care of your health and your looks and your grammar. Do not use slang words in your letters or your speaking. Now be sure Mamma is not scolding you, but you know how fussy I am about slang. Be sure to sit up straight, no round shoulders. Be careful in your movements – all of them. I am very proud of you.

[June 1] Answer all the questions I ask you in my letters. I try to think how I would like your room fixed up but every time I try I end up with Theo's trouble and I am no further along.

[June 18] Now about your hair. I do not know how to advise you as the only thing I use is sage tea, to keep the hair dark. I do know that is what I used when your hair had a falling out spell. I wash my hair once a week in lemon and it feels fine, but you must be very careful how you handle your hair. In drying it comb it from the bottom and do not let anyone stop you from the work you are doing, not even washing your hair. Let it be on a day when you have nothing else to do except in the evening. This will give you lots of time to dry your hair and do your homework and curl your hair if you want to. Alice [Lonnon] does not bother with curls. Papa asked her the other day if she gives her hair an electric shock. Alice said she never used anything but lots of lemon for her hair, so you can try it if you want to.

All this advice followed Maud's attempt to wash her hair in soda – "it turned out horrid."

Two weeks after Theo's trial opened, Maud left Berlin to pass the summer in the country. (Family news would be even further delayed.) She spent seven weeks with a branch of the zu Dohna family, at their summer estate in the Prussian village of Malmitz as English-speaking companion to the adults and activities-director for the children. The zu Dohnas, whose family tree traces back more than twenty-five generations, were pre-eminent amongst Prussian nobility. The Malmitz branch comprised Graf (Count) Alfred and Gräfin (Countess) Marguerite, with three daughters and five sons, aged twelve to twenty-four. Maud adjusted easily to her new and very grand surroundings. Initially she relished the morning walks through the magnificent park and enjoyed afternoon tea, tennis parties, and evening parlour games. But her enthusiasm waned as she realized this was a family of noble philistines.

Before long she had introduced more creative pursuits – singing, carving, furniture painting, and even reading. She played cards, losing a few pfennigs to sixteen-year-old Nico. (As captain of a Q-ship during the First World War, Nico was the terror of Allied merchantmen plying the Atlantic sea lanes.) She attracted the interest of Alfred, twenty-four, who asked if he might write to – and see – her during the winter. She must have had good reason for refusing him as he was the family heir apparent. (He was killed in the first days of the war.)

Maud's personal appeal soon melted the zu Dohnas' reserve: on August 27, her twenty-third birthday, "everyone personally congratulated me and Herr Graf Alfred took me in to dinner. A toast for me was given by Graf Alfred and 'Hoch Hoch Hoch' was said in unison." Three days later she recorded for the first time a glimpse of the zu Dohnas *en famille*: "The nobility are just like other people after all. Frau

Gräfin can scold like any other woman and one would never dream of them being countesses of the 1st Klasse."

The highlight of the summer was the staging of war games in early September, in the presence of "His Excellency." Four days before his arrival tension began to mount and once again the façade of "countesses of the 1st Klasse" cracked: "Frau Gräfin is so very vexed over so much preparation for the officers' arrival and she is very cross." The façade crumbled completely on their arrival: "Such a hub-bub! Frau Gräfin is tearing about – so are all the servants of the place. The cook is out of temper cause he don't know when to get dinner. Herr Graf thinks it improper for me to stay in the Villa alone when all the officers are there. So do I."

Among the officers was a Lieutenant Semerack, "not very nice looking, but he keeps looking at me." Lieutenant Semerack was smitten on the spot, as the diary entry for the next day shows:

> The evening is almost over. The girls noticed that Lieutenant Semerack was very attentive to me and the girls remarked on it, so I told him I would only dance with him during the evening once more. His eyes were on me the whole time and he never sat with a young lady but that he could always watch me. I was very uncomfortable. I hate anything like that. The military band played beautifully from 5 to 7. His Excellency came at 9:30. Soldiers were guarding the house and while he ate dinner in the Green Room the band gave the low long drum roll, then played and then again the low long drum roll, and then went away. Wore my blue dress with chiffon this evening.

Two days later, in miserable weather, Maud joined nine gentlemen and the eldest of the zu Dohna daughters at 6 A.M. to set out for the war games. "Battle was slow but parade was fun. Did not see the attack."

During the summer Maud received copies of the *San Francisco Chronicle*, including the issue of July 26 describing a scene during the jury selection. (More than thirty-six hundred veniremen were examined before twelve were accepted by both prosecution and defence lawyers.)

Mrs. Durrant came in late and every neck was craned to see her. One man forgot to chew his gum for at least a minute, and a woman swallowed hers. [Theo] Durrant had been looking impassive before his mother came in. Now and then a cynical and rather disagreeable smile distorted his mouth as he talked with the deputy who undertook to amuse him. When his mother came in, she leaned from behind his chair, kissed him in a lingering way, smiled and pressed both his hands. When she raised her head the face of her son was flushed and his eyes were bright with moisture. It was a full five minutes before the calm expression he assumes fell like a mantle over his face, and he was the impassive, stony faced man again.

Mrs. Durrant wore a pretty, modish black gown yesterday, and looked as though she had made a careful toilet. She is a woman who knows the value of detail and does not intend to let anyone say that Mrs. Durrant looks worried or unhappy. She intends to keep her courage up and look as though she hadn't a trouble in the world, and her indomitable spirit keeps her face bright and cheery to the very moment of adjournment for the afternoon. It is a great pity, so far as Durrant is concerned, that Nature did not set upon him the seal of his mother's face instead of his father's. If he had inherited her brown eyes, her animated face and good features, people would not have been prone to think evil of him. If he had had his mother's mouth – firm, mobile, delicately molded, like the line of a marble statue, people would have said "He has the look of innocence." The smiling face might have concealed a world of things, but surface observers would have continued to believe in him.

But as soon as the trial got under way, Mrs. Durrant's confidence – in private at least – crumbled. "My dear," she wrote in the first letter Maud received upon returning to Berlin early in September, "you can't imagine what I have been through these last two weeks. I try to keep up, but it is very hard. I have cried all day because things look so black for Theo."

Such a comment threw Maud into a panic. "Oh! I am so afraid," she wrote after receiving this letter, "that she will not hold out through this awful trial. What shall I do if anything happens to her?"

As the trial drew to a close, Maud took to prayer. "Oh Heavenly Father, protect me from what seems inevitable. I am so afraid I will lose Mamma if this ends sadly. My heart is so heavy." On November 1, the verdict was returned: guilty of first-degree murder with no recommendation for mercy. How or when Maud learned of this verdict is unclear, as her diary makes no mention of it. But twelve days later, on November 12, the tension proved too much even for her:

> I can not settle myself. Oh I feel that my poor dear Brother is lost now to us for ever. O how can I bear it? What shall I do without him? It seems cruel – cruel. Why was I not at home to be with him those fatal days? Oh Heavenly Father why, oh why, is this awful trial placed on us? Dear Mamma has always striven so hard to do right and has done so much for us all. I cannot understand it all. It is hard to see where we will benefit by such a sorrow. Where is Justice? Have the people no heart? To let an innocent suffer so as poor Theo is? Today for the first time since the Blow came I broke down before anyone. Oh! I feel so depressed I can not work or anything. I feel as if I were going to be ill all the time. My head and all over. Have been home all day. Carrie [Bowes, a fellow San Franciscan on a visit from Leipzig, before whom Maud probably broke down] called Heute [today].[18]

On November 22, a "fat fateful envelope," postmarked November 7, arrived. It contained two pencilled notes and a longer letter. The first note was from William Durrant:

Dear Maud,
    Don't worry about these stories that you see in the

papers, they are all lies. We proved Theo's good character and the Police could not find one person who swore against him. Be brave and cheer up, we will come out all right in the end, but it will take a while longer.

Mamma is brave and keeping up remarkably well. Our friends are stronger than ever and we have more than before. I started work this week. I will get half time, that is better than nothing.

Now, my dear, cheer up. We are very hopeful we will surely get a new Trial. We have not had a fair show at all, but we intend to have it at all costs.

Loving Papa.

The second note was from "Pop" Perkins:

Do not worry, we will get a new trial. We have a new witness who saw Theo on Webster Street April 3 between 4 and 6 o'clock, we will probably get more. [This witness disappeared.] Mamma is keeping well but worries about you. Dickinson and Deuprey will fight to the bitter end for Theo. We did not have a fair Trial. Our friends are more numerous than ever. Be brave and cheerful and all will be well.

Her mother's letter was somewhat more informative:

My Darling Maud,

Fate seems to be against us. You will know by now that your darling brother has been found guilty by twelve men that we thought looked like intelligent men. It was an awful blow as we thought they would disagree. They went out on [State Attorney] Barnes' speech and remained out only 15 minutes – the papers said 24. Oh, it was awful, still, we have to live on.

My poor darling, if he keeps up under the strain, he will be wonderful. I am so afraid his health will break down. I will send you the paper and that will tell you more than I can tell you. I have had a great many callers and a great many letters, and Theo has had many, too.

Cheer up and do not come back under *any* circumstances

now as it would only make Theo feel he was the cause of blighting your prospects and you do not want to make him feel worse than he is at present, but rather act to tell him you will study all the harder to fit yourself to help him along. Now do. I think it is the most fortunate stroke of luck that you were away.[19] If it is so bad that you will have to take a last look at your brother why, then it will be time enough for you to think of coming home, but we do not think it will be so bad. God bless my pet and keep her out of harm.

Mrs. Durrant was correct in saying that the papers "will tell you more than I can." The *Chronicle*'s full-page account on November 2 described the return of the verdict of "the greatest murder case this city has ever seen":

For a moment nobody moved. The silence was deadly. Durrant made a move as if to rise and instantly, from the crowded rear of the room there came a roar, low, sullen, throaty, guttural, the sound of the mob-law type of lawlessness. This time it was the roar of approval, and it came from the men, a gratuitous sign that the work of the jury had been well done. The sound was torn about the edges by a salvo of hand clapping, the treble voices of women, and a few hysterical laughs. It was not so much gloating over the prisoner as a general expression of approval that Justice had been done. It left no doubt as to public sentiment.

Almost instantly the Courtroom was brought to order, but not the prisoner's mother, who had thrown herself forward, half fainting, against her son. From her lips, white with agony, the agony that comes from someone loved far beyond oneself, came a shriek that died in an agonizing sob. The prisoner had put his hands on the back of General Dickinson's chair, as if to address the jury. He spoke to Dickinson, who sat crushed and speechless, sunk in his chair. Then Mrs. Durrant threw her arms around his neck and drew him back into his seat. What he would have said in that unguarded moment, when all his soul lay bare, may not be known. Mrs. Durrant sat inert with her face against the cheek of her son, her frame shaken with sobs that tear away the hopes of a mother, and leave behind desolation. The prisoner devoted himself entirely to looking after his mother. His own eyes were dry and hard; he was his own master again. His mother pressed her handkerchief to her lips and his, as much alone with him as if they had been in a world of their own.

Throughout all this heart-breaking scene, the father was not in the room. Mr. Durrant finally came in [he had gone for a walk, confident that the deliberations would end in a hung jury] his stern face quite as impassive as his son's, who is so marvelously like him. He walked straight up the aisle, with eyes that seemed to see nothing, and took his place aimlessly. Mrs. Durrant's friends closed in around her.

The parting of the mother and son was touching. There was one long kiss, passionate and endlessly sad. It was as if both realized there was now an end to their caresses. But in the mother's eyes still shone the faith in which there was no hope.

She believed in her son yet. His eyes were gray, noncommital. As he left her side he was surrounded by a guard of deputies and policemen twice as large as before. As he passed through the doorway, his last gesture was a familiar one as he twirled his moustache. It was the same Durrant, cool, contained, and as placid as ever.

Later, when giving his first interview as a convicted murderer, Theo related his impression of the day's events:

They say that my dear mother screamed today when the verdict was announced. It's all like a dream to me. The first thing I remember was that her arms were around my body. Everything else was so cruel, so sudden. I felt safe in her arms. I could stand any wrong, any injustice, but for my mother and sister.

Upon her return to Berlin from Malmitz, Maud began to confide in three or four German-speaking elder ladies with whom she passed much of her free time. They invited her to various and, on occasion, grand social events, in an obvious attempt to lend her the maternal support she missed. She also began to gather around her a coterie of student friends, the closest being May Hamaker, with whom she would pass two summer holidays.

According to her diary, her social activities at this time were diverse but not colourful, her relationships with her fellow students – and boarders – amicable but not intimate. (Both colour and intimacy lay ahead.)

As for her studies, she was "resolved to do better." As the trauma of Theo's trial proceedings evolved, she dissimulated as best she could the nervous strain she was suffering. She resumed her routine, her interest in singing unabated. The day after her return to Berlin, "dressed to kill," she had called on Professor Knudson. Admiring her get-up, he said that "I ought not to have any trouble to marry a Prince and then I would have money to pay for lessons." (It seems that he temporarily declined to give her more lessons gratis.) He also told her to improve her German and invited her "to come when I have time and listen and sing – a little." Deaf to his hints, she revisited Professor Knudson four days later with well-deserved discomfort: "My dress was so tight I could not half breathe, and I sang only a little" – no doubt to Knudson's relief. She heeded, however, the professor's advice to improve her German, and arranged to exchange daily language lessons with Martin Phillar, who was anxious to improve his English. Phillar was by way of being an actor and appeared, fleetingly, in Leipzig and Berlin theatres at the turn of the century. Maud mentions him occasionally in her diary with regard to the corset business, as if he were in charge of scheduling specific activities.

Her diary also provides glimpses of this strange character. "I must ever maintain my dignity with him," Maud noted soon after the lessons had started, "or he will get silly. How I do get tired of men is not understandable to me. How coarsely he laughs! by making such noises in the nose. Ugh." At another session Phillar told Maud she was "of a very cold nature. Do I like that? I am not a cold person, yet it is just as well he thinks so." In what was probably a last-ditch effort at conquest, Phillar took to flattery: "I should not allow him to call me 'kind goddess,' but somehow there is some satisfaction in it," Maud reflected. The relationship remained amicable, although Phillar threw out disturbing hints that he knew about Theo. The language lessons lasted a few months. Eventually Maud spoke immaculate German.

While her diary records regular attendance at the Hochschule and enjoyable piano lessons with Professor Peterssen, it also indicates that she gave little time to the piano, at least on a regular basis. Even so, she was progressing well. On November 6, she wrote of a bursary: "I ought to be happy for one thing tonight. I have for this term a half free Stellung. How my heart trembled when Peterssen told me to go to [Administrator] Blankenburg – and when he did tell me I had no words to respond, I was so surprised and glad and astonished, too. But what soll Ich machen? Can I by willpower overcome the difficulty which Peterssen speaks of? Why not? If only I could get the proper willpower into my stupid old head!" The problem was stage fright, which, she noted several times, prevented her from participating in prescribed student recitals. Although she never overcame "the difficulty," she managed, somewhat perversely, to control it as a dancer.

As the year 1895 drew to a close, Maud summarized her thoughts:

December 30: Oh how quickly the days are going and yet still no end in sight to our troubles. This A.M. I received a long loving letter from dearest Mamma – poor little dear how her heart must ache. Poor brother, how does he bear his position, and Papa, how can he work with that weight of sorrow? Oh! to think that February 21 has been set for the time when those cruel men will take my poor innocent brother's life to avenge the wrong. God save all of us – protect us from the climax that seems upon us. Bring forth some proof – before it is too late – that will bring Theo back to us. Oh heavenly Father have mercy. Cleaned skates, practised.[20]

December 31: Practised all A.M. At midnight the church bells were ringing and everyone hollered "Prost." The New Year doesn't bring me the joy I felt at the beginning of last year, yet I hope it will end happier than this.

It did not.

MAUD BEGAN 1896 with a burst of energy that lasted till the summer holidays. Perhaps because of the immediate appeal of Theo's conviction, delusive hope replaced debilitating uncertainty; perhaps she decided to ignore the problem for as long as possible. In any case, during this period her diary rarely refers to her family. She seems to have been more concerned with her voice; upon taking her first lesson with Professor Knudson after a lapse of some time, it was a "little husky." But the greater her enthusiasm ("I am so interested in singing that I can hardly wait for the next lesson") the worse the results. Occasionally she had reason to be pleased, as when Knudson declared "it was wonderful how I was gifted with the trill" (to which she added, "If only I could get the runs, darn it") or when, after she sang before her fellow students, "all were amazed and said I was extremely musical." (She may have misunderstood their amazement.) More frequent, however, were self-appraisals ranging from despair – "I am so discouraged, I sang worse than a cow" – to bafflement – "I don't see why I should sing so sharp one time, so flat another."

Nonetheless, she felt at home in Berlin. Some indication of the extent of her identification with her surroundings is given in her opening diary entry for April 6 – "Easter Monday, as we Germans call it." That this comment was neither totally affected nor facetious is illustrated by a unique experience recorded in her diary some weeks later:

May 1: My, we are all excitement. While fixing my account book May [Hamaker] came in to say that the whole Hochschule was to appear before the Kaiser [Wilhelm II] and the Kaiserin before the Neue Museum opposite the Schloss tomorrow at 3:30. . . . [Administrator] Blankenburg, after asking me if I understood German, invited me to be one of the eleven ladies to greet their Highnesses at the head of the steps. They were supposed to be all German girls, and I am the only Auslander. I am quite proud. After supper fussed over my dress.

May 2: Well, my part of "court lady" is over and everything seems like a dream. It was all too short. At noon took vocal lesson and didn't get home till 1:10, dressed, and at 2:15 was at the Hochschule. We rode down in private carriages – closed – black horses. My! the crowd of people on the Unter den Linden and the Museum! The other students took their places behind the ropes and we eleven in the middle by the Entrance. . . . The whole Court came and passed in. Students from all the academies with banners and in costume came, and all was excitement till 4, when the Kaiser and Kaiserin came. . . . The royal pair looked so nice and not stuck up at all. Ha! we girls followed the royal party, saw and heard everything. We made a Court bow, and were driven home at 6 P.M.

The Kaiser read his address and spoke in his throat. His left arm is shorter than his right, and in fact he has very little use of it. A number of teachers from the Hochschule received Orders.

A few days after this event a letter from Theo arrived, describing an equally unusual albeit grotesque display outside his prison cell. "Yesterday," he wrote,

I had a party from the Great Mormon Choir to see me and they sang two songs and the leading lady sang *The Last Rose of Summer*. Oh, it was exquisite. Although they were not divided into equal parts, it was something grand. There were about forty in the party, and such rosy cheeks and healthy girls I never saw before. Every note came forth as from one instrument and each and all sounded like some monster organ or symphony orchestra playing in unison. All off hand work, too. I never heard the like before. There are 1200 in the Temple Choir and 150 of them are here on a trip

for pleasure and have been prevailed upon to give concerts.
. . . What substantial healthy girls they were! They were
accompanied by male members also. They were pleasantly
disappointed with me and have changed their mind about
me. I was sorry Mamma was not here to hear them but then
Mrs. Coleman was, however. After, some of them called up
on her and came out to see Mamma.

P.S. You had better not marry a Dutchman unless he is a
rich prince and willing to do *your* will.

At this time Maud met Arnold Holtz, neither a rich
prince nor willing to do *her* will, but an Austrian army
officer and her first German-speaking avowed admirer. He
first paid excessive attention to her at a masquerade ball,
which he attended as a lieutenant of Frederick I's day. Maud
and two fellow boarders dressed "as children with hair
flying." Holtz escorted the three girls home; upon taking his
leave he greatly impressed Maud by gallantly kissing her
hand – and no one else's. Late that evening, expressing an
urge that foreshadows the climactic moment in *The Vision of
Salome*, Maud recorded a passing impulse: "Don't tell, little
diary, but I think he has the sweetest mouth, and I would
like to kiss it."

After a three-month absence on military duties, Holtz
reappeared in July and following a dinner party made his
first pitch suddenly, secretly, and dramatically:

We sat at the table from 3 to 6:30. I had to laugh at the way
Holtz kissed my hand at Mahlzeit so that the others would
not see him. I was, though, thoroughly astonished when, a
few minutes later, he asked me not to leave with May and
Frau Praetorius. He seemed so in earnest that I began to
wonder why, but a few minutes later he told me. He loves
me and wants me for his own. I told him I did not love him.
Poor fellow, he cried and is all broken up. I told Frau
Praetorius and she arranged for him to see me on Tuesday
at 1. Poor fellow, what shall I do with him? He is a good
fellow – but. At 8 P.M. we left, Holtz broken hearted in a
bedroom upstairs. I feel so sad and heavy hearted.

"He seems to be head over heels in love with me," noted Maud following the Tuesday meeting. "I like him but do not love him. He says he will wait and see if he can make me love him. He is willing to risk it and says that if he can, his life's luck is found. Poor man, he knows, too, that I have not a cent to my name. We talked it over and decided to get to know each other better. We are to correspond."

But Holtz wanted Maud, not her letters or the opportunity "to get to know each other better." No doubt because the Hochschule term was coming to an end and Maud was about to leave Berlin for a holiday, he decided to wine and dine her. The evening was colourful, but unsatisfying. "It was so interesting to hear him converse with Nico the Greek merchant. The Greek wine was delicious. I didn't like A. making a fuss over the goose, though. I couldn't smell that it was tainted. He had managed to pick the bone pretty clean before he noticed it was tainted. Later, we refreshed ourselves with a rare Wiesbaden wine and bread and cheese."

The next evening Holtz took her to the ballet (about which she made no comment); but both were tired from the previous evening, and Maud was angry because Holtz arrived with a cigarette in hand and chain-smoked without once asking her permission. "That one act has lowered him a heap in my estimation." Although the two met again after the summer holidays, Holtz gave up his pursuit. For a short time Maud tried to renew his ardour, only to realize his previous avowals were fictive.[21]

The vacation was spent in the Thuringen mountains, a popular northern tourist area. Maud travelled with three companions: May Hamaker, May's mother, who was visiting from the United States, and a Mr. Bauer, a rather well off German American who served as guide and, on occasion, host to all three women. The party's main activity was day-long hiking, its first destination being Oberschonnen, "a funny little town where pigs, horses, chickens, cows and people all live in the same house." The two girls immediately began a daily regime of "two quarts of delicious milk, hot from the cow."

During the next six weeks the party moved from village to village in a vain attempt to avoid the rain. Before long, the happy band became fractious. Mr. Bauer reprimanded Maud for inventing some kind of "Chinese dance" in a village street.[22] Maud's relationship with Mrs. Hamaker went from bad to worse, leading her to contrast the woman with her own mother: "Though Mamma has not had all the advantages that Mrs. Hamaker has had, yet she is far superior in many ways, always pushing me on to elevate myself, to use well every minute, and not spend my time in unfine talk or rude thoughts. Mrs. Hamaker is only interested in jokes and stories she tells, and falls asleep when someone else tells a story." This would have been most offensive to one whose talents as a raconteuse would become celebrated.

During these holidays several letters reached Maud. In one, Theo commented upon a compliment Martin Phillar had paid her in a conversation with Mrs. Hamaker. His reaction and confused syntax (he was habitually so meticulous) hint at the nature – later if not already the subject of widespread rumours – of his infatuation with his sister. "Of course," he remarked, "my sister is all he said she was and a thousand times more, too, and she doesn't know a tiny bit how Teddy loves her. He never half appreciated her worth till I found her gone." This remark, no matter how well intentioned, how endearing, may have added to Maud's later burden of guilt.

To another letter of June 26 Theo added the following postscript:

Nell Partridge [sister of Harry, one of Theo's contemporaries at Cooper Medical College] and Ma spend today with McCulloughs at Colma San Mateo Co. Cal. I am so glad and Nell is such a grand girl. She runs up so often to see Ma, ain't she good tho – I had the greatest dream you ever heard about her. I dreamed we were all at a picnic and were about to return home and she has left us tho everyone saw us picking our strings up. I turned back and saw Nell coming towards me and she was eating what appeared to be rubber balls, but they were rubber balls with whiskey in them. I smelled it when she came up close and she was "full as a goat." Whew but wasn't she tho.

I looked in astonishment and she began to reel and it began to rain and she appeared to be dressed in a beautiful bathing suit which by the action of the rain was all washed off leaving her à la statue. I was in a great way as to what to do, but in looking down I discovered I had a blanket in my hands which I used to encircle her, then taking her up in my arms I looked for a place to go. I seemed to have left the picnic grounds and was behind a fence which shut off a lake. It was terribly warm and the sun beat down on the lake and in a corner by the fence, yet it rained.

I found a lot of straw or hay and made bed and at this juncture the rain ceased and sun became hotter so I laid her upon the bed and she began to steam and in a moment the blanket all steamed away (again à la statue recumbent). The heat diminished and I was in a terrible stew. I didn't know what to do. She got up and came and put her arms around me and clung to me. I then made her a skirt of straw not being able to remove a stitch of my clothes for some reason or other and in a few minutes we found a flying machine into which we got and were landed upon her own roof at home from which I carried her down and into her house. Wasn't that a great experience? Ma told Nell and Alice [Lonnon] and I had to tell Alice again when she came down. Now don't breathe a word of this to a soul over there or here, but tear it off from where mark is and destroy, see.

Mrs. Durrant's letters were more inclined to practical advice: "If you always stand as if you were standing on the balls of your feet, that is all you need to do. Just raise on the balls of your feet and then come down on your heel very gently, then always keep in that posture. There you have it in a nutshell. I try to keep straight but my back hurts and so will yours."

At the beginning of September, Maud and May returned to Berlin. There, for the duration of the school year, they shared a room in the pension of Frau Ilgenstein, a divorced mother of six. May then moved but, at her mother's insistence, Maud remained until a few weeks after her brother's execution in January 1898.[23] She had returned to Berlin in fine physical fettle, but remained sick at heart. Her diary makes no reference to Theo's case; thanks to his lawyers' delaying tactics, it was then dormant. "The vague feeling of uneasiness is leaving me," Maud recorded, "but the feeling of insignificance is getting stronger. I shall go crazy if it continues much longer. I must rouse myself and be somebody. Why am I so afraid of people? I certainly can do a lot if I say 'I can,' and stick to it. I can't expect other people to do for me or to bother with me. I must work my way alone. Practiced a bit, sewed, indulged later in a fit of the blues."

Her depression was obvious to Professor Peterssen, who warned her that it might affect her studies. Depressed or not, she was losing interest in the piano, if the total absence of comment about practising or progress is any indication. She still dreamed of an operatic career and persuaded Berlin's leading voice coach, Frau Emilie Herzog, to audition her. Frau Herzog accepted her: 60 marks a month for two lessons a week. Maud's first lesson took place nearly two months later. "I tell you she is such a little person," Maud inaccurately noted, "but my, how she can sing and act. My lesson went OK but I still came away a little husky." After half a dozen lessons the impoverished student left Frau Herzog.

"I am launching into a Reform dressmaker, wouldn't Mamma laugh if she could hear me talk!" wrote Maud in November. She was referring to the corset project, which seemed to be getting off the ground.[24] The business took up increasing time but probably supplemented the meagre allowance her parents somehow scraped together. (Between

September and the year's end they sent her a total of 180 marks, or about $45. She paid Fran Ilgenstein 65 marks a month for her room and board.)

As an antidote to her discontentment and as a diversion from the corset business, she started to frequent informal evenings for music students, organized by music-loving families. It was probably at one of these gatherings that she first met the very young Artur Rubinstein, who had recently arrived to study in Berlin. In his delightful autobiography Rubinstein writes at some length about such evenings and unabashedly recalls his youthful crush on Martha Drew, an American student from Philadelphia and, like Maud, some years older than he. Maud mentions Martha Drew three times in her diary.

Her diary for these months also contains a number of unusually revealing entries. Her reaction to a now lost letter from her mother two days after returning to Berlin from her summer holiday indicates the melodramatic determination with which she faced her singular situation: "Poor Mamma," she noted, "she thinks I have lost courage. Have I? Dare I? NO! I must work, no matter how discouraged I grow. I have a duty to perform and I must do it, or die in the attempt. God helping me I will succeed."

In mid-November another letter from her mother, apparently repeating similar upbraidings supplemented with disconcerting hints about Theo's prospects, shows another aspect of Maud's terrible conflict:

> Dear darling Mamma, she is trying so hard to give me all the advantages I crave, and I must reward her by doing well and not throwing my time away. What if I should receive word to come home ["for a last look at your brother," as Mrs. Durrant had written many months earlier]? No, I could not go. They would be so disappointed. Oh for the lacking power to succeed [a Germanism]. I must. From this day on I have given my word to not miss any of my work, come what may.

Her diary does not indicate whether she fulfilled this vow.

Yet another entry, four days later, elaborates on her feelings should she be summoned to return to San Francisco: "Somehow I feel so anxious about Theo. I am so afraid I will have to go home, but then I must not lose my courage. We will get a new trial and all will turn out to our satisfaction. I would be such a disappointment to them all were I to go home now."

This was followed, the next day, by a sudden meditation, unique to the diary. Totally ignoring the preceding entries, it opened with a rhetorical question:

> What is music study? Real hard work? In America we have an altogether different picture in our minds of study in Europe. We think "Oh for a chance to study abroad," and yet when we are here we seem to lose the picture from out of our sight and work along in a semi-earnest fashion and then when everything goes slowly and we make little progress, we blame it on lack of talent etc. Much talent is thrown away just so – through wanting to do with little work.

On Christmas Eve, Ernst, the eldest of the Ilgenstein children, returned from Hamburg, where he had been a student. He at once became spellbound with his mother's new boarder. "We made time spin this evening," runs Maud's diary for December 26, "in fact all day. We had Living Pictures. Ernst and I presented 'Lebensmüde' ['Tired of Life'] and was good, so the others say. Everyone joined in, even [twelve-year-old] Heinz. Ernst has taken upon himself to be my champion, and now the first to say anything that don't suit him (about me) he is up in arms."

In choosing "Lebensmüde" as the theme of their living picture presentation, Maud and Ernst no doubt intended to personify the spirit of deep-seated ennui, so popular a pose with their generation. However, Maud's participation in this living picture is of particular interest for two reasons. The first relates to her later success as the Salome Dancer.

For Richard Wagner and Charles Baudelaire, two of the progenitors of the Decadent movement, an ennui so deep-rooted as to be more a disgust than a tiredness with life led them beyond the conventions of social behaviour and creative expression. The affinity of Maud's art with the Decadent movement, which flourished throughout the last third of the nineteenth century, is very clear. Much of her sensational success lay in her daring projection of such feelings, from her unique portrayal of Salome (already a cult figure for the Decadents) to her intensely personal version of Salome's story. It may be argued that, although the Decadent movement culminated sociologically in Oscar Wilde's downfall, its last aesthetic expression was Maud's forgotten *Vision of Salome*. The "Lebensmüde" tableau, therefore, was a primitive, unconscious foreshadowing of the daring originality of *The Vision of Salome*.

The second element of interest has to do with psychological insight, a faculty the skilfully manipulative Maud possessed far more with regard to others than to herself. As she appraised the year 1896, her strength of character reinforced by the haunting dread of failing her mother's expectations no doubt prevented any persistent feeling that she was "tired of life," even though she had many reasons to be so.[25] Instead of enjoying the Christmas holidays in Berlin with her darling mother and beloved brother, she was passing it as the impoverished boarder in a modest Berlin pension. Instead of completing his medical studies in Berlin, Theo was a condemned murderer in San Francisco, the outcome of his appeal for a new trial increasingly uncertain. Instead of advancing in her piano studies, Maud had been warned that her state of mind threatened to impede her progress. Instead of feeling at ease with the American colony in Berlin, she shunned all but a certain Mrs. Rice, terrified lest she be asked about Theo. Finally, instead of being begged to return home in this time of crisis, she had been ordered by her brother to remain in Berlin.

Little wonder, therefore, that the Ilgenstein family and Maud's fellow boarders were impressed by the "Lebensmüde" presentation: by putting her heart and soul into the presentation she had, unknown to her audience and very probably to herself, given vent to her innermost feelings. In the years ahead, precisely the same psychology would prevail in her dancing career, particularly in her performance of *The Vision of Salome* and her "visualization" of Chopin's *Marche funèbre*. The permanent imprint of the family tragedy upon her creative imagination produced compelling and inimitable performances.

No doubt those present on December 24, 1896, knew nothing of the reasons that led her to pose with such personal conviction. Throughout her life she presented a convincing façade, although at times she would be cloaked in an inexplicable reserve, at others in a disturbing moodiness. The willingness of the Ilgenstein family to accept her, even though she grew to disdain them, must have been an enormous comfort.[26] After all, where else could she go?

ERNST'S CHAMPIONSHIP had immediate effects. Maud became smitten with this young man, "so full of flame and fire." (When Ernst's sister surmised that he was falling in love, Maud's reaction was "Ha! Ha! life is short!") Within the first week of 1897 she was giving him English lessons and had a "cosy chat" with this "real jolly boy, but if I don't watch out he'll get sentimental. I know one thing, I must be stricter and not allow him to look so lovingly at me, yet he is a good boy – and smart, too."

Harmless spice was added to the budding relationship when May Hamaker started to flirt with Ernst's younger brother Fredy, and all four became fearful that the new servant girl might "squatch" on them to Frau Ilgenstein. But when, very quickly, the English lessons turned into talks on "social standing etc.," and when Maud took to rising early in order to see Ernst before he left for the day, Ernst seems to have got cold feet.

"I wish," she noted in early February, "Ernst would tell me what worries him." When she mustered courage enough to ask him, Ernst replied, "Liebe Maud, don't alter your manner to me," a request that prompted the reflection that "with all his faults – he is not handsome – yet he draws me to him and to tell the truth I find him an enjoyable companion. I wish he were older. He is not what since a child I have held as my ideal, yet there is a sympathy between us that I can't explain. . . . He is not like most young men – frivolous – but earnest and sensible." This was a curious change from her original view of him as "so full of flame and fire."

Ernst then started to flirt with May Hamaker. Upon catching the two together, Maud became "so blue that my whole demeanour changed and my face grew hot. Why am I so? He is nothing to me." And yet, the very next day, she ventured into his room on the pretext of "asking him something," only to be confronted by an irate Frau Ilgenstein, who "opened fire and Ernst took my part! The war was hot for a good half hour when we all made up. But now I know that Ernst thinks a great deal of me, having quarrelled with his mother over me." A week later, however, Maud quizzically said to Ernst at the dining table, " 'All men like the attention of women – especially actors' – he gave me such a look that I had to leave the room at the first opportunity."

This adolescent relationship – so different from her liaisons following her brother's execution, fizzled in a characteristic fashion. One evening, when May was absent, Ernst was "very nice to me." Thereupon Maud cut him short, told him she had a letter to write, and bade him a brusque goodnight. "He looked queerish at me – just what I wanted." To what purpose only Maud could fathom. Thereafter she emotionally exiled Ernst from her diary until, on New Year's Eve, 1898, a week before her brother's scheduled execution, she accepted from Ernst "a goodnight kiss – a brother's kiss as assurance of his friendship."

Meanwhile, for almost the first three months of 1897 her diary has but one concerned reference to the family problem. On March 24 she received a cable reading "Await today's letter." She at once assumed this was a summons to return home.[27] Yet she makes no reference to that assumption, her family, or that letter, for a whole month. Even then she records only that her newly found voice teacher, Frau

Corelli, told her that, following denial of a second appeal, Theo's execution date had been set for June 11. "Why don't they write and tell me?" Maud asked reasonably enough.

One reason they had not told her was that they were busy writing articles for the *San Francisco Examiner*. In its issue of June 6, the newspaper headlined two statements related to Theo's scheduled execution. The first of these articles, accompanied by a large portrait of Mrs. Durrant, was titled "Why I Will Be Present At My Son's Execution." The second, a two-paragraph statement in Theo's handwriting, bore the heading "Why I Am Willing That My Mother Witness My Execution."

In her article, Isabella explained her two-fold purpose. The first was that "he will know for as long as he is conscious of anything in this world, that Mamma's sweetheart will not die alone. The second is almost too sacred to be put into words. It is to claim the remains of my loved one. The moment the law is finished with him he is mine, and as sacred to me as every darling boy is to his mother. Mine, mine, he will be then, all mine!"

After more sentiments of this nature, and reminiscences of his childhood and adolescence, Mrs. Durrant declared that "those who know Theo consider him a martyr. Instead of being the greatest criminal of the century, he is the greatest martyr."

Theo's statement is equally ghoulish. He supported Isabella's wishes simply because he always obeyed his "loving, tender, devoted, and trusting mother."

At the last moment he won a reprieve – on legal grounds rather than as a result of these statements, although they no doubt brought in some much-needed funds.

Exactly two weeks later, after the execution date had been advanced to November 11, the *Examiner* published the following article by Maud:

AN AMERICAN GIRL

AND HER GREAT SORROW

SOMETHING OF THE LIFE AND HOPES OF MAUD

DURRANT, SISTER OF THE CON-
DEMNED STUDENT

On the other side of the Atlantic, in the German capital, Miss Maud Durrant has for two years been waiting to hear the fate of her only brother. Little has been said of this sister, far off in a foreign land, and only the most intimate friends have realized the extent of her suffering.

There has been considerable surmise as to why she did not hasten home immediately after the arrest of her brother, some time during the trial, or after the sentence. People have wondered whether she would or would not be here at the last, if the extreme penalty of the law be imposed. But no stranger knew, and the Durrants remained silent. They have been careful from the first to keep their daughter in the background, screening her from public view. Even the close friends of the family are not aware what course the daughter will pursue, if everything goes against their son. It is the general belief that Miss Durrant will not return if her brother goes to the scaffold; that she will stay in Berlin and perhaps never come back.

The truth is that the sister across the water has never for a moment thought of neglecting her brother if it should become necessary for him to give up his life. Miss Durrant intends to be here to give her lifelong comrade all the support and affection a sister can give at such a time. "Mamma, Mamma," she kept on writing, "if it comes to the worst send me word in time. Don't leave it until it is too late." At first the parents opposed the return of their daughter. They feared the nervous strain, the terrible shock, would be too severe a tax on her health. They advised her to remain where she was. But in loyalty to her childhood playmate, Miss Durrant threw advice to the wind. "If it comes to the worst, I shall go home to my brother," she wrote, "I could not be satisfied otherwise."

So the parents consented. They felt they could not say no. The money for her fare was forwarded to Germany, and several times during the last two months Miss Durrant has packed her trunks and prepared to start for home. Each time she was prevented by favorable news from home. The young lady has been in constant communication with her parents by post and cable since the first day of their great sorrow.

Mr. Durrant has prepared two special cables and the daughter understands her movements are to be guided by them. One reads "Everything favorable. Stay where you are." The other is "Come home immediately. Will telegraph you in New York."

Alone in a great city at a time when she should have been surrounded by loving friends, Miss Durrant experienced the intensest kind of sorrow. No one in the gay German capital knew at first that the beautiful American girl, who has been studying at the Royal School of Music, was the sister of the San Francisco medical student charged with the Emmanuel Baptist Church murders. For a time the girl guarded her secret well. She dreaded notoriety and could not bear to have anyone know that her brother was accused of diabolic crime. However much she grieved in private, she kept up bravely before the world, but it was not long before everyone in the American colony in Berlin knew of Miss Durrant's sorrow. She had many sympathizers, but she was reserved about her brother and people respected her desire not to talk about her brother. It was not until the Supreme Court handed down its adverse judgement that the sister broke down and opened her heart to friends.

During her two years' residence in Berlin, Miss Durrant has become a favorite in American and German circles. She is a bright, attractive girl with a winning manner and a cheerful disposition. She is of the blond type, and is considered beautiful in form and face. When scarcely five years old she displayed unusual musical talent. She had to be lifted on to the music stool, but when once there she stayed for hours playing popular tunes by ear and improvising little melodies. Before she went to Europe she composed several very pretty ballads. The young lady is now in her last term of her second year at the Royal High School of Music. It is her intention to take a four-year course. Miss Durrant is accomplished in other lines of art. She is something of a sketch artist and an expert at wood carving.

Through all the dark days the Durrant family has passed through during the last two years, the sister has never wavered in her belief that her brother is innocent and this is the message she sends him: "I have as much love and confidence in you today, Theo, as the morning I kissed you goodbye and whispered 'Be a good boy, dearie, and be sure to graduate.'"

This statement is remarkable, given the circumstances, for its apparent forthrightness, its controlled anguish. The possibility of returning to San Francisco is, to judge by the extant personal papers, spurious: pride, understandably enough, got the better of truth. The arrangements for advising her of Theo's fate may have been made but broke down lamentably.

If there runs throughout the statement an uncertainty as to whether she should or could return to San Francisco, the reason is simple. Theo had remained adamant that she remain "at her work." He and she would be spared the horror of meeting in a prison cell – maybe the notorious "condemned cell" to which he fleetingly referred in one of his letters.[28]

Yet nothing reveals her anguish or lays bare her soul as does her diary entry of May 17, 1897, three weeks prior to the publication of the article written at her mother's urging: "How I long to be free of the chains that are binding me. I want to fly away from my surroundings, away, away. No one knows my feelings and no one shall know them. I am going to worry myself ill, I know. Oh, why am I so tormented? What have I done?"

She never freed herself. Yet through her unique, intensely personal art, she ultimately found a means of loosening some of those chains.

Notes

1. "The first day that Blanche Lamont's disappearance was discussed at church Theodore came home and wrote to his sister Maud, giving a full account of it. The next two days he sent her marked papers containing the newspaper reports of it. Would a man guilty of her death do that?" (statement of William Durrant to the *San Francisco Examiner* of April 18, 1895). Earlier, during an interview with the *Examiner* while returning to San Francisco from Mount Diablo, Theo remarked, "I liked Miss Lamont very much. She was so much like my sister – so active and jolly." The Dillon *Tribune* (Blanche's hometown paper) of April 19, 1895, described Blanche as "bright, vivacious, pretty. She had a fair complexion, large brown eyes and brown hair. She was tall and slender, and not very strong physically."

On April 20 Maud noted in her diary receipt of "letters from Mamma and May and a note from Theo. They all spoke of the disappearance of Blanche Lamont. I am so unhappy."

2. On Sunday morning last the sunlight flashed the news from Telegraph Hill to a point high up on Mount Diablo that the first of the victims of the Emmanuel Baptist Church had been found.

   The flashes are sent in "dots" and "flashes," a quick flick of the mirror being a dot, and a slow a dash. The points selected were too far removed from one another to permit flag signalling, and the detachments of the corps carried only the appliances necessary for "heliographing," as the writing by sun is called (*San Francisco Examiner*, April 16, 1895).

The procedure was all the more exciting because this was said to be the first (and probably the only) time heliographing was used for nonmilitary purposes.

3. Theo attended this meeting, held at the home of Dr. Vogel, a dentist. He arrived one hour late – at about nine. In Dr. Vogel's words: "What Durrant said when he came here was that he had been out with the horses and got his hands dirty. I took him to the washstand and there he washed his hands and brushed his hair, which was somewhat dishevelled. We all noticed his forehead was covered with perspiration. He read

a letter from his sister, who is abroad" (*Examiner*, April 15, 1895).

4. On October 13, 1895 – after she had given her testimony and some three weeks before the trial ended – Mrs. Noble made the following statement, reported in the *Los Angeles Times*:

> On Friday at 9 A.M. Durrant called on us with *The Newcomes*. [Blanche's sister] Maud answered the door. He asked if Blanche was at home, expressed no surprise at seeing Maud, who would ordinarily have been at school. When told she was not at home, Durrant said, "I thought I might see her." Maud closed the door and said, "Auntie, I believe he knows that Blanche is missing. Why should he come to see her at this hour? It is past schooltime and he acted strangely . . . " A sickening realization came to me and I said, "Durrant killed that girl." That was before noon on Saturday.

5. Blanche seems to have come well protected, albeit unintentionally: "She wore more underclothing than the ordinary woman burdens herself with. Besides a suit of undergarments with an extra pair of black equestrienne tights, there was a corset waist, a pair of corset covers, a black sateen combination petticoat and waist, and a pair of stockings discovered in the rafters [of the church]" (*Examiner*, April 15, 1895).

6. In a letter to Maud dated September 28, 1897, Theo paid tribute to "General" Dickinson:

> There is one man who is grand, noble and everything applaudable. He is General Dickinson. What he has done for us has been tremendous and were I acquitted tomorrow, half a lifetime of service could never repay him.
>
> The greatest part of all the work has been done in his office under his direction. However, the others have worked nobly as has young Louis Boardman also and ex–U.S. District Attorney Gartin in our favor. We hope everything will turn out well in the end. We have every reason to hope and think it will.

Theo had little respect for Eugene Deuprey, who took over the deed to the Durrant home in payment for his services. The parents remained in the house until about 1900, when they moved to what Mrs. Durrant described as "a shack" of three rooms.

7. "For six weeks or more San Francisco has been the theatre of a carnival of blood by which the most crime-stained period in its earliest and most lawless days sinks to insignificance. Day after day the press has been forced to record the history of murder after murder, suicide after suicide, until at last the climax has been reached in the brutal butchery of two young girls" (Fresno *Republican*).

These excerpted editorials were published in the *Examiner* of April 20, 1895, under the heading "The Interior Press." In the days following, the *Examiner* published scores of readers' (usually unsigned) letters about the case, few of which doubted Theo's guilt.

8. Two days earlier, the *Times* had headlined its report of the case "He Can Smile and Smile and be a Villain still." This aptly describes the essence of his peculiar charisma that was so similar to his sister's.

Dr. Barrett, who performed the autopsies, told the *Examiner*:

> The Williams girl was undoubtedly strangled first and then the cutting was done. I found the chest filled with blood, and there were three punctures in the heart from between the second and the third ribs. There was also a hacked wound in that space, and also one in the space between the fifth and sixth ribs that also went into the pericardium but did not pierce the heart. Both wrists were cut, the radial and ulnar arteries being severed. (*Examiner*, April 15, 1895)

The previous day, the *Examiner* had published similar details – in more blood-curdling language:

> The autopsy showed how atrocious had been the crime. Both wrists had been hacked to the bone so that the hands were nearly severed from the arm. Down the middle of the forehead, ending at the middle of the nose, there was a wide irregular cut that was frightfully disfiguring but was the further removed from fatal injury than any of the others.
>
> On the left breast were three long cuts and stabs that appeared to have been inflicted in a crazy manner. Two of them were so deep that they reached the heart and it was in these gaping wounds that bits of the broken knife blade were found.

A piece of her clothing had, so it was also reported, been stuffed down her throat.

9. A critical element in the circumstantial evidence was that no blood was found on the clothes Theo was wearing when he attended the Christian Endeavour meeting the evening of Minnie's murder. The following paragraph from Isabella Durrant's letter to Maud of June 1, 1895, gives the probable reason:

> I called on Mrs. Howell as I came home today and she told me something that was too ridiculous for anything. I will tell you to show you what to expect when the trial opens – that is, from the prosecution's side. It was this: one day, one of the married women of the church wanted a book of reference and met Theo, so the story goes. Theo is supposed to have said, "Come to the church and I will get it for you." So they went and when she was up on the ladder she happened to look around and lo and behold, there was Theo perfectly nude. She ran out and never stopped until she got home. She never told her husband until she heard of the present situation, and he said, "You go down to the Chief of Police tell him what you saw." Think of that! I want to laugh. They want to find something that will do because they can not find any blood, so this is one of the stories that will do instead, making out he committed the crimes in a nude state. So, be prepared for anything you hear and don't worry.

This incident was duly reported in the press, with the added report that other women had had similar experiences.

In none of Maud's extant papers is there any direct acknowledgement of Theo's guilt. A number of casual comments, some cited in this biography, indicate, however, that both Mrs. Durrant and Maud conceded to themselves but to no one else the possibility that Theo had committed murder.

It appears that the police intercepted Mrs. Durrant's letters to Maud. Several obscure references to this occur in Maud's diaries and her mother's letters, of which the following, all from a very long letter of May 6/8, 1895, are the clearest:

> You had better burn all letters after you have read them – that is, Theo's and mine – as I do not like the idea of my badly written letters being read by others. Then it won't be necessary to send us the letters, only the envelopes to let us see how

they were opened. We will try to find out about them – if they had the right to do such a thing . . .

My darling, I hardly know when to stop writing letters once I start, but I want you to send home the envelope and letter that was cut open. Be very careful that you mark just where it was cut open and keep right on sending your letters disguised. I am so very sorry we were not more careful. I told Papa I was afraid that would happen but he said they would not dare do that. They dare do anything they want to do.

10. "I was not afraid of being lynched on the boat, but when the crowd ran after me on Market Street, I saw the possibility. When I saw the people ready to fall back as soon as one of my guards showed a pistol, I was re-assured, and I am confident I will come out of this all right" (*Examiner*, April 15, 1895).

11. The day following the guilty verdict, the *Examiner* carried a lengthy article by Dr. Forbes Webster, "probably the greatest alienist in the world." It read, in part:

From a study of his physiognomy I should say he is a youth of determined character and of a class frequently met with whose parents and friends have been loth to recognize as being of unsound mind until some crime has been committed which brings his real condition to the world.

. . . The form of mental disorder from which, in my opinion, Durrant is suffering may occur suddenly or may become irresistible, or the passion may have been nursed for some time until it obtains dominion over everything else. His facial expression, contour of skull, physiognomy and general condition lead me to regard this youth as one not altogether to be regarded as a responsible individual.

12. No doubt the very devout Theo would have appreciated a visit from Dr. Case or one of his colleagues. He expressed bitterness that his own pastor, Dr. Gibson, did not visit him; but the complaint was in part politically motivated, as Dr. Gibson had been suspected briefly to be the murderer.

On October 10, 1896, Isabella concluded a letter to Maud thus: "I have no use for the churches, they are only for those that are well, not in trouble. Not one of the ministers has been near Theo in a year, and if they wait until I ask them they will wait a long time, for I do not think that if he should die tomorrow I would call one in to speak over him."

The Salvation Army befriended Theo, but a Catholic priest, at his request, accompanied him to the gallows.

Mrs. Durrant was as good as her word. After the execution, when Theo's body was returned to the Durrant home, the Salvation Army led the mourners in hymn singing.

13. The reference to the third body was absolutely incorrect. At first, the disappearance of a Mrs. Forsyth some weeks earlier was wildly attributed to Theo. The error forcefully hints at the frenzy following the discovery of the murders.

14. This is the first of several comments indicating that despatches from San Francisco outlining the crime appeared in Berlin newspapers.

15. Nowhere in her diaries or in the family letters is there reference to any hope of acquittal. Only once – some four years after Theo's execution – does Isabella Durrant mention as her goal "getting life" for him. That goal was ironic as well as pathetic, for by the time Theo was executed he seems to have been riddled with tuberculosis. Moreover, had he been acquitted, he might have been charged with the murder of Minnie Williams. However, his lawyers were evidently scheming that, because with all the delays over the Blanche Lamont murder sentence, the Statute of Limitations might have been operative by the time such a charge would be made.

16. Ernst Praetorius (1880–1946) was a registered student at the Hochschule and later became a well-known musicologist. When he fled Germany in 1934, he was general music director at Weimar. He fled to Ankara, Turkey, where he was active in music education and in broadcasting. Maud's diary refers to him occasionally; but while she was boarding with his family he was too young to be of much interest to her.

17. May Hamaker, a student of the violin and voice (she introduced Maud to Professor Knudson), became Maud's confidante. It was she who broke the news of Theo's execution. In later life she married an American naval officer by the name of Henley. The Norfolk, Virginia City Directory for 1954 listed her as a "widow." She kept a diary throughout her years as a music student in Berlin, and Maud once wished her own diary were as "amusing" as May's. Efforts to track down these diaries have been unsuccessful.

18. Little wonder she broke down. Two days earlier, she had recorded the following dream:

> The *Weekly Chronicle* seems to throw a cloud over my brother's head. That dream I had some days ago (I have not mentioned it before now) troubles me greatly. I dreamt that I saw the newspaper with a large centre picture – a coil of dirty rope and underneath was written "The Fate of Durrant." My God, if such be the case, what shall I do? Phillar called for English lesson today. Practised.

Perhaps her imagination was playing tricks, as it is possible that the *Weekly Chronicle* did feature such a "centre picture."

Both Maud and her mother were interested in dreams, and Maud noted in her diary her intention to write down her "queer" dreams. Years later, she told Manya Cherniavsky that her then-deceased mother had appeared to her in a dream, telling her, "I am watching over you."

19. Maud disagreed with this viewpoint. In addition to the November 12, 1895, diary entry (quoted in text), she made several comments that her absence from San Francisco made her feel responsible for the crime ("If I had been at home during those fateful hours he could have come to me") or at least caused her great anguish.

20. The tendency to write so intensely of her concern for her brother or her parents and then to record the most mundane of activities is peculiarly characteristic of Maud's diaries.

21. Theo's reaction to Maud's account of her evening with Holtz was given in a postscript of a letter dated August 12: "So Canuck met Greek did she, and tasted Tokay? Look out for it and them!" Maud dutifully sent Holtz postcards while on holiday, but received no reply. Upon her return to Berlin in September, she sent Holtz a note demanding an explanation for this rudeness. After ten days of self-induced tension (answering the doorbell at every ring in hope of receiving the much wanted explanation) a note arrived, advising her he had no interest in meeting her.

22. This is the only reference to dancing (other than an occasional evening of social dancing) in her diaries.

23. Although her relationship with Frau Ilgenstein became terrible, she followed her parents' orders: "You know," her

mother wrote on May 29, 1897,

> I never think it wise to be moving about when you are alone.
> It does not look well unless you have good cause, and if you
> move, people will say "what's wrong with that girl? She does
> not stay long in one place!" No, I do NOT want you to make any
> change until this trouble is over, it will never do, do you see it
> as I do. Your Papa says the same, you like the people and they
> like you, so stay where you are and be content.

After the execution, Maud could "take no more" and left.
Her mother made no known objection. In her diary Maud says
she does not tell her mother of the troubles she was having
with Frau Ilgenstein lest she worry.

24. Her diary refers to interest from professional buyers,
arrangements for a "travelling" exhibition of corsets, and
finally, "I must say the terms are hard" (January 15, 1898).
William Durrant, speaking to journalists at the time of the
execution, mentioned that Maud had made money from a
corset patent. Her mother had earlier sent money for legal fees
to prepare a patent.

25. On September 1, 1897, following her return to Berlin from
a summer vacation, she wrote, "I am sick of life. What am I
good for?" This is the only time she expressed such thoughts
in her diaries.

26. In the weeks immediately leading to Theo's execution,
Maud dismissed the Ilgenstein family as "unsympathetic,
frivolous, unloving," little realizing how difficult it must have
been to have her in their midst. At that time, too, she had a
very unpleasant dispute with Frau Ilgenstein over, it seems, the
Frau's financial interest in the corset project and her disap-
proval of Maud's relationship with Artur Bock, discussed in
Chapter 3.

27. March 24, 1897:

> I am so broken up I can hardly think straight. I was prepar-
> ing to go out when I received a telegram from Mamma
> reading "Await today's letter." Of course that means "come
> home." Oh, why are we so persecuted? Oh Theo, you are
> innocent, why can't we prove it? I haven't been able to do
> anything all day. All the family knows now, and they are so
> good to me. Frau Corelli came to see me this evening. She,

too, was so nice. Ernst and I, May and Fredy, we have just returned from a short walk. I don't expect to sleep, but I will try.

On June 5, 1897, Theo wrote:

I am happy tonight because of the good news I received from the Court of California from whence issued a writ commanding all intention on the part of the authorities as regards what was to take place on the eleventh of this month, to be set aside and proclaiming a stay of all proceedings until the case is further investigated by the U.S. authorities.

. . . Fear nothing, dearest sister, all will be well yet. I am not going to detail the horrors of the condemned cell and death watch, all that is past and gone. The prison officers Capt. Edgar and Jamieson and others (et al.) are so very glad to see me snatched from out that horrid room. They even took me out fifteen hours or more before the official notice was presented, and put me back in my old quarters in front of the great garden, saying I was sufficiently capable of watching myself and that it was a hard task to be compelled to place me under death watch. They are all so kind and believe in my case and treat me as best they can.

3

Turning Point:
1897–1903

N JULY 1, 1897, Maud and May Hamaker left Berlin for a two-month holiday in northern Thuringia. After an overnight train trip they arrived in Thal, a small resort town and traditional site of the Walpurgisnacht of the Faust legend. The day after her arrival Maud met "Herr Artur Bock, a nice young sculptor," with whom she would have her first, probably her longest, and possibly the most meaningful of her many liaisons with men.

For at least eight years Bock waited to become her husband. Like others, he was smitten at once, declaring his love in a darkroom, as he developed her photograph. "He told me he loved me from the first morning he saw me. I felt almost lost. I like him well, and told him so. He is satisfied. No one knows yet. We enjoy each other's society, never thinking of the future."

Nor, would it seem, did she think much about the present, for during the sixty-one days she spent in Thal, she made only sixteen diary entries. She recorded day-long hikes, including a visit to "Bach's house – nothing much" (Artur's uncle was voluntary curator; today, it is a major tourist attraction), one dispute ("immediately made up and became as sweet as honey"), and hours in Artur's studio, where he worked on a bust of her. Fortunately, later diary entries and a handful of Artur's letters provide a clearer account of their relationship.

Maud was unforthcoming to her family about Artur. Occasionally Theo would ask how the bust was progressing or comment on excursions she and Artur took together.[1] What little she told about Artur – that he had a large studio in Dresden and his works had been exhibited – prompted Theo to recommend *Romance of Two Worlds* by a best-selling novelist of the day, Marie Corelli, in which the artist is a painter, the heroine a sculptor.[2] Maud dutifully read but did not comment on the novel, little realizing that Theo's enthusiasm for it would in later years acquire an awful irony.[3]

Maud's reticence about Artur was unnoticed by Theo, who boasted he was well fed, well housed, and well treated in San Quentin's Murderers' Row, to where he had been transferred in April 1897. ("This hotel is one thousand per cent better than that coop in the City.") Moreover, he had become enthralled by a recent revelation: "A gentleman was searching our family history and found we still have noble blood in our veins. The line of Barons etc. are of the same name Durrant – our own precious spelling, too. I always felt it, now I know it. The Baron's motto is *Labes pejor morte*, which means "Labour is worse than Death" [*sic*]. The coat of arms is most beautiful in design. The motto is somewhat short but perfectly correct."

IN A LATER letter, Theo enclosed his hand-drawn copy of the crest and corrected his mistranslation of the motto to "A Dishonouring Stain is Worse than Death." Although he was jumping to unsubstantiated conclusions, his certainty was strong enough to inspire him to "die like a Durrant." At his execution he astonished more than two hundred witnesses – and the hangman – with his bravery.[4]

Maud returned to Berlin on September 1, "dumb-founded" to learn that Professor Corelli, who had become and remained a good friend, did not intend to continue her voice lessons. Moreover, her piano teacher Professor von Peterssen had acted on his warning, issued some twelve months earlier, that her personal distress was seriously affecting her studies: she was refused readmission to the Hochschule. (After the initial shock she seems to have taken this blow in stride, as if realizing that von Peterssen had acted in her best interest. She was readmitted a year later.) Worst of all, Theo's letters began to reveal an ebbing confidence. In one twelve-page letter he scrawled an incoherent analysis of his defence and in others, writing of his resurging religious faith, he urged Maud to care for their parents.

The pressure on Maud finally came out in a nightmare. "My dream," she noted on October 2, "was awful. I saw Theo being taken for a murd[erer]. Cut off fingers, etc. were in my room, to make the Police think I had done it." During the day, however, she dutifully continued practising the piano and, under the direction of a Dr. Brosswetter, who paid her the occasional 50 marks, worked on a never-published translation of Charles Dickens' *Little Dorrit*. Moreover, Artur Bock arrived in Berlin, where, except for a visit to his family over Christmas, he remained some months.

Artur's visit had its own frustrations. Maud was very depressed, Artur very busy, and Frau Ilgenstein, where Artur was taking his evening meals, very suspicious. Maud's diary gives only a glimpse of their relationship at this stage. One Sunday afternoon they went to the National Gallery. "I wanted to ride back as it was very foggy and doing my cold no good, but Artur wouldn't give in, so like a fool I walked. I ought to manage him, instead of him managing me."

For all her love of the dramatic, no episode in her life is more dreadful than the weeks surrounding her brother's execution. Theo's lawyers had successfully delayed that event in June 1897. For the next five months, much to the disgust of the press and the dismay of the judiciary, they used a plethora of legal ploys as grounds for appeal to state and federal courts. This resulted in judicial chaos,[5] which was temporarily (if dramatically) resolved when, late in the afternoon of November 10, the state supreme court ordered postponement of Theo's execution scheduled for the next morning.

Theo and his parents paid a heavy price for their lawyers' delaying tactics. For more than six months they rode an emotional roller coaster of thrilling relief and shattered hopes. For Maud, the lawyers' arguments could be followed only through condensed (and in all likelihood garbled) reports in the New York *Herald*. Bewildered and distressed, she seems to have consciously attempted to ignore the whole affair to avoid speculating on the uncertainty of Theo's fate. Between June and mid-November (when she abandoned her diary for a month) her diary records are generally mundane, with minimal reference to either her family or "the Blow."

In a sense she had spent all her emotions. In April, shortly after Theo had for a second time been formally sentenced to death (with execution set for June 11) she sent an emotional, extravagant appeal to governor Budd of California. The appeal, however, fell on deaf ears and then became irrelevant when, on June 3, the U.S. Supreme Court agreed to hear (at its fall session) "an application for leave to appeal." This effectively annulled the scheduled execution date of June 11.

However, early in November, days before the Supreme Court was scheduled to hear it, the California State Prosecutor successfully challenged the validity of the Application, thereby throwing the entire case back to the State courts. As a result, on November 10 Theo was for the *third* time formally sentenced to death with execution set, with unseemly and, more to the point, injudicious haste, for November 11. (Throughout the proceedings, so the *Examiner* reported, Theo "stood like a wooden statue.") Eugene Deuprey thereupon successfully challenged the legality of the execution date (arguing that his client had the right to thirty days between the date of the Supreme Court decision and the remittitur) forcing referral of the entire case back to the United States Supreme Court. The affair had become a legal – and in the view of some observers an insoluble – quagmire. Amidst all this confusion, on November 17 the *Examiner* published Maud's appeal to the governor. The opening and closing paragraphs are indicative of its tone:

Esteemed Sir:

A grief stricken sister, who thousands of miles away from all who are dear to her heart, from the scenes of her childhood and girlhood, from where she passed the happiest days of her life – days spent without care or grief in the companionship of the most care-taking, considerate, and loving parents and brother, kneels before you and pleads, prays for the life of her brother. Oh sir, if only you knew as I do, if only you could take one look into his past life, one look unbiased by the contemptible reports that have been circulated about him in the San Francisco papers for the last two years you, too, would say he had been a true, noble, model boy.

Eight more paragraphs climaxed with "Give my brother the benefit of the doubt. Reverse the decision of the Supreme Court and keep him on this earth." Maud ended the letter:

Kneeling before you in closing as in the beginning, and praying that the impulse will be given you who have the final words to utter in behalf of my precious brother to save him from the terrible fate that is hanging over him, I am, with the deepest regard for your judgement and decision, yours in sorrow and affliction, Maud Durrant.

A month after the dramatic stay of execution, the *Chronicle* reported, on December 16, that "there was a big crowd in Judge Bahr's court yesterday when Theodore Durrant for the fourth time was sentenced to be hanged [on January 7, 1898]. The prisoner appeared much less concerned than many of the spectators." Three days later Maud made a significant entry in her diary. "I shall have to resign myself to the inevitable."

Christmas week was funereal. "How sad and down-hearted have I been all this day!" she exclaimed on Christmas Eve. "Oh, how I have longed for my parents, my home, my Theo! No one can realize what I have been through lately. We had a tree but I did not enjoy it at all. Oh, for the Ruhe [peace] of last year!" Christmas Day was "very queer, in fact none at all. I have such fears for those at home." On Boxing Day, she attended the "very simple but impressive" funeral of Mrs. Rice's husband. The next day her thoughts were for her family: "Oh! how I wish Theo were here to meet all my friends. What a favourite he would be. Poor boy, alas, that cannot be yet awhile. My poor parents, God protect them and give them strength. Dear Lord, rather than have my dear brother suffer so, take him away to You before that day."

The entry for New Year's Eve, 1898, ended with a touching gesture from her rejected admirer, Ernst Ilgenstein: "Would that this year would never end unless the new one has good news and brings joy to us, to Theo. This evening we were very quiet. The clanging of the church bells made me unhappy. I thought of poor Theo who perhaps will never again hear those bells. . . . Oh Father! Take him to Thy loving care before that day. Save him! . . . Ernst gave me a goodnight kiss – a brother's kiss as assurance of his friendship. We have taken the tree down, cleared the salon. Now to bed."

Contrary to her earlier pleas and their professed intentions, Maud's parents did not summon her home "to take a last look" at her brother. To have done so would have been against Theo's wishes – and common sense. Following the stay of execution in June, Theo had become a pawn in a game of judicial chess, in which his attorneys' purpose was a stalemate that would spare Theo the rope. For the legal profession, the tactics of the defence made the case both important and frustrating. The press enthusiastically covered the attempts to save Theo: challenges to the conduct of the trial, questioning of the circumstantial evidence, and appeal after appeal.

Their job was made easier by Theo and his hysterical

parents, who, in a desperate bid to raise and obtain public support for commutation to life imprisonment, for the last six months of the affair deliberately invited rather than shunned public attention. Thus, on the morning of July 7, with the warden's permission the operator of an animatoscope, a primitive precursor of the movie camera, arrived at San Quentin Prison and proceeded to the garden outside Theo's cell, where he set up his equipment. Theo, having rehearsed his performance the day before, emerged from his cell and took up several poses, such as picking and smelling flowers. "Most of the pictures," reported the San Francisco *Call*, "were of the kind showing animated scenes, and Durrant appears in a variety of poses."

According to the *Call*, "if the prison officials do not object, phonographic messages and animatoscopic scenes of Durrant may be expected with regularity." Apparently, the prison officials did not object. In a letter of September 28, Theo reported to Maud that "the phonograph with the first little talk of about 150 words or less netted nearly $1000 or $1200, half we got and it went on the case and elsewhere." Theo then suggested, "You would be, with a piece played on the piano into a phonograph or a talk, a great drawing card no doubt." As he explained:

> That letter of yours [to Governor Budd] created great sympathy and I think a few tunes or a duet with your prof, a song or a talk or reading would perhaps get $800 all told, when the excitement is on again. Read into one cylinder a piece or a couple. Into another sing, if you can, a pathetic song or get Frau C[orelli] to play for you. Play into another or into two cups or cylinders as they are called. If you and Frau C. or May sing with you they could get some of the returns.
>
> I think the plan a good one. Let an announcement be made into it first that so and so will play or speak. I think we can raise much help from it.

Although committed to helping Theo in virtually any way possible, Maud rejected the scheme.[6]

Equally offensive were two other of Theo's fund-raising projects. Under the heading "Writes About His Emotions. Durrant at San Quentin Pens the Story of his Life," the *Call* of October 6 described Theo at work:

> Durrant's cell is not over large and the little ray of light that manages to creep in is just sufficient for him to see the paper. There, surrounded by stone on three sides with roof and door of iron, the murderer writes for hours at a time. Occasionally he stops and paces the floor when some knotty question arises in his mind; then back he goes to the work of compiling the history that some day may become public property.

The history was never published. However, for its *Sunday Magazine* of November 21 the *Examiner* printed excerpts from *Azora*, Theo's incoherent novel of some 70,000 words. *Azora* was a very poor roman à clef, featuring Maud as the crudely idealized heroine. Such publicity was reason enough to keep Maud away from San Francisco. Much as she no doubt yearned for her family, she seems to have accepted remaining in Berlin.

It was just as well. On December 24, General Dickinson formally charged with contempt of court one of the jurors in Theo's trial. He complained that "small, peppery, and peculiar" Horace Smyth had based his verdict for conviction on information he received outside the courtroom. The *Examiner* printed the formal complaint against Smyth but refrained from publishing the "alleged expressions used by Juror Smyth in characterizing Theo Durrant as a monster," on the grounds that "they are not intended for delicate ears and belong in the domain of the abnormal." During the contempt proceedings that followed, three witnesses, all attorneys, testified that Smyth had indeed declared that "Durrant was a moral monster, and came honestly by it. Smyth then repeated the disgusting gossip he had heard about the Durrant family." After a day-long hearing in court, Smyth was discharged, only to be sued for slander by the Durrant parents, who demanded $50,000 damages. Nothing came of this action.

Given the desperate attempts of the Durrants and their attorneys to forestall due execution of the law, this affidavit against Smyth might be dismissed as the acme of bad taste and judgement. There is evidence, albeit circumstantial, as in Theo's own case, that the rumours were more than mere gossip. The public record, as preserved in the press accounts of the entire drama, strongly hints at an unhealthily intense – one might say unnatural – relationship between Theo and his mother. The circumstances, nature, and obscure motives of the two murders suggest that Theo was without doubt emotionally unbalanced. Finally, there remains the comment of Leo Cherniavsky, who preserved Maud's personal papers after her death. Maud had an intense relationship with Leo for some three years; thereafter she was friends with him and his brothers and sisters for more than forty years. Leo remarked to both his sister Manya and, later, to his brother Mischel that, in deference to Maud's memory, he had de- stroyed certain of Theo's letters in which he clearly referred to his intimate relationship with his mother.

No matter what view one takes of the foregoing, had Maud been in San Francisco on Christmas Day, 1897, pub- lication of the charges against Smyth might well have destroyed her. On January 24, 1898, she noted in her diary: "Wrote to General Dickinson requesting him to open suit for me against my insulters."

Maud spent the first week of the New Year in "a state of excitement that was dreadful." She yearned for older com- pany than that of the "frivolous, unsympathetic" Ilgenstein household. "I am so unruhig, I kann nicht [I am so unhappy I can do nothing]. What," she asked herself again and again, "will become of us? I must urge my parents to go to Australia." Two days before Theo's scheduled execution, she ventured to Lloyd's Reading Rooms but "found nothing new" in the American papers there. She took to practising the piano, but even this escape was frustrated when "the people living upstairs" asked that she stop, as a family member was ill. On January 6, she went to meet Artur, who was returning from his Christmas visit to Thal. She braced herself for the cable her parents had promised they would send if the Supreme Court in Washington acted in Theo's favour. But no cable arrived.[7]

On January 2, Theo wrote to Maud from his death cell in San Quentin Prison. Complaining that "there isn't a speck of news at this time," he commented on the weather ("delightfully free of rain"), the "splendidly passed" Christmas holidays, and other studiously dull topics. He made only one unintentionally chilling lapse from bland fantasy: "Booth Tucker, the Commander of the Salvation Army, is to be here today. I wonder if he will think it worth his while to visit the condemned men."

On the eve of his execution, Theo, in his fondness for the melodramatic (and, no doubt, for a fee), granted the last of the several interviews to Alice Riz. Under the banner headline "Durrant will Hang Today," the *Examiner* devoted three full pages to this skilfully designed interview, featuring Theo's signed assertion of his innocence: "In conclusion, I will say this in my last interview. That my hands are free – free from all stain of crime. I am glad to again proclaim Alice Riz has heard in this, my last interview to earthly mortals, my cry of innocence. This I strenuously and loudly proclaim."

Other papers did not exploit the melodrama so extravagantly, but waited with bated breath for Theo's long-expected, long-demanded breakdown. Even the *Los Angeles Times* headlined the Associated Press report on his condition:

Broken in Spirit and Devoid of Hope
Paces his Narrow Cage
Praying for Deliverance from the Gallows.
Passes a Very Uneasy Night.
But Says the Murders Will Come out in Time.

Maud's diary records how she spent January 7, the day of her brother's scheduled execution:

This day is over. Oh God, comfort mein Eltern. Give them strength to stand by this trial. I feel sure something has

saved my darling brother. Received letter from Mamma and
Theo. How cheerfully Theo writes, dear boy. At 12:45 May
and I went to Frau Professor [Corelli]'s. I worked quite a bit
on my handkerchief and listened to pupils taking lessons. At
7 went to May – she wasn't feeling well. Artur was also
there, so we chatted till 8, then took the bus home. A fine
fire is raging in the district of Moabit, an iron works, I
believe. The sky is beautifully lit by it.

The next afternoon, while on her way to exchange the
skates he had given her for Christmas, she met and had a
"pleasant talk" with Artur. That evening, however, after
declaring in her diary "Oh to know, to know with certainty, my brother's fate," she went on to wonder, "Am I
doing right in this matter between Artur and myself? For
the sake of my parents I can not marry such a poor man."
She devoted the next day's diary entry to this hitherto
unrecorded matter, making a decision as fateful as it is
revealing: "No, every day it seems clearer to me. I am, as
they say, 'a lady born,' and will I ever be able to be happy
with him? He is good and talented and has no bad habits and
he loves me dearly – more than I love or can ever love him.
Yes, as a brother I could love him – but not as a ––– . No I
feel sure of myself. We have such varied tastes, too."
Two days later, during the afternoon of January 10, May
Hamaker broke "the dreaded, dreadful" news for which
Maud's reason had long told her to prepare, despite the
protests of her heart:

I can bear it, but my parents, how do they? Darling,
innocent brother, would to God I could have seen you once
more before you were taken from us. Rest, my darling, I
believe in a Wiedersehen [afterlife]. We *shall* meet again in
the Happy Land of our Heavenly Father. God spare my
parents and let it be Thy Will to give us many happy,
prosperous years together. Herr Bock came this evening and
filled me with gentle words of comfort. I am so tired, so
weary, so sad.

She was briefly spared the lurid accounts of the execution in the San Francisco press, although when Artur called the next day he brought "what was printed [on the front page] in the New York *Herald*, Paris":

One of the most remarkable cases recorded in the criminal annals of the country terminated today in the execution of Theodore Durrant . . .

Sentence of death was passed four times on Durrant, but on each occasion a stay was obtained and justice was cheated.

At last the execution was fixed for today, and the scene of many motions and stays was transferred to the Supreme Court at Washington this morning, where an application was made for a writ of *habeas corpus*.

Then was enacted one of the most exciting incidents ever witnessed in that august chamber. After the condemned man's lawyer had advanced his arguments, the Court retired at noon to deliberate . . . After thirty-five minutes had elapsed the doors were opened and the announcement was made that the Court had unanimously denied the writ.

This ended all hope for the condemned man, and the crowd, manifesting its approval, quietly retired. The decision was wired to California, and the hanging took place at 10:30, "I am innocent," being the last words spoken by the convict.

"It is so unhuman," Maud noted that evening in her diary. "How could they take his life? Darling Theo, we believe you innocent and ever shall." Indeed, she was possessed by that belief for the rest of her life.

Stupefied, she made only intermittent diary entries thereafter. On February 2, she marks the receipt of the January 8 issue of the *San Francisco Examiner* "from an unknown. My darling brother, you were brave, thank God. Who would be so heartless as to send this to me? I wish I had gone home. He died with his sister with him, that gave him courage."

She had good reason to wonder who could be so callous as to send her this vividly written account of Theo's last hours. Yet the paper's editor was not solely responsible for the lurid coverage. The behaviour of both Theo and his parents invited sensational treatment. At his son's request, William Durrant and more than two hundred "invited" guests attended the execution. Before the event, Mr. Durrant publicly discussed disposition of Theo's corpse, which no local cemetery or mortician would touch, for fear of public outrage.

Although Mrs. Durrant was officially forbidden to attend the hanging, press accounts describe her as being hysterically morbid; she publicly kissed her dead son's lips and, after the body was delivered to the family home, spent hours "talking" with Theo. Later she kept in contact through mediums.

But Theo upstaged both parents. Standing, stone sober, with the noose around his neck ("Don't put that rope, my boy, until I talk. Well, don't tighten it, then"), he asserted his innocence and forgave all – including, quite specifically, the local press. That morning, Father Logan, who had regularly visited him in prison, had accepted him into the Roman Catholic Church. (Father Logan proved a source of great spiritual strength to Theo and was one of four clerics who offered to accompany him to the gallows.)[8]

"I'm the descendant of a race of people who never flinch," Theo told the prison doctor on the eve of his execution. "They never flinched at anything. My ancestors could face death itself, and if I have to go up those steps tomorrow, I'll go as a Durrant, and die like a Durrant." He was as good as his word.

"He died the bravest man I have ever seen," said Amos Lunt, the hangman. "His legs were just as steady as they could be. All the others bent at the knee. I have never seen such nerve, and never expect to see anything like it."

Maud obliquely referred to the most heart-breaking detail in her diary. "His father," said Isabella, describing her last moments with Theo for the *San Francisco Chronicle*, "gave him a little memento from his sister. She intended it for New Year's Eve, and I dreaded Theo seeing it, for it was a little locket with her picture. I thought he might break down. He put it round his neck and said 'Now we are together again.' Those were the last words he spoke. He took my arm from his neck and laid my hands in his father's and pushed us very gently out of his cell."

So traumatic were the closing hours of Theo's drama that, in spite of its sensationally lurid treatment of the case, the *Examiner* editorial conceded that "the execution can not be regarded as the triumph of justice. The best that can be said of it is that Justice has not been beaten down. After three years' delay, if the execution is not a victory for Justice, it is so near a defeat that it brings little credit."

Later that month the last of Theo's letters to Maud, written hours before his execution, arrived, together with one (not extant) from Mrs. Durrant.[9] Her mother's, according to Maud's diary, proved the more distressing, for enclosed was a letter that Frau Ilgenstein had written to her concerning Maud and Artur. "Frau Ilgenstein's brief was so widerrichtig [so contrary to truth]," noted Maud in her diary, "that I can never forgive her. Poor darling Mamma, what will she think of me?" Isabella took it in stride, explaining in a letter of February 8, 1898, that she understood Frau's concern yet, pending answers to some earlier questions, approved of the relationship with Artur. But to this she added a caveat: "Tell him that Mamma is a very little jealous of anyone who may try to steal our only daughter from us. Perhaps I can hear you say 'How do you expect me to say such a thing, Mamma, to a gentleman of such short acquaintance?' Oh, I am only going by what Frau Ilgenstein told me and am waiting for an answer – that's all." Having lost her only son to the gallows, she had no intention of losing her only daughter to marriage. She got her way.

Mrs. Durrant had opened this letter with an expression of her feelings regarding Theo's execution:

I was so glad to hear you speak so bravely about our loss, I can not take it so. Well, it is not the taking of his life that makes me feel so badly but the three years of torture with us hoping, and then to snap him off. Oh, I shall never become reconciled to it, no, never. Their justice is so hard to bear. Oh my poor darling, no, everything was not done that could be done and no one thinks so. If we had had more money we could have done more, yet even with what we had there were mistakes made in the beginning and those mistakes were the cause of our defeat all the way, and we could not seem to overcome them . . . we have to look at it as all for the best but I can not look at it in that light. Still, we have to live on.

William Durrant, in only the second extant letter since Theo's arrest, wrote at greater length, more informatively; he also made some radical charges:

My dear Maudie,
You must not think it strange that Papa does not write to you oftener . . . You know that I think of you always. Mamma writes to you often and tells you all the news, leaving nothing for me to say. All I can say now is what you have already said about dear Theo. He is with the angels and wears a bright star in Heaven. Oh, if only you knew how gently he bore all his persecutions, you would be amazed, he was always brave and manly and kind to everyone about him. He was a favourite of all the prison officials who were extremely kind to him and made his burden as light as possible. Some of them cried for him and would have if they could have let him have his liberty. They gave him every-thing that he needed. They believed him innocent and during his very last moments he made a most wonderful speech to the world declaring his innocence. He convinced them and all right minded people that he was truly inno-cent. Hundreds who believed the newspapers now believe Theo's last words. You can see by the clippings we send you what the press thinks of the San Francisco dailies. The *Examiner* was the cause of all our troubles. It was they who accused Theo first and kept the case constantly before the public and kept them at the boiling point and also kept the

Governor intimidated. He is a moral coward and all our friends say so. There is one thing I can say – if it had not been for Mamma they would have taken Theo two years ago, and that is sure. She has worked night and day and oh, so hard, I cannot tell you all she has done to try to save our dear one.

Mamma interviewed all the best attorneys in San Francisco and got pointers from them and spurred our attorneys along and made them fight every inch of the way as we went. Do you know what the press of the country call your Mamma? Well, I will tell you. She is the Mother of the Century, as the Spartan Mother who never faltered, not even at the last and is still brave. She is honoured by everybody. Mamma has received hundreds of letters commending her for the brave fight she has made both publicly and privately. You don't know what a mother you have. Everybody is proud of her, I could not have done one half if I tried ever so much, though I did my best. Mamma had some of the best men in the State see the Governor and they worked hard with him but it was no use. You may ask why. I will tell you.

Budd wants to be U.S. Senator [in fact he retired from politics] and he thinks that by standing with the rabble he will be sent to the Senate. That is his ambition as it is also that of the *Examiner*. To help send him there he would also save a man's life if he thought he could gain anything by it. Dear Maudie, I cannot begin to tell you how good Theo was and of the many good words he has written these last three years. He has astonished his friends by his writings to the Press which were published from time to time. Everybody says he was exceptionally smart, and a braver and a truer man never died in this country. He was a perfect marvel to everybody. The *Examiner* wanted him to make a confession and implicate [Rev. George] Gibson and offered him three thousand dollars to do so. They also offered me the same to have him do so. All they want is a sensation to make a few nickels. If they could get Theo to do that they could arrest Gibson and have another sensation to go on. While we

would like to see Gibson arrested we want to have some
tangible proof to go on, and while Theo did not know
anything about the crimes, he was not going to accuse
anyone with his last breath for the sake of money. He
scorned their dirty money, that's all for the present.
Your loving Papa.
P.S. You must thank all our friends for their kind consider-
ation of us. Now Maudie, have you lost your heart in that
far-off land? If so, you must wait till Mamma comes to you.
I see you like him and give a good account of him. Are his
parents well-to-do? You must look out for that as well as for
other things. Remember me kindly to him, and thank him
for the care he is taking of you.

In mid-February, Maud left the Ilgenstein pension. Between that move and June 28, when her diary stops, she
made only twenty-five entries. "The fact is," she explained
to herself, "that I have been too sad of heart to write down
what to me has been so uninteresting." And yet, during that
time she passed an examination for readmission to the
Hochschule and found a new, unidentified voice coach. She
continued, also, to see Artur Bock – she was by no means
finished with him – but, above all, she waited for her
mother's arrival.

Although she ceased making daily entries in her diary, she
continued to record in exquisite detail her daily expenses
(but not her earnings). From March 1, for instance, she
itemized her daily grocery expenses together with a
monthly rent: for the first time she was cooking for herself,
living on a bare minimum. While she may well have made
some money from the corset business, a postcard among her
personal papers establishes one source of earnings even more
off-beat. "Dear Colleague," wrote a Dr. Penn (in German)
to a Berlin publisher:

As my reminders have been ignored so far, I am forced once
again to despatch a messenger "by express" to come and
pick up "egoism" as well as "final stages of development."
I need these quite urgently, as the printer is waiting for

them. Furthermore, please contact, if necessary by pneumatic post, the lady who did the illustrations on fertilization and ask her to get in touch with me tomorrow between 1 and 2 or between 4 and 6, as I will be able to place various orders with her. I assume she lives in Berlin, is capable of drawing from models, and is not too busy.

Dr. Penn was the author/editor of *Illustriertes Konversations-Lexikon der Frau*,[10] a sex manual for women; Maud was his illustrator.

While Maud undertook such unorthodox money-making projects, two major considerations delayed Mrs. Durrant's departure from San Francisco. One was financial. As a first step to solving this problem, she sold all her furniture, save the piano and Theo's "things." ("All your brother's clothes Papa I suppose may as well wear as it is so hard to keep the moths out of them," wrote the ever practical Isabella.) Eventually she scraped together enough money, but not before pointedly warning her daughter:

> You are going to have a disappointment if you think Mamma will cook, or think she can cook, for I have gotten out of that domestic habit. It is too late for me to start thinking of living in one room as I did in California, cook and live in one room I might have done that if you and Theo were over there for just one year and then he was going to take us all over. I would then have been happy, but as things have gone I can not be counted on to pinch and scrub in one room. I can't do it, I won't do it.
>
> If I am going over there it will be to do what is most agreeable to me. I am tired of living and if I can't do something I have always talked to Theo about and what I have looked forward to, then I will stay here where at least I have room to breathe. I am tired of domestic work of any kind, and I simply won't come down to do it in one room. I would simply die.

The second reason for Mrs. Durrant's delayed departure concerned her husband's state of mind, although it would appear hers was the more troubled. She refused to leave San Francisco until her husband was gainfully employed, given all he had been through. In the early summer of 1899, he started work at his old trade of shoe making.

In the meantime, Mrs. Durrant issued her daughter an insightful reminder and orders – both verging on emotional blackmail – that she would successfully fulfil, albeit in a fashion Mrs. Durrant would never have approved of:

> You have an opportunity that you must not overlook, for in it lies your whole future success. Your sorrow with your personality ought to give your playing a charm that can not be taught. Now don't lose the opportunity to allow the public to judge what you can do. Your dear brother would not allow you to be disrupted even to give him the comfort of knowing you were helping his mother get life for him. Now it will break my heart if you allow anything to prevent you from carrying out his wishes. You must make a name for yourself if you wish to gladden our last days [Isabella was forty-five], for nothing else will make up for our loss but showing the world that you as well as he were ambitious. Now, my dear, close your teeth tight and say I WILL, even if it takes every minute of my time, I will, I shall I MUST and NOTHING will prevent it!

In a letter dated April 24, she wrote sentimentally of her beloved Theo, little realizing that she was letting slip circumstantial evidence that Theo had committed the murders:

> Just think it was four years ago on Easter Sunday that they took your brother away from us. We went into Theo's old room and took in the view. We could see the steamers in the bay so clearly. It did look so lovely after the rain. Then we thought of the first time they took our darling to that dreadful place and as he left he said, "I wonder if this is my last look at the beautiful hills where I have known so many happy days." Then his throat ached, poor darling, and it was all he could do to keep back the tears for if he should shed

any, the hounds would say he was breaking down. Oh, how I wish I could see into the beyond. I would love to know he has what he was denied on earth.

Isabella finally joined her daughter early in the summer of 1899 and remained with her some eighteen months. She arrived, so Maud confided to Mischel Cherniavsky's wife Mary, some twenty-five years later, with a little urn that she took with her everywhere. The urn contained Theo's ashes.[11] Very shortly after Mrs. Durrant's arrival, she and Maud left Berlin for the summer, spending their first three weeks in Thal with Artur's family. By November they were back in Berlin. In the spring of 1900, they began their long-delayed tour of Europe, the highlight of which was Florence. Maud insisted in later years that it was seeing Botticelli's *Primavera* in the Uffizi Gallery that inspired in her the germ of her later art.

Although Maud's private record of these months is extremely scanty, consisting of two or three months' record of daily expenses but no place-names, William Durrant's six extant letters from July and August 1899 provide at least a glimpse of how he, his wife, and his daughter were managing. Contrary to his wife's fears, he reported he was thriving. "Don't worry about me, I am OK and well," he insisted in the first of these letters, "never felt better in my life, not a bit lame. Eat and sleep well."

In other letters he urged his wife "to get something for those night sweats" and informed her that the clairvoyant had said "Theo wants to talk to you himself, and he won't talk through anyone else, you understand me." He expressed concern for Maud's health – "30 lbs is a lot of flesh to lose" – and with his wife's depression. "Now, Maudie, Mamma used to talk like that when she was here, that she did not have interest in anything. Well, I did not blame her then, but now she must pick up and live again. She must brighten up and be spry."

During her visit, Isabella met Artur Bock. A handful of his letters to Maud, three of them written during her

mother's visit, have survived. While chiefly about his struggle as an impecunious sculptor in Hamburg, these letters
provide evidence of his relationship with Maud as it evolved
after Theo's execution. In the first, dated December 31,
1899, Artur writes of a forthcoming visit, remarking that
"this will be wonderful, we will love each other, you only
have to be good." This may be an innocent enough remark,
except that six months later Artur wrote: "How are you my
sweetheart? Are you well behaved or ? This morning, when
I woke up, you had just finished talking to a man when I
heard you say, 'When shall we meet again?' Naturally, I was
very sad, but at the same time happy it was only a dream."
(Artur may have been inordinately jealous, but Maud's later
record suggests he may have had grounds for his suspicions.)
In the last of the six letters, Artur reassured Maud that she
had no grounds for *her* professed jealousy, at times sounding
like a scene straight out of *La Vie de Bohème*:

> No, my sweetheart, this is nonsense. Tell me where, and on
> what occasion. No, the only female being with whom I have
> had the opportunity to exchange ideas, is my little model,
> and she hasn't been posing for three weeks. Last night, for
> the first time in a long while, she came to see me to bring
> me my clothes (socks, underwear, etc.) she had mended for
> me. She didn't want any money for it and has done this work
> before for me for nothing. She told me tomorrow is her
> birthday, so I decided to give her a dozen handkerchiefs at
> the cost of four marks, she wanted them so badly. You surely
> don't have to be jealous of this plain little girl. She is a poor
> deplorable thing who has to support her mother, too, which
> isn't easy among the few artists here. See, my darling, you
> can take a glimpse everywhere, into the most hidden
> corners of my heart. I only love and live for you, so that you
> may feel happy and comfortable with me. This is my great-
> est wish.

That wish was never granted, although exactly when
Maud threw him out of her life is unclear (probably not until
she had no further need of the monthly "allowance" that,

his letters show, he so generously sent her from his meagre earnings). His sculpture *Salome*, for which she was indisputably the model, is dated 1905/6. For many years – he married only in 1923 – Artur Bock was profoundly hurt. Yet in the long run his career was the more successful – certainly the more enduring – and his life more stable. Between 1905 and 1914, he was by far the best-known sculptor in Hamburg. Although his artistic importance is largely regional, he is one of the most important German sculptors of memorial monuments prior to and following the First World War. By the time of his death in 1956, he was living in considerable affluence. That year Maud Allan also died, obscure and impoverished.

Some time before her departure for Germany, Mrs. Durrant had determined the practical purpose of her trip. "Yes," she wrote Maud, "when I come over we will see what is best to do, as to what or when we shall do first, in a way making a new beginning, won't we?" Isabella may have been taking too much for granted; by this time Maud knew what she wanted to do, although she may have needed her mother to push her to do it. Her goal was to study with Ferruccio Busoni, one of the most prominent pianists and pedagogues of the day. He was also director of the Meisterschüle in Weimar, a position once held by Franz Liszt.

In the opening paragraph of "My Weimar Days," chapter six of her autobiography, Maud writes of her "keen desire to be directed in my musical studies" by Busoni. When she received "an affirmative reply to my letter asking if I might attend his classes, I felt as though I could shout my joy from the house tops" (p.67). An educated guess might suggest that her mother made Maud write that letter. Busoni must have known, or at least known of, Maud as one of his admirers in Berlin, where he frequently gave piano recitals.

To judge by "My Weimar Days," the "delightful, free-and-easy days of hard work and bon camaraderie" that summer bore happy memories second only to those of her childhood in San Francisco. "The most delightful relations," Maud writes, "existed between Busoni and his pupils. To us he was something much more than a great master of his art. We really might have been his children, and when our work was done we seemed to share quite naturally in his family life with his wife, the dearest of women, and his two beautiful children" (p. 68).

During that summer Maud forged a lasting friendship – which probably included a brief liaison some years later – with Ferruccio Busoni, based on a mutual appreciation of musicality and aesthetics. Ivor Dent, author of a biography of Busoni written under the watchful eye of Busoni's widow, Gerda, was told by Maud Allan how one evening, with Busoni at the piano and with a shawl borrowed from Frau Gerda over her shoulders, Maud danced for the first time. The Busonis were enthralled.[12] It was this evening of experiment, Maud told Dent, that spurred her on to explore her hitherto secret urge to dance.

Great as Busoni's encouragement and intimate as his friendship may have been, it was of far less practical importance than that of her first and most important mentor, Marcel Remy (1870–1906). Remy was on the periphery of Busoni's circle – in his extant correspondence Busoni occasionally refers to Remy as a critic and visitor.

Maud's first meeting with Remy, at a dinner in Berlin following a concert by Busoni, was a turning point, for Remy helped Maud realize her concepts, supervised her research, and served as her agent/manager. Above all, he suggested the approach and wrote the music for her chef d'oeuvre, *The Vision of Salome*.[13]

The nature of Maud's personal relationship with Remy is unknown, but in *My Life and Dancing* she pays generous tribute to this strange man. She recalls how, during that dinner, when "spontaneity was the order of the evening," she spoke to him "of my idea, my ambition – dancing as an art of poetical and musical expression":

Marcel Remy was interested at once. As well as being a musician, he was a savant, a Greek scholar. It was a happy inspiration to confide in him. The sculptor, the artist, and the man of learning range more widely in quest of subjects than the musician pure and simple. Remy spoke of dancing, in the true Hellenic spirit, as a dead and forgotten art; of the unending possibilities open to one who should endeavour to re-create a lost art of expression. His encouraging words were as fuel to fire. Very generously and wholeheartedly he offered to assist me in the matter of research. So I came to have the assistance of one who was not only a scholar and critic, but artist to his fingertips. (p. 74)

In her autobiography and elsewhere Maud stresses the enormous effort she made between her initial, bold decision to abandon the piano – she did not tell her parents until just before her debut[14] – and her first performance, almost exactly two years later, of "musically impressionistic mood settings." At no time does she mention the influence or example of her precursors or contemporaries. Maud was convinced that she had created her own art, so in her view no such influence existed; however, dance historians are correct in refuting so categorical a denial. She would concede that her study of classical Greek dancing was of enormous significance to her art, as it was to all "classical" dancers, the most influential if not the originator being, of course, Isadora Duncan; yet Maud considered her art unique.

Although it is extremely difficult to define let alone evaluate Maud's art, an appraisal of her personal and artistic characteristics can clarify its chief features. Unlike any other dancer of the period, she was extremely musical and had a first-rate musical education. Equally remarkable was the depth and range of her imagination, which was thoroughly steeped in trauma. The effects of that trauma were most obvious in her repertoire, which tended towards grief, unhappiness, and the morbid, deliberately counterbalanced by a handful of truly joyous dances, best exemplified by Mendelssohn's *Spring Song*.

Her profound musicianship and her enormously fertile imagination, the pivots of her art, were embellished by her innate grace, acclaimed by critics and public alike. Her keen intelligence and boundless diligence in pursuit of a fixed goal successfully integrated these particular gifts with the scholarly research Marcel Remy directed her to.

Unrelated to her immediate objective yet essential to her art was her natural acting ability. Lifelong friends assert that she was a born actress, albeit untrained and of a melodramatic order. Her acting potential was particularly suited to mime, that most subtle art form.

Her aptitude for arts other than music was yet another of her remarkable assets. Throughout her career she designed her own costumes and, at least initially, was her own seamstress. Her informed awareness of lighting effects – an aspect most reviewers of her performances overlooked – originated in her knowledge of photography, learned from Artur Bock during the early years of their relationship. Her mastery of posing, first manifest in her enthusiasm for living pictures, and a crucial element in her performance, was born of her deep appreciation of the aesthetics of sculpture. This was, no doubt, a core theme in her conversations with Artur Bock; but she also had considerable expertise in wood carving and clay modelling, lifelong hobbies she took up in San Francisco.

After two years, during which she "worked, worked, worked, harder than ever, giving days to research and experiment, delving among libraries for old postures, studying poses on some ancient vase, jar, or amphora," Maud gave her debut on December 24, 1903, at the Theatre Hall of Vienna's Conservatory of Music. With Theodor Szántó as her accompanist,[15] she presented herself as Miss Maudie Gwendolyn Allan. The program opened with her dance interpretation of Mendelssohn's *Spring Song*, which would later enthrall her London audiences, and featured Chopin's *Marche funèbre*, possibly her favourite work. The program included other Chopin works, Schubert's *Ave Maria*, and Rubinstein's *Valse caprice*, also a later favourite of London audiences.

The performance was reviewed by a number of papers. In a letter of December 31, 1903, Isabella Durrant remarks on "the good criticism you had, my five out of seven, that was very fine indeed. You need not have any doubts as to your success after that. I feel sure all will be well."

Two reviews, both unsigned, appeared in the *Illustriertes Wiener Extrablatt*. Although the performance failed to thrill these reviewers – as a nervous neophyte she may well have floundered on the stage – both commented on personal attributes that ultimately became the object of public and critical acclaim. Neither considered her a beauty, yet one was struck by the expressiveness of her hands and face, and both remarked upon her slim figure. Both, too, recognized her grace of movement and her obvious originality. In the first review the word *young* appears four times; in fact, she was thirty years old, scarcely young for a dancer.

It is not surprising that both reviewers were puzzled by her performance. This, after all, was the debut of a new artist and a new art. Maud put her particular physical attributes and innate grace at the service of her imagination, her musicality, and her thwarted passions. This integration provided the basis of her dancing, which remained unchanging and unique. However, dancing was solely a means of Maud's very personal expression; she had no formal training and insisted she had no interest in the "terpsichorean art." Thus, no would-be disciples could emulate her; nor could she establish a "school." This is one reason some informed observers considered Maud's dancing more phenomenon than art, a remarkable fluke of no enduring significance to twentieth-century dance. Ironically, these same observers were the first to proclaim Maud an artist.

Her reactions to the reviews of her debut are unrecorded, although she never did learn to tolerate criticism. Nonetheless, she sent her parents an elaborate ticket/invitation and a glowing account of the evening, which had ended with a banquet provided by an unidentified source.

Her mother could scarcely contain her joy over the news

of this sufficiently successful debut. Soon she was issuing instructions on how to deal with her fellow San Franciscan in Europe – Isadora Duncan – whose fame so rankled Maud.

Notes

1. These excursions included an encounter that prompted the following from Theo:

> How your mind must have floated back to the ages long ago when just such laurel-crowned white-robed maidens danced and marched to the tune of Greek and Roman instruments, at the sight of the procession you saw at Ruhla [a nearby hamlet]. Remember there is beauty in primitiveness and always pick out the good points to tell about, and if there are bad points, treat them kindly in speech and writing. How beautiful is the perfect satisfaction and contentment you tell about in these people, compared with the vulgar dissatisfaction and grabbing and wishing-for-more sentiment so loudly crying in America.

2. In a letter of May 22, 1897, Theo wrote:

> How I should love to take the hand of Frau Prof. Corelli, bless her dear heart. Perhaps I may some day, who knows? I have read a number of Marie Corelli's works – is your Prof Corelli any relation? I have enjoyed many an hour with Corelli (in her books) and hope to spend hours with your Prof. Corelli.

3. In early 1918, Marie Corelli sent a note to Noel Pemberton Billing, a right-wing member of the British Parliament, artfully casting doubt on Maud's loyalty and morals. This led to published statements culminating in the infamous "Black Book" libel case Maud launched, and lost, in April 1918. Corelli considered *Ardath* her best novel. (See Sir Daniel Eyers Godfrey, *Memories and Music: 35 Years of Conducting*, London: Hutchinson, 1924, p. 165.)

4. Theo was claiming kinship with the Durrant baronetcy of Scottow, Norfolk, created in 1784; there is no known connection. However, Theo (and, to a lesser extent, Maud) seems to have drawn strength from the claimed connection with aris-

tocratic ancestry. Perhaps Theo had in mind some unknown facts about Mayor Sutro's ancestry. (Sutro's father was a wealthy businessman.)

On August 25, 1895, he wrote to Maud, who was spending the summer with the zu Dohna family: "I am so glad the Count and Countess received you so lovely – be your own sweet self, stately and queenly as you always are. Remember that we hail from noble French and English stock, and that our tree dates far back and that not so long ago a Princess sat at the head of the table. We are of noble blood, too. Recollect our wealthy relations in England – esq. Durrant of Norfolk, England."

5. Under the heading "Badly Mixed," and quoting an Associated Press wire, the *Los Angeles Times* of July 3, 1897, reported that "the Durrant murder case has resolved itself into such a state of confusion that it will require the combined efforts of the State and United States Supreme Courts to restore it to the proper legal condition." Theo's execution was that resolution.

6. In a letter dated November 27, 1897, Theo remarks: "Your idea of and in relation to the phonograph is good. Let it rest, as you say."

7. "Miss Durrant, the murderer's sister, knows her brother's fate. The family had arranged to cable her at Berlin if the application to the Supreme Court was successful. By the nonreceipt of a cable on Friday, January 7, she knew the end had come" (*Chronicle*, January 9, 1898).

8. In her later years Maud told Manya Cherniavsky that her mother had met Father Logan on board ship en route to England. Maud said that Father Logan told Mrs. Durrant that in his confession Theo had admitted to the murders. It is possible that Mrs. Durrant met Father Logan on board ship, though it is less likely that even she could break Father Logan's vow of silence. Maud often found it difficult or inconvenient to differentiate between truth and falsehood, reality and fantasy.

9. Theo's letter, dated January 6, 1898, opens:

> My very precious sister,
>   Oh, how it does rain tonight and how it did rain all night. It is practically the first rain of this winter and the farmers are

crazy with joy. At the present moment it is quiet and looks as though it may clear up. This A.M. I took a great hot water "swim" in the cell and after a good exercise had a good lunch. And now I am feeling splendidly, in mind, body, and spirit, and feel as healthy in one as in the other, but in the latter I feel way above ordinary things and trouble seems to have been lifted from my soul. Oh! How I wish that all of you could feel the same buoyancy and faith that I do. You know the just shall *live* by faith in God.

There follows a vigorous assertion of religious faith and two paragraphs on "the wonderful study of psychological conditions in our inner self." The letter ends:

I haven't any news except that the lawyers have been working with tremendous energy. Mr. Deuprey was just here, on business to Mr. Hale, the warden. He gives me much hope and when he went away he left me in good spirits. We hope soon, we don't know just when, but some time, to have some readable news for you. As yet, however, there is nothing new. Everything is being strictly attended to and nothing will be left undone.

Now, with much love I will close this time.
Love from all in abundance.
0-/30 or thereabouts is the time o' day.
Au revoir for a time.
Affectionately, Theo.

10. Published in two volumes by Martin Oldenburg (Berlin, 1900).
11. This is contradicted by the following passage from Mrs. Durrant's letter of April 1, 1899:

I am going to write you a letter before I leave San Francisco telling you where I have left Theo's writings. I will not take them with me for I am so afraid something will happen to them.

I will leave them in a safe until we are settled again, when we will set to work to have them put in order, won't we? I will also leave what is left of our loved one in a safe place, and when you have had your success we will build a monument in Southern California and then we will lay them to rest, won't

Maud Allan photographed in Hamburg, c. 1900.
Staatliche Landesbildstelle, Hamburg.

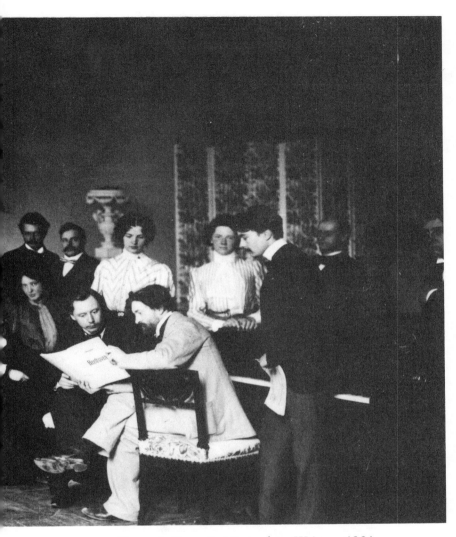

Ferruccio Busoni's Masterclass, Weimar, 1901.
To the immediate right of the vase stands Maud Allan,
behind the young Egon Petri and Ferruccio Busoni, seated.
Deutsche Staatsbibliothek, Berlin.

Convicted murderer Theo Durrant. Self-portrait, c. 1896.
Author's Collection.

Letter from Theo Durrant to his sister Maud, April 19, 1896.
In it he reports on a visit of the Mormon Temple Choir to the prison.

Artur Bock, sculpture, 1901.
Dr. Hans Bock, Tubingen.

*Artur Bock's sculpture of Maud as Salome with
John the Baptist's head, 1905.* Dr. Hans Bock, Tubingen.

Marcel Remy, composer of score for "The Vision of Salome."
Dance Collection, New York Public Library.

*Franz von Stuck's work study for his portrait of
Salome, 1906.* Lenbachhaus, Munich.

Franz von Stuck's Salomé, *1906.* Lenbachhaus, Munich.

Maud Allan as Salome in Budapest, 1907.
Hungarian Dancers' Association.

Managing Director - - Mr. ALFRED BUTT.

11/5/1908

Programme - - 6d.

The Management politely request that where necessary Ladies will remove their hats in order not to obstruct the view of those sitting behind.

1.	March ... ... "The Bull Fighters" ... ... *Kottaun.*	8.0
2.	MISS ANITA EDISS Comedienne.	8.5
3.	BELLE DAVIS and her Southern Piccaninnies	8.15
4.	SAM ELTON The Man who made the Shah laugh.	8.25
5.	THE JUGGLING McBANS (*Last Week*).	8.35
6.	PRINCESS TRIXIE introduced by W. H. BARNES.	8.45

The only animal in the World known to be possessed of responsive intelligence. Members of the audience are invited to go on the stage during this performance.

7.	MISS MARION WINCHESTER	9.5
8.	R. G. KNOWLES America's Peculiar Comedian.	9.15
9.	Intermezzo	9.35

Selection "Vive la Danse" ... *Arranged by Herman Finck.*

MATINÉE OF THE FULL EVENING PROGRAMME, INCLUDING
MISS MAUD ALLAN, SATURDAY NEXT AT 2.

10.	MISS MARGARET COOPER	9.50

Will sing at the Piano—
(a) "Ypsilanti" ... H. G. *Pelissier.* (b) "Bobby Dear" ... *Charles Scott-Gatty.*
(c) "In the Dingle Dongle Dell" ... *Clare Kummer.*
The Pianoforte by CHAPPELL.

11.	First Appearance in England.	10.5

MISS MAUD ALLAN
In Selections from her famous Classical Dances.
(a) CHOPIN'S ... ... Mazurka. | (b) RUBINSTEIN'S ... Valse Caprice.
(c) "The Vision of Salome."
During Miss ALLAN'S Engagement she will present further Selections from her Répertoire of Classical Dances.

12.	ARTHUR PRINCE And his Sailor Boy "JIM."	10.25
13.	THE BIOSCOPE	10.50

Shewing the World's Events from Day to Day.

Victoria Cup, Hurst Park, May 9th, 1908.	Types of British Battleships, &c.
The Naval Disaster in the Solent.	Whimsical People.
Coaching Revival:—Mr. A. G. Vanderbilt's	Yachting in a Stiff Breeze.
"Venture"- London to Brighton.	Students' Jokes.

Incidental Music by HERMAN FINCK.

9th SPECIAL MATINÉE.

Owing to the continued unprecedented demand for seats, it has been decided to give a Ninth Special Matinée

Wednesday next, May 20th, 1908.

MISS MAUD ALLAN

will present an extended répertoire of her Classical Dances including "The Vision of Salome."

Miss MARGARET COOPER will Sing at the Piano.

SEATS CAN NOW BE BOOKED.   NO SMOKING.

Treasurer—Mr. THOMAS MILLER.   Stage Manager—Mr. FRANK DAMER.

NOTICE.—The Public can leave the Theatre at the end of the performance by all exit and entrance doors which open outwards. Where there is a fireproof screen to the proscenium opening, it must be lowered at least once during every performance to ensure its being in proper working order. All gangways, passages and staircases must be kept free from chairs or any other obstructions, whether permanent or temporary.

The order and composition of this Programme may be varied as circumstances require.

BOX OFFICE open from 10 a.m. to 11 p.m.   TELEPHONE No. 6834 GERRARD (2 lines).

The Pianofortes used at this Theatre are by Messrs. John Brinsmead & Sons.
Toilet Table Appointments throughout the Theatre by Hinde's, Ltd., London and Birmingham.
During the Overture a Series of Pictures are shown by the World's Advertising Co., Ltd., of 248, High Holborn, W.C.

Musical Director—Mr. HERMAN FINCK.   Acting Manager—Mr. E. A. PICKERING.

London's Palace Theatre programme, 1908.
Author's Collection.

The Salome Dancer in full regalia, as used on a greeting card.
Message inside reads "Thinking of You." 1908.
Author's Collection.

Maud Allan, 1908. Author's Collection.

MAUD ALLAN

AND

LEO. JAN. MISCHEL

CHERNIAVSKY.

Programme.

1. LEO, JAN. MISCHEL CHERNIAVSKY.
   Trio for Pianoforte, Violin, 'Cello . . . . *Bache*

2. MAUD ALLAN.
   (*a*) Am Meer (By the Sea) . . . . *Schubert-Liszt*
   (*b*) Valse A minor, Op. 34 . . . . *Chopin*
   (*c*) Spring Song . . . . *Mendelssohn*
   (*d*) Moment Musical . . . . *Schubert*

3. MISCHEL CHERNIAVSKY.
   (*a*) Vito . . . . *Popper*
   (*b*) Scherzo . . . . *Van Goens*

4. MAUD ALLAN.
   Peer Gynt Suite . . . . *Grieg*
   (*a*) Morning
   (*b*) Ase's Death
   (*c*) Anitra's Dance
   (*d*) Dance of the Gnomes

INTERVAL OF TEN MINUTES.

5. JAN CHERNIAVSKY.
   Rigoletto . . . . *Verdi-Liszt*

6. LEO CHERNIAVSKY.
   (*a*) Ave Maria . . . . *Schubert*
   (*b*) Spanish Dance . . . . *Sarasate*

7. MAUD ALLAN.
   Blue Danube Valse . . . . *J. Strauss*

Maud Allan will be accompanied in all her Dances by the Cherniavsky Trio.
Accompanist: Frank St. Leger.

A DIFFERENT PROGRAMME WILL BE SUBMITTED AT EACH CONCERT.

NOTICE.—The Management reserve the right to make alterations in this Programme.

Manager - - - HOWARD EDIE.

Electrician - FRED. W. MITCHELL.   Treasurer - H. I. COHEN.   Advance Manager - W. A. LOW.

The MAUD ALLAN Company under the Direction of W. Angus MacLeod.

No. 1.

DAILY TIMES PRINT.

Programme for the Maud Allan/Cherniavsky Trio Company tour,
1913-1915. Author's Collection.

*Studio pose for Tchaikowsky's
Fifth Symphony, Los Angeles,
1926.* Author's Collection.

At the races: Alice Lonnon places a bet, while Maud Allan looks on, shocked. The Cherniavsky brothers, Leo, Jan, and Mischel, stand to Maud's immediate right. Manila, 1914. Author's Collection.

Leo Cherniavsky and the tour director on Christmas Day, 1914. Author's Collection.

The Cherniavsky Trio at work during their Australian tour, c. 1927.
San Francisco Archives.

*Holford House, c. 1918. West Wing, where Maud
Allan lived – the rest of the mansion was occupied by
the Baptist Training College – is near the top
left-hand corner of this photo.* Royal Commission on
Historical Monuments, London.

Music room in the west wing of Holford House. The Maud Allan statue in the bow window is by Jacob Epstein. Author's Collection.

Maud Allan seeking the shade in Alexandria, 1923.
Author's Collection.

we? Then I shall be content and not until then.

While his wife was visiting Maud in 1899, William had the urn on his mind. He wrote on July 23 to Maud: "Now tell Mamma not to worry about the receipt, it is all right. If I should lose it that would not matter as they have my handwriting in the office in their books, see, and you or Mamma can get it by proving your identity, understand me."

Theo's writings (and ashes) were no doubt swallowed up in the earthquake of 1906. However, his name lives on. In 1949, twelve American mystery writers collectively wrote *The Marble Forest*. At a loss for a pseudonymous author, they chose the name of Theodore Durrant, to whom the work is also dedicated.

12. With regard to the relationship between Maud and Busoni, Etienne Amyot, founding director of the prestigious BBC Third Programme in 1946 and a friend of Maud Allan in prewar London, writes:

> I knew Gerda Busoni fairly well in her last years, meeting her originally at Schloss Berg, the music centre of Madame Langenhan, in Switzerland. She never said an ill word against Maud. I had the impression that she believed Maud and Busoni had at one time had an affair. (The reason Maud took to me when she first heard me at some London [piano] recital was that she thought I played like Busoni – an absurd exaggeration of course for he was not *one* of the greatest pianists of this century but THE greatest. Maud told me the first time she danced was to Busoni, Gerda, AND Richard Strauss – which was the reason Strauss wrote his *Salome* opera. But this surely was once more an instance when Maud was proclaiming something to be true that was in fact fantasy – so often indulged in in the last years. (From a personal communication, June 22, 1988.)

13. Remy was a native of Liège, the son of a music-loving notary. As a teenager he organized various musical groups, one member of which was Hubert Goossens, father of Eugene and Leon Goossens, renowned conductor and oboist respectively. Hubert Goossens was later associated with Carl Rosa, founder of an opera company bearing his name that thrived in England until 1958. Carl Rosa's daughter, Violet, became Maud's first-

known personal secretary and accompanied Maud to the United States in 1910.

As a schoolboy, Remy was impulsive, disorganized, and full of fantasy, with a natural talent for improvisation. He moved to Paris in his early twenties; there he eked out a living as a music critic and correspondent for Belgian newspapers. In 1897 he moved to Berlin as political correspondent for *Le Temps* of Paris, for which he was eminently unsuitable. He took to writing horror stories and provided *Le journal de Liège* with a regular column titled *"La vie à Berlin."* In it he reported on the activities of Belgian artists in Berlin, in particular Eugène Ysaÿe, the great violinist and teacher, and César Thomson, a less-remembered musicologist; Maud came to know them both.

In Berlin, Remy became very poor and at one time was forced to take work as a representative of Thomas Cook and Son, the first international travel agency. He died in January 1906, at the age of thirty-six, ten days before Maud's debut performance of *The Vision of Salome*. He became totally deaf and neurasthenic before his death, and may well have committed suicide. (Such deafness is a common symptom of advanced syphilis, to which his lifestyle may well have exposed him.) The Belgian papers briefly reported his death, ascribing it to meningitis. Remy's brother and Maud were the only mourners at his interment. (See Marcel Kunel, "Marcel Remy, Critique et Conteur liégeois," in *La Vie Wallone: Revue mensuelle illustrée*, June 15, 1923, pp. 452–65. The author is indebted to Lacey McDearmon, Curator, Dance Collection of the Performing Arts Research Center, New York Public Library, for providing this reference.)

In a letter to his wife dated July 17, 1902, Busoni mentions Marcel Remy:

> It is raining horribly now. . . . The pieces that Remy brought are just like the weather today. He – Remy – has the defect common to all Frenchmen of being patriotic. He likes to find fault with what is German and to praise what is French, although he tries to be just. But in this respect he is not altogether successful, for his Latin superficiality and impetuosity stand in the way. His judgement is always formed too quickly, and clever at the expense of truth . . .

Such was the composer of the music for *The Vision of Salome*.

14. Maud referred to her parents' initial reaction during an interview with the *Daily News* of Perth, Australia, on September 26, 1914: "The world lost a promising musician when she decided to become a dancer. At the time she adopted her strange and impressive art, she was a pianist with a brilliant record at the Berlin and Leipzig [*sic*] Conservatories. Justly enough, her parents were not overpleased when she gave up the piano and danced under a light in classical raiment." In her *Jottings* she wrote, "My parents' first knowledge of my new career."

15. Theodor Szántó (1877–1934) was a member of Ferruccio Busoni's master class of 1901, which Maud attended. He later became a champion of such modern composers as Bartók, Debussy, and Kodály.

4

First Steps: 1903-1907

*T*HE CONTRAST BETWEEN Berlin and Vienna at the turn of the century was at least as great as that of Toronto and San Francisco. Berlin was recognized as the greatest industrial and commercial city on the continent of Europe; Vienna was the intellectual capital of Austria and in many ways the cultural pacesetter of the continent. Few European capitals had more valuable art collections than Vienna, few had an older university (Vienna's was established in 1365) or a more renowned medical school. Few, if any, had so cosmopolitan and heterogeneous a population, pleasure loving, genial, and possessed of a *bonhomie* that distinguished it from Berlin's hard-working but dour citizens.

An unabashedly modern, efficient city, Berlin lacked indigenous culture.[1] Vienna had the richest of cultural associations, particularly with the great composers from Haydn to Mahler (director of the Vienna Court Opera – later the State Opera – and a powerful influence on the city's cultural life) to Richard Strauss (on the threshold of an equally important career).

For any neophyte dancer, Vienna was the indisputable

fountainhead of the terpsichorean world and the only viable venue for a debut. All the more so for a modern, experimental, and, in her own view, unique dancer such as Maud Allan. Had she been critically damned, she probably would have had no alternative but to return to her mother, who was reluctant to have Maud live in San Francisco, with its awful memories. Indeed, Isabella Durrant warned her in a letter of December 31, 1903, "You must not think of coming home for a number of years as you would not be happy after what has happened, so make your plans accordingly, as this is not the place for you for some time."

As it turned out, Maud was able to rationalize her reception, which was far from enthusiastic, as sufficiently positive to indicate that so determined, talented, and desperate an individual should persevere. A dancing career is difficult at any time, but for Maud, a woman of thirty, it was treacherous. Indeed, her career would prove more stunning than lasting.

Maud's debut astonished and delighted her mother, for it fulfilled her quasi-mystical faith in her daughter's gifts. Isabella's joy, however, was gradually tempered by a persistent uneasiness that she might be losing her "darling baby," as she often called Maud. This mixture of fear and delight is well illustrated in a letter of December 31, 1903. It begins with an outburst of heartfelt thanks to those who had helped Maud prepare for and launch her debut and then reports the opinions of two close family friends. Pop Perkins, she reported,

> is so happy with your success. He says that where you will be able to outshine Miss Duncan is that you have received an excellent education, you have your art at your command, and can create a new one while she is finding out the old masters. Many people think she is going too far now, and will be classed a fanatic. I hope not, poor girl, for she has worked hard. But not as hard as you have, in such a short time. I just think you are a wonder.

Mrs. Durrant next passes on the views of Dr. Thrasher, who had been such a stalwart friend throughout Theo's troubles:

Dr. Thrasher is delighted but also, I may say, mad at your name being changed, but when I showed him the advisability he cooled down and said it was well enough to make your debut so that you could be seen on your own merits, but he would not have that do, and now you must take your own name, for it is a beautiful one and it is for you to lift the stigma that has been so unjustly put upon it. I told him it would be done as soon as you had succeeded as you wished.

I do hope you have a grand triumph when you appear before the general public. You must not let one doubt enter your mind when that happens. The great secret of your debut was, as you say, that you were sure of yourself. That is what both the Doctor and Papa say is the secret of all success in life. So, when you have gotten independent for your own self and your art, you can snap your fingers at all those who would go to see you for what you were [Theo's sister].

I did so hope we would be together again this Xmas, but it has passed once more. I suppose that but for your new art you would be married by now or with us. Speaking of marriage, Dr. Thrasher says it would be better not to get married. Of course you could, but the ideal purity of your work is so much better portrayed by a virgin than by one who has been contaminated by man. The thought is beautiful in the mind while witnessing the movement of the old masters by a lovely maiden. Not that marriage is not beautiful by its own standpoint but I would not care to have you do this work if married – any other work but dancing for a married woman.

This letter also clarifies William Durrant's status and prospects. For $2.50 a day he was making trunk trimmings and handles – without getting his hands stained as he had when he worked with shoes. He had also, with his wife, completed a correspondence course in optometry and was now awaiting the next state board examination.[2] "To further your Papa's interest," Isabella explained, she had paid $1.50 for him to attend the local association's annual dinner, where he had been the centre of attention. So many of his fellow optometrists said they had long wished to meet him, presumably as the father of California's most celebrated murderer.

After reporting Pop Perkins's prediction that "you will either make big money or nothing as the fad goes," Mrs. Durrant returned to the safest of topics – Maud's debut. This time, however, her thoughts were not on Maud alone:

> I wonder how Miss Duncan likes to have a rival, or did she know you were preparing to be her rival? Dr. Thrasher is afraid that your giving the whole evening alone will be injurious to your health and very fatiguing. I told him I did not think it would be much more than were you to play the piano for the same length of time and, of course, you do not perform evenings in succession, therefore you will have time to rest in between. I think the after-hours before retiring are likely to be more harmful than the performance itself. I do not believe Miss Duncan spends many moments before retiring after an evening performance and my dear, heavy eating is very bad for one who wants to keep her youthful looks, so retire after a light repast in order to save your nerves.

By March, Maud's exhilaration over her Vienna debut had ebbed, overwhelmed by a wave of self-pity: her "public" debut – Maud had already given recitals for the staff and students of the Hochschule, so she claimed in newspaper interviews – was suffering delay after delay. In a letter of March 26, 1904, her mother showed little sympathy:

> First of all it was no hall to be had and now it is the war [an obscure reference, perhaps to deteriorating relations between Austria and Serbia]. The latter we can understand but as for the former, we never could see why some place could not be obtained at once after your debut. You had the

money, all that was necessary was the go-ahead. I think you had better come to America to learn how to get a move on. The longer you wait the more time will it give Miss Duncan to give you trouble as you write she is doing.

If it is that Miss Duncan has recognized who you are and is trying to injure you, let me know the truth, but it must be true, not hearsay, and I will give it to the press to show her up. I would pass it in just as you would write it, so be careful. Let it tell what she is doing or saying against your coming out in her work. On the other hand, if you are under obligation to her, and you are not keeping your word, you know best. We can not see her object in trying to injure you. No artist can expect to monopolize the world. Does she think the whole world belongs to her? Or does she think she has a patent on her work?

I hope your next letter will be brighter and you in better spirits. I would not indulge in tears any more if I were you, it will do you no good.

At the height of Maud's success and until her second tour of the United States in 1916, Isadora Duncan loudly insisted that she had "helped" Maud in Berlin, a claim that Maud initially refuted and then minimized. On one occasion Maud recalled that she had interviewed Isadora Duncan in Berlin, before Isadora had become famous, and that this interview had been published in a San Francisco newspaper, for which Isadora never thanked her. They disliked each other intensely. According to Manya Cherniavsky, Maud deplored Isadora's failure "to take her art seriously." Perhaps this was another way of deploring Isadora's willingness to publicize her private life, while Maud, of course, was so secretive. Her *Jottings* show that the two met (or at the least crossed paths) in Berlin, Paris, and New York.

Her public debut finally took place in Brussels, probably at the very end of 1904. Although there are passing references to it, no press reviews have been found.

Maud's first documented public recital took place on

January 2, 1905, in Liège (Marcel Remy's hometown) and was warmly reviewed. Maud's account of the evening prompted the following scene in San Francisco. Her mother wrote:

> I took your last two letters for Papa Perk to read. Cormack [Perkins's housekeeper] must hear them and then had to go for a handkerchief, she was crying so. Had to wait till she came back, for she had to weep to think our girls are both successful now and at the same time. She has a big heart and is so impulsive. Pop Perkins kept saying "Well, that's fine, better than any letter from Alice [Lonnon, his daughter]," so we are all thinking good thoughts for Friday – but we know it will come out all right.

Mrs. Durrant was referring to Maud's public debut in Berlin, which took place on March 4, 1905, at the Artists' Club, followed by another performance ten days later. The reviewer for the *Berliner Tageblatt*, while confessing to boredom after the first three items and declaring the performance to be imitative of Isadora Duncan, nevertheless conceded that Maud had "greater musical talent, her movements are in better accord with the music, and she seems to have better control over her body" than her fellow San Franciscan. Maud had reason to be hopeful. Yet, to judge by the tone and content of her mother's next extant letter of March 25, Maud was depressed. "We read your letter this A.M.," Mrs. Durrant began, "we were so anxious, it's five weeks since your last one." Mrs. Durrant then threw out an idea that her daughter must have read with mixed feelings:

> I wish I could be of use to my little girl, if I could, I would be with you very quickly. Sometimes I think that as long as you make Berlin your home, until you are further along in your art it would be a good idea for me to go there and take a flat, thus making ready for Papa to come over and open his office in our flat. I have no doubt we could get some two or three roomers in the meantime to reduce our expenses and

yet have a nice home. I think there are enough English speaking people in Berlin to give Papa and me plenty of business in our work.

The rest of the letter covers a range of topics, such as:

Do not keep late nights if you value your good looks. Late suppers in ill-smelling, badly ventilated restaurants with *wines* will sooner or later give one a dissipated look and manner, which in a measure will court a familiarity that at other times one would not permit. You did not say how your Berlin friends took your work.[3] We would have loved to have heard more about your evening in Berlin as we know how very hard it is to receive kind notices from those creatures, the critics. You must feel favoured to have them even kind to you. Were there any Americans, or did anyone know or make known who you were?

Of all Isabella's letters, that of November 1, 1905, is the most remarkable. Evidently there had been a move among Maud's friends to inquire whether the University of California at Berkeley would be prepared to sponsor her in recital. Mrs. Durrant, although violently opposed to the idea, sought the advice of General Dickinson, the prominent attorney who had fought so hard and long for Theo. Two weeks later she gave a detailed account of her conversation with the General. Incredulous at the mere suggestion, his first question was whether it would be Maud's intention to perform "that dance" (presumably Chopin's *Marche funèbre*). When Mrs. Durrant answered "I don't know," the General struck at the heart of the matter:

Does not your daughter understand her friends would be severe in their criticism at her appearance in such a work, when she remained away during your deep affliction so that she might perfect herself in other branches which to my mind would be more in harmony with the pathetic side of the whole affair? A dance is a dance, and sooner or later it will be given in the Variety Halls. You have only to look at that girl Fuller's dance.[4] It is given in the ten-cent show as also in the free beer dives by painted up beer handlers. Your daughter would not want her name sounded as the Fuller's when mentioning the dance.

Dickinson also warned that the "Church people" would be up in arms, even if the entire project were funded by the university. Moreover, Dickinson pointed out – and this surely clinched the argument for Maud – the university would not pay for the performances, as all profits from any university-sponsored event went into the university's coffers. "Write and tell her what I say," concluded the General, "then should she come she cannot say she has not been forewarned as to what people will remark of her dance."

So strong a reaction from so respectable a source led Mrs. Durrant to plead that Maud return to her parents, but as a daughter, not a dancer:

> Well, my dear, if you do not get along you have your parents who will give you a warm welcome when you are tired of trying. We are getting along in years now [Isabella was then fifty-three] and would be happy, if only with three rooms, to be near each other. Why not do as I always wanted you to do, give up trying to come before the public, take what we could give you. I ask you again, what is the use of it after all?
>
> Of course it will be like beginning all over again, but it must be one way or the other sooner or later, why not now? We are living very humbly so as to live within our means, but so long as we have our health, that is all we ask other than to know what our little girlie is doing when we lay down at night.

From this incomplete collection of letters Isabella emerges as a domineering, practical, insightful, clever, and desperately lonely woman, tormented by at least two inner conflicts. She had first to reconcile herself to Maud's decision – quite possibly the first Maud ever took independently of her mother – to abandon her piano studies for what her mother clearly considered a questionable occupation. The more intense and subtle conflict was her realization that the more Maud pursued success, the less likely would she ever be content with a life of domesticity.

With the end of Isabella's extant letters, the only records of Maud's fortunes until that memorable matinee of her London debut in 1908 are the reviews and accounts of certain incidents related to her performances on the continent. Some of those records, though far from complete, are very colourful.

In 1906, before her debut of *The Vision of Salome* in December, Maud performed in Hamburg, Cologne, Leipzig, and Berlin. To judge by the generally appreciative reviews, she had reason to persist in her new art. By far the most interesting of these recitals was that of April 4, in Berlin, where she seems to have given more than one recital. Among those attending was Professor Altmann, Artur Rubinstein's beloved tutor. Professor Altmann was an unusually cultured person and not given to flattery, so his review of Maud's performance in the *Nationale Zeitung* of April 6 was encouraging:

> Miss Maud Allan presented mood settings that were extremely appealing to the eye. By refined gestures and her way of dancing, the young artist is extremely successful in reflecting the mood of the musical work in question. Her interpretation of Mendelssohn's "Spring Song" was superb. Her rendition of Schubert's "Ave Maria" showed devotion, her representation of Chopin's "Funeral March" stirring emotions. Miss Allan's settings are bound to fascinate even wider circles than Miss Duncan's presentations.[5]

The only other documented event of Maud's life in Berlin in 1906 appears in an interview she gave at the height of her fame in London, two years later. In the midst of this interview she revealed far more of her real self than on any other occasion. She related how, at the time of the San Francisco earthquake and fire (April 18, 1906), she had no word from her parents for more than ten days:

She was at the time resting and en pension, and many of the pension's habitués extracted an agreeable excitement from watching her with lynx eyes to see whether she showed any feeling. And as she neither went into hysterics nor wept uncontrollably on some dowager's shoulder, they decided she was a very hard and unnatural person. At the end of what seemed to her an endless ten days, a telegram reached her and was given to her as she was passing through the hall, where suddenly they all crowded around her and bombarded her with questions. She read the telegram, folded it up again with a deliberate exactness that should have told them something of her benumbed state, made her stiff lips form the words "They are safe," and went quietly to her room, while they whispered loudly that it was very strange that she could receive such news without fainting. And they were so aggrieved at being cheated out of this agreeable break in the monotony of their lives that they never quite forgave her, and believed most firmly henceforth that she was a person devoid of natural affection.[6]

There is no question that between her debut in Vienna and her first performance of *The Vision of Salome* two years later, Maud had to struggle to keep body and soul together. Although her occasional recitals were appreciated by a small circle of cognoscenti, they were far from remunerative. That struggle came to an end – although notoriety preceded affluence – with the first performance of *The Vision*. This work, undoubtedly her chef d'oeuvre, although by no means her favourite work, was a sensation in London and brought her international fame as the Salome Dancer, an epithet she deeply resented as unworthy of her unique artistry.

The Vision presented Salome as a *femme fatale* and as decadence incarnate. Both views were modern. For centuries Salome had been approved by the Church and was a popular subject for artists in many disciplines. The traditional view, carefully nurtured by the anti-feminist policies of the Church, was simply that she was an evil woman responsible for John the Baptist's death.[7] In the mid-nineteenth century, however, artists began to view her as the archetypal *femme fatale*. Heinrich Heine, Gustave Flaubert, and, a generation later, Oscar Wilde, wove elaborate fantasies around her, and in so doing removed her from traditional associations. Some half dozen composers including Alexander Glazunov and Jules Massenet had written operas based on her story long before Richard Strauss composed his masterpiece. Foremost among painters fascinated by the figure was Gustave Moreau, whose *Tattooed Salome* was considered his masterpiece during his lifetime. Moreau (1826–1898) became obsessed by the figure of Salome. After his mother's death, he confined himself to the apartment he had shared with her, attempting to paint Salome out of his system.

All these nineteenth-century artists focussed on Salome's sensuality, perverseness, and seductive powers. By the end of the century she also personified the decadence of an old society on the brink of radical reform or dissolution.[8]

The most immediately important influence on *The Vision of Salome* was Max Reinhardt's production of Wilde's play *Salome*, first given in Leipzig in 1904. From a theatrical point of view – and *Salome* was nothing if not *fin de siècle* drama – Reinhardt's production was daringly innovative. The subject was, if not sacred as in England, then certainly considered unsuitable for the stage and, in the notorious Wilde's treatment, scandalous. Both Marcel Remy and Maud saw this Reinhardt production in Berlin.

Choreographic treatment of the story was not original. A number of Maud's contemporaries had enjoyed considerable success with dance interpretations of the drama. As early as 1895, Loie Fuller was performing a *Salome* composed of three short dances. However, Remy's treatment of the material was highly original and daring, as it exploited Maud's personal experience. Remy caused Maud to identify the Baptist's execution and, more forcefully, his decapitated head, whether papier mâché or invisible, with that of her brother. In effect, Maud was giving vent to her fierce passions with the aid of her intensely vivid imagination.

Therein lay the effectiveness of her performance and the reason it could not be successfully imitated.

Maud's debut performance of *The Vision of Salome* took place on December 26, 1906, before an invited audience. Two other dancers, much younger than the thirty-three-year-old Maud, were also performing – for the first time – in Vienna. Ruth St. Denis, one of the most important figures in the evolution of modern dance, was appearing at the Ronach Theatre. (Some thirty-five years later she and Maud would be working in the same California aircraft factory, Maud as a draughtsperson, St. Denis as a riveter.) The other dancer was destined for a shorter career, greater notoriety, and a more unpleasant end: Mata Hari, executed in 1917 (unjustly, according to some modern biographers) as a spy by the French government of "Tiger" Georges Clemenceau.

The reviewer of the *Illustreites Wiener Extrablatt* summarized *The Vision of Salome* as "a few interesting movements by the extremely talented Miss Allan." Predicting that her "honest attempt to invent a new dance is bound to fail," the reviewer nevertheless added, "Why should this be of any concern to the directors of variety shows?" His point was valid enough, for it was at the Palace, London's leading variety theatre, that Maud had her enormous success.

Ten days earlier, this newspaper had reported that at a dress rehearsal "this beautiful dancer, allegedly a native of San Francisco, had caused concern due to her piquant lack of costume." At the demand of an unnamed princess deeply committed to supporting the Court Opera and as deeply offended by Maud's perceived nudity, a second rehearsal was held, attended by Court Opera director Mahler and senior members of his staff. This time, the newspaper reported, "Maud Allan's body was covered by more veils while she danced *The Vision of Salome*, to the accompaniment of [Remy's] authentic Arabian music." The controversy no doubt provided good publicity.

Maud's next engagement, at the Kiraly Theatre, Budapest, indicates the response *The Vision of Salome* could gen-

erate from a public audience. On January 4, 1907, she was
a guest artist in *The Sho Gun*, which had been a Broadway
success. During the second act she performed several dances
and an excerpt from *The Vision*. She was apparently an
overnight sensation, for her engagement was extended to
three weeks. According to newspaper accounts she was also
invited to perform "Greek" dances to the music of Chopin
and Rubinstein at private evening parties.

The day after her debut in Budapest, Maud and her local
agent, M. Szydow, were interviewed by a journalist from
the *Magyar Szinpad*.[9] On entering her hotel room, the journalist was struck by Maud's grace: "She walks towards me
with marvellously rhythmic steps; her walk is beautiful, her
upper body follows her every step with exciting movement." Szydow took over the interview, for Maud was
exhausted. Only at the end did she speak of her studies and
her admiration for Wilde's *Salome*. Finally, she gave her
account (not necessarily accurate) of what had happened in
Vienna:

> We were called in by Mahler. At the rehearsal he was
> delighted. Everyone who saw it was conquered. Then the
> police brought up some moral questions. They said my dance
> was immodest. I invited the members of the city council and
> performed the dance for them. They were in awe and
> congratulated me after the dance. Nevertheless they decided
> I had to wear a leotard. Never! I chose rather to leave. I do
> not make compromises. No! Never! I signed a contract with
> the Carl Theatre [Vienna]. Then I received an offer from
> Laszlo Beothy. It appealed to me but was difficult. The
> Kiraly Theatre [of which Beothy was owner/manager] had
> to pay a lot of money for me. We shall see if it is worthwhile
> for Beothy. My feeling is that they will appreciate me
> here.

Later in the week the same journalist interviewed eleven
members of the Budapest theatrical community and published their views on the "naked dancer." Opinion was
sufficiently mixed to allow Maud to defend her stage cos-

tume in a letter to a newspaper, a letter clearly designed both to attract publicity and to serve as a credo. "The dancer's body," she argued, "is her instrument, the raw material, just as the violin is to the violinist, and clay is to the sculptor. Is it really possible to cover up this raw material when it is precisely this that brings about the desired artistic effect?"[10]

Controversy over her state of undress was not the only result of her debut recital in Budapest. Six months later, on June 30, 1907, the *Herald* of Augusta, Georgia, printed a story (the last paragraphs of which, continued on another page, are missing from the newspaper's records) titled "The American Girl Who Danced Salome With a Real Head." Although the tale has all the markings of a press agent's invention, there is no question that the more credible part of the tale took place and a real possibility that melodrama also occurred. The credible incident was reported in a Budapest daily,[11] and is noted in Maud's personal *Jottings* made in the late 1930s ("Budapest: I dance in a lions' cage"). It was vividly related to close friends in 1945, when Maud demonstrated how she had "hypnotized" the lions by the skilful use of her marvellously expressive hands.

The Augusta *Herald* story ran as follows: prominent among the leaders of the high-living nobles of Hungary was a certain Count Géza Zichy, scion of one of Hungary's most powerful families.[12] His shibboleth, as the *Herald* put it, was courage. During a dinner given in Maud's honour, the conversation "turned to the manifold virtues of courage and its multitudinous manifestations."

"It takes tremendous courage," said Miss Allan.

"What does?" chorused the nobles.

"Why – to come out on the stage before hundreds with feet bare, with shoulders bare, with little dress," she said.

"Ha, ha, ha," laughed Count Zichy.

"It does indeed," said the little dancer earnestly. "Every time I appear, until the spirit gets into me, it is as though I were about to undergo martyrdom. Don't you think that is courage – to fight down and go out and face the thing you dread?"

"Ha, ha, ha," laughed the Count again, thinking doubtless of boar hunts and duels and other blood curdling specialties.

"Hundreds peering at you from the darkened house," said the dancer. "Eyes of men, eyes of women. In how many are there other lights of contempt – of desire? Each time I dance I think of it and I dread it."

"What you call in America brag," said the Count. He was not in a very good mood tonight.

"Ha, ha, ha," laughed the Count unpleasantly. "You would think you had the courage to dance in a den of lions. Pouf!"

Miss Allan thought for a moment, while the nobles laughed with the Count.

"How much will you bet?" she said suddenly.

"That you won't dance in a den of lions? Ten thousand Marks," replied the Count.

"Done!" said Miss Allan.

The upshot was that Maud, "robed as Primavera" (presumably a reference to Botticelli's *Birth of Spring*, which, Maud always maintained, first inspired her art), arrived at the appointed time and, in front of Count Zichy and his cronies, entered and immediately began to dance in the lions' cage. Shortly thereafter entered "two little cubs, gamboling and playing like a pair of kittens. . . . There was a perfect cyclone of laughter from the crowd. Count Zichy was mad all over. It was a fraud, a Yankee trick. He would not pay." But he did pay in the end, so the story goes, and Maud turned over the 10,000 marks to the hospital. So much for known fact.[13]

To obtain his revenge, Count Zichy invited Maud to give a private performance of *The Vision of Salome* in the hall of one of Budapest's great palaces. Towards the end of the performance, reported the *Herald*,

to Maud Allan, swaying like a passion flower in the last steps of the Seven veils, a giant negro brought upon a great salver Johaanan. Her eyes half closed, the dancer raised by its dank hair the ghastly prize of Herodias' daughter. She leaned towards its lips. Gently the severed head touched her wrists, and there shot through her a terrible tremor, a shivering of the soul. Upon her white flesh were the stains, dark crimson clots. It was blood. Her body rigid as though carved in marble, the dancer slowly forced her eyes to the face she held aloft. It was the face of a man not long since dead. As one from whom life passes very quickly, she crumpled to the floor. From her hands dropped the head. It rolled upon her breast and fell beside her, leaving upon her white body a crimson trail. So was the dancer Maud Allan taught that it is not well to jest with a Noble of Hungary.

Zichy may have devised the scheme as an original if cruel prank, but circumstantial evidence suggests another, more sinister, possibility. Twelve years earlier,the *New York Times* of December 26, 1895, had reported that Count Géza Zichy was quietly married in New York's St. Stephen's Roman Catholic Church. "Count and Countess Zichy drove to the Windsor Hotel, where the latter has been living since she returned here from South Dakota."[14] Blanche Lamont was from Dillon, in the neighbouring state of Montana, which she left only a few weeks before she was murdered by Theo in April 1895. The following November, Theo had been found guilty of her murder. It is therefore reasonable to suppose that the new Countess Zichy was familiar with the "Crime of a Century" proceedings, which were reported throughout the United States, and she recognized Maud Allan as Theo's sister. If she resented her husband's interest in Maud, what more diabolically horrifying means of terminating a liaison, real or imagined, than to confront Maud Allan with the most intense of her private feelings?

In April, Maud travelled to Munich for an engagement to include *The Vision of Salome*. However, the Munich Men's Club for the Fight Against Public Immorality got wind of its controversial nature and successfully persuaded city authorities to ban her performance. With the active support of the artistic community, led by two prominent painters of the day – both of whom did at least one portrait of Maud as Salome[15] – a "libel action" was launched against the club. The result of the action is unclear – other than that Maud was well publicized, and the whole imbroglio inspired a piece of doggerel titled "Something New About Salome" published, on April 22, 1907, in the *München Neuest Nachrichten*.

Later in the month Maud went ahead with her scheduled recital – without *Salome* and without the success she sought. "First of all," reported the *Berliner Tageblatt*, which had covered the affair in a series of brief despatches,[16] "she did penance for her Salome sins by presenting Schubert's *Ave Maria*. Other pious dances followed" before a sparsely filled house.

On May 7, Maud joined the program of Le Théâtre des Variétés in Paris. Her debut in Paris was deliberately timed to coincide with the Paris premiere of Richard Strauss's opera *Salome*. The Strauss work, conducted by the composer, caused real excitement; Maud's debut attracted favourable attention without reference to Isadora Duncan. The critic of *Le Figaro*, for example, praised her grace, her mime, her dramatic feeling, her modesty. Maud was on the threshold of conquest.

Following this encouraging engagement, she toured France as a member of Loie Fuller's troupe; but, according to her *Jottings*, she had business problems ("the manager who tried to frighten me into a contract; I return – broke – to the Berlin of my student days"). In her autobiography she writes at some length but not specifically of her bitter experiences with her early managers; she omits any reference to her humiliating return to Berlin. Maud does not write directly of her association with Loie Fuller, who had done her an unidentified good turn a few years earlier, though in a paragraph of cunning charm she very thinly disguises a reference to Fuller and a companion – probably Gabrielle Bloch, her lover, or Mary Bran, a concert agent, a proud and unabashed lesbian:

Another time, two women, one well known in the theatrical profession and to the world, too, cheated me out of my rightfully due money and now said, "If you think we owe you money, go legally to work to get it." And this sentence, uttered by the shrewder of the two, was accompanied by a smile verging on a sneer, while her hands, as usual ungloved – we had met again at the house of a mutual acquaintance in Paris, and were now waiting for a cab – were stuffed into the outside pockets of her very mannish looking coat. But it seems to be the principle of these two women not to pay debts, unless positively cornered. I believe their hotel bills in Marseilles are still owing, and that was two years ago exactly. (p. 91) [17]

When she wrote this, in October 1908, Maud was affluent beyond her wildest dreams. In later years, such charges would pale beside her own ruthless and devious financial practices.

By the time of her sojourn in France, Maud had struggled for almost five years to make a name – and some money – in Europe. How she survived during the long intervals between her occasional engagements is not known. Although her parents awaited her with open arms, Maud would be ashamed of returning home without having achieved significant success after a ten-year absence. The tragic associations of San Francisco were additional reasons to rule out such a move. Besides, with its artists, its aristocracy, and its cultural heritage, Europe was her spiritual home. Thus, whatever pressures her mother may have put upon her to return to San Francisco, whatever personal hardships she had to bear, Maud drew upon her formidable reserves of willpower. She was determined to wait for the break she was sure would come; if it did not come unaided, she would bring it about, were it in her power to do so.

That break came in an opportunity to dance privately before King Edward VII at the fashionable spa of Marienbad (now just inside Czechoslovakia), where the king was on holiday in September 1907. There are no fewer than five accounts of this episode, three by Maud at different periods in her life. The first comes from *My Life and Dancing*, published scarcely one year after the event. According to this account it was while she was staying at the fashionable Hôtel de Londres near the Place de l'Opéra in Paris that she met the great chanteuse Yvette Guilbert, well known for her generosity towards aspiring performers. Guilbert arranged for her to appear in a charity matinee at the Théâtre Sarah Bernhardt.

"It was," Maud added, "through the generous efforts of this great artist and her husband Dr. Schiller that I was enabled to dance for His Majesty . . . An introduction to Princess Murat and through her to Mrs. Hall-Walker, further paved the way" for the latter's husband (later Lord Wavertree) was a close friend of the king. Thus it was that in September 1907 Maud "was in Marienbad awaiting the command to appear before the King of England. It was the happiest moment of my life when he took my hand and with his calm dignity told me he considered my art a beautiful one, and my dances worthy of the word classical" (p. 86).

The second of Maud's accounts is so contrived that it deserves little attention except that its distortions hint at the pathos of her later years. It was written in 1921 as one of a series of "reminiscences" she composed for a San Francisco newspaper. In this account she writes that her audience included King Edward VII and his cousin Kaiser Wilhelm II of Germany. "I was overwhelmed at the thought of appearing before so great and revered a monarch as the King of England. I cannot say I felt an equal sensation with reference to the ruler of Germany."[18]

Recalling how she was presented to the two sovereigns after her performance, Maud conjures up a scene sure to impress her socially unsophisticated readers:

King Edward smiled upon me with that kindly smile that so became him and, taking my hand, said "Your art is a most beautiful one. In every way your dances deserve the word 'classical.' If there is anything I can do for you, ask me."

I felt suddenly in the position of Salome when Herod uttered those tremendous words – "Ask . . . even to half my kingdom."

Always impulsive and without thinking of court etiquette and other dreadful complications, I said without hesitating "I should like to dance before your Queen Alexandra. Then my happiness would be complete." His Majesty peered gravely at me for a few moments. Then he said "You shall. When you are in London you shall come to Buckingham Palace and give Her Majesty as much pleasure as you have given me."

From the German Emperor I received many kind and flattering words spoken in English with a very guttural accent.

The last of Maud's recollections is a simple note from her *Jottings* made some thirty years after the event. "I learn that King Edward is at Marienbad: a friend in need. I meet Lady Wavertree who arranges for me to dance before the King. The King as audience. Prince Francis of Teck."[19]

In contrast to these personal recollections are those of E. Romayn Simmons, for twenty years the accompanist and business manager of Lillian Nordica, a celebrated American-born soprano, published in a short article in *Dancing Times* in 1967, and those of Sir Frederick Ponsonby (later Lord Sysonby), at the time private secretary to King Edward vii, published posthumously in 1951 under the title *Recollections of Three Reigns*.

According to Simmons, Edward vii had invited Madame Nordica and some of her friends to join him for a few days at Marienbad. Shortly after Madame Nordica's arrival Lady Wavertree told Simmons to arrange for an after-dinner recital featuring the unknown Maud Allan. Simmons thereupon contacted Charley Little, "the popular social editor of the *Daily Mail* and an excellent pianist," asking him to join him as Maud's accompanist. Simmons then called on Maud, "a charming young girl who had not yet danced much in Europe and was frankly glad of an engagement." Simmons did not tell her for whom she would be dancing, although Maud knew perfectly well.

Maud opened her performance with "some Rubinstein Waltzes in Greek costume" and then disappeared for some minutes. Simmons recalled that, just as the king was getting restless, Maud reappeared:

> When she made her entrance I sensed an extraordinary tension in the atmosphere which I at first mistook for admiration. But just then Charley stopped playing and I looked up to see what was wrong. His monocle had fallen on the floor, his jaw had dropped, and his eyes fairly popped out of a crimson face. I managed to keep the music going, but was in a frenzy to find out what it was all about . . .
>
> Salome's heavily jewelled Oriental dress seemed to concentrate around the wrists and ankles, for there seemed to be nothing much anywhere else. She wore a diminutive bra, doubtless inherited from Mrs. Tom Thumb, and a ditto string of diamonds, designed for a midget's baby.
>
> . . . And seven veils as well. Adjusting my glasses I looked again and saw a small chiffon handkerchief of seven different shades floating from a red rose that must have been glued to her bare flesh. It was a more than effective get-up where the women were all clothed to the ears.

After the performance Maud was presented:

> The King was all graciousness and compliments. "You're a very fine artist. Why have we not had the pleasure of seeing you dance in London?"
>
> "Only, sir, because I have never been asked."
>
> Turning to his equerry, Sir Stanley Clark, the King said "Please write to Alfred Butt and say we would like him to engage Miss Allan at the Palace Theatre so that the English public may enjoy her performance as much as we have."
>
> This genial gesture placed Miss Allan as a headliner in the famous Music Hall, where she became so popular that she

remained for four [*sic*] years and was an idol of the London public for many more.

Simmons's recollection is much nearer the truth than Maud's self-serving memories. It does not, however, seem as accurate as that given in Sir Frederick Ponsonby's *Recollections of Three Reigns*. With no reason other than discretion to alter his diary entries, Ponsonby's recollections of the event are probably the most reliable:

One evening the King dined with Mrs. Hall-Walker and after dinner a new dancer came, by name Maud Allan, who had never danced in London. The King expressed a wish to see her dance, but I was rather doubtful as to whether it would be right for his Majesty to do so. I had been told that she danced more or less naked, and I was afraid the English press might get hold of this and make up some wild story. I therefore went to see Mrs. Hall-Walker and said I had heard that Miss Allan danced with only two oyster shells and a five franc piece, and questioned whether it would be quite wise for the King to see her. Mrs. Hall-Walker replied that Miss Allan was a great artist and there was nothing offensive about her performance. The question was to get the music, and finally Little, the correspondent of the *Daily Mail*, and the leader of the town band were made to play duets for Miss Allan to dance to. I at once went to Little and explained to him that he was coming in as a friend, and I trusted that he would not report any of this in the *Daily Mail*. He roared with laughter and said he would of course treat it quite confidentially. The dance was very exceptional, and I must say Miss Allan was really wonderful. Her dance of Salome with the head of John the Baptist was really most dramatic, and although I cannot say she wore many clothes, there was nothing the least indecent about her performance. The fact of her having danced before the King was used later as an argument with the London County Council to allow her to continue her performance in London.[20]

The credibility of this account is suggested in a number of particulars. For example, Ponsonby's concern about the possible inappropriateness of the performance is characteristic of the author's position and background as a courtier who had served three monarchs. King Edward VII himself was in this regard the antithesis of both his mother, Queen Victoria, and his son, George V, who saw Maud dance – though possibly not *The Vision of Salome* – at least twice when he was Prince of Wales.

Characteristic, too, is the author's specific request that the *Daily Mail*'s social columnist refrain from reporting the evening's entertainment, his vagueness about the musical arrangements that were made so quickly, and his evident awkwardness in describing Maud's costume. Finally, his closing reference to difficulties with the London County Council is accurate enough. Were it not for the known support of the king, the council may have acceded to demands that *The Vision* be banned from the London stage.

Beyond question, this performance before Edward VII was the break any aspiring performer would dream of. As Maud was remarkably skilled at turning matters to her advantage, it is certainly possible that, with an introduction to Mrs. Hall-Walker, she travelled to Marienbad determined to ingratiate herself with anyone whose position might further her aim. Whether the king on his own initiative referred Maud to his friend Alfred Butt or whether he did so at the prompting of someone such as Mrs. Hall-Walker is immaterial. He obviously enjoyed Maud's performance enough to give her encouragement. A number of Maud's later friends inferred from passing hints that in return Maud did not hesitate to grant appropriate favours. Whatever the price, the outcome proved satisfactory – at least to Maud – for the initial London engagement was to be the peak of her career.

Notes

1. According to Artur Schnabel, who first came to Berlin at about this time, "there was only one opera house, perhaps three playhouses, three concert halls, one variety show and one light opera – all addressed to one group of 10,000" (*My Life and Music*, p. 51). On the other hand, Vienna was for Schnabel marked by an "atmosphere of jesting defeatism and precious, playful, morbidity" (p. 35) – in other words, a centre of thriving Decadence.

2. The archives of the American Optometrist Association do not show Mr. Durrant as a registered optometrist, although there are records that he passed the exam.

3. Maud never forgot the lack of support most of her Berlin friends gave her when she started her career as a dancer. In later conversations she would recall how they told her she was wasting her time. She mentioned this occasionally in interviews. One of her supporters was Joseph Joachim.

4. Together with Isadora Duncan and Ruth St. Denis, Loie Fuller was one of the pioneers of twentieth-century dance. She was well known for helping aspiring dancers. In a letter of July 28, 1896, Mrs. Durrant refers to the *Scarf Dance*, one of Loie Fuller's early and celebrated dances:

> Now I will tell you what Alice [Lonnon] told me not to tell anyone, but as you are so far away and I know you will not mention it to anyone, not even to her as it might get to her father and he, poor dear, feels badly enough about her going on the stage at all. But as Alice is cut out for that, there is no need to oppose her in the matter. One evening she went out to a party where she danced the Scarf Dance, and as she had asked Phil [her brother] to call for her, he said he would attend. She showed me how she danced, my, but she is as graceful as a faun but look at the grace she has and her figure is not bad, is it?

5. This recital was advertised in the *Zeitung* of April 4. In it, the reference to Gluck is unique in all of Maud's programs and may have been put in as a direct concession to Isadora Duncan's dances to this composer's music. If so, this would be good reason for Maud to be viewed, at least at this stage in her

career, as an imitator of Duncan. There is also a "Vokal Quartette Abend" announcement, with Artur Schnabel as accompanist to his wife, Schnabel Behr. At the top of the page a new program advertising a Variety Circus lists "Will Rogers, Lassowerfer."

6. "Maud Allan and her Dances," in *Pall Mall Magazine*, July 1908, pp. 699–709.

7. Some idea of the mystique surrounding the Baptist is suggested by a despatch from Rome in the *San Francisco Examiner* of January 3, 1904:

> Pope Pius has just ordered one of the most precious relics of Rome restored to the church of San Silvestro, from which it was removed to the Vatican in 1880, when the church was besieged by Italian troops. The relic is the authentic head of St. John the Baptist. . . . The relic is contained in a silver reliquary weighing one hundred pounds.

8. Bram Dijkstra, in *Idols of Perversity: Fantasies of Feminine Evil in Fin-de-siècle Culture* (O.U.P.) p. 379 defines Salome as "the true centrepiece of male masochistic fantasies."

9. Maud recounts her dealings and subsequent quarrel with Szydow in *My Life and Dancing*, pp. 89–91.

10. January 17, 1907. The Budapest press was divided in its opinions. The *Theatre Week* of January 11 deplored her perceived nudity; the *Sunday News* of January 13 welcomed her as "a pioneer of a new dance style – as distinct from that of Isadora Duncan." The *New Times* concluded a lengthy and convoluted discussion with the declaration that "the artistically sensitive will recognize and support this as art." There were, no doubt, many other newspaper commentaries.

11. *Tolnai Vila*, "Lady Dancer in a Lions' Cage," January 20, 1907.

12. Géza Zichy (1849–1924) was not merely a bon vivant. The one-armed count was also a left-hand piano virtuoso and composer. His teachers included Franz Liszt, with whom he on occasion appeared in double recitals, featuring a three-handed arrangement of János Bihári's *Rákóczy March*. From 1890 until 1894 he was president of the Hungarian National Academy of Music, and from 1890 to 1892 administrator of the Opera House. His first act was to restrict Gustav Mahler's rights as

operatic director, whereupon Mahler resigned. Zichy later became president of the National Conservatory. As a musician, he would have been struck by Maud's musicality, as a gallant by her sexuality. Maud, of course, would have been attracted to his patronage.

13. She was not, to be sure, the first to dance in a cage of lions. The *San Francisco Chronicle* of April 1, 1897, reported that "Mlle Bob Walter, who is doing the serpentine dance in a cage of lions at the Gaietie Paris, is a very pretty Parisienne who makes up to look like Loie Fuller, even to the blond wig, in wild confusion. The lions in whose cages she dances are whelps, big enough and old enough and ugly enough to be dangerous." There is no reason to suppose Maud knew of, let alone recalled, this item, unless she had read it in one of the "papers from home."

She may well have known, though, of the following incident in Paris, reported in the San Francisco *Bulletin* of January 17, 1904: "Darius Coulet, a lion tamer, has had to appear before a 10th District Magistrate because his twelve-year-old daughter danced a cake walk in a lion's cage. M. Coulet pleaded the lion was toothless and paralytic and unable to move. But he was fined, the magistrate remarking that the little girl should not make the acquaintance of even a toothless lion."

14. His bride was the daughter of the well-known cartoonist George Curtis Wright and the former wife of Fernando Yanaga, whose sister was Consuela, Duchess of Manchester. "Count Zichy's family ranks very high among the Hungarian nobility. He is wealthy in his own right and is the eldest son of his parents. It is understood the ceremony did not meet with the full approval of his people."

15. Franz von Stuck (1863–1928), an independently wealthy artist, was known in Germany as "the painter prince." He did at least three paintings of Maud as Salome, one of which holds pride of place in the Munich Municipal Gallery where it was for years incorrectly identified as a portrait of Tilla Durieux, the German actress who took the lead role in Reinhardt's celebrated production of Oscar Wilde's *Salome* in 1904." Following an early period of German romanticism, centred on fantasy and legend, he became a successful portraitist. He and Frederich von Kaulbach (1860–1920), an equally successful

artist of the day, were Maud's most prominent advocates in Munich. Von Kaulbach was likewise a well-known portraitist; his subjects ranged from the aristocracy to artists including Maud, Isadora Duncan, and Joseph Joachim. Both painters' names appear in Maud's *Jottings*.

16. In April 1908, a lawyer's letter protesting the critical attack of W.T. Titterton in *The New Age* stated that Maud had performed at the New Theatre, Berlin, and had given special matinees at the Kammerspiele Theatre, and that both theatres were sold out for all performances. As this is a formal statement challenging Titterton's statements as false – if not libellous – there is little reason to question its accuracy. No specific dates are given.

It may have been at the Kammerspiele Theatre that Maud studied and got to know the great Italian actress Eleonora Duse, about whom she wrote a radio script some thirty years later. She greatly admired this actress.

17. In her *Jottings* Maud also noted "Loie Fuller and Gabrielle Bloch in Marseilles."

Mary Bran had come from Russia to Paris with Sol Hurok as a business partner. Subsequently, when the partnership dissolved, Mary Bran specialized in managing dancers and dance groups, while Hurok specialized in musicians, eventually becoming the most powerful of American impresarios.

18. This was the same kaiser who had received her at the entrance to the Neue Museum on May 2, 1896. The account is totally false.

19. Francis of Teck was the brother of King Edward's daughter-in-law, later Queen Mary, consort of his son, George v. He was a notorious horse gambler. "Although he and his family are poor, he recently bet $1000 with a well-known bookmaker on a favorite – which lost," reported San Francisco's *Evening Post* on July 20, 1895. The debt, so the *Evening Post* reported, was paid by, "Prince Adolphus of Teck, who married the Duke of Westminster's very rich but very ugly daughter." It may have been by this somewhat circuitous entrée that Maud became the mistress of the second Duke of Westminster, in 1909 or so.

20. Sir Frederick had reason for concern about press reports, as he explained in his *Recollections of Three Reigns*. A few days earlier, the king innocently went to the local Marienbad

theatre to see "Die Holle" ("The Underworld"). What he assumed would be a melodrama proved to be a music-hall show, featuring "songs and recitations" of political and "improper" content. The king left at the start of the second act. "The next day the papers were full of this incident. . . . The Bishop of Ripon wrote a letter to the King expressing the satisfaction of the whole Church at the protests the King had made against obscene musical comedy. . . . When I asked the King what reply I should send, he said, 'Tell the Bishop the exact truth. I have no wish to pose as a protector of morals, especially abroad.' "

The Court Circular of September 2, the daily record of the royal family's activities, stated that "the King regretted exaggerated reports regarding his departure from the theatre on Thursday night. The play was of mediocre quality and according to one account a German version of *The Hound of the Baskervilles*."

The next day the Court Circular reported that "Miss Maud Allan, an American, had the honour of appearing before his Majesty in some classical dances." *The Vision of Salome* was barely "classical," but, after a hard day's shooting in cold weather, it no doubt took the king's mind from the 180 brace of partridges his party had shot that day.

5

Conquest of London:
1908–1910

*T*HREE DAYS AFTER performing for King Edward, Maud began a two-week engagement in Prague. According to the German-language newspaper *Bohemia*, her dancing caused a sensation, culminating in her performance of "the fantastically brilliant Salome scene":

It is as if a wildly jerking sensuality were driven into the slender body, as if it began to blossom and swell forth and glow through her skin . . . In naked sensuality, her body calculating, she meets the eyes of Herod; the rhythm of her motion accelerates; she knows what she wants,[1] and suddenly in its grisly horror the head of the prophet is handed her from the cistern. With the natural motions of the wild ash she dances Salome, the demivierge of the perverse instincts, gaze now focussed on the pale head in heated ecstasy. Wildly she revolves her head in jerking madness; her eyes and fingers groping in the cramps of love, they fantasize about unheard-of desires; shame seems to have vanished from her perspiring body; one draws back from the flame of this passion. Finally abrupt shock overcomes her, freezes her motion, forces her to lay aside the dead head and to be

paralysed in the numb pose of nameless self-disgust. . . .
Only the curtain fall releases the spell of this unique vision.

From Prague Maud went to Bucharest, where she gave
four recitals, and then to Leipzig in January 1908. This
engagement, which garnered good reviews, brought to an
end the first stage of her career.

For five years, while her career had been in the hands of
well-meaning amateurs at best and of dishonest managers at
worst, Maud had struggled to acquire her own identity as a
unique artist. Her career had not foundered, nor had she
been stigmatized as a mere camp follower of Isadora Duncan, then at the height of her fame in Germany. Too puzzled
by the originality of her performance to treat her as a
serious artist, reviewers were probably awaiting further
developments.

When she introduced *The Vision of Salome* – a work original in its intent, story line,[2] movements, intensity, costume,
and music – her direction became clear. If critical recognition was to be denied her as a serious interpreter of classical
works, then hers must first be a *succès de scandale*. *The Vision*
raised strong opposition – and support by leading members
of the cultural community – in Vienna, was a sensation in
Budapest and Prague, was appreciated in Paris and, possibly,
in Berlin.[3] Here was an obvious means of satisfying her
mother's ambitions for her.

Yet Maud remained unwilling or unable to relinquish that
peculiarly earnest commitment to the art of "classical"
dance interpretations. This uncompromising attitude and
her refusal to provide the general public with any hint of her
private life made her difficult to market.

Maud and a companion arrived in London on a rainy day
in February 1908 for a two-week engagement at the Palace
Theatre.[4] She promptly called on Alfred Butt, whom, so she
humorously recounts in *My Life and Dancing*, she first mistook for the theatre's doorman. At thirty years of age, Butt
was London's leading impresario. During his long career he

would manage the London debuts of Anna Pavlova, Maurice Chevalier, Paul Robeson, and Fred and Adele Astaire. (Unfortunately, little is known of his business dealings, for he insisted that all his files be burned on his death.)

What took place between Butt and Maud can only be surmised; the outcome was Butt's decision to present Maud as one of his "discoveries." Prior to her debut before invited representatives of the press, government, and the peerage two days before her public debut at the Palace Theatre, an illustrated pamphlet promoting this "discovery" hit the streets of London's West End. As no copy of this pamphlet seems to have survived, it is likely that Butt realized that its contents could be extremely damaging to sustained success and acted swiftly to destroy all copies. Excerpts do survive, however, in quotations in the press. Presenting the Toronto-born dancer as coming from "a land where the fires of the French temperament glow ardently through the icy purity of the People of the Snow,"[5] the booklet went on to describe Maud's physical attributes:

> Her skin is satin smooth, crossed only by the pale tracery of delicate veins that lace the ivory of her round bosom and slowly waving arms. Her lovely face has the small pointed nose with sensitive nostrils, while her mouth is full lipped and ripe as pomegranate fruit, and as passionate in its ardent curves as that of Venus herself. Her velvet eyes are set in clear opalescent blue whites. They are eyes as frank as a child's. They are eyes that caress with love, flash with hate.

In describing Maud's performance of *The Vision of Salome* (the pamphlet seems to have mentioned no other dance) the writing became openly erotic:

> Her feet, slender and arched, beat a sensual measure. The pink pearls slip amorously about the throat and bosom as she moves, while the long strand of jewels that float from the belt above her waist float langorously apart from her smooth hips. The desire that flames from her lips and bursts in hot

flames from her scarlet mouth infects the air with the madness of passion. Swaying like a white witch with yearning arms and hands that plead, Miss Allan is such a delicious embodiment of lust that she might win forgiveness with the sins of her wonderful flesh. With her hot mouth parched for kisses the impeccable saint had refused to give her, she lures an invisible Herod to grant her fiendish prayer.

In the very height of her furious exaltation at winning her request, the change comes. Before her rises the head she has danced for, and the lips that would not touch her in life she kisses again and again.[6]

Whatever Maud may have thought of such fulsome hyperbole, such advance publicity was certainly different from any she had so far experienced.

Somewhat more to the point, instead of sharing the evening with one or two other artists as had been her custom when not giving solo recitals, she was one of a dozen or more performers in a variety program. Although her ranking changed, it seems, from time to time, she was clearly a star attraction; her name was regularly advertised in the *Times* in heavy print. The original troupe included "Sam Elton, the man who made the Shah laugh," R.G. Knowles, "America's most peculiar comedian," and a number of other names that today mean nothing. Had Alfred Butt added Maud Allan to the Palace program in a routine fashion, the chances of attracting serious attention would have been negligible. This is why he arranged the private matinee recital on March 6.[7]

Such a recital was the safest way of introducing so unusual a performer to London. After all, Maud was engaged for only two weeks: if critical reaction fell short of expectations, the patrons of the Palace Theatre would soon forget Maud – and Butt's error of judgement. However, if the matinee were a success, Butt would have launched a brilliant career.

The press reviews of this special matinee, followed by those of her public debut two days later, were ecstatic.

Maud Allan was hailed as an artist personifying grace and elegance, those two supreme ideals of the Edwardian era. Under the head "A New Canadian Dancer," the March 8 edition of the staid London *Observer* exulted over her performance.

> She is a reincarnation of the most graceful and rhythmic forms of classic Greece; but in her the grace and rhythm of Greek art are changed into exquisite movements from the frozen forms in which they appear on Greek vases and reliefs. Miss Allan, however, not only is sculpture brought to life, but music turned into moving sculpture. Her supple, pliant, apparently weightless body "enacts" Mendelssohn's "Spring Song" in such a manner that it seems a fresh thing, full of poetic suggestion. Surprise and delight at the marvels of Spring, the sense of balmy air, blossoming trees, trilling birds, are not suggested but clearly explained in her dance. Even more entrancing is her interpretation of Rubinstein's "Valse caprice," as a wild Bacchantic intoxication of joy; whilst in *The Vision of Salome* her writhing body enacts the whole voluptuousness of Eastern femininity.

If the *Observer* paid scant attention to *The Vision of Salome*, the *Times* of March 10 treated Maud's performance of the work as an artistic triumph:

> There is no extravagance or sensationalism about Miss Allan's dancing; even when crouching over the head of her victim, caressing it or shrinking away from it in horror, she subordinated every gesture and attitude to the conditions of her art. It will, perhaps, be fair to say that her dress as Salome is daring; it would be unfair to Miss Allan not to add that, like her performance, it is absolutely free of offense. There is not even the feeling that she is pulling chestnuts out of the fire, so completely is she justified in her art.

Some weeks after the initial excitement had passed, the performance and the action of the work were more calmly discussed in the *Labour Leader* of June 26:

The Vision opens with a young girl standing in a beautiful Eastern garden. All around are tall, sombre trees and obelisks; the light is the vague and shadowy light of the moon.

Suddenly she glides forward, the dance begins. Her hands move like the weeds swaying to and fro in gently moving water; her arms remind one of the gleaming crest of an idly undulating wave; her body is tortured into inconceivable postures. One moment she is the vampire, softly lulling her victim to sleep with rhythmical movements of body and piercing eyes holding him spellbound; next she is the lynx, crouched to spring. Always the fascination is animal-like and carnal.

She sees the head of John the Baptist standing near. Seizing it, she places it in the centre of the stage, and falls down before it. Her slender and lissom body writhes in an ecstasy of fear, quivers at the exquisite touch of pain, laughs and sighs, shrinks and vaults, as swayed by passion. One moment her dancing is hot, barbaric, lawless; the next, grotesque, sinister, repulsive; one moment she enervates, with a gliding sweetness; the next she stabs with a terrible attitude.

She kisses the head and frenzy comes upon her. She is no longer human. She is a Maenad sister. Her hair should be dishevelled, her eyes bloodshot. The amazing crescendo ceases, she falls to the ground a huddled yet wondrously beautiful mass.

The wonder of it all is that throughout this fantastic mockery, this enchanting insistence upon the flesh, nothing is extravagant, nothing discordant. London has never seen such graceful and artistic dancing. It is of a magical beauty. But the beauty is magic; and the magic is black and insidious.

The truth was, of course, that only her intensely imaginative response to the scenario coupled with her commitment to artistic perfection disguised the fact that *The Vision*, sensational and extravagant, was an inferior product of *fin de siècle* decadence. This disguise helps explain the success of

The Vision in London. The audience could marvel at the artistry and power of Maud's performance or indulge in its suggestive sexuality: *The Vision of Salome* made her both an artistic and a sensational success. Her dance interpretations were widely appreciated, but they lacked the daring excitement of *The Vision*. Maud's dance interpretations of, for example, Chopin waltzes were not part of her popular success, although her *Spring Song* was immensely popular.

Yet, despite the praise that so quickly evolved into a skilfully managed boom of some eighteen months, much of Maud's success was fluke. So much of what she offered was fortuitously attuned to the prevailing social and artistic ethos. One critic remarked, "She has the wonderful gift of expressing by means of the dance the very feeling and meaning of a period. Now she is a maiden who might have stepped out of ancient Athens again, now the very siren who danced before King Herod."[8] So, too, did she express the essence of Edwardian England.

Off stage, her grace and charm opened wide the gates of society; on stage, she put those gifts to the service of her tremendous musicality and imaginative insights. The "poetry of motion," recognized as a fundamental element of her innovative art, had its counterpart in that recent invention, the bioscope, as the moving-picture projector was known. A regular feature of the Palace and other London variety theatres, the bioscope brought to the public a new awareness of motion (although on the screen it was anything but graceful). Maud's dance interpretations poetized this new awareness of movement. The public was able to marvel at the artistry of her performance while relishing, in *The Vision of Salome*, what her performance made so marvellously real – the passion, sensuality, and eroticism of Herod's daughter and the object of Maud's intense desires.

There is yet another aspect of Maud's success. Maud made herself appear – and gradually she became – British to the hilt. She felt at ease in society (whose patronage was so important to public if not critical success), and society felt at ease with her, which it rarely did with music hall entertainers. That Edward VII had in a sense discovered her was no doubt helpful, too.

Finally, there were significant factors in the way she portrayed Salome that fascinated her public. In presenting her as an apparently innocent girl who, while experiencing a "vision," liberates her perverse and repressed emotions to the point of catharsis, Maud made Salome a mystifying mixture of the erotic and the exotic, artfully shrouded in a veil of Edwardian discretion and good taste.[9] Her London audiences, supposedly more proper than most of those on the Continent, willingly mistook her bare feet, her painted toenails, her lack of tights, for various degrees of nudity. For many women she represented an enviable freedom, although Maud was the least emotionally liberated of women. For many men, she was little more than a delightfully refreshing sex symbol.[10]

Hailed by leading members of London's cultural establishment as a profoundly musical and imaginative artist, sought after by London society, and celebrated by London's West End patrons more interested in entertainment than in art, Maud Allan became a household name. She also became a tempting target for conservative clerics for whom her audacity was a cause for alarm and topic for sermons. For, ever since Cromwell's time – and indeed until 1964 – the portrayal of biblical (and royal) characters on the stage had been forbidden.

The attacks, which were not long in coming, were reported in the San Francisco press. The *San Francisco Examiner* of April 26, 1908, ran a banner headline, "Great Fuss over John the Baptist's Head," and asked whether it is "proper or even good art for a beautiful young woman, a dancer of voluptuous figure, to appear bare-footed in a single diaphanous garment – no tights or undergarments of any kind – with the head of St. John the Baptist the object of amorous pantomime?" Of the leader of the anti-Salome protest in London, the *Examiner*, which never identified Maud as Theo's sister, continued:

Her principal English critic, Archdeacon Sinclair, is at present the most talked about example of England's "muscular Christianity." He is a giant and an athlete, given to delivering in his sermons stern and harsh truths to London fashionable society. The suggested voluptuousness of Miss Allan's dance would be abhorrent to him even in the absence of the Baptist's head. She is a woman, and no woman may depart from the Saviour's ideal of women. In one of his recent pulpit addresses on this subject he said: "The principle from which Christ proceeded to denote the position of woman, who in Greece was a drudge, in Rome a chattel and among the Jews a recluse, was that of absolute uncompromising purity." If *The Vision of Salome* must be given, the Archdeacon declares that it should be given without the Prophet's head, "which is an unwise and unnecessary accessory."

In London, these attacks attracted restrained attention, for no editor cared to tangle too closely with so fashionable a cleric.[11] In her autobiography, however, Maud colourfully, graciously, and with a touch of humour – she was a most skilful raconteuse – recounts her attempt to assuage Archdeacon Sinclair's distress. He emerges as more effete than muscular, more ridiculous than persuasive, especially as she lets slip that he declined to see her performance. The image of her parents joining her for tea with the archdeacon adds a final comic touch:

> One of the objections I have encountered, and one that I would love to overcome, is that of kind Archdeacon Sinclair. Although he has not seen my portrayal, he was quite shocked at the thought of dragging Salomé from the pages of the Bible and flaunting her crime before the public. . . . Accordingly, one afternoon I went to see him at the Chapter House [of St. Paul's Cathedral], and I shall never forget his kindness and courtesy. His dignity and gravity impressed me greatly. . . . "I am pleased to see you," he said, and I bowed my thanks as gravely as he had spoken.
>
> Appreciating that his kindness was great in seeing me at

all, I did not waste time by explaining much of the preliminaries. "I hear that you object to my *Vision of Salome*. I have come, knowing that you would be just enough to tell me why."

"So I will, and do not for a moment think that I have at any time said that your work is not artistic, for I am sure from all I hear and have read that it is, and from your manner I should judge both you and your work quite serious; but," he continued, "I feel there are Christians in my flock who may be repulsed at the thought of Christ's forerunner being made the subject of a scene for the stage. Or for that matter any Biblical story being put on the stage. . . . "

I explained my views and he listened so kindly that it would have been an extreme pleasure to me to have given in to his way of thinking immediately, had it been in my power to do so. But we parted friends – good friends. . . . Not long afterwards I had the great pleasure of attending service at beautiful St. Paul's and of being, together with my parents, his guest at the Chapter House for tea, and then I met his charming sister and many of his dearest friends. (pp. 98–99)

Together with the critical and clerical reactions to Maud's dancing are the recorded opinions of members of her audiences. Perhaps these are the most revealing of all. One of the "first Californians to see Maud Allan dance in London," Charlie Forbes, an engineer, declared in an interview:

Everybody who sees Miss Allan in the Dance [*The Vision of Salome*] comes away with one of two opinions – that it is really "the limit" or that it is "so artistic." There is no middle opinion. Many go to see her because they think it is the most improper thing ever put upon the stage. Just as many regard the performance as the highest expression in motion of the pure and chaste. The performance struck me as indecent but performed in such a way as to make it appear perfectly modest. From a certain French point of view such an achievement is high art.[12]

A society lady described her impressions upon first seeing Maud dance at a private recital in honour of the Khedive of Egypt:

> We heard the first note of Mendelssohn's "Spring Song" and Maud Allan appeared. She danced as the nymphs dance in the forest because it is Spring time, the world is beautiful and it is a joy to be alive. I was in the forest with the nymphs, I smelt the crushed grass and thought I heard a blackbird. The illusion lasted only a few minutes, but it was wonderful to have felt it. Afterwards, Miss Allan interpreted Chopin's "Funeral March" swathed in grey draperies that concealed her features and all the pain, the loneliness in the world seemed concentrated in her little figure. I know I had to wipe my eyes.[13]

To balance the books, as it were, the comments of a dance historian of the day must be noted, for they define her technique and explain the effect – and purpose – of Maud's performance:

> One of the felicities of her accomplishments is her ability to pass with the music from the major to the minor key or vice versa. When a phrase first occurs in one key and then in another, it is repeated in her dances with just that modification of aspect and accent which express the change of mood. The faith with which her movements follow the mood of the composers is only probably fully recognized by those who are musicians as well as connoisseurs of the dance. Her translation of music has not seldom the rare quality of translations, of being finer than the original.[14]

For nearly two months the London press was mesmerized. Then, on May 2, a critical attack appeared in *The Academy*, edited by Alfred Douglas, Oscar Wilde's former lover. This ill-tempered article, titled "All We Like Sheep," was by a writer with the uncannily appropriate name of Christopher St. John. This was the recognized pseudonym of Christina Marshall, Ellen Terry's secretary/editor and lifelong companion of Terry's daughter Edith Craig. St. John complained that some nine years earlier Isadora Duncan had, with no fanfare and little success, introduced to London the very art that Maud, in a *Daily Mail* article, had claimed to have originated. This was a reprehensible stance, St. John argued, as Maud had yet to acknowledge publicly (she eventually did) that she had attended Isadora Duncan's recitals in Berlin long before she decided to become a dancer. St. John contended, furthermore, that thanks to effective publicity all London had been duped into believing Maud was a "genuine dancer," when "some of the adulation given Miss Allan should be transferred to her as a hypnotist. She makes the audience think she is wonderful. As it takes two to make a great work of art, is not the thought of the audience as important as the skill of the performer?" St. John's concluding paragraph was less critical than contemptuous:

> Miss Allan is a very earnest young lady with a sincere conviction of her mission. She dances like a revivalist preacher and makes as many converts. It would be stupid not to admire the character which has brought about so great a success. But it would be just as stupid to mistake this American "grit" and "bluff" for beautiful art. There is very little art in Miss Allan's performance. She herself admits this when she says she has never learned to dance. Perhaps this is one of the secrets of her success. The English people dearly love a Lord. The English Lord (and the class he represents) dearly loves the amateur.

Confronted with the threat of a libel action, Douglas beat a hasty retreat and printed a limp apology. He did not escape Maud's fury, however, if indeed she grossly insulted him at the garden party and then, on being reminded that her brother was a murderer, slapped him in the face.[15]

Douglas's rejoinder did not become common knowledge in London, for the London press evidently considered so searing a family disgrace irrelevant to Maud's success and did not mention it. (The truth only came out a decade later when Maud, bringing another libel action, was maliciously crossexamined about her relationship to Theo. By that time, the personal pain was far greater than the damage to her professional reputation, which had fallen into irreversible decline. In the United States, of course, reports of her London success were regularly linked to mention of her brother's execution.)

Lord Alfred's knowledge of Theo's disgrace undoubtedly came to him through his brother, Lord Sholto Douglas, who was living in California throughout the proceedings against Theo. Accounts of Sholto's escapades and reports of Theo's case more than once appeared side by side on the front page of San Francisco papers.[16]

Quite possibly at the time of the garden party incident, another foolish conflict received wide press coverage. Maud had contracted to perform in Manchester's Palace of Varieties during the West End's summer doldrums, as part of a scheduled six-week tour of the provinces. The theatre manager in Manchester dutifully sought approval for Maud's engagement from the local Watch Committee. (Established some months earlier, the committee had banned as indecent a "living statue" act by Milo, a well-known poseuse of the day.) In spite of a recommendation of approval from Manchester's chief of police, who had, with two others, gone to see Maud's act, the committee banned her engagement for its purported nudity and indecency.[17] A number of other city councils – Liverpool and Bournemouth among them – followed suit.

Manchester's ruling received scathing mockery from the London press and inspired several cartoons featuring Maud, for the Watch Committee had banned as indecent an act that King Edward VII had commended and leaders of London's social, artistic, and political communities had applauded.

Whatever the diverting and profitable publicity this farcical decision may have provided, the next challenge was decidedly offensive. The *New Age*, in its issue of June 27, published "The Maud Allan Myth," by W.T. Titterton. His description of Maud's *Vision* ("Her flesh gleams with dusky light under her gleaming jewels. The eyes of her pulsing breasts [a reference to her scanty costume?] scorch us, her hot pursing lips suck out our soul") dismissed the work as a mere belly dance and Maud's art as a myth. Titterton charged that her repertoire was unchanged from that of three years earlier, asserting that "with a rechauffée of her past" (Maud must have cringed) she had conquered London thanks to ill-informed, ill-considered critical acclaim. Then, as if to emphasize that his view was balanced, he conceded that, although the Salome dance was "detestable," and the *Marche funèbre* of Chopin "worse than ever," "one or two" of Maud's movements were superior to Duncan's, whom he had earlier praised with as much gusto as he now condemned Maud.

Maud's reaction was predictable: a lawyer's letter protesting that she had never performed "the Salome dance in the way described;" moreover, to suggest, as Titterton had, that the king would have condoned such a performance was, without a formal apology, cause for legal action, as were other misrepresentations of facts. The *New Age* issued an apology. The attack had no discernible effect on Maud's phenomenal run at the Palace Theatre.

In October, seven months after her sensational debut, Maud had a bad fall on stage. Following a suspiciously long recuperation – more than three months – she was welcomed back warmly – but not wildly – in February 1909.[18] Her engagement continued, no doubt with unrecorded breaks, until November. By then, hindsight shows, the boom was sinking although her international fame kept her career afloat for a few more years.

During this time Maud amassed a considerable fortune. "She's not a rich woman," Butt told a business colleague in 1913, "but she can sign her cheque for £25,000" – a large sum in those days. At the height of her success she was receiving £250 a week from the Palace Theatre. (Harry Lauder, the foremost entertainer of the day, was earning a little more than £300 a week.) In addition to her scheduled appearances at the Palace Theatre, she gave many private recitals – for a minimum of £250 each.[19] (Thus she was able to live in grand if austere style while these funds lasted.) At the Palace Theatre, all box-office records were broken during her engagement, and the shareholders received 33 per cent dividends. (One Saturday night there were eighty applications for boxes from the social elite of London.)

Flower-pot statuettes of Maud in her most striking poses were for sale in many gift shops of fashionable Bond Street. Fashion-conscious women adopted sandals – even, on a dare, in ballrooms – and went about their daily routine bare-legged and bare-footed. The smart dress of the day was skin-tight, the lining forming a divided skirt, with a large square tab of embroidery in front. Even costume jewellers looked to Maud for inspiration. Their best seller was a large string of beads worked into a shaped design and adorned with three immense jewel-covered bosses, two of which were worn as breastplates. The popularity of sequins gave way to bead fringes and bead trimmings.[20] (Meanwhile, Maud took care to dress with impeccable taste off stage. She soon became, if not an arbiter, a prominent figure in the world of fashion.)

Other signs of her success were numerous burlesques and parodies of *The Vision*. The Alhambra Theatre featured a very successful *Sal Oh Mee*, and the well-established parodist Pelisser had a field day imitating Maud's performance. To these off-shoots neither Maud nor the Palace management took exception.[21]

Amongst those inspired by but not competing directly with her was Lady Constance Stewart Richardson, a refreshingly deviant member of the British aristocracy. She held advanced views on religion, radical but not very fruitful ideas on education, and original opinions on women's place in society, all vigorously expounded in her book *Dancing Beauty and Games*. Lady Constance was also an outstanding swimmer. In the summer of 1908, her hobby horse was classical dancing. In July, she was invited to a weekend house party to meet King Edward VII. After dinner Lady Constance suddenly appeared, wearing an exact replica of the Salome costume, right down to the bare limbs and barbaric jewellery. Her impersonation duly applauded, she dramatically threw herself at the king's feet and rested her head on his knee. During the silence that greeted such familiarity, Lady Constance looked up at the king and firmly said, "Sire, I claim the head of Sir Ernest Cassell," one of the wealthiest men in England and father of the late Countess Mountbatten of Burma. An embarrassed titter ran through the room until it became obvious that the king was unamused. He was sensitive about such close friends as Cassell. At this point the hostess bravely stepped forth to suggest the bridge tables be set up, a diversion that soon restored the king to good humour and Lady Constance to his good graces.

With her social skills, her mysterious appeal, and the king's interest, Maud was quickly accepted by London society. One of her more consequential contacts was Herbert Asquith, who had become prime minister of a Liberal government in April 1908. Equally well known was her intimate yet indefinable relationship with Asquith's wife, Margot.

Before she became widower Asquith's wife, Margot had freely associated with a group of unorthodox women dubbed the Souls. Even as the prime minister's wife, she attracted a distinct coterie of female friends, among whom, for a time, was Maud Allan. Both Asquiths took her under their wing. On one occasion, for example, the prime minister seated her between the Austrian ambassador and himself, as she was graceful and charming, fluently bilingual, and a very good listener. On another occasion – Maud delighted in recounting this incident – Mrs. Asquith placed her next to Winston Churchill at dinner. Affronted that Churchill took no notice of her, Maud broke the ice as she left with the other ladies for the drawing room. "Well," she said to Mr. Churchill, "we do not seem to have found much to say to each other this evening." Mr. Churchill looked at her indifferently, nodding stiffly. "But," Maud pointed out, "we have at least one thing in common." Barely giving Churchill time to ask, Maud explained: "We are both the rejected of Manchester." Shortly before, about the time

Maud had been banned from performing there, Churchill had lost a parliamentary by-election in Manchester.

Maud's relationship with Margot Asquith caused talk if not open speculation in social, diplomatic, and political circles. Official guests so frequently saw her with Mrs. Asquith at formal receptions that diplomatic egos were hurt.

Whether or not Mrs. Asquith was the hostess, she was probably present at a Salome dinner/dance held in August 1908. The *New York Times* of August 8 published the gist of the rumoured story. The Salome dance had

> so fired the imagination of society women that one of the great hostesses of the Metropolis a few weeks ago issued invitations to twenty or thirty ladies whose names figured in Court and other fashionable lists, to attend a Maud Allan Dinner/Dance which would be undesecrated by the presence of any man. The guests were bidden to appear in Salome costume. The idea created intense interest and much enthusiasm amongst those honoured with such invitations. Each of the ladies proceeded to outvie her sisters in providing herself with a costume matching in all details the undress effect of Miss Allan's scanty costume. The party passed off successfully and beyond the hostess' fondest expectations.
>
> Dinner was served to the accompaniment of Salome music, tinkled by an orchestra behind the fortification of palms and flowers. And when the cigarette and coffee stage was reached, some of the more graceful members of the party demonstrated that they had not only succeeded in matching Miss Allan's costume, but had learned some captivating steps in movements.

Prime Minister Asquith's friendship with Maud had particular risks. Many of his supporters were political nonconformists who already looked askance at him because he had invoked closure to allow passage of reformed licensing laws. Asquith's opponents in the Liberal Party also were suspicious of his association with a dancer. For some, the very word was synonymous with "naughty"; for others it connoted the oldest profession. Had some political opponent chosen to capitalize on aspects of Maud's private life – as would happen a decade later in an obvious attempt to discredit Margot Asquith – the danger for the prime minister would have been immediate.

In October 1908, to mark the 250th performance of *The Vision* at the Palace Theatre, *My Life and Dancing* was published. Free copies of this autobiography were distributed to the audience that night. (At the same time appeared *Maud Allan and Her Art*, a folio of thirty-six pages comprising photographs, an analytical essay, a tribute by the journalist Frank Harris, press notices, and even sonnets – among them two by Aleister Crowley, the high priest of black magic, the unspeakable, and the unthinkable – celebrating Maud's art.)

My Life and Dancing is a polished version of the serialized memoirs that had already appeared in London newspapers. Naturally, Maud camouflages her family background, but she writes of her youth with genuine affection, taking pains to ooze the charm that would appeal to the sensibilities of Edwardian readers. Maud sprinkles her *Life* with occasional comments on such matters as the meaning of art and the devotion of mothers, as if she wishes to establish that hers is a mature personality, "not a kind of floating, airy, effortless, butterfly kind of process" some perceive her art to be. This impression of maturity is sustained by hints of a mysterious, pervasive sadness countered by outbursts of gratitude for her reception in London.

My Life and Dancing was by no means the only publication generated by Maud's success. Four known cartoons, by far the most interesting being "Pas de Fascination," appeared during these months as well as numerous press interviews. Most were tiresomely platitudinous, but that published in the July issue of the *Pall Mall* magazine was captivating. Maud's father was briefly interviewed; he spoke of his daughter's many talents, mentioning that he had just brought over "from overseas a cabinet she had carved at home, to be installed in her Berlin studio."[22]

Maud's answers to personal questions were singular, to

say the least. She stated that both her parents were eye specialists and her brother a doctor. An uncle (presumably Dr. T.E. Clarke, the family friend who had persuaded Theo to study medicine and who is listed in the 1895 San Francisco City Directory as residing with the Durrant family) was "a surgeon of distinguished ability." Maud ended the interview with a graceful rhapsody on flowers followed by a trance-like outburst, persuasive and possibly sincere, on "the rhythm of things. I can't find the words I want – only it is music to me, the April smell and the springing uplift of growing things and a sudden glimpse of blue in the sky, and the swift outlining of a white cloud in living silver by a flash of the sun. It is all music, and the echo is dancing." Her aesthetics, throughout her life, remained equally metaphysical, and were one reason why she left no followers or school.

Possibly related to the "Pas de Fascination" cartoon was a playlet, "Salome and the Suffragettes," that appeared in a small weekly magazine, *The Referee*. The main characters in this silly symphony are the leading politicians of the day and Maud Allan. It takes place on the spacious terrace of the Houses of Parliament, the site of regular afternoon teas for politicians and their guests. Amongst those present are Prime Minister Asquith, Chancellor of the Exchequer Lloyd George, and a nervous Winston Churchill accompanied by his oversolicitous mother. As they settle down to a leisurely tea and conversation sprinkled with political allusions of the day, the Suffragettes' motor launch, under the command of the indomitable Flora Drummond, heaves into view, set for a frontal assault. Suddenly finding themselves under attack, Asquith attempts to protect Maud with his umbrella, Churchill rushes to protect his mother, and Lloyd George, preoccupied with preparing the annual budget, finds himself pelted with strawberry jam.

Amid the panic Maud is kidnapped. Asquith thereupon receives a message from the Suffragettes that they will hold Maud ransom until "You have given us a solemn pledge to bring in a measure for the enfranchisement of women at once." Enter Alfred Butt, who, upon hearing of Maud's abduction, demands the army be called in. "There are," he explains, "five crowned heads quarrelling over the State Box. Sir, as Prime Minister of this country," he tells Asquith, "you must restore Salome to the Palace or I will not answer for the consequences."

Asquith capitulates and promises the vote for women. Maud is rushed under police escort to the Palace Theatre at the terrifying speed of sixty miles an hour.

The playlet is worthy of mention only as it indicates the peculiar eminence Maud Allan enjoyed during her conquest of London. It exemplifies her imprint upon the society and, peripherally, the politics of the day.

There were two quite extraordinary publications as a result of Maud's prominence. The first is *Salome and the Head*, a painfully indigestible novel by E. Nesbit, the much-admired author of children's books.[23] This novel touches on certain aspects of Maud's lifestyle and fame. It describes in careful detail the "savage simplicity" of her grandiose residence, West Wing (referred to as "The House of No Address"),[24] records the effect of her performance as the "Salome dancer," and gives a view of her character only a shade less repulsive than that of her greedy entourage, who gloat with her every night over the day's rich tributes of jewellery.

The virtually incomprehensible plot revolves around the rivalry of two men: the adoring Denny, handicapped composer of the *Salome* music, and Mr. Templar, a wealthy country gentleman come to London in hot pursuit of Sylvia/Sandra, as the heroine is named. At the climactic moment of the Salome dance Sylvia recognizes Mr. Templar in the audience, collapses, and drops the prop of the Baptist's head, which shatters.

A heavy parcel containing a replacement prop is delivered to "The House of No Address." Sylvia puts the parcel on her pillow. When she retires for the night, she lifts it to put it away in a cupboard – "not a nice thing to have in one's bedroom." The parcel is soaking wet – with blood: "The

head she held in her hands was the head of a dead man."
Sylvia falls into a swoon and the plot into disarray.

This tasteless, melodramatic, and grotesque episode is surely based on the incident in Budapest, which Nesbit must have learned of as gossip. In all likelihood Count Zichy himself spread the story, for he was in London at this time.[25]

While the only known copy in North America of *Salome and the Head* has been gathering dust on the shelves of the Chapel Hill campus of the University of North Carolina, another novel, titled *Maudie* and republished in England in 1985 as "a notorious erotic frolic of the Edwardian era," stands on the shelves of London's few tame sex shops. *Maudie*, like *Salome and the Head*, is inspired by the reputation or knowledge of Maud Allan's private life, which, this novel suggests, was secretive and far more colourful than her public life.[26]

Maudie is the mistress of a grand estate at Staines, near Windsor, and of four admirers who gravitate there for a weekend. She sets out to satisfy their – and her – sexual appetites with great panache, described in boring pornographic style, and amidst great luxury: "The house was not so much a tart's but rather like that of a great lady of fashion . . . paid for by the wealth of Bertie Evans-James ('Tubby'), the fat cheery son of a Lancashire millionaire."

Maudie is the perfect hostess – and more. On one occasion she performs "the Dance of Emancipation" (a suggestively oblique reference to *The Vision of Salome*); on another she invites her guests to join in photographing nude models – a prelude, of course, to more erotic pleasures. (Under Artur Bock's instruction Maud Allan had become an enthusiastic photographer during her early years in Germany.) There is even a passing mention of the Manchester Watch Committee.

The identity of the men who share all that Maudie has to offer cannot be documented. However, in later years Maud openly spoke of her liaison with the second Duke of Westminster, head of one of the wealthiest families in England. Maud asserted that the duke had asked her to marry him, but this is doubtful if only because each of the duke's four wives was from a suitably aristocratic background.[27] (Besides, she was by no means the duke's only mistress. Nor was the duke Maud's only lover during this period, as her jottings of later years may suggest.) On occasion, too, she would conversationally hint that she had been a member of King Edward vii's entourage during a number of his private visits to Paris.

Both the foregoing novels, published in 1910, make much of Maud's living quarters. Probably she had just moved into West Wing, part of Holford House, a sprawling villa overlooking London's Regent's Park. Rather than take on the responsibility of so expensive a lease (by the mid-1930s nearly £600 a year), Maud persuaded Margot Asquith, an independently wealthy woman known for her impulsive acts of generosity, to do so. Margot met the obligation at least until her husband's death in 1928, after which she cut back expenses, including in all likelihood the leasehold of West Wing.[28] By the mid-1930s, Maud was again responsible for the lease, which at one time was £5,000 in arrears.

Maud also persuaded Margot Asquith to pay for the installation of floor-to-ceiling mirrors in what became her well-known drawing room/studio. After the renovation of this magnificent room was completed – in 1912/13, it would seem – Maud took a journalist on a guided tour. Referring to some "new dances" that required "special lighting effects," she explained that:

> In order to perfect herself in these dances special environment has become necessary. No ordinary dancing room would do, so she decided to turn the largest room in her new home in Regent's Park into a private school for herself. It is 42 feet by 32 feet. Ranged along one side is a great mirror with folding wings which, when opened, measure 24 by 8 feet, and the wings can be put at any angle so that the dancer has three views of herself. On the floor is spread a soft carpet of dull green. There is little furniture and what there is has been picked up by Miss Allan on her travels. A

lion skin and a head, a leopard skin and a head came from
Rhodesia [toured in 1911]. A Paris firm is ransacking France
for two old chandeliers for the electric light to match the
two that have already been found. A piano stands near a
window and from the music room one can walk on to the
spacious lawns. Every morning from 10:30 to 1 the lessons
and exercises are learned. The mirrors tell where a hand is
too stiff or an elbow too sharp for an expression.[29]

Over the years, Maud altered the furniture and added a
statue of herself, believed to have been the early work of
Jacob Epstein.

From West Wing, with its gorgeous gardens, Maud
would sally forth to patronize public functions or fund-
raising projects, such as that for visiting athletes gathering
in London for the Olympic Games of 1908. Heading a group
of entertainers, she participated in a special performance
that raised £300. On another occasion, to the delight of "all
London," she danced in a specially constructed wooded
glade at the Veterans' Fete in the grounds of Chelsea's Royal
Hospital – a performance recorded in a two-page sketch of
the *Illustrated London News* of July 23, 1908. In brief, she gave
generously of her time and art to worthy causes, as long as
her name or presence proved an attraction.

Maud's conquest of London was as total as it was unusual.
Acclaimed as the sensational interpreter of *The Vision of
Salome*, she was sought after as an artist by the most influential members of London's cultural community. At the same
time she was acclaimed as a music-hall artist by the general
public and welcomed as a bewitching presence by the most
eminent members of London society. Yet the very nature of
her dancing and the intensity of her success assured that her
conquest would be transitory. Given her age, much of it was
illusory; in later years it became an act that only an individual of her enormously diverse talents and energy could
sustain.

Behind her public mask was a woman who was able to
live as befit "a lady born," yet sought recognition as a

"great" dancer. "The Salome Dancer" had brought her fame and wealth but little satisfaction as a serious artist. During the next two decades she toured the world in a search of recognition as a "great" dancer. Yet her quest was doomed, perhaps because she mistook her indisputable uniqueness for greatness.

Notes

1. Both in real life and in the role of Salome: in a postscript to a letter of October 10, 1896, her mother remarks, "Maudie knows what she wants and Maudie is going to have it, is she not?"

2. Maud seems to have "explained" the story line of Salome to suit the tastes of her audiences. Initially, she insisted Wilde's play was her main source. In England, she gave the plot a psychological twist; in the United States, she frequently insisted that the Bible was her model.

3. As previously noted, Maud very probably shared a theatre in Berlin with Eleonora Duse. The great Italian actress was Isadora Duncan's rival for the affections of Ellen Terry's son, Gordon Craig, the innovative stage designer. When in the mid-1930s Maud prepared six short radio talks on persons she had known, for the New York radio station WINS, she paid generous tribute to Duse:

> The genius of this woman inspired me beyond words to express. . . . She was a born artist, not one created by the rigid rules of the academy. She *was* art. Instinctively she did the right thing, translated the character for us flawlessly. The lessons I learned studying her at these rehearsals and the advice and help she gave me in my own Art, will ever be treasures to guard for evermore.
>
> One day she said to me, "Quiet movements and silence are often more expressive than violent action and many words."
>
> A true artist knows instinctively how to respond to natural impulses and to give full expression to the spiritual state. No one can teach her. She listens to the "still small voice" and

follows it. So it was with Duse.

And so, quite obviously, it was with Maud Allan.

4. Ferruccio Busoni was very probably her travelling companion. Within days of Maud's debut he gave a London recital and then went on a tour of the provinces.

5. Quoted in the *Pall Mall Gazette*, March 11, 1908.

6. These excerpts are quoted in *The Pelican*, March 11; *Truth*, March 18; the *Pall Mall Gazette*, March 11; and the *Daily Telegraph*, March 7, 1908.

7. Butt engaged Maud over the objections of his board of directors. This became public knowledge after the shareholders meeting of the Palace Theatre in September 1908, when a shareholder asked who was primarily responsible for engaging her. The chairman said the whole board took the decision, whereupon Alfred Butt publicly claimed full credit.

8. Undated cutting from the clippings file of the Dance Collection, New York Public Library.

9. In his study *La Femme Fatale* (New York: Mayflower Books, 1979), Peter Bade remarks that Wilde's play, "however fatuous, did give definitive form to a particular type of destructive female: the young girl in whom perversity and virginal innocence are piquantly mixed – the paedophile's femme fatale" (p. 16). The description might have been written of Maud, it fits so well.

10. In 1967, for example, the brother of Dora Winnifred Black, Bertrand Russell's second wife, demonstrated a puppet-like figure – two fingers wrapped in a handkerchief – which as a lusty youth he and others toyed with in emulation of Maud Allan's entertainment at the Palace Theatre.

11. One London cleric, the Reverend Macdonald Docker (of unknown denomination) expressed his objections more colourfully, as if unable to repress a secret relish in the erotic overtones of Maud's performance. According to the *San Francisco Examiner* of July 12, 1908, Docker declared in a Sunday sermon: "There can be nothing to please an aesthetic public in the suggestion of the pitiful head of a saint spotted with blood and dripping with gore as it comes from the executioner's blade. . . . And can the posturings, however beautiful, justify the terrible sacrilege and hideous horror?"

As late as 1913, Salome was a thorn in the side of Canon

Newbolt, of St. Paul's Cathedral, London. On August 25 he preached that:

> the current evil is the indecent dance, suggestive of evil and destructive of modesty. I urge parents to assert "I will not allow my daughter to turn into a Salome even though Herod were to give me half his kingdom and admit me into the most coveted society of a world which has persuaded itself that immodesty is artistic and that anything is inartistic that removes the intolerable monitoring of its pleasures.

In an editorial of August 26, 1913, the *New York Times* concurred: "Canon Newbolt spoke directly to the point. . . . His example should be followed in all the churches of England and the United States. We are drifting toward peril, and the peril must be checked."

On September 3, 1908 – at the height of Maud's success in London, and only weeks after Gertrude Hoffman's imitation in New York – the *New York Times* published an editorial titled *The Salome Pestilence*: "What we most object to is the shockingly bad taste of it all. It is rampant vulgarity."

12. From an unidentified clipping in the Dance Collection, Performing Arts Research Center, New York Public Library. This report concludes: "According to Mr. Forbes no mention of the Durrant case is ever made abroad in connection with Miss Allan. The story current in London is simply that she was born in Canada and was taken to California when she was about six years old. The English consider that what her brother may or may not have done cuts no figure with Miss Allan as a woman or as an artist."

13. Vittoria Colonna, Duchess of Sermonetta, *Things Past* (London: Hutchinson, 1928), p. 86–87.

14. J.E. Crawford Flitch, *Modern Dancers and Dancing* (London: Grant Richards, 1912). Quoted in typescript of "Two Years in the Life of an Edwardian [changed in Maud's hand to "Great"] Dancer," a typescript of some 200 pages prepared in the mid-1930s by Verna Aldrich, Maud's infatuated secretary/companion of a decade. This typescript gives a good idea of the numerous facets of Maud's effect on London. It is chock full of verifiable facts and figures.

15. That incident may have been apocryphal, but the following

entry from Maud's diary of March 26, 1898, is not: "Artur called at 4:30 and we had a big row. He tore up a card (in my possession) addressed to the Ilgensteins. In my anger I gave him a slap in the face. It was unladylike and I was sorry. I sent him a Rolonpost [postal telegraph] and so now it is wieder gut [all right again], I hope."

16. Sholto, sent out to operate a forty-acre farm in California, fell in love with eighteen-year-old Loretta Addis (stage name of Loretta Mooney). Horrified at the idea of such a marriage, English friends had him arrested on a charge of insanity. During his twenty-four hours of detention, he received funds from his father, the Marquess of Queensberry, who raised no objections to his son's choice. Some weeks later, Sholto and Loretta married. Following a visit to England, they returned to live in Los Angeles where Loretta, thanks to all the publicity, was featured as a song-and-dance artiste. Her husband was retained to introduce her. (Describing his performance, the *Chronicle* of December 3 reported that "everyone screamed at one of the funniest pictures of stage fright they have ever seen.") Eventually they had five children and settled in the south of France. They divorced in 1921.

Loretta's mother was interviewed by the *Chronicle* on November 28, 1895, regarding her conversation with Carrie Cunningham, a journalist who, so Mrs. Mooney said, had told her that "Durrant had asked her advice whether he should plead guilty or not; that, Miss Cunningham told me. She also told several of my children."

17. "If people were to look at women they should look at their wives" was one of the more fatuous comments of a Watch Committee member defending the ban.

18. In her *Jottings* related to her engagement at the Palace Theatre Maud noted, "My first accident on the stage." Exhaustion may well have been the cause.

Her private life may have been a factor in so long an absence. Manya Cherniavsky had heard it said that during her conquest of London Maud had an abortion. However, Manya would not assert this as a fact, adding her familiar remark, "Anything was possible with Maud Allan." Research, though, has validated every verifiable statement Manya made about Maud's life and career.

19. There is no reason to question these figures (they may indeed be conservative) or the effect of her fame on the fads and fashions of the day. These figures and effects are given in "Two Years in the Life of an Edwardian Dancer."

20. Aldrich, *passim*.

21. Among the more successful of these parodies was that of the comedian Pelisser, whose success is referred to in *The Theatre* (Sydney, Australia) of May 1, 1914, during Maud's tour of Australasia: "Miss Allan says she 'visualizes the emotional quality of music.' The late Pelisser, of 'The Follies,' visualized her for me at the Apollo Theatre, London. I always regretted not seeing her before I saw Pelisser, as it was impossible for anyone with a ribald mind to become attuned to her after. I feel I owe Pelisser a grudge for this."

Among other imitations and burlesques were:

(i) La Belle Leonora as Nautchy Sal, the High Priestess of High Art Mysteries in "Sal Oh Mee" at the Alhambra Theatre. (Photograph in "The Sketch," April 29, 1909.)

(ii) Phyllis Dare in "The Dairy Maids," featuring a child chorus of "Miniature Salomes" at the Queen's Theatre. (Photograph in "The Sketch," June 24, 1908.)

(iii) Malcolm Scott as Salome at the London Pavilion. (Photograph in "The Sketch," June 17, 1908.)

(iv) Gertrude Hoffman's direct imitation of Maud's dancing, featuring *The Vision of Salome*, in New York. (Reviewed by the *New York Times*, July 14, 1908.)

(v) "Following Gertrude Hoffman another popular dancer of the day, Eva Tanguay, offered her version of the *Salome* dance and asked for £400 a week to come to London. A third Salome was La Sylphe, whom New York persuaded to cross the Atlantic. Then there was Signora Pertina, from Canonbury, and Julian Etynge, the female impersonator, whose Salome was described as "a choice morsel in the programmes of the Honeyboy Minstrels presently in New York." (Aldrich, "Two Years in the Life of a Great Dancer," ch. 7.)

The stage treatment of Salome may be said to have ended with the following review from the *San Francisco Chronicle* of October 23, 1916:

EVA TANGUAY DISAPPOINTS

After fifteen minutes of songs with a change of costume for

each, the curtain fell while she arranged a Salome burlesque.

If the original Salome was offensive as done by Oscar Wilde, the burlesque was worse. Miss Tanguay was not vicious in the same way. She was merely busy irritating you by means of an unmusical voice reading unharmonious lines in a ragtime spirit, the syncopation of which was rhythmically wrong. To criticize it would be to shoot a zeppelin at a buzzard. The curtain fell without emotional protest from the audience.

22. The cabinet Mr. Durrant referred to is seen in the background of a photograph of Mrs. Durrant during Theo's trial.
23. Republished, presumably because as a roman à clef it appealed to readers interested in identifying the men in Maud's private life, as *The House of No Address*.
24. In its extremely brief obituary notice of Maud Allan, the *Times* of London referred to her "grandly austere" London home, which Busoni and others used to visit.
25. Count Zichy is listed amongst the guests at the annual meeting and dinner of the Royal Automobile Club, presided over by the Prince of Wales, later George V. It was held at Covent Garden Theatre on April 1, 1909. Maud was the featured after-dinner entertainer. (*The Royal Automobile Club Journal*, April 1, 1909.)
26. "*To the Reader*: 'I think you'll like "Maudie"; she's fanciful and frivolous. I should hardly call her "fast," though she does do the most dreadful things, but she does them so nicely that probably the most strait-laced of people will have to forgive her, when they read her in the privacy of their own or other people's bedrooms – not only forgive, but love her and her bad ways and her worse friends.'" (*Maudie*, London: W.H. Allen, 1985, p. 9)
27. At his death in 1947 the second Duke of Westminster had been husband to four women, including the daughter of Sir Frederick Ponsonby, later Lord Sysonby, who, in his *Recollections of Three Reigns*, had described Maud's performance in Marienbad before King Edward VII. The duke's liaison with Coco Chanel was much publicized.
28. The official records for this period are not extant, so this cannot be corroborated. Among the civil servants who at one time or another dealt with Maud's stormy tenancy of West Wing was Sir Arthur Durrant (1864–1939) of Suffolk. In 1909

and 1910 he was principal clerk, Office of Works; from 1910 until 1919, director of supplies; and from 1920 to 1929 director of lands and accommodation (of Crown holdings). He was no known relation.

29. From an interview in the Bombay *Times*, November 15, 1913. The original account of the "tour" she gave a London journalist has not been found.

6

Years of Touring:
1910–1915

ETWEEN CLOSING NIGHT at the Palace The-
atre and her departure on January 10, 1910, for her first tour
of the United States, Maud performed in St. Petersburg and
Moscow. One of her motives, surely, was to match or
eclipse the success of Isadora Duncan, who a few years
earlier had taken Russia – and the young Russian poet Sergei
Essenin – by storm. The visit proved a catastrophe. Maud
had walked into a lion's cage of critics and was badly
mauled.

Valerian Svetlov, mentor of Anna Pavlova (whose coming
international success would instantaneously undermine
Maud's renown), dismissed Maud as "a slavish imitator of
Isadora Duncan – almost a caricature."[1] An unnamed reviewer dismissed *The Vision of Salome* as a belly dance,
possibly fit for the masses seeking entertainment in a park
theatre. These reactions may have sprung from the perception that Maud was an amateur or vulgar entertainer,
presuming to perform before a paying audience used to the
best in classical or modern dance.

If she was perceived to be less than a serious artist, her
performance must have fallen lamentably short of her usual
standards. Perhaps she was overcome by nerves, by the

pressure to satisfy so demanding an audience, and by the all-pervasive cult of Isadora Duncan.[2] She had just come from nearly two years of exhausting performances in London; ahead lay an uncertain reception in the United States. Perhaps, too, rehearsal conditions for her debut in St. Petersburg proved too much for her.

"Yesterday," ran a notice in *Perb* shortly before her St. Petersburg debut, "Miss Maud Allan's dress rehearsal took place in the High Hall of the Conservatorium. Miss Allan conducted the orchestra herself. Props and decorations were brought by the artist from London."

Understandably enough, Maud glossed over her failure in St. Petersburg. She told an American journalist a few weeks later that she "had performed before a brilliant audience of the society leaders of the Russian capital,"[3] probably true as far as it went. She also gave, she stated in the memoirs written a decade later for the San Francisco *Call*, a private recital for the tsar and tsarina. This is certainly credible, as the tsar was a fond cousin of Edward VII, whose appreciation had led to Maud's debut and subsequent triumph in London.[4]

She recorded her Moscow performance in her *Jottings* some twenty-five years later with the notation "Moscow – the Conductor there." This comment would be meaningless (no record of her performance in Moscow has been discovered) were it not for another interview with an American journalist: "once when I was in Russia, the orchestra leader was angry with me for some reason or other and played horribly. First I cried and then I made up my mind I wouldn't. I ran down at him, waved my hands, told him to play it all over again, and the audience clapped."[5]

On January 10, 1910, she boarded the *Lusitania* for the United States, accompanied by the first of her three known female "secretaries." Violet Carl Rosa was the daughter of the founder of the Carl Rosa Opera Company, which enjoyed considerable success in London for more than seventy-five years; it folded in 1958. Travelling to the United States two days later, on the ss *Barbarosa*, was Ferruccio Busoni, whose concert itinerary followed Maud's closely. Unlike Busoni, who enjoyed an international reputation, Maud had little reason to feel confident of success with the American public, let alone American critics.

She had only to read the *New York Times* to learn of the suspicion with which Carl van Vechten, the dean of American dance critics, viewed the "classic" dancing phenomenon. Moreover, he was overtly disgusted with "Salomania," with which Maud (and, to a lesser degree, Richard Strauss, whose opera *Salome* had been banned in New York) was identified. Some fifteen months before Maud's most unwelcome arrival van Vechten had declared that America had had more than its fill of "classic" dancing. Had she made her American debut earlier – as had been her widely publicized intention – her popular reception, if not her critical reception, might have been warmer. However, her popularity in London precluded even the shortest of sorties to the United States, and in the interim a number of purely "classical" dancers, notably Isadora Duncan, had come and gone, with varying success and without the blemish of "Salomania." In a sense, therefore, Maud was beaten before she opened her ambitious American tour; at the very least the odds were against her.

If she was known to the general public at all, it was as the originator of "the Salome dance," not as the unique and serious artist she and critics in England and the Continent considered her to be. For American journalists, her conquest of London was puzzling: was she a concert artist or a vaudeville entertainer? (*Variety*, Maud's nemesis in the United States, maliciously published reports that she had declined offers of $3,500 to $5,000 a week to appear in vaudeville.) Had she duped London's reviewers and public by subtly catering to the baser passions in a performance that in America might be taken as obscene, or was her performance a genuinely creative work of art? Was she merely a snob, or was she exploiting the acclaim of titled and eminent members of British society for her own purposes?

Her much-publicized association with Prime Minister Asquith and his wife, Margot, was a case in point. The Los Angeles *Examiner* reported that her friendship with Margot Asquith had caused a serious strain in the Asquith marriage – speculation that Maud always took care to deny, doubtless with a certain satisfaction.

Finally, her relationship to Theo was widely known amongst American journalists. Thus, a great deal depended on her handling of the newspapermen. On the eve of her North American debut, which took place in Boston on January 19, 1910, she was interviewed for the Boston *Transcript*. Maud made two blunders: she criticized, and she boasted. She declared, "I never wear clothes that cramp me, and yet I think I never look ridiculous. That dress, for instance," she said, pointing to a beautiful gown of sealskin moiré that lay on the bed, "is perfectly healthy in its lines, and yet I do not think anyone would turn to look at it." This was a clear thrust at Isadora Duncan, whose street clothes were a version of the Grecian garb she affected on the stage.

Maud then predicted that future ballroom dancing would be based upon her concept of dancing as "a spontaneous expression of the spiritual state." (This was particularly tactless given that the *New York Times* fiercely championed traditional ballroom elegance and her New York debut was less than eighteen hours away.)

At the end of Maud's remarks the interviewing journalist observed: "I don't doubt that she's a marvelous dancer. But as a prophet, I have my doubts."

Her Carnegie Hall debut was damned by *Variety* as monotonous. Van Vechten was coolly appreciative; compared with the several classical dancers he had recently reviewed, she had "a picturesque quality which is all her own."[6] She did not perform *The Vision of Salome* at this recital.

In her interview with the *Chicago Tribune* on January 23, the eve of her debut in that city, the graceful, charming, and refined individual revealed in the London press metamorphosed into a slightly ridiculous yet captivating "barefoot dancer." According to the opening paragraph of this interview, Maud "discovered the 'poetry of motion,' thought it lovely, and practised her devotion so skilfully that members of the nobility worship at her feet." The reporter then added:

> As a conversationalist the danseuse easily has the better of the ordinary mortal. She talks three ways at once. A whole-souled eastern drawl seems all the time trying to break through the shell of an English veneer. Every now and then – when the owner grows excited – it gets out in the open and cavorts around until she grabs it and pushes it back, under its covering of rolled r's and forgotten h's.
>
> Then she talks with her eyes. These are great round green affairs that melt and flash and twinkle and sometimes seem to go out altogether. They die that way when she is most eagerly discussing the soul of motion. But while the eyes and voice are getting along pretty well within a duet comes a pair of sinuous, tapering hands doing the obligato of the conversation in a manner bewildering if not terrifying. They slip out at you and punch the commas and italics, then dart back and bump into her teeth, frequently get a stranglehold on each other and add to the general gaiety of things.

Asked to explain "the poetry of motion," Maud presumably obliged at some length; at any rate, the interviewer provided this amazing paraphrase: "If the compositions are played beautifully, she dances beautifully. If a flagelot busts, she limps. If a trumpet is out of tune an intricate gyration is likely to get tangled in the middle, while if the whole orchestra is bad, soul visualizing runs completely amuck and Miss Allan gives way to ordinary tears." (This last comment refers to the incident in Moscow, described earlier.)

Maud then completed her discourse by boasting foolishly, but not totally untruthfully, that "I never practise. While I am dancing I know nothing but the surge of the music." The interview ended with Maud shedding her "tiny shoe" and one stocking for a *Tribune* artist to sketch; when published, it was illustrated with a caricature to boot.

A few days later Maud was back in New York. Notwithstanding her assertion that she had stopped dancing *The Vision*, she devoted the second half of her recital to this work, no doubt in an attempt to capture public attention. The effort was futile, as much because of disastrously poor stage lighting as of the subject itself, which was dismissed as overly familiar.[7] Prospects of either acclaim or financial success were poor indeed.

During the next six weeks she travelled the cities of the Eastern seaboard, gaining more attention and probably giving more pleasure with her interviews than with her performances. A highlight of her way to San Francisco was the concert in Cincinnati, for the conductor was the young Leopold Stokowski, then in his first season as conductor of that city's orchestra. (Maud would run across him some twenty-five years later when he was the star of the movie *One Hundred Men and a Girl*. At that meeting he failed to recognize her or, even more humiliating, to recall this concert.)

According to the *Cincinnati Post* of February 12, the audience was, at first, somewhat apathetic to Maud's dancing, but warmed to it enough to demand a repetition of Mendelssohn's *Spring Song*. Maud was impressed by Stokowski, declaring that the Cincinnati Symphony Orchestra had "played her accompaniments in a far more satisfactory manner than any other organization that had assisted her." Originally, *The Vision of Salome* was scheduled for this concert; but protests against its inclusion from financial supporters of the fledgling Symphony Society caused it to be cancelled several days in advance. The result was a significant fall in the sale of seats. (The exclusion of *The Vision* also discouraged sales in Philadelphia and other cities.)

By the time she reached San Francisco in early April, Maud had put the disappointments and frustrations of the previous three months behind her. She was determined to be a public and critical success in San Francisco, and her dread of being viewed as the sister of the city's most notorious murderer proved groundless. By chance or design, on the day of her first concert, which was in the evening, society women had organized a matinee charity show of living pictures "depicting the court beauties of England and France during the 18th century and opening with Queen Marie Antoinette, surrounded by her ladies in waiting, her pages and flower girls."[8] The *Examiner* gave this event generous publicity, thereby indirectly promoting Maud's performance. The *Chronicle* of April 1 reported that "there is in San Francisco an intensely peculiar interest in the famous dancer who left her home almost a score of years ago and went to Europe to learn to sing." Both artist and audience were ready for a most moving experience.

In all probability her San Francisco debut was the greatest performance of Maud's career. "Last night," reported Ralph Renaud of the *Chronicle*,

at the Garrick Theatre was a night among 10,000 to be remembered, treasured and, I am tempted to say, reverenced. Maud Allan, an exile for the last 15 years that have made her one of the greatest artists, appeared in the home of her childhood and won the city to complete subjugation. Henceforth San Francisco will be to her a city of tears and a city of love and laughter. Within my time no such personal triumph has occurred here. The theatre was packed and fully half came out of curiosity. It was an audience of Americans and not of exuberant Italians prepared to applaud their favorite tenor. Yet, at the conclusion of her wonderful interpretation of the *Peer Gynt* suite the whole house, from gallery to pit, was yelling and stamping its approval. If they had not lost their senses, they had at least abandoned all dignity in a frantic appreciation that the mere clapping of palms could not express. It caused a stress and a strain which the emotions of no human being could withstand.

When Miss Allan had finished the last item on her program, the poignantly beautiful *Valse caprice* of Rubinstein, she crept forward to the footlights with moist eyes and quivering lips to make a little speech. Her voice was barely audible for the sobs she tried to suppress, but she spoke the most sincere and touching thanks I have ever heard. She referred to the happy days of her childhood here and to the dark and sad days that had so tragically followed. She declared that when she had left San Francisco she had determined never to return until she could bring back the success she had dreamed of, and that of all the cities on earth, she yearned most for the appreciation of this one.

"Take me to your hearts," she ended, with the catching breath that preceded a burst of tears, "I know you have, but oh! keep me there."

Three days later the same writer described the conclusion of Maud's dance interpretation of Chopin's *Marche funèbre*:

Black draperies hung from the hair and shoulders, trailing upon the floor. She crouched under an insupportable load of sorrow, and crept forward with anguished hands and face working in agony. As the calmer melody clarified from the sounds of the viols, her arms were raised in supplication, only to droop pitifully as the music returned to sobs and inexpressible grief. Her last movement was to veil her face. It seemed the living representation of death, if the paradox is permissible, and dramatic to the last degree.

In the course of the month, Maud gave at least seven performances in San Francisco and area; finally, with declared reluctance but at public demand, she danced *The Vision of Salome*. The critic for the *Examiner*, who, like Ralph Renaud of the *Chronicle*, had been so generous in his praise of earlier performances, found this work artistic enough but as "moral" as a "surgical operation; the rest of the program was exquisite, with every number worth a hundred *Salome* dances." Renaud found the work offensive.[9]

As in London, Maud's success extended beyond the stage. The *Chronicle* reported that upon her arrival at a fashionable déjeuner given in her honour (to be followed by a few short dances), "she looked so unique and stunning that one could forgive the many for staring at her with such spellbound interest."[10] Three days earlier she had spoken to a ladies' club about her art. The "several hundred members," reported the *Examiner* of April 28, "received her with applause approximating acclamations of bewildering emotionalism. Indrawn exclamations of o-o-oh! mingled with demonstrations of applause greeted her as, with clinging draperies falling about her sandals, Miss Allan glided on to the stage." The *Chronicle* was taken by her delivery far more than by her message: "She has a low toned musical voice, an easy natural conversational style of address, and a graceful languid manner which lent charm to the simple, unaffected things she said."

During her stay in northern California, she also gave concerts in towns on the standard touring itinerary, including Stockton and Sacramento. Her last reported performance, according to the *Los Angeles Times*, was in the southern part of the state, on May 6, the day King Edward VII died. During an interview a few years later she recalled: "Wherever I have gone, the galleries have not only been well patronized, but I have never experienced the slightest trouble with them. In California I danced before an audience of hardy, rough looking foundry workers. At the conclusion one of the leaders got up and said 'Boys, she ain't a girl, she's an angel!' "[11]

On April 12, the *Los Angeles Times* reviewed her debut there, incorporating an interview and an account of her dress rehearsal, which was:

> presided over by a tall slender young woman in an ulster, with Symphony Director Hamilton clad in a sweater rather than a coat, merely following the rhythm of her flying hands with his baton. Miss Allan, who is quite unimpressive with real clothes, has the most wonderful hands in the world. They are better than any baton. She always rehearses her orchestra – and in this manner. First, wrapped in a big coat with a basket hat far down over her face, she sat on the stage resting her chin in her hands and intently gazing at the leader.
> Then a phrase that demanded repetition sounded in her

ears. "No!" she cried, "this way – la la la la tra – that's it!"

But the fever of expression had seized her and in a moment, leaping to her feet, she kicked over her chair and was swaying in harmony with every phrase, indicating tempo and expression with both hands, singing with all the fervor of a Latin leader, and drawing out the finest points of the theme.

After the rehearsal she had a long musician's conversation with Director Hamilton, and it was mightily different from the usual conversational handout to the bandmaster. The average dancer says "Too fast" or "Too slow" and signs for the bass man to punctuate her kicks. Miss Allan talked about the inner meaning of Chopin and the possibilities of Rubinstein.

She then declared to the fascinated journalist that her real ambition was to conduct an orchestra and that she had been promised such an opportunity in London.[12] That evening the journalist attended the concert and penned this amazing account of her "interpretation" of Chopin's Valse in A Minor:

> She glided rather than stepped about the stage. She seemed listening at moments uncertainly, at other moments with bursts of joyous passion, again with little tremors of laughter; now and then with visibly embodied sighs and in a rare moment swaying as though bent by a breath of love. The incarnation of this Chopin Valse moved before you. You forgot about the dance, you forgot about Miss Allan, you merely waited for the next visualization to begin. Presently, the music stopped – and there stood Miss Allan – bowing. You couldn't tell what she had done, where she had moved, nor the way she had gotten there. She had simply alchemized a piece of music for you.

In Maud's view, certainly, her reception in California was warmer than she had dared hoped. It seems to have released tensions that had gripped her since her arrival in the United States. The differences in her personality (and in her critical reception) as reported in the West Coast and Eastern seaboard press are striking. While the former might have been making deliberate amends for its sensational and cruel coverage of "the Crime of a Century," its acceptance of Theo's sister as an individual and as an artist seems to have released in her that ineffable charm that had entranced London for nearly two years. It certainly released some remarkably honest comments in a statement she sent to the *San Francisco Chronicle* either during or after her tour of the state. Answering the "charge" that she danced for money, she boldly declared, "I do. I have found, unromantic as it may seem, that neither art nor artists can exist without it." She also defended her use of a stage name, a defence that suggests that the press did not completely disassociate her from her brother. "No one on earth has any right to attack me save as Maud Allan. To do so is cowardice beyond contempt."

The balance of the statement concerns the "morality" of *The Vision of Salome*, which was based, she insisted this time, on the Bible. She concluded on a general note: "The thought of returning after so many years was not entirely pleasant, and I did not expect such a fine and beautiful reception. But when I come back it will be with the full knowledge of how big hearted San Francisco is." She did not perform in San Francisco again for sixteen years, when she appeared in a vaudeville theatre for one week, attracting little if any notice.

Temperamental, tactless, and tense as Maud may have been in the face of indifference, suspicion, and hostility during the first weeks of her three-month American tour, she had just cause to be upset.

In an interview with London's *Daily Chronicle* on December 24, 1910, she explained that she had been in a train accident while travelling overnight between Chicago and New York. The effects were traumatic. She told the London journalist:

My poor nerves are suffering from it still. It happened early in the morning, at about 5:30, and it was being awakened with such a terrific shock and such an indescribably awful noise that did the mischief to my nerves. And on top of that, the sight of the bodies of the fireman and the driver, and their smashed train!

It really was a terrible experience, and I ought to have taken a rest and chanced the monetary loss. But I worked for six months with the memory of that scene continually forcing itself upon me, and it was only the wonderful tonic of the people's generous applause at the 85 dance recitals I gave in the numerous cities of the tour that kept me from breaking down entirely. But the strain of keeping up every single appointment of my long and trying contract, when my system was in need of complete rest, had proved too much for me, and that is the real reason I have had to delay my London appearance for so long.

Another problem was more debilitating in the short term. "I suffered," she explained, "no fewer than three times from ptomaine poisoning, and the pain of dancing and posing while the effects of this poison were acute was enough to drive me crazy." (In fact, this "poisoning" may have been the initial signs of appendicitis. Throughout her 1913–1915 tour of India and Australasia, she coped with a "rumbling" appendix, and refused to have it removed.)

She must have been exhausted both physically and emotionally, because it was only in February 1911, months after her return to London, that she again appeared at the Palace Theatre for a three-month engagement. Presented as a feature of the evening's program, she was kindly received, but that spontaneous overflow of powerful emotions that had surged through the theatre three years earlier was now but a gentle rain, unable to wash the writing off the wall.

She must have seen at least some of that writing, because she became preoccupied with a new project to replace *The Vision of Salome*. She was planning a new "Oriental" ballet, with an original score commissioned from Claude Debussy. The basic scenario for this work, eventually known as *Khamma*, had been worked out by Maud and one of her most fervently loyal admirers, William Leonard Courtney, the drama and literary editor of the *Daily Telegraph*. (Courtney had been professor of Philosophy at Oxford until public knowledge of his homosexual proclivities led to his resignation.)

Under the terms of the contract between the musician/dancer and the composer, Maud was to pay Debussy 10,000 francs on signing the contract, 5,000 francs upon delivery of the completed score, and another 5,000 francs after the fourteenth performance, as well as a royalty of 50 francs for each of the first 500 performances.[13] Debussy had undertaken this contract purely for "des raisons d'économie domestique" – and indeed the terms were generous. However, what appeared to be an impressive coup for Maud turned into a costly and frustrating blunder.

Khamma also proved something of a burden for Debussy. Until his death in 1917, he was bombarded with the insatiable demands of that "détestable Maud Allan." She had two basic complaints: that the delivered score was too short and, "as the music stands, it could never be a success," an opinion that time seems to have vindicated. In Debussy's view the complaints were ill informed, ill advised and, worst of all, ill mannered. The upshot of the acrimonious relationship was that Maud never performed the work. It was given its first orchestral performance in 1924 and was finally staged at the Opéra-Comique in Paris on March 26, 1947.

Disconcerting as this project must have been, Maud treasured the score for which she had paid so much and from which she had gained nothing. For more than twenty-five years she never let it out of her hands until, no doubt for her own "raisons d'économie domestique," she attempted to sell it. Among those approached as potential buyers were Arturo Toscanini and John Barbirolli, the British conductor who in 1936 had succeeded Toscanini as conductor of the New York Philharmonic.[14] Among her personal letters are two from Barbirolli – the first, of June 2, 1940, requests an appointment (in London) to examine the score; the second is from Vancouver, British Columbia, assuring Maud that the score is being actively studied for possible performance. Nothing came of this, and Barbirolli returned the score to Maud when she moved to California in 1941.

What became of the score is a mystery. At her death, the ragged envelope that for years she had been saying contained the original manuscript was found to contain only an incomplete manuscript version of the piano sketch, prepared by Debussy's amanuensis, Charles Koechlin. That fragment now belongs to the Music Library collection of the University of British Columbia.

In November 1911, Maud set out on a tour of South Africa. With her was her lifelong friend Alice Lonnon, daughter of "Pop" Perkins. To relieve Maud (not to mention the audience) of a full evening of pose dancing, Alice Lonnon recited passages from Shakespeare and, according to an advertisement in the Pretoria *News* of December 24, "told stories." The tour was a great adventure; the itinerary included Rhodesia and a visit to the Victoria Falls. Professionally, though, it was a failure, relieved only by social activities in Pretoria, Capetown, and Johannesburg, where they performed for a week and cancelled a return visit because of poor houses.[15]

However disappointing this tour may have been, it proved of great consequence; for it was in the famed Carlton Hotel in Johannesburg that Maud met the Cherniavsky Trio. Three years later they would extensively tour India, the Far East, and Australasia together; their friendship, and that of their sisters, Maud retained until her death.

The Cherniavsky Trio comprised three highly gifted brothers – Leo (violinist), Jan (pianist), and Mischel (cellist) – who were on their second tour of South Africa. Leo and Jan were both born (in 1888 and 1893 respectively) in the Ukrainian city of Bedichev; Mischel was born in 1894 in Uman, a smaller town near Odessa. They were part of the exceptionally musical family – five sons and four daughters – of Abraham and Rosa Cherniavsky. The three brothers, together with the eldest son, Gregor, were taken in to their father's youth orchestra at a very early age. Within a short time their father gave up his job conducting this orchestra (which played in a park bandstand) to teach his younger sons. In 1904, he obtained special permission to travel in Russia – it was a time of pogroms and travel by Jews was restricted – and took the trio on an extensive tour, including Minsk, St. Petersburg, and Yalta. There the trio performed for officials of the court. (At the age of ninety-three Jan recalled having seen two of the tsar's daughters playing in the palace grounds in Yalta.)

The family then left for Vienna, where the trio soon enjoyed the patronage of the Rothschild family. Some months later they moved to England, where, armed with invaluable introductions, the three boys were giving private performances and earning enough to support the family within a week of their arrival. Their first public concert in England was in Cambridge, where they shared the stage with the Irish tenor John McCormack and received one guinea each.

In 1908 the three boys went on tour to South Africa and Australia before returning to London.[16] In early 1911 they returned to South Africa, with twenty-three-year-old Leo in charge.

Leo was a solidly built man with dashing eyes and a dark complexion. He shaved twice a day, yet to be embraced by him was, at least for his young nephews and nieces, unforgettable for the abrasiveness of his beard. He played the violin as he lived his life – passionately, dynamically, and, it must be conceded, a trifle roughly. With an air of authority born of his responsibilities, always prepared to take charge yet unselfish and kind-hearted, he was a born organizer, trained on the job.

Jan, two years younger than Leo, was the most hard-pressed of the three. In addition to playing trios and performing solos, he accompanied his brothers in their solos until relieved by another pianist (on occasion his youngest brother, Alex). Uneasy even at the age of ninety-three if denied access to his beloved piano, he was the most musically poetic of the three, endowed with insights and a fervour that infused his piano playing and his many other interests.

Mischel, the cellist, eighteen months younger than Jan, had the greatest natural talent of the three and a tone that drew unstinted admiration from audiences and concert cellists alike. He did not develop his talents to the full, however, apparently under the delusion that discipline might damage rather than mature them.

On the stage the three brothers exuded a charisma that entranced their audiences. Gifted with engaging personalities and considerable ego, all three shared as great an enthusiasm for music as for life and an uninhibited willingness to perform anywhere, at any time, for any audience. Their most remarkable trait, both on and off the stage, was their absolute harmony and musical intuition. They performed as a trio until 1934, when each went his own way.

Maud was instantly struck by the trio's spontaneity and musicianship – her two most distinctive traits – although, unlike them, she was highly trained. She no doubt appreciated their popularity with the public. When she learned that these globetrotters (an epithet invented by Howard Edie, their dynamic agent) planned to tour India en route to a second tour of Australasia, she suggested that she join them – or, rather, they join her. They did not reject the proposal out of hand. Apart from her musical empathy, she had an international reputation that could effectively complement their more localized fame and popularity.

They may also have recalled that during their return visit to Sydney's Palace Theatre in March 1909, Miss Sarah Cuthbert, advertised as "Australia's Maud Allan," was giving nightly performances of "the Salome Dance" at Queen's Hall. (The trio's repertoire during this tour had included arrangements of Mendelssohn's *Spring Song*, Chopin's *Marche funèbre*, and Grieg's *Peer Gynt* suite, each of which was also part of Maud's repertoire during her conquest of London.) These works were, of course, featured during the Maud Allan Cherniavsky Trio tour.

As for Maud, after experiencing the personal and professional hazards of touring on her own in a strange country, joining forces with the trio was too attractive an opportunity to be missed. She loved travelling.

Apart from these considerations she had another, far more powerful, motive. Almost as soon as she had set her luminous eyes upon him, the thirty-eight-year-old dancer had become infatuated with Leo Cherniavsky, seventeen years her junior. (She had a penchant for younger persons, of both sexes.) Their liaison lasted about four years, with a futile attempt on Maud's part to revive it in 1923. Thereafter it evolved into a friendship that lasted till Maud's death, at which time Leo acted as her executor. Their relationship was tempestuous from the first, for few relished more the conflict between opposing wills than Leo Cherniavsky, and few women were more inclined to provide that opposition than Maud Allan (even though it was she who regularly gave in).

Exactly how and when it was decided to join professional forces is unclear. All that is known is that the trio went ahead, as scheduled, with a tour of India (they gave their first recital there in Bombay on December 12, 1912) and were midway through a tour of the Far East when they cabled their acceptance of a mutually satisfactory contract. Having boarded a ship in Yokohama, they arrived in London in mid-1913, and the Maud Allan Cherniavsky Trio Company was formed.

After she had become acquainted with the family and probably in order to ingratiate herself with the autocratic Abraham Cherniavsky and his offended wife, Rosa, Maud suggested and offered to arrange that Manya, the second youngest daughter in the family, board at King's House School in Highgate.[17] (The fees would be paid by the trio.) The Cherniavsky parents were planning to emigrate to North America (after one winter in Winnipeg they settled in Los Angeles). They welcomed the suggestion, both as a convenience as they settled in to a new life and as a unique opportunity for their daughter to acquire some education and social graces.

Manya attended this school for three years (Maud took particular care to familiarize her, as the only Jewish girl in so Protestant an institution, with the conventions of the Church of England). During school holidays and on occasional weekends, Manya would stay at West Wing, venturing, in spite of being intimidated, into the vast, unoccupied mansion of which West Wing was but an adjunct. (However great a debt she may have felt to Maud for her hospitality and guidance, Manya more than paid it back in later years in Los Angeles when Maud bled Manya's gratitude like a leech.)

As the three musicians and the dancer rehearsed and prepared for an itinerary such as only Leo Cherniavsky could design,[18] a problem arose among Maud Allan, the Viceroy of India, and Lord Crewe, secretary of state for India. Lord Crewe was the political superior of the viceroy, a member of the diplomatic corps who, raised to the peerage in keeping with the appointment, became Lord Hardinge. Lord Hardinge had been skilfully pressured by the hierarchy of the Anglican Church of India and decided that he was duty bound to ban Maud from touring India. He declared that her performance before "mixed" audiences would be detrimental to the "prestige of the white woman in India."[19] Even though he indirectly acknowledged that he had seen Maud perform in London, and Maud insisted that she had no intention, for both social and practical reasons, of mounting *The Vision of Salome* in India, the viceroy stuck to his guns.

For more than two months he pestered Lord Crewe and his officials with cables, at one point declaring that he had legal authority to ban Maud from entering India.[20] At first Lord Crewe did not take seriously the viceroy's concerns, although, always sensitive to political implications, he trod softly. A highly embarrassing controversy was given the issue by the English-language press in India and, shortly thereafter, in London, where the papers presented the matter as one of public decency amid wild predictions of public disorder in India. The London *Times* even published a letter from the Bishop of Calcutta, the effective leader of the protest, in vigorous defence of the viceroy's concerns.[21]

A turning-point came when Maud discovered that Roshanara, an Anglo-Indian born classical dancer, had just returned safe and sound from a tour of India, where she had included in her program versions of several dance interpretations Maud had originally made famous. Only in late October, when her departure was imminent and a ruling was required, did Lord Crewe order the viceroy and his clerical supporters to stop molesting her.[22]

No one but the Cherniavsky Trio knew that the publicity surrounding the issue was entirely the brainchild of Howard Edie, the company's advance manager. Upon hearing of the viceroy's concern, he used it to arouse interest in the forthcoming tour. He conspired with the editors of Bombay's two major English-language newspapers to concoct and reply to letters to the editor protesting Maud's visit on grounds suspiciously similar to those bruited about in the vestries and clubs of Calcutta.[23] The issue thus raised immediately caught fire, as both sincere and specious correspondents aired opinions. Neither the trio members nor Edie chose to let Maud in on the secret.

While she innocently worked her way through this controversy, the Cherniavsky Trio left for Bombay, accompanied by the tour director, a lawyer by training but impresario by choice. Throughout the fifteen-month tour, he regularly wrote to his wife in London. By happy chance many of these letters were preserved.[24] Thanks to them, a behind-the-scenes glimpse of Maud Allan the artist, her interpersonal relationships, and her character survives.

She arrived in Bombay on November 14, ten days after the trio and tour director. She was accompanied by Alice Lonnon, officially designated as her secretary/companion, and by Fred Mitchell, her electrician, who somehow survived the entire trip. Her sets were mainly heavy velvet curtains, which were frequently difficult to hang and, from the trio's viewpoint, adversely affected the acoustics. The company was completed by the arrival of Frank St. Leger, a recent graduate of London's Royal Academy of Music, whose immediate job was to accompany Leo and Mischel in their solo works. (The three brothers opened the concerts with a trio, and during the course of the evening each played two solos.) In Australia, St. Leger was also scheduled to conduct the local orchestras of major cities, which had been engaged to accompany Maud in *The Vision of Salome*. (Following this tour, he was Dame Nellie Melba's accompanist for three years; later he became a conductor and finally assistant general manager of the New York Metropolitan Opera, from which he retired in 1950.)

The tour opened in Bombay on November 24, to a sold-out house. But that evening disaster struck, throwing the tour director into a flurry of activity and admiration for Maud Allan the dancer:

> We got through our opening night with flying colours, and the *Times of India* notice is magnificent.. We lived in the theatre all Sunday and Monday and on the Monday [opening] night Maud Allan, in her very first dance, broke a fibre of the calf muscle. She was in agony all evening, but never let on, and at the end of the evening she could not put her ankle to the floor. I got the best surgeon out of bed at 2 A.M. and he ordered complete rest, so we had to cancel the Bombay season. All India is saying she has been stopped by the Government – letters and telegrams pour in daily from all quarters of the globe. She really is the most beautiful and charming dancer and when one sees her one marvels that anyone could be so filthy minded as to see any indecency – it is the acme of purity and grace – and her understanding of music must be extraordinarily deep. I am right now negotiating with the Nizam of Hyderabad for a performance for the ladies of his harem and those of two relatives.

This engagement apparently took place, because in her *Jottings* Maud noted "Dancing for a Harem in India."

While Maud convalesced in Bombay, the trio went on a quickly improvised tour, rejoining her on December 19 for the three-day train journey to Calcutta. Upon arriving in

Calcutta, Maud and Alice sped on to Darjeeling in the Himalayas, returning in time for the opening concert on January 1.

That concert was a triumph and, for Maud, sweet vindication. The theatre was packed – throughout the week-long engagement nightly receipts hovered around £200. In the audience was a journalist from *Basumati*, a Bengali-language newspaper, whose "roughly translated" review was sent on to the tour director's wife:

I think myself very fortunate to be able to see the dancing of the nude lady, which is appreciated by the Western communities, but it was a task for me when I was asked to give a perfect report of the performance. I entered the stage and found it dark on all sides. It was not like a Bengali stage, and I thought that perhaps Bioscope pictures would be shown, but to my surprise I found a very beautiful lady standing there in very thin clothing. She moved her hands and feet in a very peculiar manner which we could not appreciate. It may be a good sort of dancing but to an Indian her art is not good or attractive. [Here the writer quotes a song describing the appearance of the stage as being like a scene on a moonlit river where a lady is taking her bath half clothed.]

Miss Allan then came on in another dress, and now the stage was lighted. She began to dance in another mood, it was not like other English dances. It was something new and I believe it was appreciated by the Europeans, but we Indians had no taste for it. Then she began to express various moods in gestures and poses which again we could not appreciate because we are used to hearing such emotions in our theatres in songs.

I was given to understand she would appear in the nude but very fortunately [so much for the viceroy's fears!] she was requested by the Europeans not to come in that state and so, though she had a very thin dress on, yet the features of her different limbs were perfectly seen.

I also found some Bengali ladies and gentlemen present,

but they seemed to sit still and not appreciate the dancing and they appeared to me like so many crows among peacocks. Also the tunes played by the famous musicians were not appreciated by us.

As for the English-language press, the comment of one unidentified editor epitomizes the reaction of the British establishment in Calcutta, the original centre of opposition to Maud's tour: "I went a Philistine. I came away absolutely won over. For the rest you have my criticism of her performance."[25]

After this rejuvenating week in Calcutta, the company made a 4,000-kilometre round-trip tour of the Punjab, going as far north as Lahore. (According to Mischel's recollections in 1981, it was during this three-day trip that Maud and Leo consummated their relationship.) En route they played in New Delhi, the new capital of India – the viceroy took care to be absent – and Agra, the site of the Taj Mahal, which they visited immediately after their concert and before catching a train at 4 A.M. At the Taj Mahal she had a mystical experience – probably more imagined than real – that about twenty-five years later she would make the focal point of a fictionalized autobiography.

On January 25, the day after their return to Calcutta, they boarded the ss *Aranhola* for Rangoon, Penang, Singapore, and Hong Kong; they played one or more very successful concerts at each of these stopovers.[26] After three well-received concerts in Hong Kong, the large foreign colony of Shanghai turned out in force for the three scheduled concerts. The review of the first of these ended with a revealing complaint: "Is there any reason why the theatre authorities should not suppress whistling and catcalling in the gallery? The trick is new to Shanghai, and insufferable. It nearly marred the pleasure of an unequalled evening."

In Shanghai, Leo told the tour director about the public-relations origin of the fuss over Maud's tour of India. He also informed him of Theo's trial and execution. ("Leo says the boy was the only brother of Maud Allan and the fact is well known in America.'') In the letter in which the tour director passed on this information to his wife, he also commented on the interpersonal tensions that were evolving:

> Maud Allan is cracked about Leo and hates his brothers because they dislike her for making such a fool of him. She is always trying to get him away from them but the three are absolutely one – their affection for each other is very beautiful, as is their perfect harmony. Leo is too shrewd to go too far with her.
>
> I've had a very serious talk with the Boys about practising and rehearsing all her numbers, and they have promised to mend their ways. She says they let her down but they say that as she won't rehearse they don't know what she wants.
>
> She says she won't rehearse until they practise the music, and so they go on. She is largely to blame as she never praises them and often abuses them, and they say they are just as great artists as she is and that it was only a fluke and no clothes that made her name. (Mischel told her this!)[27]

The animosity became so intense that in later years none of the three brothers cared to talk about this ten-week sea voyage in any but the most general terms. Discretion and loyalty were the chief reasons for this self-imposed silence, but the brothers also seem to have recognized that the complexities of Maud's artistic temperament were, in certain ways, similar to their own. Certainly they responded patiently to those elements in her personality that so frequently aroused pity and terror: pity for her persistent agony of mind over Theo; and terror of the iron will that seemed part of her unquestionable charisma. To confine four such temperamental artists, two of whom were enmeshed in a stormy relationship, to such close quarters for more than ten weeks was to invite trouble.

By the time they arrived in Manila, where they gave four successful concerts, Maud's intentions were all too plain. She wanted to marry Leo, break up the trio, arrange for him to study for a year, and then tour with him. Leo's response was fairly typical of his generation: no wife of *his* would be on the stage. She would stay at home, having babies. (In fact, although he was married three times, he fathered no children.) Maud's aspirations and his growing impatience with her prompted the tour director to write the following character analysis, written on board the ss *Kumano Maru*, a "jolly little boat of 5000 tons – very steady, nice cabin, good food":

> She has innocent but dangerous blue eyes, like a child's, but she is mean and selfish, a grab all and give nothing, a harlot at heart and a humbug because she is always posing as the paragon of virtue and talks most beautifully on moral subjects, but really she doesn't care much what she does so long as she isn't found out. She has never been contradicted in her life, and so Leo has recently taken to telling her all her faults, hypocrisies, her mean and selfish ways. They have the most awful rows, but to the astonishment of everyone she always gives in. She is a clever woman who calculates her every move and I am pretty sure she is playing for something – but what?

This is an uncharitable analysis, but, as the record suggests, it is neither entirely inaccurate nor unjustified.

In the same letter the tour director reveals that Jan's and Mischel's resentments had an economic basis as well. The original contract for the tour of India and the Far East was negotiated by wire from Shanghai. (The terms for Australasia were at the time left open.) Under its terms the trio was to receive 60 per cent of the profits, with Maud taking the balance. However, in London, prior to the trio's departure for India, Maud produced a more "professionally" prepared contract drawn up by Alfred Butt. Told that the terms were the same, only the wording more formal, Leo signed on the dotted line. Later, he discovered that only 25 per cent of the profits had been assigned to the trio. Such skulduggery, coupled with Maud's overt determination to take Leo unto herself and destroy the trio – and, in his brothers' view, Leo himself – was bound to cause dissension.

In Manila, Maud added insult to injury by going out with

"a man of doubtful reputation," whereupon Leo refused to speak to her for two days of the sea voyage. The tour director, in an attempt to forestall a fateful confrontation over the unsigned contract for Australasia, took on the role of peacemaker. Warning Maud that she was confusing her personal and business relationships with Leo, he told her to leave well enough alone and let him handle business matters as was his responsibility. Leo likewise warned her that she would have "a hell of a time" if she tried to give them less than their due in the unsigned contract. Maud ignored these warnings. During a rowdy conference with Leo and the tour director, she described the brothers as "little rats." The tour director wrote home that she declared

> she would do nothing for them because they insulted her with their looks and bearing. At this point I told Leo he had better go, and then I said to her "Can you wonder at the Boys being sore – how would you feel if I induced you to travel to Australia with a promise of a salary of £700 a week and if upon your arrival I said there was nothing to bind me, and I will give you £200 a week or nothing?" I then did my best to get her to accept a compromise but finally she refused and said they could arbitrate. I have told the Boys who are delighted as they think they will win, but Leo is awfully sick as he feels she does not really care for him. He wrote her a very bitter "all is over between us" letter and has not spoken to her since. Yesterday at lunch she was nearly crying and left the table, and could not face us at dinner. The two boys are very nice to her – she is very sad – because they think Leo is safe. It is a tragi-comedy and I shall be very very sad if Leo finally gets entangled with her. Today she came to lunch very sad, and after she paced the deck alone and Leo ditto – both dying for the other to speak first but neither willing to break the ice. Is it not foolish?

On a glorious morning of March 31, 1914, the ss *Kumano Maru* entered Sydney harbour. On deck with Maud were the Cherniavsky brothers, pointing out landmarks familiar to them from their earlier tour. Immediately ahead of them was a sister ship, the ss *Sumano Maru*; milling about in the inner harbour was a mass of ships and small yachts, bedecked with flags and blowing on their sirens. When Maud commented on the colourful scene Mischel teasingly suggested that the welcome was for her. It was intended as a joke, for the company was only passing through Sydney en route to Dunedin, New Zealand. Maud fell for the bait and, as the ship followed in the wake of the *Sumano Karu,* waved graciously to the enormous crowd and official-looking group of kilted dignitaries who stood waiting at dockside. Finally, Leo explained to her that the crowds were waiting for "the Uncrowned King" – the enormously popular song-and-dance entertainer Harry Lauder would be disembarking from the *Sumano Maru*. Maud good-humouredly ceased her queenly acknowledgements.

The Sydney *Morning Herald* described the dockside scene that day:

> "Where is he?" was the exclamation of all hands.
>
> Suddenly, from a perch almost as high as the top light, came a familiar laugh with a tilt in it, and a voice exclaimed, "It's a braw morning!" Dressed in kilts with a dagger [skean dhu] in his stocking and a huge meerschaum pipe in his hand, Harry Lauder laughed himself into Australia in his own peculiar way.

Later that day, after a heady civic reception he so vividly describes in his autobiography, Harry Lauder and his wife spent a quiet evening with Maud and the trio.

During the three-day stopover in Sydney the matter of the unsigned contract came to a head. At the tour director's suggestion, Leo contacted a solicitor, who formally advised Maud that, no matter what she might argue, until the contract was signed to the trio's satisfaction they would not appear in concert with her. She had no choice but to accept the good offices of the tour director, who

> fixed up everything as it should have been fixed up on the boat. In the evening she asked me what I had done. I told

her, adding that a little explanation – an agreement – would have to be signed by the two parties. She answered she would sign nothing. Next day the agreement came – there was a scene – she wept, and said she would rather give up the Tour than sign anything that Leo could show to prove he had won a victory. I said I would get Leo to write a letter instead, so I sent for Leo and they met for the first time in days. It really was a comedy – these lovers – as I had to explain to them the matter in a cold judicial manner when suddenly she blazed forth at Leo about the low down ways of his race and he blazed back that he was proud of his race and didn't do the dirty things she resorted to.[28]

At this point the solicitor was announced, so I took Leo away, and on hearing that a letter would be as binding as an agreement, Leo consented to write one. The solicitor sketched it out, I put in all the nice kind words and turns of expression ("Why should I?" asked Leo, "Don't be a fool," said I) and finally it was written and sent to her. Later, when I went to see her after giving her some time to digest it, she said "You wrote that letter, you are a dear" – and kissed me!

With the contract finalized, the company set sail for Dunedin, where, on April 13, they opened their Australasian tour. That concert was, in the director's words, "the best we've given so far." His exhilaration was short-lived, however; four days later Maud reported "a slight pain in the old place," her lower leg or ankle, and on doctor's orders rested a week – at the cost of the Dunedin season. Once recovered, she gallantly fulfilled a hectic schedule of one-night stands in the small towns of New Zealand.

It was in Auckland, New Zealand's capital (where six profitable concerts were given in the first week of June), that the most memorable incident of the tour occurred. On June 1 the legendary Ellen Terry, in poor health and in her sixties, arrived from Australia to continue her world tour of recitals. (She described them as "just talks or chats to my friends, and they are merely the means by which I express the result of a life's study and training in Shakespeare, while at the same time they allow me to introduce the scenes I am able to read instead of act.")[29]

Writing of Miss Terry's arrival, the tour director (who had managed one of her tours in England a few years earlier) remarked: "The poor old thing is very ill, utterly prostrated by the heat of the sea voyage, and can't get right again." In any case, "She had four big receptions in Melbourne, but could only attend one for a few minutes. Thousands met the ship but she would not get off till all had gone. She can't see a soul but lies in her room all day. I hope I will see her for a minute, dear soul."

He did indeed have occasion to see her, as his remarkable account of June 5 attests:

On Tuesday when I got back from the theatre I got a message to say I was to go up to see her [Terry] at once, so I went up to her flat and found her in bed, looking much better than I had expected, but still very old. She was delighted to see me, said the rest was doing her good but that she longed to be home again but would fight on to the end as she couldn't bear to think that the people who had brought her out would lose money. She said she was quite sure she would die in the Red Sea. I advised her to go home by the Cape – she is not a bad sailor but hates the confinement on board.

How wonderful she is, her brain as quick as ever, talking on a dozen subjects at once, keenly interested in life, merry and cheerful and chock full of humour and charm. "I hate my body" – and that is just it – you feel that Ellen will never die, that her spirit will simply take flight to another sphere. I told her I had first seen her as Lady Macbeth. "I'm sorry for that," she said – and then I added I had next seen her as Beatrice. "Ah, it all seems like a dream – that this old hulk could have been Beatrice!"

On Friday night she came to the theatre. She was much relaxed and got out of bed and came down and sat in the stage box. She was enormously excited afterwards and I took her round to the back stage and introduced her to

Maud Allan and the Trio. "Wonderful, wonderful boys," she exclaimed, "you have dragged the soul's soul out of me. I wish I were mother to you all, I must kiss you each" (and does so). "And you, Maudie, Queen Maud, how you've *improved*! But then no one had such music to dance to, as you've got. I could have danced myself, no one could help it." (Imagine Maud Allan's fury!) "And you, Jan, your touch is like falling petals and Leo, why now you are laughing – but when you play you look as if you had all the sorrows of the world on your shoulders, but perhaps it was the accompanist [Cyril Towey], he had not quite your temperament. Well, good-bye, I must come again tomorrow though I shan't sleep tonight. I haven't been so moved for years."

Well, she did come on Saturday night and I sat with her and watched her face. You can imagine how the Boys played for her, and she sat there with all sorts of expressions flitting across her face, every now and then a little laugh (like a child's) at some beautiful passage, and then at something tender and sad the tears would come running down, and out would come the handkerchief.

"Oh, I can't bear it, I can't bear it," she would say. It was an experience that showed me more clearly than anything else the secret of her power to move an audience to laughter and tears.

I saw her only once more, just before we sailed. I took Leo around to say good-bye. She gave us each a photograph and to me her book of her life and on the photo of Beatrice she inscribed "In remembrance of Ellen Terry." She asked us all to see her in London, and to stay with her in Kent but, she said, she had a feeling she would see me again, but never "those dear boys."

Some twenty-four hours later the company launched their Australian tour in Melbourne, opening "to big business and terrific success. I have never seen a more enthusiastic audience," wrote the tour director – only to add that the next four nights brought in abysmal receipts. The sixth performance, on a Friday night, featured *The Vision of Salome* and attracted a sold-out house, with £372 in receipts. However, he wrote, "the Trio was wildly, Maud Allan only politely, applauded; she creates a feeling of disappointment every time, except for a few. . . . They say she doesn't dance." (In New Zealand she was even referred to as "Fraud Allan.")

The next engagement was in Sydney, where the opening night was again sold out and enthusiastically reviewed. Advance bookings were heavy enough to announce an extra matinee performance. But on the third evening, Maud tripped over a fault in the stage and damaged the cartilage of her right knee. The balance of the Sydney engagement was immediately cancelled and Maud was hospitalized for a week. She did not dance for another ten. Mischel Cherniavsky recalled that, while in hospital Maud was visited by Ellen Terry, in Sydney waiting for her boat to Vancouver, British Columbia. Meanwhile, the trio toured on their own and rejoined Maud in August for a month's rest at a resort hotel in Wentworth Falls, some kilometres from Sydney. The tour director recorded:

> There is a beautiful drawing room in this hotel with a fair piano and every day after tea Jan and Leo play us Beethoven Sonatas. Every morning, from 10 to 1, the trio practise, the three instruments going all at once. Maud Allan loves it as it reminds her of her student days in Berlin. After lunch Jan and Mischel play tennis on the good hard court, Leo and I walk.
>
> Maud Allan's illness has cost her about £1,000 loss since Sydney and she hasn't much left to lose and doesn't know if she can get any more money from London because of the War [which had broken out some three weeks earlier, on August 4]. She has just recovered from her illness, but she can't walk much yet and complains that the muscles around the knee are weak, but she does not feel pain in the joint itself, so we may be all right, but naturally we are very worried about her.

At the end of August the company set out for western Australia; en route, Maud visited a specialist in Melbourne, who told her the bitter truth: her right leg would never be reliable again until the cartilage was removed, but the leg might be permanently stiff. "I don't think," commented the tour director, who had accompanied her to the doctor, "she can dance much longer. She is quite out of condition, is very fat (weighs 168 lbs.) and the knee is very painful." He underestimated Maud's tenacity: she gave her last concert twenty-two years later, at the age of sixty-three.

Maud's reception in Perth was lukewarm, partly because she was understandably restrained in performing. She was a trifle less cautious with a journalist from the Perth *Daily News*. In an interview published on September 25, the day before the first of three scheduled concerts, Maud seemed to be aware that her success had been mild: "My work is something so different from what the people expect that probably, at first, they will be taken aback. They will probably look at one another and look at me and say, 'This isn't dancing.'" Thereupon she launched into her stock exposé of her method as a revival of the ancient Greeks'.

When asked her opinion of Australian audiences, she failed to hide an underlying condescension:

Australians? They love music – but they don't understand it. It would be unreasonable to expect a people engaged in the work of building up a country to become educated in the arts at the same time. But the love is there, and a better appreciation and fuller understanding is to come. Why shouldn't you people love music? With such a beautiful country and sunshine, it could hardly be suppressed.

When asked *his* view of Australian musical standards, Leo Cherniavsky gave the same reporter a statement that clearly delineates the strange composition of the company as well as his own blunt honesty:

What Australia needs is young men and women who will train students on the latest ideas of the Old World conservatoriums. If I had my way, I would bring these teachers to this country and, after a time, I would replace them with another batch of still more modern ideas, and in this way you would have the benefit of all that is the most up-to-date in musical training. You want opera houses and symphony orchestras under government or municipal control, not composed of butchers, for instance, who cut the meat in the morning and take up the fiddle in the evening, but professional artists who would mold the taste of young people.

It is true that you have orchestras in your principal cities but there is a tendency to rush things – to tackle ambitious works before mastering less intricate ones. Then too, I believe much can be done by visits of great artists. It is true that Australian audiences are most appreciative, but one sometimes wonders if they are discriminating audiences. I am afraid they are sometimes attracted by a great name rather than the message the artist has to deliver. Personally, however, we have no reason to complain, for Australian audiences have been most generous and, if my memory serves me rightly, none more than audiences in Perth.[30]

If the three Perth concerts were lacklustre, the one that followed was certainly colourful. Even the two concerts Ellen Terry attended in Auckland and the one that Dame Nellie Melba graced with her presence in Melbourne a few weeks later, however meaningful, lacked the originality of opening night in Kalgoorlie. (In her *Jottings* Maud noted "Kalgoorlie – the audience there"; she delighted in anything ridiculous.)

Originally the campsite of prospectors who in 1893 discovered rich gold deposits on the edge of the western desert, Kalgoorlie was a boomtown within two years. (Today it is a ghost town, preserved for tourists.) Thanks to a succession of remarkably far-sighted pioneers, Kalgoorlie enjoyed a decade of astonishing yet responsible growth. By 1909 it boasted an impressive town hall and a 1,200-seat theatre, both built of stone from nearby quarries. It also had a horse-racing track and a prestigious School of Mines. (Herbert Hoover studied there, while under contract to manage two nearby mines.) Kalgoorlie also boasted the only official brothels in Australia, tolerated because so many of the 25,000 residents of the town and surroundings were single males.

Kalgoorlie's cultural reputation had become great enough, between 1908 and 1914, to attract such world-famous artists as Nellie Melba, contralto Clara Butt, and Harry Lauder. During their tour of Australia in 1909, the trio had performed there, and the company expected typically appreciative audiences.

The first-night audience on October 6 was appreciative, but scarcely typical, for a good many in it were mystified miners. Inadvertently – or was this another of Howard Edie's publicity stunts? – the advertising posters had announced that on opening night Maud would feature *The Peer and the Gypsy*.[31] Mischel Cherniavsky fondly recalled that, while Maud made her graceful way through her performance of Grieg's *Peer Gynt* suite, there echoed through the theatre cries of "Open up yer legs more, darlin' " and "Get down on yer back again, Maudie," and similar urgings of a decidedly nonartistic intent.

The Kalgoorlie *Miner* euphemistically reported that "to the majority of the spectators last night Miss Allan proved novel and delightful," leaving unsaid the minority opinion. News of the true nature of Maud's performance spread quickly: "Good second night but no miners," reported the tour director.

Two weeks later the company arrived in Sydney for six concerts, to make up for those that had been cancelled after Maud's accident. The best that Sydney's *Daily Telegraph* could say of Maud was that "she charmed everyone with the culture and grace of her dancing." The trio was much better received.

During this week an action against Maud for breach of contract came to trial before a judge and a four-man jury. It was brought by William Anderson, manager/lessee of the theatre in Sydney where Maud had had her accident. Although Maud's case was watertight, the trial dragged on for three days and was reported in major Australian newspapers. The jury found in Maud's favour but awarded her only court costs.

She chose this "episode" for one of the six radio scripts she prepared but never delivered some twenty years later for the New York radio station WINS. Its main thrust was to promulgate an alleged friendship with Ellen Terry. After recalling intimate if fictitious visits to Terry in Auckland, Maud claimed that, just as the jury was returning to announce its verdict in the Anderson case:

> who should enter the Court but Ellen Terry! Quite out of breath, she said, "My dear, I have just arrived from New Zealand and hearing of the case, I have come directly from the boat. Can I help you any?" [an expression that Ellen Terry would never use – Maud should have known better than to attribute it to her]. Impatiently she waited for the Jury to return and then said, for all to hear, "Why, it is quite simple; you were injured, and the stage did have a hole large enough to cause such an accident, so why on earth are the Jury slow in deciding?" She was quite willing to gate crash the Jury room!
>
> I had to rush off to give a matinee, but Ellen Terry waited for the decision, and about an hour later I saw her and the opposing Counsel, of all people, standing in the wings, waving her hands and blowing kisses to me as I floated across the stage, to the strains of an enchanting Chopin Waltz. I didn't have to ask who had won!
>
> In summing up, the learned Judge side-stepped and congratulated me on my "tidy mind," to quote him, and the way I had helped to defend myself. He then said, "If you ever decide to give up dancing, Miss Allan, I suggest you read for the Bar. I consider you eminently suited for such a profession." I was flattered indeed.

In light of Ellen Terry's personal integrity and other evidence, Maud's account, although disarmingly narrated, is patently false. Only the compliment of the "learned Judge," although highly irregular courtroom practice, did occur. Mischel Cherniavsky remarked that Maud's lawyer was "not much good" and hers was not an easy victory, even though the evidence (which included the deposition of Sydney's most eminent doctor) was conclusively in her favour. It would seem, therefore, that the judge handed out this deserved compliment as a means of reproving Maud's lawyer without directly criticizing a fellow member of the legal fraternity. As the case was reported in many Australian newspapers and covered in considerable detail in the Sydney press, the reproof was barbed, indeed.

The successful outcome of this case in no way alleviated her financial situation. The tour director, who by this time had little use for her, recorded:

> Maud Allan is short of funds with back debts and forward expenses to pay. She said she wouldn't pay the Boys and had no money here except the £200 due from her accident insurance, and no money at home. I got wild and told her not to talk such nonsense. She said, "It's true, I have no money." "Then," I said, "Alfred Butt is a liar." It was like a blow between the eyes. She gasped, "What do you mean?" and I said, "Before I signed my contract I asked Butt if you would be able to meet your obligations, and he replied, 'She's not a rich woman, but she can sign her cheque for £25,000.' When Frank St. Leger owed Mrs. Collie a few pounds, you used to read him a lecture about the indignity of not paying his debts; when the Boys were hard pressed for money in Bombay following your accident you refused to put up another penny till you saw the colour of their money, and said that if they have not got it, they must borrow it, but you never offered to lend them a penny.[32] Now you are owing money all around – £150 to the Boys, saying you have no more because you don't like disturbing your investments!" Of course she burst into tears but later came back with a smiling face, having gone round to see her lawyer.

The fact remained that Maud was barely making £50 a week, although for the last ten weeks, thanks to some "splendid" contracts, her weekly profit had risen to about £100.

To make even small profit, she had been compelled to swallow her pride. She deeply resented being known as the Salome Dancer, preferring to dance to Chopin waltzes, which quickly bored the average audience. Yet every time she performed *The Vision*, receipts went up by 40 per cent. Thus, for the last part of her tour, *The Vision* was a regular part of the program.[33]

The road to Brisbane was littered with one-night stands in more than a dozen small towns. Business varied from an abysmal £12 to "good," thanks mainly to the trio's popularity, to judge by the tour director's report that "Maud Allan is a great failure everywhere in this country." (Two years earlier, he had managed an Australian tour for the Danish-born ballerina Adeline Genée and a corps de ballet, so he had some basis of comparison, although Genée visited only major cities and was rapturously received.)

From Brisbane, where the hot weather affected attendance although the reviews were positive, more one-night stands led to Melbourne. Everyone was getting tired and discouraged, and tensions were mounting. Leo and Maud were not on speaking terms – a fairly common occurrence – and Jan's and Mischel's patience with Maud was running thin. Maud sneered to Jan, "I suppose you are afraid your brother will marry above his rank," to which Jan shot back, "No one is too good for my brother."

The Melbourne season opened on December 26. Newspaper reviews confirm the tour director's report:

A great success in the new Tahiti Auditorium that seats 2,000 and, they say here, is the finest concert hall in the world. It was a gorgeous program – Maud Allan gave the *Peer Gynt* suite, *Blue Danube*, Chopin, with *Spring Song*, and the *Barcarolle* of Chopin as encores. The Boys played the Tchaikowsky Trio and received an ovation. Melba was present and was most complimentary. Maud Allan was to stay with her from Sunday to Saturday but got bilious and cried off. All of us spent the day with her last week. Her place is magnificent, about 30 miles from Melbourne, at Lilydale.

The importance for Maud of Melba's presence is revealed in another of her six radio scripts ("A Tribute to Nellie Melba"). It is tempting to assume she embellishes the facts to the point of fantasy; however, her account is corroborated by the tour director's comment and the review that appeared in *The Argus* of December 29: "The most enthusiastic member of the audience was, perhaps, Mme. Melba, and certainly no greater compliment can be paid to a great artist than the demonstration of affection from another."

Maud's script begins:

A pleasurable surprise awaited me on my opening night in Melbourne. The atmosphere was electric, the large concert hall was packed with an eager audience, and I wanted to give my best. But I was tired.

Just before I stepped on to the stage my tour director brought me the news that Mme. Melba was in the audience. I nearly passed out because I was so tired, I suppose. I had appeared before many great people and for Mme. Melba many times in London but Melba in her home town seemed somehow different.

All went well, and I turned at the close to bow to the Queen of Song. To my embarrassment she was leaving her box. Can you imagine my feelings? The blood rose in my cheeks and I wanted to cry, but bowing bravely to the enthusiastic audience, I left the stage. Continued applause made my return to the stage necessary, and then I saw Mme. Melba and a bevy of young ladies laden with flowers come smiling down the centre aisle. At her command I was showered with these gorgeous blossoms from the stalls, more from the corner boxes of the Circle, till the stage was a huge flower drift in which I was standing almost knee high. She did this to show her appreciation of my art.

After making a quick detour to Tasmania ("The most beautiful island I ever visited," recalled Mischel), the company headed for Adelaide. There, after giving the last of three performances on January 23, the tour ended. Maud returned to England via the United States; the trio remained in Australia to tour on their own, and the tour director took a ship for London.

Recalling in his old age the trio's more than fifteen months of touring with Maud Allan, Mischel Cherniavsky was purged of any animosity he may have felt towards her. His impression of the Maud Allan of 1913–1915 had altered little during the forty years he knew her.[34] He said only that "she was a very nice, charming woman, quite good-looking. There was something mysteriously nice about her – she had a very pleasing manner and a beautiful smile." On Maud the artist, he was more specific:

She had no technique, you understand, but enough to get by for what she was doing. Of course, we improvised a lot – we used to call her improvisations "change of program," because we never knew what step she might take, but somehow we were always able to follow her, which is why, I suppose, we toured with her successfully, all things considered. She was also an actress, you know. We saw this at the very first rehearsals we had with her. We knew she wasn't all that young, but it was marvellous how she appeared as a young girl of twenty when she was made up, with a chiffon. Her whole face lit up! She was, also, a wonderful mime – that was perhaps her greatest gift – and don't forget her hands! She knew how to express a whole range of feelings through her hands alone. They were, perhaps, the most remarkable of all. Her hands, her facial expression, her body, her musicianship, they all came together in a performance that was, somehow, intriguing. But after a while it became boring. You must remember that she was all alone – not like Isadora Duncan, who had her girls to fall back on. It was like a restaurant with a very special menu for $500 – you had to be a certain type and from a certain background to enjoy her art fully.

For Maud Allan, this tour was a gruelling experience, but she had seen the world and given pleasure to a broad audience. At forty-one years of age she had toured with artists almost a generation younger, whose outstanding trait both on and off the stage was unbounded vitality. Despite the personal tensions, despite her accidents in Bombay and Sydney, Maud had, through willpower and courage, kept up with (if not thrived on) the Cherniavskys' hectic energy. Moreover, although her reception, especially in Australasia, had scarcely advanced her reputation, she saw no reason to be discouraged, as she never doubted the significance of her art.

A few months later, having completed their tour un-encumbered by Maud Allan, the Cherniavsky brothers took a ship for Los Angeles. (En route they gave a concert in Suva, capital of the Fiji Islands. There Mischel met a young Canadian who would be his wife for more than sixty years.) One evening in Los Angeles, so his sister Manya recalled, the boys described Maud Allan's dancing for their adoring family. Mischel, with his elder sister, Claritta, disappeared from the music room and returned, Claritta's shawl draped around his shoulders and two half grapefruits somehow attached to his chest. To the accompaniment of his brothers, Mischel "demonstrated" Maud's poses and movements. In his enthusiasm, he slipped and gracelessly slid under the grand piano. No one present, said Manya, ever forgot that hilarious evening. Although Mischel never mentioned this incident to his sons, they all recall how, when looking for something, he would sometimes stoop, his eyes bulging and his arms outstretched, in clear but silent parody of Maud. Having accompanied her for well over one hundred dances, neither he nor his brothers could take Maud Allan the performer all that seriously. Yet this did not diminish either their appreciation of her profound musicality or their lifelong puzzlement by so gifted an artist and so enigmatic an individual.

Notes

1. Quoted in Max Niehaus, *Isadora Duncan: Leben und Wirkung* (Wilhemshafen: Heinrich Shofens, 1981), p. 52.

2. When Maud arrived in Bombay to start a much-delayed and much-publicized tour of India, she was interviewed by *The Advocate of India*, on November 21, 1913. Asked if she anticipated a success in India, she replied:

> I hope I shall be successful. I will give the public the best I can. I shall try to win their favour. I shall know the minute I step on the stage, because I can feel the atmosphere. But I am always very nervous; not nervous whether I shall be a success or not, but nervous that I shall not do myself justice in my own eyes. I know every time I do a wrong thing, and that worries me. Very often I have to be pushed on to the stage! I see the curtains before me and become nervous, and someone behind me has to give me a push.

3. Indianapolis *Star*, January 1910 (exact date not available).
4. In her *Jottings* Maud noted "The Zar," together with "King Edward" and "Kaiser Wilhelm." Elsewhere in these disjointed notes she wrote, "I dance for the President." This reference remains as obscure as the indication that she danced for the kaiser, although the kaiser was interested in dance. (During the first decade of this century he composed and at great expense mounted two ballet productions, both embarrassing failures. It is therefore conceivable – though it would be somewhat surprising, given his conservative tastes – that he saw Maud dance in Berlin at the start of her career.) It seems that Maud met President Woodrow Wilson in California in 1916; she may have danced for him then. There is no record of her having done so in Washington.
5. *Chicago Tribune*, January 23, 1910.
6. *New York Times*, January 21, 1910.
7. Carl van Vechten wrote of this performance:

> Yesterday's representation differed in no marked respect from that of three years ago [in Paris] and the stage setting was the same she used in London. It is true that in Paris she had caressed the severed head of St. John the Baptist. Yesterday the head itself was left to the imagination but none of the caressing was. However, New York has seen so many dances of this sort by now that there were no exclamations of shocked surprise, no one fainted, and at the end there was very little definite applause.

In her *Jottings* is the following, which may clarify van Vechten's comment on the Salome dance: "My first American tour – customs officers – the head of St. John the Baptist is smashed – a new head with the flavour of comedy."

8. *San Francisco Examiner*, March 27, 1910.

9. Acclaim for Maud's performances was not unanimous amongst San Francisco's many reviewers, although the praise the *Examiner* and the *Chronicle* lavished on her dancing overshadowed the adverse criticism. To the writer of "Town Talk" in an unidentified publication, her performance "all seemed rather absurd." A writer for *The Argonaut* compared her unfavourably with the nautch girls of the East and Hawaiian hula dancers.

10. Fourteen years earlier she had attracted the same attention in the streets of Berlin: "Sakes, how the people stared at me today, my lips and cheeks were extra rosey." (*Diary*, April 24, 1896.)

11. Perth (Australia) *Daily News*, September 28, 1914.

12. This is very possible. Maud was a lifelong friend of Henry Wood, then one of London's most interesting young conductors. He was subsequently the founder and director of the famous Albert Hall Promenade Concerts.

13. According to a notation on the cheque Maud wrote for 10,000 francs, the sterling equivalent was £395/17/7 – a substantial sum – for the first instalment on a musical score.

14. In a letter of April 1987, Etienne Amyot, who knew Maud well in the 1930s, recalled that "Maud showed me the *Khamma* manuscript. At least that is what she *said* the bulky manuscript was. She wanted me to sell it to Toscanini, whose daughter I knew! I believe she got 'advances' on it from *many*, but where it is now I have no idea."

Mr. Amyot's recollections are confirmed by the following comment from Verna Aldrich, Maud's secretary/companion during the 1930s. Writing from California on April 15, 1939, she remarked: "It was a pity the *Khamma* deal fell through, that would have straightened up your financial problems and given you something to go on with. But cheer up, dear, I think things are going to be all right soon, that is about as much as I can tell you now."

Manya Cherniavsky recalled that the manuscript had lots of

pink markings scribbled in – presumably dance notations. She recalled Maud giving it to Josef Szigeti, who during the late 1940s tried to interest New York publishers in it.

15. In the typescript of her unpublished autobiography, Doris Langley Moore, the distinguished Byron scholar and costume historian, recalled seeing Maud Allan dance in Johannesburg:

> It was when I was about nine that Maud Allan came to South Africa, an exponent equal in renown to Isadora Duncan, or rather, more famous still in English-speaking countries. My parents had admired her in London and were anxious that I should have the benefit of a display regarded as rich in cultural significance. Every seat in the theatre was booked in advance, and I was thrilled with the sense of occasion, but my love of spectacle was much disappointed by the absence of scenery. There were only grey velvet curtains between which, in the simplest of classical drapery, the dancer slipped on to the stage.

16. The trio enjoyed enormous success during their first tour of South Africa and Australia. In its January 1909 issue, the music critic of *The Triad*, New Zealand's leading arts journal, wrote, "Let me beg all my readers to hear these wonderful boys, and they will arise and call me blessed." When in 1914 he next heard them in Auckland during their tour with Maud Allan, this same critic urged the three brothers, "no longer children, yet enormously gifted," to retire for a year or so for concentrated study, advice that they would have done well to follow, had circumstances permitted. Many years later, when Jan commented that the trio had been exploited, Mischel vehemently disagreed, arguing that, to support the family in London, they were obliged to tour during these years.

17. During her first visit to the Cherniavskys' modest but spacious family home in London, Maud – sole resident of grandiose West Wing – asked how so numerous a family could live in such cramped quarters. After Maud's departure, Leo's mother remarked that if Maud spoke like that before she was Leo's wife, what would she say *after* she had become his wife? Leo took the hint.

18. The original itinerary for the first segment of this tour included Malta, Alexandra, Colombo, *Bombay*, Poona, Banga-

lore, Madras, *Calcutta*, *Allahabad*, *Lucknow*, *Agra*, *Lahore*, *Cawn-pore*, *Delhi*, Karachi, and *Rangoon*. Because of the controversy outlined in the text, time permitted concerts only in those places italicized. Some ten years later, Maud would perform in Malta and Alexandra.

19. Lord Hardinge first broached the matter in a telegram of August 14, 1913, to Lord Crewe:

> There is a matter which has been raised by the Metropolitan [head of the Anglican Church in India] of which I was quite unaware. He informed me that Maud Allan, the dancer, proposes to arrive in Calcutta next November and to dance in public. He was much concerned at the prospect. I entirely share his views, and consider that [these] dances, such as I have seen performed on one occasion at a London Music Hall, would have a most unfortunate effect in India. The Bengalis would be delighted and would crowd the theatre to witness what they regard as the public degradation of an English woman.

To this, Lord Crewe telegraphed on September 4, 1913:

> I will see what can be done to check the export of Miss Maud Allan to India. She is all that is reputable in character, it is said, but that is no excuse for her to appear before a crowd of grinning Bengalis attired in a few beads, nothing else. I am glad the Metropolitan mentioned it.

20. "We have heard that she is an American, but have not been able to verify," wrote Lord Hardinge on September 20. "If so, we could remove her under Act III of 1864 as an undesirable foreigner. The facts might be ascertained."

In his telegraphed reply of September 20, Lord Crewe pointed out that Maud was Canadian.

(Manya Cherniavsky clearly recalled Maud had – and showed her – two passports, one American, the other British, which was all Canadians could have in those days. When I asked her how this was possible, Manya threw up her hands and said, "Anything was possible with Maud."

21. I say without a shadow of a doubt that Miss Allan's visit would be beneficial neither to the position which we, as Englishmen, occupy in this country nor to the cause of moral-ity amongst the Indians which is so unmistakably struggling

forwards, but only with the greatest difficulty and in the face of tremendous hindrances. I have only just left Calcutta, where the subject was being freely discussed in the clubs, and I was assured that men of all kinds were agreed, almost to a man, in deprecating the visit. (London *Times*, October 9, 1913)

22. On October 8 the viceroy's secretary despatched a letter to the Bishop of Lahore, the Right Reverend Henry Bicker-steth Durrant (no known relation to Maud), one of the metropolitan's strongest supporters. The letter virtually orders all further protest to cease.

21. Howard Edie struck gold in these editors, both violently critical of Lord Hardinge, who, in his memoirs, *My Indian Years* (London, 1948) wrote: "As for the two principal English journals of Calcutta, the *Statesman* and the *Englishman*, from the time of the Durbar [1911] and until my departure [to the new capital of Delhi] the virulance [sic] of their attacks upon me and my administration were without precedent, one of them likening me to the infamous Suraj ud Dowleh, known as the Scourge of Bengal" (p. 68).

With diplomatic inaccuracies, he also gives the following account of the whole imbroglio:

> Public opinion was at one time torn by the news that Maud Allen [sic] was coming to dance at Calcutta. I was pressed by the European community to prevent her entry into India, but the objections of the Europeans to some of her dances as being unsuitable for Indians to see induced her to modify her clothes and dances to such an extent that when she came even the Europeans considered them dull and uninteresting. Anyhow, I gave full marks to Miss Allen for her behaviour. (p. 88)

24. The tour director's son excerpted passages from the extant letters, on condition that his father not be named.

25. Quoted in *Theatre Magazine* (Melbourne, Australia), March 2, 1914.

26. During this segment of the tour, Maud occupied a cabin alone. Alice Lonnon shared with a Mrs. Collie, the wife of a Bombay doctor who seems to have come along for the ride (and whom Maud would successfully use a few years later).

27. Maud's only documented reference was the following: "I have not danced before to the accompaniment of the Cherni-

avskys, but we had several rehearsals in London, and I am sure we will combine well. I found them very quick in understanding what I wanted done, and they appreciated my interpretations of the music. They are very clever musicians" (Interview with *The Advocate of India* [Bombay], November 21, 1913). In her *Jottings* she lists the trio twice. On the other hand the trio was very forthcoming in its public praise of Maud Allan.

28. While en route to India on the ss *Arabia*, the tour director wrote to his wife: "I listened to a long and interesting conversation last night between Leo and Ramsay MacDonald [a future prime minister of England] who is on board, on the subject of the Jews in Russia. Ramsay MacDonald is one of the Commission the Government is sending out to inquire into matters they don't understand in India." (This was the commission's second visit; they were in Bombay in December 1912, when the Cherniavskys opened their first tour of India. Perhaps Ramsay MacDonald had met the trio at that time.)

In later years, Manya Cherniavsky maintained that Maud was fundamentally anti-Semitic.

29. *New Zealand Star* (Auckland), June 1, 1914.

30. At the time, Leo was planning to open a music conservatory in Sydney. It would have been an innovative operation, to say the least.

31. To publicize Maud's visit, Howard Edie set all the schoolchildren throughout Australasia to writing essays on classical dancing for prizes of books. He also arranged for an expensive reception in Melbourne, for which Maud received the bill some weeks later. Thinking the bill a big joke, she prepared a radio script ("An Amusing Incident") about it. The joke, of course, was on her.

32. In London, while negotiating tour managements with Maud, Leo remarked to the tour director that one had to employ "bluff." He added, "Do you think Maud Allan would have agreed to the partnership if she knew we had only £700?" (For Mrs. Collie, see fn. 26)

33. Mischel Cherniavsky did not comment – perhaps deliberately so – on his view of the *Vision of Salome* score arranged for the trio. Perhaps it was this arrangement that made him insist that Maud's dancing was more fit for the vaudeville than the concert stage.

34. These conversations occurred before the tour director's letters came to light, and therefore lacked the direction those letters would have given our discussions.

7

The Years of Decline: 1915–1930

PON HER ARRIVAL in California in February 1915, Maud lived for about a year with her parents in a bungalow on Lucille Avenue, in a seedier part of Hollywood. During the summer she played the lead role, which featured excerpts from three dances (including *The Vision of Salome*), in a silent movie titled *The Rugmaker's Daughter*, no copy of which has, much to the chagrin of dance historians, been found. To judge by the reviews, this "romance" had few redeeming features: one reviewer complained that it was "too much of a melodrama to be a good burlesque, too much of a burlesque to be any sort of drama." In all likelihood Maud agreed with the critical consensus: in later years she rarely referred to the venture.

En route to London in the spring of 1916, she had an emergency appendectomy in New York. According to press reports, she nearly died. This was, of course, the "ptomaine poisoning" of her 1910 tour of the United States, which had intermittently flared up during her tour with the Cherniavsky Trio, as the tour director's correspondence attests. Her parents joined her in New York during her convalescence. The family posed for a photograph in Central Park: Isabella

Durrant has taken care to stand on the curb, with the result that she physically dominates her famous daughter.

Before sailing for London, Maud opened a concert agency, primarily designed to manage (possibly because no one else would) her second tour of North America. (Maud later indicated that, in a moment of passion, Sol Hurok had offered to manage this tour, but got cold feet.) This tour was scheduled to start in September and was to feature Debussy's *Khamma* ballet score. She was determined to conquer American dance critics and the American public, despite her failure in 1910, as she had conquered England in 1908. From London she organized an orchestra of forty, engaged conductor Ernst Bloch, who was impatient to get away from war-isolated Switzerland, and selected a supporting cast of eight dancers and extras.

This tour started and ended badly. For whatever reason, and probably at the last moment, Maud did not use the *Khamma* score. She replaced it with *Nair the Slave*, a full-length "pantomime opera" by two minor Italian musicians. (She examined the completed score for the first time only when she arrived in New York.) She declared: "This dance is so new and appealing that I could not resist the temptation to let the public see it at once." With barely two weeks before her opening performance, she rehearsed her neophyte company, with Stafford Pemberton (whose brief dance career seems to have ended with this production) taking the male lead.[1] The work was generally dismissed as a pale pastiche of *Sheherazade*, which the Diaghilev Company had presented with such success a few months earlier. Indeed, she narrowly escaped wholesale ridicule: this work was originally titled *Ham*. "I have heard of lassies being enslaved by booze, dope, horrid men and recalcitrant ideas, but never, never before by ham," observed *Variety* in its ongoing campaign to find fault with anything to do with Maud.

Proclaiming herself – for the first time – a "symphonic dancer," Maud started her tour in Albany, New York, on

September 28. "Her *Peer Gynt* number had charm; the Strauss [*Blue Danube*] provided opportunity for some charming work, and in her oriental number Miss Allan is alluring," wrote the local critic. Such unenthusiastic comments were among the kinder she received from the American press. Ernst Bloch was immediately recognized as a fine accompanist, conductor, and composer. (In addition to accompanying Maud, he provided orchestral interludes, on occasion his own compositions.)

From Albany the company ventured into Canada, performing in Ottawa, Montreal, and Toronto. In Ottawa, Maud lunched with the governor general, the Duke of Connaught, whom she had met in London; in Montreal she was appraised by S. Morgan Powell, the foremost Canadian reviewer of the time, who discussed her art and her three performances with great perception:

> The art of Maud Allan is something that cannot be easily expressed in terms of art. It eludes definition because it is largely evanescent. . . .It seems as if she were the disembodied spirit of poetry, the essence of poetry expressed through the medium of perfect grace in motion, in poise, in repose. For this graceful woman can convey to you as much in a moment of absolute relaxation, absolute immobility, as she can in a moment of supreme intoxication of passion.
>
> It is an artless art that directs her dancing, for you never lose the perfect illusion of the dramatic or poetic moment. She never suggests Maud Allan acting a part in a set scene. She is the part: she lives the role, and her audience enjoys the completeness of her visualization the more because there is never any suggestion of artificiality about it.[2]

In Toronto, she ran into unnerving difficulties:

> "I simply won't go on," [she told the Toronto *Telegram*] "unless the stage is properly arranged." The tone was indignant and we gasped to think of the sensation which would be created out there in the audience if things were not re-arranged and Maud should refuse to appear.

"I expect I sound pretty cross," she said, "but everything was wrong. The lights were wrong – the whole arrangement was wrong, and it ruined the effect. Why," she went on, "in that last scene every bit of the scenery is of exquisite silk, but it may as well have been of canvas, the lights were so bad. And look at this exquisite material," holding up some of her silver gauze and jewelled draperies, "it didn't show at all. They might have been ANYTHING."[3]

From Toronto, a handful of one-night stands brought the company to five performances in New York City. The reviews ranged from patronizing to rude. The consensus was that if there were a redeeming feature to the program, it was the scenic setting of *Nair the Slave*; if there were a praiseworthy performance, it was the orchestra's under Ernst Bloch's fine direction.

The transcontinental tour ran out of funds in Buffalo and closed at the end of November. The company trekked back to New York and the seedy Palace Theatre, home of vaudeville in a city where vaudeville lacked the prestige it enjoyed in London. Both Maud and the company were reviewed with cold civility. She remained in New York over the winter, organizing an abortive conservatorium of dancing and music. In April of 1917, just as she was about to leave for London, she learned that her father – or, as she oddly identified his photograph many years later to Manya Cherniavsky, "the husband of my mother" and "a man of few words" – was dying in Los Angeles. She rushed back to see him on his deathbed. At the same time, so it was reported, her mother fell "critically ill." She survived, though, for about another twelve years.

While Maud was in Toronto, she issued a statement "definitely" denying any plan that she and Leo Cherniavsky were about to marry – as had been reported in both the North American and London press. (Manya later mentioned that their impending marriage was announced in London when she was at King's House School, which she left in 1917. At least one London paper had scathingly referred to

Leo as "Mr. Maud.")[4] These reports were as conflicting as they were erroneous, although there is no doubt that at one time Leo definitely wanted to marry her. Doris Langley Moore recalled Leo telling her that when he mentioned this intention to his father, old Mr. Cherniavsky merely remarked that Leo surely knew he would not be the only man she had lived with. To this Leo replied that he "would rather be the last and not the first than the first and not the last." Though he certainly was not the last person to live with her, he was certainly the first to refuse to marry her, just as he remained the only man Maud wanted to marry.

By the winter of 1917, Maud was back in London, and in November appeared for a short season at St. Martin's Theatre with a solo pianist and a "little symphony." She was neither featured nor greatly praised. However, her next appearance on the London stage attracted far more attention than anyone expected or Maud intended: she accepted the lead role in Oscar Wilde's *Salome*.

She was offered this role by J.T. Grein, drama critic for the reputable *Sunday Times*. Grein, one of Maud's foremost admirers in 1908, was the driving force behind the Independent Theatre Society. This group, founded in 1891 to present the London premiere of Henrik Ibsen's daring *Ghosts*, specialized in modern and controversial plays. As they were presented before private audiences, they were exempt from the Lord Chamberlain's censorship.

Wilde's *Salome* suited the society particularly well. Written at the height of the Decadent movement by the most publicly disgraced Decadent, *Salome* had never been performed publicly in England – as much because it dealt with a biblical character as because its author was Oscar Wilde.[5] Private performances by such stage societies were common enough in London, but the decision to produce *Salome* in the spring of 1918 was politically unwise. In France, the Allies appeared in danger of defeat. French army units were in open mutiny, and charges of treason, both within and outside the army, were rampant.

In England, politicians refrained from publicly blaming

one another, but as Maud would discover, there was no lack
of political intrigue. Among the backbenchers in the British
House of Commons was Noel Pemberton-Billing, elected in
1916 on a platform of a vigorous air policy. (His views on a
viable Air Force were as advanced as his "morality" was
reactionary.)[6]

He was feared by cabinet members for his persistent
questions on a wide range of politically sensitive matters,
particularly corruption, real or perceived. He aired many
of these concerns in his weekly political broadsheet, *The
Vigilante*. The January 29, 1918 issue asserted that one reason
why things were not going well for the Allies was that many
of England's leaders were under threat of blackmail. The
article stated that Prince William of Wied, the Allies'
puppet King of Albania, had a "black book" detailing the
depravities of some 47,000 English persons of both sexes.
These ranged from the wives of cabinet ministers (a veiled
reference to Margot Asquith; Herbert Asquith was by this
time leader of the Opposition) to the men in the Royal Navy.
The latter allegedly frequented the dives of major seaports
where enemy spies, by means of illicit sexual favours,
extracted information about ships' movements. (This particular claim was never mentioned by the press during the
legal proceedings that followed.) This fantastic story was
intended to create a political crisis, subtly based on the
controversial reputation of Margot Asquith, whom Pemberton-Billing and his sympathizers hated. All they required
was a catalyst.

In February 1918, Grein announced the proposed production of *Salome*, with Maud in the title role. George Relph,
who later enjoyed a distinguished career in London's West
End, would take the part of Herod; British composer Gran-
ville Bantock would provide the music for Salome's dances.
At least one performance, which was briefly reviewed in the
Times, was given in mid-April at the Royal Court Theatre.

Amongst those who noticed this announcement was the
popular novelist Marie Corelli, whose *Ardath* Theo had
urged Maud to read some twenty years earlier.[7] Marie

Corelli sent the announcement to Pemberton-Billing, suggesting that "it would be well to secure the list of subscribers to this new 'upholding' of the Wilde 'cult' among 'the 47,000,'" adding: "Why 'private' performances?"

Within a week of Grein's announcement, Captain Harold Spencer, one of Pemberton-Billing's colleagues and author of the Black Book story, commented in *The Vigilante* of February 16. Under the heading "The Cult of the Clitoris," he remarked that "to be a member of Maud Allan's performance in Oscar Wilde's *Salome*, one has to apply to a Miss Valetta of 9 Duke Street, Adelphi, W.C. If Scotland Yard were to seize the list I have no doubt they would secure the names of several thousands of the first 47,000."

The selection of Maud as the target was a brilliant stroke. Through *Salome*, she had identified herself with Oscar Wilde, whom she had visited in Paris shortly before his death. Wilde's reputation provided crucial emotional validity to the wild innuendo of *The Vigilante*. Second, Maud had been the model for *Maudie*, "a notorious erotic frolic of the Edwardian era" that surely would have been known to Pemberton-Billing or his supporters. Third, no matter how offensive the insult to Maud's reputation, the profession on which that reputation rested had yet to gain respectability. If only through guilt by association, she was less respectable for being a dancer, and hence the more vulnerable. (Mata Hari had been executed as a spy.) Finally, Maud was a publicly recognized friend of Margot Asquith, who rarely restrained her behaviour and who had become the target of a smut campaign suggesting that she and her circle were sympathetic to Germany.[8]

In previous issues of *The Vigilante*, deliberately libellous statements against many public figures had appeared, but all had been studiously ignored. Maud, though, impulsively sued for criminal libel. For Pemberton-Billing her decision was surely welcome, as it allowed him to advance his political aims and personal biases. Maud was undoubtedly resolved to defend and protect the family name; after all, for a Durrant, "A Dishonouring Stain Is Worse than Death." Also figuring in her decision would have been her love/hate relationship with the law; her thirst for excitement, and possibly her delusion that, by launching and winning the case, she would once again enjoy public acclaim. The decision proved catastrophic.

The proceedings, which started in Magistrates' Court on April 6, attracted immediate attention. *The World* described the next day how

> in a downpour of rain a queue some fifty yards long formed outside the Bow Street Police Court. The people composing it were mainly associated with the theatrical profession, and they were eager to hear exactly what it was that Miss Maud Allan and Mr. Grein alleged against Pemberton-Billing, whom they had summoned on a charge of criminal libel; Miss Allan, wearing a black fur cape with spangles on the bodice, sat with friends in the front row of seats usually reserved for witnesses. Mr. Grein was at the solicitor's table, where Mr. Billing had also seated himself.[9]

As her counsel, Maud retained W.E. Hume Williams and Travers Humphreys, both of whom went on to distinguished careers. The trial date was set for May 30 at the Number 1 Court of the Old Bailey; the proceedings were presided over by Judge Darling, the incarnation of Victorian prudery, who little understood much of the salacious evidence presented. The trial lasted five days – an excessive length of time for a case of this sort. It was reported in detail by all the London press, from the most sophisticated, such as the *Times*, to the most sensational tabloids.

The allegations of illicit sex, the crude hints of political intrigue, the questionable sanity of one witness, the apparent perjury of at least one other, and the testimony of that old roué Lord Alfred Douglas provided a welcome respite from the tensions regarding the outcome of the war, which so agonizingly hung in the balance.

Nor has the trial lost its fascination.[10] One book, two

plays, and various radio and television programs are based on the case, and it has been regularly included in anthologies of scandalous trials, so richly entertaining is it.[11]

In none of these treatments is Maud Allan given more than a minor role. Not only has she fallen into obscurity, but the entertainment lay elsewhere: in the posturing of Pemberton-Billing, who conducted his own case; in the raucous behaviour and irrelevant testimony of his principal witnesses; and in the unsubtle references to political intrigue that gave the whole affair far more significance than it deserved.

The comic relief lay chiefly in Judge Darling as he attempted with prurient rectitude to define for the jury sexual practices he did not understand. In his charge to the jury, for example, he defined sadism as "passions exercised over dead bodies," and fetishism as "when you have a longing to possess a shoe, a glove, or a flower or a bit of hair that belonged to a woman you love, and if you desire it greatly, why, then, that is fetishism."

In its article on Darling's otherwise distinguished career (he later became Lord Chief Justice), the *Dictionary of National Biography* refers to his conduct of the case as "a shocking example" that went far to lower the status of the bench.   Darling accepted the prevailing view of the time, referring to Oscar Wilde as "a great artist, possibly, but certainly a great beast, there is no doubt about that."[12]

If for others the affair was amusing, for Maud Allan it was traumatic. Many years later she spoke of Pemberton-Billing as "the worst man that ever was." The proceedings turned into a nightmare when Pemberton-Billing – with Judge Darling's permission – introduced the irrelevant matter of Theo's trial and execution, on the astonishing premise that the vices that led to Theo's crime were hereditary. He sadistically led Maud through Theo's history and then discussed with her various sexual "perversions," each of which he claimed to find in *Salome*.

Equally painful was the testimony of Captain Spencer,

who claimed that when he was a child Theo's case was "one of the dreadful tales they used to frighten us with in Canada," although Spencer said he was born on the American side of the Great Lakes. He remarked, under oath, "I regard Miss Allan as a very unfortunate hereditary degenerate." When examined at great length about the genesis and contents of the "black book" that he claimed to have studied in Prince William's Palace in Durazzo, Albania, Captain Spencer's testimony moved from viciousness through blatant lies to the colourfully absurd.

Judge Darling made no serious attempt to control this testimony. Nor did he attempt to control such other defence witnesses as Lord Alfred Douglas, only too happy to denounce Oscar Wilde and, perhaps, to repay Maud for the slap in the face at the garden party some ten years earlier. Defining Wilde as "the greatest force for evil that has appeared in Europe during the last 350 years [presumably a fanatic's reference to leaders of the Protestant Reformation], the agent of the Devil in every possible way," Douglas capitalized on his "expertise" as translator of *Salome*. The lengthy discussion of the play by Douglas and Pemberton-Billing was little more than the self-righteous philistine and the self-serving reprobate cooing a mutual horror of Oscar Wilde and his works.

The closing addresses of Billing and of Hume Williams were exactly what one would expect. The former's was aggressive, irrelevant, and effective; the latter's was respectable but ponderous. In his charge to the jury, Darling meandered as in a London fog, further distorting the thrust of the issue. This is scarcely surprising: the testimony he had heard clearly bothered him, Pemberton-Billing's bullying tactics had bewildered him, and Maud Allan had certainly not bewitched him. It would have taken a far firmer and braver judge to withstand Pemberton-Billing and the political pressures that pervaded the affair.

The jury found the defendant not guilty. Pemberton-Billing emerged from the Central Criminal Court a popular hero; Maud left by a side door, as befits one who had failed to disprove that she was a "lewd, unchaste, and immoral woman."

One of Maud Allan's most remarkable traits was to mask over any personal bitterness she felt about the various misfortunes of her long life, beginning with Theo's tragedy. Particularly striking in this regard is her account of the Pemberton-Billing case in her *Memoirs*, serialized in the San Francisco *Call and Post* in 1921. Of the article in *The Vigilante* that sparked the action, she wrote: "It contained an outrageous attack upon my character, and in a very peculiar way introduced the names of people who were very high in the land. The whole was a subtle suggestion that anti-British influences had surrounded the wife of the [former] Prime Minister." Having admitted that "never in my whole life have I spent such a hellish time as I did during those slow, dragging hours at the Old Bailey," she evokes the atmosphere in the court:

> The Court was packed to suffocation and it was said that everybody who was anybody in London had managed, by hook or by crook, to get inside the trial room. Besides the occupation of every seat, a number of persons jammed themselves around the walls of the Court, making the atmosphere unbearable and trying the temper of everyone engaged in the case.
>
> Right from the start there was an atmosphere of nervous tension that affected the Judge and perhaps the Counsel as well, for it is admitted that while Justice Darling is an excellent judge, he did not shine on this occasion. Indeed, after the verdict was given the comments of the leading London newspapers were exceedingly severe, containing such sentences as "a weak judge," "the Judge seemed to have completely lost his head," "the judge seemed cowed by the blustering vehemence of Mr. Billing" and so on.

Maud's surprisingly balanced account of the proceedings summarizes the "fantastical" story of the "black book." She also claims that at the close Judge Darling declared "Miss

Allan leaves this court without a stain upon her character."
However well intentioned, this remark – if, in fact, it was
ever made – proved wide of the mark.

Not surprisingly, Maud does not mention the cruellest
element of the trial – the long discussion in open court of
her family's dishonouring stain. Her failure to disclose this
past to her lawyers was her greatest blunder. Had she done
so, or had they been less taken in by her charm and more
aware of her private life and the rumours that swirled
around it, they surely would have advised against taking
legal action. As things turned out, there was little they could
do against Pemberton-Billing, who both conducted his own
defence (allegedly with expert advice from a lawyer whose
identity remains unknown) and gave direction to the entire
case.

The immediate outcome of the debacle was that Maud
Allan was shunned by her public and by theatre managers,
who bluntly advised her not to appear on any London stage.
She still had "important" acquaintances, but a number at
least lacked the stamp of respectability and social cachet of
her earlier associates. Yet the loss of other socially prominent
friends was not a great one, for she certainly felt more at
home culturally with creative artists of all kinds, who dismissed the "black book" affair as an aberration of British
justice rather than a reflection upon Maud the artist or
hostess.[13]

One of her staunchest friends at this time was Ferruccio
Busoni, who stayed with her during one of his visits to
London, no doubt to help her through the traumas of the
affair. While he was there, Bernard Shaw visited West
Wing one day for afternoon tea. After Shaw's departure,
Maud recalled in later years, she and Busoni sat on the
staircase, laughing heartily at their visitor's inability to stop
talking and at his attempt to impress them with his musical
knowledge.[14]

Shortly thereafter, Maud went to visit her mother in
California, where, presumably, she wrote the *Memoirs* for
the San Francisco *Call and Post*. Titled "How I Startled the

World," these *Memoirs* are ambiguous and chronologically and factually distorted. The bulk of the twenty-four instalments are tasteless fantasy, clearly designed to appeal to her readers' prurient interest in hints of sexual propositions from the exceedingly rich (for example, Indian princes) and the socially prominent (such as King Leopold I of Belgium, who, she implies, fell in love with her and attended all her recitals in Brussels). While these can be dismissed out of hand, on some matters – witness her account of the "black book" trial proceedings – she seems reliable enough. Those instalments concerning her plan to become an actress, probably developed following her return from America, are of real interest:

> I had for some years had a very strong desire to act upon the legitimate stage. In this aspiration I was very much encouraged by the late Laurence Irving [son of the great actor Sir Henry Irving], one of my truest friends and whose untimely death was a very great grief to me.
>
> I discussed with him many times my keen desire to appear in the legitimate [theatre], and at length it was arranged that we should take what was then called the Independent Theatre in London for a short season of Shakespearean plays, in which I would take the part of the heroines. We went over the plans in fullest detail, and I began to study the parts allotted to me. Everything seemed very promising, and I was keenly interested in making the project a real success.

This project was to begin after Laurence Irving's return from a North American engagement and Maud's tour with the Cherniavsky Trio. However, in May 1914, while Maud was in New Zealand, Laurence Irving and his wife boarded the ss *Empress of Ireland* en route to Canada. (Their tour was to open in Montreal.) Just outside the Gulf of St. Lawrence the ship struck an iceberg and sank within minutes. All but a handful of the 400 passengers drowned in the icy waters.[15]

Of all Maud's professional mishaps, this was among the more devastating. Without doubt she had great potential as an actress, provided she could rid herself of her penchant for the melodramatic and her adulation of the rather outdated acting style of Eleonora Duse. That Laurence Irving seems to have committed himself to giving Maud leading roles is evidence of her potential, as his own wife was an aspiring actress.

Although no record of Irving's plans for Maud exists other than in these *Memoirs*, Maud's account does seem plausible. In all likelihood W.L. Courtney – who had actively worked on the scenario for *Khamma* and had been one of Maud's most enthusiastic critics in London – introduced her to Laurence Irving. Courtney had been Laurence's older brother Henry's tutor in Philosophy at Oxford and may have recognized in Maud a kindred spirit for his protégé. Whether Courtney was aware of Maud's familiarity with such matters is unknown, but he must have recognized her fascination with the morbid. One of Laurence Irving's interests was the criminal mind; he wrote extensively on the subject.[16] Early in his career the aspiring actor had played *Markheim*, adapted by Courtney from Robert Louis Stevenson. It was a study in the remorse of an educated man who committed a criminal act for love of money.

(Coincidentally Theo, in an interview with the *San Francisco Chronicle* on December 23, 1895, about six weeks after his conviction for murder, remarked:

> I have been reading these last few days Robert Louis Stevenson and have just finished *A Close Call*. In many ways it reminds me of my own case. Stevenson says the case is an authentic one, as it is a matter of record. It refers to well known cases of innocent men facing the death penalty. It refers here particularly to the one of Richard Wagner of Maine, whose unjust death was followed by repealing of the law for capital punishment.)[17]

Recuperated from the trauma of the "black book" affair, in the spring of 1920 Maud set out for a tour of South America with her mother in tow and in pursuit of Leo Cherniavsky, who was touring Argentina with his brothers.

Very little is known of this foray: in her *Jottings* she noted "Revolution in Chile 1921"; and Mischel Cherniavsky described Maud's series of concerts in Buenos Aires in the summer of 1920 as "so-so." On board ship on her return journey was Artur Rubinstein. In his autobiography he mentions Maud as a fellow passenger, although he neglects to mention that upon boarding the ship presents from admirers – a huge basket of flowers for Maud and a case of champagne for him – awaited them. Nor does he relate, as Maud later told Manya Cherniavsky, that during the trip he played poker with fellow passengers, including an English aristocrat whom he caught cheating.

Shortly after her arrival in London, Maud appeared at the London Coliseum. She shared the program with Tamara Karsavina, star of the Diaghilev Ballet, and with the great French clown Grock. The London *Times* found her tiresome, and, compared her with Karsavina, "the true comedian of the ballet," she was "the tragedian." Given that the audience had had its fill of tragedy during the war, this was small recommendation.

This reception did not discourage her from continuing her career. Leo Cherniavsky recommended Doris Langley Moore to assist her. A few years earlier Moore had worked diligently for the trio as their advance manager in England; in later years she was a novelist, a biographer (notably of Lord Byron), and a distinguished historian of costume whose expertise enhanced many theatrical and film productions.

In her typescript autobiography, she wrote of her early days in Maud's employ:

When there was nothing specific to attend to, I sat in a very quiet grey room [in West Wing] upstairs, sorting out newspaper clippings and feeling so remote from the flow of human affairs that I looked forward to the butler bringing me a tray of tea as a rousing event, though he was the most taciturn of men. When Miss Allan went away to give performances in the West of England, the silence and the solitude were oppressive beyond words.

All reference to crime and punishment was taboo in her presence, and we made swift diversion when strangers innocently touched upon murder cases prominent in the newspapers. An atmosphere of extreme decorum surrounded her, the watchful decorum of one who is conscious of things to be lived down. Her face was still pretty and her smile a charming one, which showed her dimples and her good teeth. She was polite and wholly indifferent to me.

In the spring of 1923, before Doris had much time to wonder if her services might still be needed, she was offered the assignment of advance manager for a tour of Egypt by Maud and Leo and Mischel Cherniavsky, accompanied by Mischel's wife, Mary. (Jan was in Vancouver, awaiting the birth of his first child. His place was less than successfully taken by a pianist from London.) "It would be my task," wrote Doris, "to handle all publicity, ensure the transport of costumes and effects, verify facilities for correct stage lighting, supervise the printing of programs and the hanging of posters and a dozen other duties, not omitting contact with local notabilities." She was twenty-one years old.

En route to Cairo, she stopped off in Gibraltar to prepare for a concert by Maud and her colleagues. According to Mischel, the arrangements went badly awry; when they arrived in Gibraltar, they discovered the concert had been thoroughly advertised – but the theatre had not been booked! Nevertheless, the engagement was fulfilled, after an exhausting round of negotiations, and they sailed on to Cairo. Doris Langley Moore's recollection of the opening concert there provides a most accurate picture of Maud Allan's performances:

> It was the very end of the season and the overwhelming heat did nothing to fill up the empty spaces on the theatre plan of the Kursaal booking office. The opening concert was well attended, but the success modest. I had not seen Maud Allan dance since my schooldays in Johannesburg and I watched her with a reluctantly critical eye. That she had grace, vigour and musical sensitivity no one could deny.

Two tributes I must pay Maud Allan. She really had the art, which Ruth Draper perfected, of making one forget the stage was empty of anyone or anything but herself.[18] When she stooped to gather flowers, one took it for granted that they were there, and when she held out her arms towards a branch of blossom [in the *Spring Song* of Mendelssohn] it hardly seemed invisible. She was no longer doing her *Salome* fantasy, but she had other items in her repertoire which could hold the most blasé audiences. Her rendering of Sibelius' *Valse Triste* could give me a frisson even when seen frequently from the wings. In this she appeared as a dying woman who hears in the distance music which brings back the joy and sorrow of her life. She is drawn by it to get up from her couch, and although I am sure there was no couch on the stage, I have always seen Maud in my mind's eye slowly rising from it. She begins to waltz with blind and trance-like movements which become more and more febrile until they end in the throes of death. Mischel Cherniavsky's wife, Mary, said she always half believed that Maud would really fall dead in that dance.

Doris went on to Alexandria, where she made arrangements for three concerts (more successful than those in Cairo). From there she moved on to Malta to set up concert dates there and await the artists' arrival. This assignment proved a baptism by fire:

I have never been in an environment where outmoded rules of morality were so rigorously enforced as in that island in the early 1920s. Bare legs, even male, were not to be seen on the stage and when an Italian opera company played *Lucia di Lammermoor* at the Teatro Reale, all the kilted Scotsmen were compelled to wear bright pink tights.

The question of allowing a dancer to present herself bare legged at the knees was a matter of consternation, but with the patronage of the Governor General and several other influential people, I felt I could count on the objections being overcome as they had been, elsewhere, a long time ago. But I had a lot of bother about the posters. These were large and represented Maud Allan doing one of her dainty tripping poses in a modest opaque dress with a skirt several inches below the knees revealing bare legs. It had been designed in Maud Allan's palmy days and was every Edwardian's idea of a nymph at play. As fast as these posters went up, I was told they had to come down. Some were torn down which, as they were very expensive, was a worry to me. I had to guarantee that, for every performance, one box would be reserved for the Police and the censor.

Mischel recalled sitting next to the censor during rehearsals (at first Maud had refused to perform at all) after she had been advised not to lift her legs too high for fear of offending the official. (Leo suggested she wear a pair of his trousers!)

Throughout the tour Maud was distraught over Leo's unwillingness to reanimate their liaison. Her misery provided Doris Langley Moore with a rare moment of personal contact. It was in Malta, Moore recalls, that:

I used to hear her crying at night, her bedroom being directly above mine. One evening, when I was reading an autobiographical novel by Strindberg, whom I found depressing enough without the accompaniment of sobs, I determined to risk her displeasure by offering what comfort I could – a daring venture because, as I have said, I never was intimate with her. I went upstairs and she received me with no disguise of her grief, indeed with such candour that I was able to clear away her idea I had no idea she entertained – that I might have been the cause of Leo's lessening attachment. My reassurances were sincere, for although I felt gratitude and friendship for Leo, and he was cordial and considerate to me, there was not the least sentiment between us.

Upon her return to London, Maud procured for the week of September 25 an engagement at the Alhambra Theatre. The reviews were, to say the least, cool. The *Times* condescended to one brief sentence; but *The Encore*, a theatrical publication of mercifully small circulation, was cruel: "Maud Allan's physical development does not add to the dignity of her prancing." If Maud could not take the hint, booking agents did, and she never again danced in London.

Unable or unwilling to admit that her career was at an end, Maud sent Doris Langley Moore to the Continent to organize concerts in Brussels, Paris, and Lyon. In Brussels, the concert was under the patronage of the British ambassador; in Paris (as a benefit concert for a charity) by *la crème de la crème* of Parisian Society. In the audience at Lyon was the mayor of that city, Edouard Herriot, future prime minister and revered elder statesman of France.[19] Shortly after completing this assignment, Doris left Maud's employ and met her again only on one or two casual occasions.

Maud then returned to the United States. On November 10, 1925, she danced on the stage of the New York Metropolitan Opera House, from which she had been barred from performing in 1910. Attitudes had greatly changed, as had Maud's reputation. Presenting herself as a "mimeodramatic" dancer, she shared the evening with the Stony Plain Vocal Ensemble, a group of vocalists sponsored by socially prominent New Yorkers. (This concert, publicized as the first in an extensive itinerary, was the ensemble's first and last performance.)

Maud then went on to California, where in March she appeared with the Los Angeles Philharmonic and, in August, became the first noninstrumentalist to perform at the recently opened Hollywood Bowl.[20] Finally, in June 1927 she procured a one-week engagement at a San Francisco Vaudeville Theatre. The California press seems to have ignored all these appearances.

Maud returned to London, accompanied by her mother, whose health was in serious decline. By selling the last of her jewellery, Maud told Manya Cherniavsky years later, she was able to provide Isabella with full-time nursing attendance and the care of prestigious Harley Street specialists. Under their care, Mrs. Durrant lingered for two years or more.

Although preoccupied with her mother's declining condition, Maud hungered for the stage. In 1932 she snacked on a minor part, that of the Mother Superior in Max Reinhardt's lavish production of *The Miracle*, starring Diana Cooper, Leonard Massine, and the Austrian-born actress/dancer Tilly Losch. To judge by her *Jottings*, mingling once again with distinguished persons of the theatre thrilled Maud: "*Miracle* days – Lady Diana, Tilly Losch, Reinhardt, C.B. Cochran [London's leading theatre agent of the day]."

This engagement led to her final appearance on the English stage. "Coming out of retirement," as the advance publicity of the Manchester *Guardian* put it, she appeared in *The Barker*, a play about an American circus troupe. (It had enjoyed considerable success on Broadway in 1927 and, a year later, was well received in London's West End starring Claudette Colbert and her husband, Norman Foster.) Maud received star billing for her role as a Hawaiian dancer. The production ran for one week at Manchester's Repertory Theatre.

The critical reception was tepid. On September 11 the *Guardian* commented that "the little we see of Maud Allan's dancing reminds us certainly of her skill in that art, as does her elocution, that acting and dancing are rarely combined in one personality." The Manchester *Evening Chronicle*, perhaps hinting at a melodramatic element in Maud's performance, remarked that "she shone in the tenser moments of the play." Whatever hopes she may have had of this acting opportunity came to nothing; this was the swan song of a career in England that had started with such eclat twenty-five years earlier.

It was probably during this period that Maud formally established the West Wing School of Dance – perhaps in part as a means of keeping herself occupied while her mother's health declined. Very little is known of this project. Its failure was regrettable, for Maud was indisputably a gifted teacher. Moreover, her professed motives in establishing the school were socially benevolent and, from her viewpoint, artistically legitimate. Besides, with its elegant Music Room

fitted with the costly floor-to-ceiling mirrors, and its magnificent lawn and gardens, West Wing was an ideal locale
for such a school.[21] However, her art was unteachable to
anyone not in complete empathy with her aspirations.

In an interview the *New York Times* published in September 1935, Maud outlined the aims and curriculum of the
operation. Whether the curriculum was seriously pursued
is open to question, as it is difficult to suppose she would
promote ballet, for which she had so obvious a disdain.
Whether her interviewer took her account all that seriously
is likewise doubtful:

> She tries to prepare children from the London slums who
> show an aptitude for dancing, to make a career of it in the
> most practical way. Though she continues with the teaching
> of her artist pupils in her own method of dancing, these
> youngsters are taught in addition ballet and tap, so that they
> can have some hope of earning a living in some choreo-
> graphic branch of the theatre. They are also taught diction,
> and in her drawing room they are allowed to get an insight
> into how people behave who have not been handicapped by
> a background of poverty.[22]

There may well have been a financial motive for this
operation. Margot Asquith had decided to stop paying the
expensive leasehold on West Wing. Unwilling to live elsewhere, Maud may have visualized the school as a source of
funds. She could not expect "slum" children to pay fees and
her own fortune was depleted; however, there was no
reason why she might not seek financial support for so
benevolent an operation from her rich friends and acquaintances. Maud had on at least one occasion already resorted
to a stratagem that was, to say the least, opportunistic.[23] In
the years ahead she would repeat this manipulative practice
with increasing frequency and characteristic yet progres-
sively desperate determination.

During their travels with her, the Cherniavsky brothers
had become accustomed to Maud's way with money. It

became a standing joke that she would open her purse in their presence only to prove it was empty, even when she had no serious financial worries. Some fifteen years later, when Mischel and family were living close to Maud's grand quarters, the joke got out of hand. On several occasions Mischel was called upon to settle West Wing's utilities bill and once he was asked to lend £100 for some alleged emergency. Another time, Mischel, Mary, and Mary's mother, on a visit from Vancouver, dined at West Wing. A few days later the overseas visitor invited Maud to tea at her hotel. Maud arrived punctually, carrying a huge basket of freshly cut flowers from her magnificent garden. With truly theatrical flourishes (so Mary Cherniavsky's youngest sister recently recalled) Maud presented these flowers to her hostess from whom, at what she unsuccessfully calculated to be an opportune moment, she asked for a loan.[24]

Far more extraordinary in Mischel's recollection was Maud's behaviour following her mother's death, which occurred about this time. At her request, the Cherniavsky Trio played at the funeral service, held in the Music Room of West Wing. The trio first played "Aase's Death" from Grieg's *Peer Gynt*. Then Jan Cherniavsky was asked to play Chopin's *Funeral March*. The Cherniavskys and their wives (Leo was married by this time) were greatly taken aback when Maud, dressed in massive black veils, suddenly performed her dance interpretation of the *Funeral March*. In a melodramatic finale, Maud threw herself on her mother's open coffin. Following the ceremony Mrs. Durrant, "lying in a beautiful heavy box," was carried away in a hearse drawn by four magnificent horses, draped in black. All this grandeur, Mischel added, "was never paid for."

Notes

1. Pemberton's dancing career up to this engagement was undistinguished. Earlier in the year he was publicized in the

Los Angeles Times as "the matinée idol of the New York Winter Garden," who planned for Los Angeles a similar entertainment, featuring the *Spring Song*, and "thirty pretty social girls of this gay city of angels."

I assume nothing came of this project, as there seem to be no reviews extant.

The female cast included Claire Macmillen; Maud's "manager" for this tour was Charles Macmillen. On November 2, 1905, Maud had given a recital in Elberfeld, Belgium, with Francis Macmillen, violinist. For many years Charles was his brother Frances' manager. Presumably Claire was related.

2. Excerpt from his review in the Montreal *Star*, October 3, 1916. Morgan Powell was the only professional critic to review her with considered insight during this abortive tour. He paid her a genuine tribute in "The Ballet and Maud Allan," one of a collection of critical essays published in *Memories That Live*. (Toronto: Macmillan, 1928).

3. The Toronto *Telegraph* of October 7, 1916, reported the following audience reaction:

> "Whatever made Miss Allan give such a thing as Chopin's 'Funeral March' at a time like this in Canada?" [A reference to the slaughter of Canadian troops on the Western Front.] So ejaculated one woman who watched Maud Allan last night.

This comment prompted from Maud a long and defensive response that ended with: "I have always loved to do the 'Funeral March,' but it never was so wonderful to me as now, when I have so many dear friends at the Front. It seems like a sacred thing."

4. In Toronto her manager distributed a statement, signed by Maud, that she "definitely denies" the report, although some months earlier they had publicly stated that they planned to marry.

5. From Queen Elizabeth's time until 1964, representation of any biblical character was forbidden on the British stage. Whereas the Lord Chamberlain made no attempt, in spite of publicized protests, to ban *The Vision of Salome* (presumably because Edward VII had seen and approved it in Marienbad), he banned Strauss's opera *Salome* for almost three years. In 1910 Sir Thomas Beecham finally produced it, but only after toying,

at the demand of the Lord Chamberlain, with the text. His account of how he and his cast dealt with these demands, related in his book *A Mingled Chime*, is hilarious.

6. Noel Pemberton-Billing (1880–1948) "was among the earliest Englishmen to realize the potentialities of the aircraft in wartime," according to his obituary (November 12, 1948) in the London *Times*. *Defence Against the Night Bomber* (London: Hale, 1941) was one of three insightful books he wrote on the topic. Upon election to Parliament, as an independent, he made "purity in public life" his chief concern. He resigned his parliamentary seat in a letter to the Speaker of the House of May 27, 1921. The *Times* published the letter in full.

He fought – and lost – four by-elections in 1941 and sued a Conservative candidate at the first of these for allegedly saying that a vote for Pemberton-Billing was a vote for Hitler. He lost the case, but was told he had conducted his argument "with propriety and skill." His first wife, who died in 1923, was Lilian Maud Schweitzer, a cousin of Albert Schweitzer.

7. Marie Corelli lived in Stratford-on-Avon, with Miss Vyver, her lifelong companion. (Her home is now used by the Shakespeare Institute in Stratford-on-Avon.)

8. In her diary for June 2–6, 1918, Lady Cynthia Asquith records having discussed the Billing case at some length. "The cruel thing is that, to the public mind, the mere suggestion of such things is in effect the same as though they were proved. Adele said the shop-women sort of strata were saying, 'We always knew it of the Asquiths, and we're so glad they're being exposed.' Margot, of course, attributes the whole thing to an anti-Asquith plot – to make it impossible for him ever to return to office – and I should think there is a good deal of truth in this theory" (p. 445).

"Poor Margot, her indiscretions are so naive, so childlike, that they ought in themselves to furnish a certificate of innocence" (p. 446).

9. J.T. Grein seems either to have joined Maud in this action as a matter of principle or to have been persuaded by her to do so. Billing dealt brutally with him, implying he had pro-German sympathies because he had not returned at the outbreak of the war a medal awarded him by the kaiser in recognition of his efforts to promote cultural ties with Ger-

many. Billing also emphasized that Grein was a naturalized British citizen, having been born in the Netherlands. Although Grein played only a minor role in the affair, he was ruined by it. In 1987 a literary prize bearing his name was established in London by a group of British journalists.

10. The affair reached the highest levels of government:

> Lord Curzon drew the attention of the War Cabinet to the publication in the press of the evidence taken in the Pemberton-Billing libel action, and stated that, in his opinion, such publication was doing more harm than anything that had appeared in this connection for many years. Opportunity was being taken to attack every section of society, and the social effect must inevitably be bad. Insinuations and accusations were being made against public men without a shred of foundation. Lord Curzon asked if nothing would be done, by means of censorship or otherwise, to prevent such publications by the press in the future. (*War Cabinet Minutes*, 1916 Meeting 225, Item 17)

At a subsequent meeting (No. 429) Lord Curzon was advised that nothing practicable was possible.

11. In 1977, *Salome's Last Veil: The Libel Case of the Century* was published. This book gives a comprehensive account of the proceedings, placed in the context of the intense political intrigue of the day. In New York, *Dancing for the Kaiser*, a play "based on an actual case," was produced in the 1970s by the Circle Theatre. In 1980, Peter Gale's *The Inadmissible Crime of Maud Allan*, a direct representation of the proceedings, was privately produced in London.

12. Darling had chosen to preside over the case. As senior judge he had the right to select his cases. His mishandling of the proceedings discredited his practice of making witticisms and jokes in court.

13. In a letter of April 24, 1984, Etienne Amyot recalled Maud's hospitality in the early 1930s: "At her house you met everyone – arts, politics, whatever. She entertained simply but well. Knew how to mix people and get the best out of them in the way of interesting talk. I admired her greatly, was fascinated by her elusive graciousness – it wasn't so much beauty as a sort of mysterious and sympathetic flow." Among her friends were "G.B. Shaw, King Alphonso of Spain, Lord

Astor, Sir Henry Wood, Jacob Epstein, and others of like celebrity of the times." All further remarks of Mr. Amyot are from this same letter.

14. This is confirmed by Busoni's detailed account, in a letter to his wife dated November 1, 1919, of Shaw's conversation when invited to tea at West Wing. See *Ferruccio Busoni: Letters to His Wife* (London, 1938), p. 279.

15. Miss [Ellen] Terry was nearly prostrated with grief after receiving news of the death of Laurence Irving. Needless to say, the actress has been intimately acquainted with all the Irving family. Both Mr. H.B. Irving and Mr. Laurence Irving have been known to her since their boyhood. While appreciating the undoubted ability of Mr. H.B. Irving, she always pinned her faith upon Laurence, of whom she was exceedingly fond. Throughout his theatrical career she had been convinced that he would develop into a truly great actor, and worthily carry on the work of his illustrious father. "We kept the news from her as long as possible," said Miss Terry's travelling companion. "It was terrible when she heard the news," she added. *New Zealand Star* (Auckland), June 1, 1914)

16. Henry Irving was the author of *Studies of French Criminals in the Nineteenth Century*, *A Book of Remarkable Criminals*, and the Introduction to the Everyman edition of *Crime and Punishment*.

17. "A Close Call" is not included in Stevenson's *Collected Works* (1933).

18. Ruth Draper was a superb "dramatic monologuist." Like Maud, she was inimitable, leaving no known disciples. She was active from about 1915 to 1955. She was the sister of Paul Draper, the maestro of the harmonica and friend of Artur Rubinstein.

19. Of the Lyon engagement Doris Langley Moore recalls:

the disfavour I incurred when I kept an astonished Frenchman standing in a corridor before I would admit him to Miss Allan's dressing room. He was a Monsieur Herriot who was accustomed to instant homage, being the holder of some great office. Not that I had the slightest notion of it while I tried to appease him with polite conversation until Miss Allan consented to see him – which she would have done immediately if I had recognized the name.

20. Manya termed this performance "memorable." Maud featured her dance interpretation of Tchaikowsky's *Pathétique* Symphony and closed with the *Blue Danube*.

The orchestra was directed by Alfred Hertz who, on January 22, 1907, had conducted the debut performance of Strauss's *Salome* at the Metropolitan Opera in New York. J.P. Morgan, a member of the Metropolitan's Board of Governors and the Metropolitan's 'landlord,' was deeply offended by the work. Encouraged by his daughter Anne, he cancelled the three scheduled remaining performances. The furor that followed only contributed to the outbreak of "Salomania" that swept the United States in 1908, following Maud's sensational success in London.

In her *Jottings* Maud entered "Hollywood Bowl – Alfred Hertz 120 musicians."

21. Maud had used the premises for seminars given to select groups of aspiring dancers soon after she had taken possession of the property. The school may therefore have been a natural outgrowth of these seminars.

22. Neither in her personal papers nor in any interview did she refer to the School of Art that in 1937 she attempted to establish, presumably to complement the dancing school. The instructor of this short-lived project was Dr. Curt Sachs, to whom Maud, so her diary records, gave English lessons in 1895. ("He knows no English at all.") Fleeing Germany in 1933, Dr. Sachs, already an internationally known musicologist, moved to Paris, where he taught at the Sorbonne and researched at the Musée du Trocadero (now the Musée de l'Homme). The school ran only a few months, partly because Dr. Sachs moved to the United States in 1938. It had but two students, one of whom was Mr. Edward Roberts, a sculptor now living in Exeter, Devon. Mr. Roberts was greatly impressed by Maud's insistence upon "the value of hours and hours of practice in order to produce anything of excellence, whether in dance or in art." He attended the school three afternoons a week and on Saturdays, for lessons in drawing and painting. (From a personal communication with the author.)

23. One of the few friends of Maud Allan whom Doris Langley Moore met while working for her at West Wing was Mrs. Collie – the Bombay doctor's wife who had travelled with the

company for a good part of their Indian itinerary. "I had no idea," Mrs. Langley Moore recalled in a letter dated July 3, 1986, "that this lady had financed the tour we made in 1925 – after which Maud began to drop her. I was astonished last time I travelled on a liner to see my parents in South Africa to meet Mrs. Collie, travelling second class while I, then married to a rich young man, was in the first class. We had a conversation in which Mrs. Collie disclosed to me how ruthlessly she had been treated. This was in 1933."

24. "Maud Allan came to see me, bringing the first lilies from her garden, and then asking me to lend her money! Very uncomfortable" wrote that generous patron of the arts in her diary (May 17, 1930). On another occasion during this visit she noted "Mischel busy selling Maud Allan's jewellery."

Maud's garden *was* magnificent. In her *Jottings* she listed thirty species of flowers and sixteen "flowering shrubs and trees."

8

The Final Years:
1930–1956

*T*HERE IS NO QUESTION that without her mother to push her, without her determination to satisfy her mother's expectations, Maud would never have reached the giddy heights of her success. That she did fulfil her mother's demands and was welcomed in the most "refined" surroundings may have satisfied Isabella Durrant, but would not necessarily affect the power of such strong psychological ties forged in Maud's early years. In her *Jottings* she noted a "special bond between Mamma and me" and listed four occasions on which her mother had appeared in a vision.[1] The best evidence of the relationship between mother and daughter is provided in the extant letters her mother addressed to Maud during those terrible years in Berlin.

Moreover, while Isabella Durrant's death may not have significantly affected those ties, it did affect Maud's psyche. Deprived of the role of submissive daughter, Maud gradually and awkwardly – because vestiges of her former self remained – took on the role of dominant older woman. She became the lover of Verna Aldrich, her secretary/companion, some twenty years her junior.

Verna lived with Maud, at West Wing, for at least ten

years, until 1938. She clearly loved her employer. In the early 1930s, however, she had briefly been engaged to a suitably wealthy English widower. Maud broke off this engagement by threatening to reveal her relationship with Verna and, failing that, to commit suicide.[2] Thereafter, Verna devoted herself to Maud's well-being.

Verna's mother had known Isabella Durrant in San Francisco and evidently tried to dissuade Verna from going to live with Maud. Maud, though was adamant, and Verna infatuated. Against such resistance nothing could be done. Related to an extremely wealthy family but not rich herself, Verna spent what private funds she had on maintaining Maud's tenancy of West Wing.[3] Beautiful, elegant, and innocent when she joined Maud, she had lost these qualities by 1938 when she returned, permanently, to California. From the handful of extant letters Verna addressed to her, it is clear that Maud came to treat her as a chattel, to be disposed of when of no further use.

The first of these letters, written from West Wing on June 23, 1936, to Maud in Los Angeles, indicates the nature of their relationship. Maud had apparently been hospitalized:

> Darling Maudie,
>
> Well, I have had an anxious few days trying to get news of you – I feel quite exhausted. This evening I got the cable and it is some reassurance – but I can't imagine you having gallstones – you never have had. I hope I got the truth of it all and that everyone is not lying, for I would much rather have the exact truth, I would worry less then. Anyway, dearest, I am so sorry you have been ill – and I can tell you I feel far away when you are ill – even cables take an interminable time. Anyway, Maudie dear, I didn't know how much I love you until I heard you were critically ill. Now take care of yourself and don't do anything startling.

A later paragraph in the same letter gave forceful advice to Maud, who, living in her late parents' bungalow, was intent upon making her mark on Hollywood: "Nella [an unidentified friend] was out here to supper last Sunday and we discussed you and she said to tell you that she says on no condition are you to leave Hollywood. You must stay there – conditions are more favourable to you there than here according to her stars and you have only laid the pipe or rather threaded the needle and if you come home now it will all go for nothing."

"Now about the difficulties I have here, I have plenty, believe me," is how Verna introduced her proposal that West Wing be let to her – furnished – for £687 a year. Verna's point was that if the Crown, the owners of the property, "make any trouble, they can whistle."[4]

Maud ignored Verna's proposal, perhaps because she did not trust it. Certainly she was busy, preparing for what proved to be her last public recital. This took place at Redlands Bowl, under the sponsorship of the Redlands Community Music Association. (The founder of the association, Grace Mullen, later helped launch the careers of Jerome Hines, Ruggiero Ricci, and Leontyne Price.) Maud was then sixty-three; her fellow soloist and accompanist was Etienne Amyot, then thirty. Mr. Amyot recalled that Maud rehearsed in a large room in the home of Jimmy Whale, a well-known Hollywood director. "I knew she was at least sixty (and looked it)," Amyot writes. "But the moment she started to move, it was as though she had recaptured youth."

Amyot had first met Maud in the late 1920s, when he was an aspiring concert pianist; he was introduced to her by the British composer Arnold Bax. On that occasion he saw her dance "in her large and lovely garden to a gramophone. In the soft twilight air it was something to watch. What was so essentially different from . . . most other dancers was her extreme musicality: that absolute and perfect co-ordination between movement and the rhythm of the music – whether of the hands, the eyes, the swing of the neck, the twist of the neck. All was absolutely in time."

In early 1936, he got to know her and her ways all too well. At that time he met her in New York, at a post-recital

reception given in his honour by a member of the Rocke-
feller family. Maud, making a grande entrée on the arm of
Anne, J.P. Morgan's daughter, was among the guests. (This
was the same woman who, some thirty years earlier, had
convinced her father to ban Strauss's *Salome* from the Metropolitan Opera's repertoire after its debut performance.)[5]

Maud, who was en route to California, invited Mr.
Amyot to be her guest at the ranch she had rented from
Ginger Rogers outside Los Angeles; she assured him that she
would get him plenty of interesting work in Hollywood.
Mr. Amyot took the bait and spent two months in Maud's
company. When, shortly after the Redlands recital, he
decided to leave, "I naturally said I would like to contribute
to some of the expenses of the house she had rented." Maud
took him at his word and before he knew it, he was paying
the entire rent! Being a man of private means, "I didn't
blame her for conning me. I thought it was rather a joke."

So, too, was the way he left. Aware of Maud's Circe-like
powers, he called Manya Cherniavsky, saying, so she recalled years later, "You've got to help me because if my
family finds out, I'll be disowned! I want to get a ticket to
return to England and arrange things. Please come over
early tomorrow morning and keep Maud busy while I make
my escape, so I won't have to say goodbye!" When Maud
discovered he had gone, she seemed indifferent, merely
remarking, "Isn't that nice? I'm so thrilled he has gone back
to England."

In a recent letter recalling the episode, Amyot remarks
"Manya always giggled when we spoke of my departure
from Los Angeles. I had concert dates in Austria, Holland,
and England which I naturally had to fulfil, though dear
Maud thought I could chuck these for some astronomical
sum to be earned in Hollywood. She always visualized LARGE
sums."

Some months after the Redlands performance, while
Verna struggled with financial problems in London, Maud
was evidently bemoaning her lot in Los Angeles.

"Darling," wrote Verna on March 29, 1937,

I know how hard it all is but you must be brave and carry on like my little soldier – I have the same to do at this end but know you have all you can carry so I do not unburden all the little things to you. But I want you to unburden to me as much as you want. Darling, you must grit your teeth and be happy even if it is only to take a walk with the little wee doggie. I am so sure – I can't tell you how sure I am – that the end of next year will see our troubles far behind us. That does not mean I think we must wait another year – I think they are dawning now!

Verna also suggested, in a tone strangely akin to Isabella Durrant's, that Maud should set about writing her autobiography:

Really and truly darling, I will not have much patience if you don't make the effort – write your opinions about anything that occurs to you. You have had a wonderful life – and more than all else you are a wonderful person yourself and you must not let a feeling of pity and lethargy overwhelm the real, fine brain that is down under all this trouble. Darling, you don't think I would have loved you all these trying, worrying years if you had just been a vain shallow creature – there is something in you that is great – and overcomes, that is not mastered by circumstances, but masters circumstances! Now, my Maudie must overcome the circumstances of the day! The little girl in you must not be afraid to cry – she must be great! You have a definite work to do, now do it!

In a half-hearted fashion Maud acted on her secretary's suggestion: she bought a little blue-covered notebook in which she wrote names and places as they came to mind. These are the *Jottings* that have proven so invaluable in the writing of this biography.

Verna's next extant letter opens with a salutation a shade less affectionate, a veiled warning, and a reminder: "Dearest Maudie: Well, I don't seem to get any letters from you, pretty soon, if you don't keep in touch with me, you will

fade in my thoughts to just that of a distant friend – so it's
up to you to keep the memory green."

She then writes about financial matters which, she explains, she had "bridged for the moment." The Crown was
getting impatient, having learned of an enquiry to purchase
the lease on Holford House, all of which, save West Wing,
was standing empty.[6] That enquiry had come from the art
dealer and patron Lord Duveen, who visited the house one
day. Verna told Duveen's agent that:

> We didn't want to sell, that it was not necessary and we
> wished just to live here, but if they wanted to buy they
> would have to pay well for the privilege since West Wing
> is the key to the whole property. We asked 40,000 pounds –
> expecting of course to come down considerably. They were
> told they would have to negotiate with the Crown for the
> rest of the property. Immediately the Crown began to
> bother me about the arrears and to worry about the next
> quarter's rent.

For two pages of this single-spaced, typed letter Verna
details the stratagems she had followed "to leave the big
wolf at the door." These stratagems included a phone call
to Robin, a wealthy friend, and later Etienne Amyot's wife,
on holiday in Austria. Robin agreed to guarantee Verna's
overdraft for the amount of the rent.[7] Verna's troubles,
though, were not over: "At about four o'clock the crazy
bank manager or rather clerk telephoned to say he couldn't
do it unless my overdraft came out of it. He was quite
adamant and I didn't know what to do."

At the last moment Verna had a brilliant idea. She contacted Mr. Stevens, Robin's bank manager. What followed
illustrates how business could be conducted in prewar England for those with proper credentials or wealthy connec-
tions:

> He said, "Come over in the morning and we'll fix it up." I
> went over and we had a talk and he certainly is a real person
> and so kind and businesslike. He and the solicitor fixed it up

and today the guarantor's signature should have arrived. He didn't ask me anything about whether you had a lease or not – or pry into our affairs at all. He said he had been up here not long ago and had thought of coming in. "'But," he said, "I thought that if I went in they would think I was coming because of the overdraft, and I'm not going to bother them. I would like to go on helping Miss Allan, but five hundred pounds was just the limit I could go on with."

In due course, as the debtors would discover, Mr. Stevens changed his tune.

Meanwhile, in California, in an attempt to make some money, Maud offered the public two master classes of twenty hours each during the summer of 1937. The courses – the first in Berkeley, the second in Los Angeles – would be called "The Art of the Dance." Nothing other than a formal announcement found amongst her papers is known of this project, but it may have been the impetus for Maud to be invited by a group of wealthy admirers to serve as consultant/director of a dance studio in Los Angeles that was to be affiliated with a cello studio under Manya Cherniavsky's direction. (By this time Manya, long-time resident of Los Angeles, was the wife of a doctor and the mother of three teen-aged daughters. She had become increasingly active in musical circles. A fine cellist, she had a number of private students and was regularly consulted on musical matters by Twentieth-Century Fox executives.) Space at Normandie and Sixth Street in downtown Los Angeles was rented – fortunately on a monthly basis – and renovations got under way. Maud's chief concern was the mirrors, indispensable to any dance studio. Only mirrors of the highest quality, such as those that Margot Asquith had paid for in West Wing some thirty years earlier, would satisfy Miss Allan. But her demand was ignored as premature, as was her demand for a salary appropriate to her status as a "great" dancer.

Kind as everyone had been, she complained to Manya, "they want to do it their way, not mine, and that's just not good enough." Try as they might to reach an agreement, Maud would not, she declared, compromise her art. She would take only highly talented students, for whom only the best would be good enough. She may have been determined to prove that, although she might be in her sponsors' debt, they would bow to her will. Instead, they threw up their hands in despair and withdrew their support.[8]

Those on the periphery of this project doubted that Maud ever intended to run a studio in Los Angeles. Had her demands for the mirrors been met, they surmise, she would have contrived some further objection. For years, she had spoken of opening a studio but had made no attempt to do so. The same fate awaited projects suggested to her; she would welcome each idea, say she would think about it, and then never mention it again.

After the grandeur of West Wing, her late parents' bungalow on Lucille Avenue was modest accommodation indeed, but even it was too costly, as the house was still mortgaged. Consequently, the bungalow was rented out for $50 a month, and Maud made the rounds of friends, most of whom had been her guests at West Wing. For several weeks she was a self-invited guest at the home of Manya Cherniavsky, until Louisa, the middle daughter, exasperated beyond endurance by Maud, bluntly told her to leave, during an evening meal. With studied deliberation, Maud wiped her lips with her napkin, which she folded with memorable grace and went upstairs to her bedroom. (Louisa's father, failing to suppress an understanding smile, gently reproved his daughter for her outburst.) A few minutes later, with battered suitcase in hand, Maud made a grand theatrical exit.

Maud then went to live with her childhood friend Alice Lonnon, who in the early 1920s had homesteaded on Mount Palomar in San Diego County. She was living with her brother Phil, a retired dentist who in his youth had been Theo's intimate friend. Before long Maud left Alice and moved to the home of a wealthy friend, Alice Millard of Pasadena.

Known to Maud as Pitter, Mrs. Millard was the widow of a rare-book dealer who had died in the early 1920s. Mrs. Millard had developed her late husband's business successfully, establishing lucrative ties with the Huntington Library in Pasadena. Attached to her Pasadena home was a museum of fine books and china, which was open to interested scholars. The house and the museum were designed by the young Frank Lloyd Wright and are among Wright's masterpieces of domestic architecture.[9]

The sojourn with Alice ended abruptly in January 1938. The two women were involved in a serious car crash; Maud was at the wheel. For Maud, who was quite seriously hurt, the accident was a source of terror, as her *Jottings* attest: "Accident – Act of God – Duress – Panic" is scrawled across the page. Mrs. Millard never recovered, and died two months later.

Maud then returned to her lifelong friend, Alice Lonnon, at which time she was inspired to write a forty-page typed autobiography, fictionalized in the fashion of late-nineteenth century women's novelettes. Despite its obvious shortcomings as a work of art or fiction, "A Rainbow Out of India" has some remarkable insights into Maud's psychology.

The maudlin plot concerns the meeting in San Francisco of an aged Dr. Herold and Octavia Lockburn, who has been seriously injured in a car accident: "It was something that couldn't occur – but did," she tells Dr. Herold. "Something took the wheel out of my hands and that same something let me live, by a miracle. You see my back was broken in five places, to mention only that."[10] The point of the plot, comprising narratives by both Herold and Lockburn, is Dr. Herold's gradual recognition of Octavia Lockburn as the beauty he had observed dancing in the grounds of the Taj Mahal thirty years earlier. (He had gone to the Taj Mahal to kill himself because of his failure to track down this very beauty, whom he first glimpsed passing by in an open limousine in San Francisco. The dance at the Taj Mahal saved him.)

Octavia Lockburn then relates her life story, the central

experience of which is that visit to the Taj Mahal with her female companion – "mother, duena, manager, secretary, lady's maid, alter ego," a figure based on Alice Lonnon. A young, world-renowned pianist, she was in Agra

> for a single recital, simply to have an opportunity of seeing the Taj Mahal. We were gloriously rewarded by the view of it at sunset, then we hurried back to the concert hall. After the performance we went to see the Taj Mahal again, to see its exquisiteness by moonlight. . . . In sheer enchantment we stood still and breathless on the platform, gazing at the scene down the long, flowered lanes between the pools until the beauty of it paralysed us with ecstasy. . . . I felt a premonition come over me, I was impelled to dance. Notwithstanding the fact that I had no interest in dancing, nor received the least training in its rudiments, I found myself performing the most expert and difficult manoeuvres. My clothes hampered me. Without a moment's thought I cast off most of them, and found the freedom so delicious that I threw myself into it with increased understanding. I have never been able to do again what I did that night! I have been four and a half decades trying it.

She heard "a choir in the sky – singing while I danced." She lost all awareness of her physical body as the heavenly choir increased to deafening volume and then gradually diminished into silence. Dr. Herold had seen her initiation into the mysteries of the art of the dance.

Once committed to dancing, Octavia "worked as few artists have ever worked," with the result that she became known as the creator of interpretive dancing:

> I was the Toscanini of my art. This combination of talents brought me universal acclaim. I came to live for dancing as formerly I had lived for music. Everything was subordinated to my art. Friends, home, country, I became the essence of selfishness. Not the slightest distraction was permitted to hinder or annoy me, I overstrained friendship and bank credit alike, without compunction or record of the trans-

gression. I borrowed carelessly of time and money from all-too-willing friends and colleagues.

My travels and researches were expensive. My mode of life was necessarily luxurious because I required absolute concentration in my search. I had to retain the semblance of youth, youth itself, in order to attract audiences, without whose stimulus an artist does not exist.

I earned a large fortune, and the last of it is gone now. What I had not given away as I went, I used to defray the expenses of my accident.

The accident is a blessing (however obscure) in disguise: "It answered the question which made my life a trail of doubt." It leads Octavia to a decision to join that beloved companion, who had been with her to India. (She, with her dentist brother, retreated from the world and lives in the backwoods of San Diego County. In fact, Alice Lonnon lived there to escape the asthmatic attacks that plagued her elsewhere.) "I am glad that the time has come," Octavia reflects out loud. "She will be glad to see me, and her brother will be pleased. Yes, they will both be glad, when they know I am coming. And they will be wiser, even as I am. We were children together. Once more we will be together – to the end."

"A Rainbow Out of India" describes the physical Maud Allan with indisputable accuracy. As an attempt to rationalize the terror of the car accident it is not persuasive, but it is revealing as the description of the way Maud Allan would have others see her and as she saw herself. Maud Allan did, indeed, visit the Taj Mahal after the concert at nearby Agra, and she did dance there. With her, however, apart from her "female companion," were the Cherniavsky Trio and the very wealthy Maharajah of Cooch Behar.[11]

According to Mischel, who often referred to this visit to the Taj Mahal as an experience of pure serenity, the maharajah made little secret of his interest in Maud and, indeed, asked her to dance there that night.[12]

In spite of her expectations in "A Rainbow Out of India,"

Maud did not spend the rest of her days with Alice Lonnon. She returned to West Wing in November 1938, her fare paid by two of the wealthy women who had attempted to sponsor the School of Dance. At about the same time, Verna left London for California. It was apparently understood that if she could not resolve the financial problems of West Wing, Maud would re-join Verna in California. Absence from her beloved home had made Maud's heart grow fonder; but for Verna, distance quickly provided a new perspective. "Really, you know," she wrote from California on December 7, 1938, with unusual insight, "I am beginning to think that place hypnotizes us both – it is so lovely out here and life is so much less expensive." Such hints, however, Maud could not appreciate. War rather than words, worries, or warnings would be needed to end her love affair with West Wing, monument to her glory days.

More distressing was Verna's hint that she could not sue Alice Millard's estate for the car accident. At Maud's behest Verna had sought legal counsel on the matter, only to be told that, as the driver of the car, Maud was responsible. "If you had been an employee it would have been different," Verna explained, "but driving at Mrs. Millard's request did not constitute employment . . . Awfully wrong law, I think." (To add insult to injury, Verna reported that Mrs. Millard's estate had all gone to her mentally incompetent daughter.)

Some idea of the desperate state of affairs at West Wing is provided in the closing paragraph of Verna's letter. "Well, my dear Maudie, how I wish I could peep in on you. My dear, don't stay there and be miserable. You know you can sell the furniture as per the estimate and perhaps you can get more than £8 for the little piano."

Each of the eight extant letters Verna wrote between January and September 1939 is several pages long. They indicate clearly that she felt at home in California and reveal her growing, justifiable impatience with the problems of West Wing. Maud was unconscionably implicating everyone but herself in the matter of the annual leasehold payments, which were by this time seriously in arrears. Moreover, despite explicit instructions to the contrary – "I told you a long time ago that you must never, under any circumstances, appeal to him for help," Verna wrote on January 2, 1939 – Maud had cabled one of Verna's wealthy relations for funds to cover "Verna's personal overdraft." Verna was infuriated. That debt, she reminded Maud, had been incurred solely to "meet immediate property obligations that had to be met in order to save the place for you at all. I gave your interests many years of my life and I think it is a poor return that you do this."

Three weeks later matters worsened. Mr. Stevens, the bank manager who had seemed so charming less than two years earlier, demanded proof of Verna's ability to pay off her overdraft within three months. Failure to provide such proof would necessitate Maud signing away her interest in West Wing. Appended to the copy of a letter Mr. Stevens had addressed to Verna in California was a handwritten transcript of "a horrid little note" to her from Robin, the wealthy guarantor of that overdraft, with whom Mr. Stevens had been in contact. "You knew," Robin had reminded Verna, "Maud's financial position before you left England, you therefore knew she is in no position to pay 600 pennies let alone 600 pounds to me or anyone else."

While Verna worried herself sick ("I've had a hard time this winter, much harder than anyone has realized"), Maud did little to alleviate the situation. To judge by Verna's letters, Maud simply chose to ignore such distasteful matters as selling the lease on West Wing. She was evidently much more anxious to know why Verna had allowed the gardener to dismantle the glass house. Verna's answer was to the point: As it was unlikely that Maud would remain much longer in residence, such decisions were of little moment. However, her observation prompted a peculiar personal request: "I wish," Verna wrote on March 1, 1938, "should you leave West Wing, you would have someone level the little graves where the doggies are buried. If they are level no one will disturb them but if they are plainly graves, they might dig them up."

Verna's letter of March 12 all but lays bare her resentments and regrets as she summarizes her thoughts on West Wing:

> It seems so good to be out of all the nightmare of worry –
> it seemed so endless – I don't see why you ever went back to
> it. It hypnotized me while I was there – I thought the house
> was all important, but now that I am away from it I realize
> that if we had both washed our hands of it years ago, we
> would be much better off today. I can't understand how,
> when you were away from it for a few months, you ever
> wanted to go back to it. I do hope you can sell the lease for
> something this Spring – no matter how little.

As the financial screws tightened, Verna's stance became more adamant. "I just can't do anything right now," she wrote on March 23, "and it's useless to bombard me. I'm very sorry, but there it is. I can't do what I can't do, can I?" Such comments angered Maud; they bordered on *lèse majesté*.

Had Maud suspected some new influence on her secretary/companion, she would have been justified. Verna was living in a family-style hotel in Hollywood, operated by a Miss Kenner, who, like Verna, was a Christian Scientist. Miss Kenner was an immense help and source of strength, Verna explained in this letter of March 23. "I feel I must prove to myself that I can take care of myself, on my own. I want to feel independent. This is for my own self-respect. Oh, how I wish I had dropped it all years ago and started on some line independently – then today would be a different story." Clearly she was following advice rather than, as heretofore, her own impulses or Maud's orders. The immediate result, it seems, was an ominous silence on Maud's part: "I hope you will write soon," poor Verna added as a postscript to one letter. This was followed by the sudden severance of what had been an intense relationship of at least ten years' duration. That Verna had not resolved irritating financial problems was, it would seem, just cause for dismissal.

Without an awareness of her underlying ruthlessness,

Maud's accusation against Verna would strain credulity. Verna, who had given Maud so many years of her life, the best part of her reputation, and, no doubt, most of her private means, was accused of being a thief.

The original grounds on which Maud based this absurd accusation were, admittedly, provided by Verna. She explained in a letter of March 12, 1938, that, while unpacking her steamship trunk in Los Angeles, she had made an "unfortunate discovery." This she reported with an equally unfortunate lack of tact:

> I remember now doing it when I thought I was packing up everything for good and that we were both returning to California. I packed your little brown trinket case in my trunk. I did not want to send it to storage but thought I would give it to you when I met you out here. I have sealed it with sealing wax and will deposit it with a bank or anyone you would like me to leave it with. It costs four dollars a year to leave it in the bank, but I would prefer to do that than keep it with me. I will send it if I get a good opportunity – but if I send it through the post you will probably have to pay duty, so that's no good. They would probably charge you as much for the things as they are worth. I could have kicked myself when I found it.

In her grander days Maud had collected many costly pieces of jewellery from her rich admirers. She sold the last of these to provide her mother with the best of care during her last years. Nevertheless, Maud claimed to the end of her days that her faithful and naive secretary had stolen her remaining valuable jewellery. Indeed, it was only with great difficulty that Manya Cherniavsky dissuaded her from launching suit, soon after her arrival in Los Angeles in 1941, against Verna for theft of these nonexistent valuables. Those familiar with Maud's character were appalled, but not surprised, by her reckless cruelty.

So outrageous a charge did have one benefit: it cured Verna of her pathetic infatuation, and she died in 1970, having lived the rest of her days in relative peace.

With no further letter from Verna, there is a virtual blackout regarding Maud's life in London between 1938 and 1941, although it is a fair guess that she became a modern-day Miss Havisham grieving for her past.[13] She did have two visitors. Michael Cherniavsky, Mischel's eldest son, remembers how gaunt and drab both she and West Wing looked when, with his father, he unexpectedly called on her in 1940. Mischel, of course, was an old friend, for whom dissimulation by Maud was neither appropriate nor necessary.

On August 7, 1940, when Maud visited the Crown Estate office regarding the future of her beloved West Wing, her dissimulation was total. This is revealed in a document in the office's files dated August 8, 1940. It is addressed to a Mr. Meadows "for his information" and bears the initials of an anonymous civil servant.

According to this report and other relevant documents, Maud disclosed her intention to build a new residence on the property. She even submitted a photograph of the structure she contemplated: a pseudo-Tudor cottage displayed at the *Daily Mail* Ideal Home Exhibition in 1938.[14] The civil servant must have been nonplussed, as much by the design of the structure as by Maud's taste. However, by this time he may well have given up dealing seriously with the wily tenant; in the office files is a carefully ambiguous letter to a Crown official from Lloyd George's private secretary, clearly indicating that Maud had successfully appealed to Lloyd George with regard to the civil servants' threats of eviction.

By the late 1930s, without Verna and her funds, Maud turned to Etienne and Robin Amyot for financial help. Before long, the Amyots were "being made more and more responsible for various debts which in the end amounted to a great deal." Nor were they the only ones from whom she extracted funds. Etienne Amyot recalls "a Brigadier General in Montgomery's 21st army – Maud got £500 out of him. So much for charm and that quality she had of mesmerizing and enchanting others!"

The tug of war between Maud and the civil servants

ended in a draw on October 9, 1940. During one of the very
first air raids on London that evolved into the Battle of
Britain, Holford House suffered serious bomb damage.
Maud Allan was not alone in West Wing; Mr. and Mrs.
Amyot were with her. Nineteen years later Etienne Amyot
recalled that evening in a letter to Manya Cherniavsky. The
letter was dated February 22, 1959, and was written following an afternoon spent with Mischel Cherniavsky talking
about Maud Allan and the many artists they had both
known:

> I was telling your brother how one night my wife and I were
> in the Regent's Park House when about five bombs fell on
> the other end of the house and in the garden. There was no
> gas, no light. So – it was about 4 A.M. and we were frozen
> – I walked with a torch to the ballroom, and found it in
> ruins, with the lovely old ceiling on the floor. I picked up a
> bundle of laths, brought it back to Maud's Music Room,
> made a fire with it, put on a kettle, and we had a delicious
> cup of strong tea. What a life that was!

A few days later, solely for reason of safety, Maud bade
a fond farewell to her beloved home. (According to a report
made shortly after her departure, West Wing was rat-
ridden and riddled with dry rot; an old motorcar was found
in the basement.) Maud then lived with the Amyots for some
months, working as a volunteer chauffeur and ambulance
driver.

In mid-1941, she decided to return to Los Angeles. The
Amyots paid off her considerable debts, purchased her fare,
and provided her with funds sufficient to last for six months.
("She said she would be living in her parents' old home and
would be 'comfortably off.' ") That she, a private citizen
aged 68, with no special claim to priority treatment, procured air passage to Lisbon is, to say the least, astonishing.
At the height of the Battle of Britain, when flights were few
and far between and space extremely limited, space was
found for Maud Allan.

When she arrived in New York in mid-August she was briefly interviewed by the *New York Times*, which identified her as "the dancer whose Salome was once considered sensational." Maud told the interviewer that the British government had taken over her London home, which was true enough, and that her "extensive library on the dance had been lost when a bomb fell on her country cottage," a fabrication.

In Los Angeles she took an evening course in drafting and worked for the Douglas Aircraft Company for the balance of the war.[15] She never complained of her change of fortune, never openly pined for West Wing; but this, of course, was in accordance with her resolve, made many years earlier and steadfastly adhered to: "No one knows my feelings and no one ever shall."

In April 1949 a draft letter to her lawyer, Robert Gifford of Pasadena and his wife Evelyn, set out her plight.

Dear Evelyn and Robert,

This is the most difficult letter I have ever had to write, and I want you to forgive me if I impose too heavily on your friendship, which I have treasured these many years. I am in great financial distress and must open up to someone. I don't know what will happen to me if no relief comes. It is worse than going through those years of war and tragedy. From affluence and a beautiful home and honour to a small ugly room without proper conveniences – no work – no money, no outlet for my talents. I can't take it any more. I'm ill with worry and fear. I know I should know that God is my protector and supply, but darling it is hard when in my present plight to keep firm hold of what I know is true.

I have worked when work is available but on the whole only young people are wanted. Also the aircraft plants are discharging workers rather than taking any one.

I can receive no money from England – only at intervals – the last was almost a year ago – 125 pounds or $500 [from the Amyots?]. By living so very modestly, going without necessities, clothes, and proper food, I've managed to reach today. I have just 13 cents left and don't know when I will get my next amount from England.

I wrote today to my lawyer to sell the greater portion of my possessions in London to recover my fast dwindling money. The loss of my home there and now the discontinuance of the School which had an earning capacity and which bore my name and from which I drew a good steady income since I came to America, has made my security almost a thing of the past.

I owe three months' rent and had I not an understanding landlord (a Christian Scientist) who knows the difficulties attending getting money from England, I would have been evicted a long time ago with no place to go. Now he asks for the rent of over $100, for he truly needs it. He is not a rich man.

When I had to give up my parents' home in 1945 where I could have taught Music and Dancing, rented part of the house and sold the three lots 60 × 150 each and paid off the mortgage in a short time, I had to store all my things – furniture, lots of lovely books and china which Mrs. Millard gave me, music, records, stage costumes, etc. The last link between me and a new life of promise was gone. I wept bitter tears.

Now the storage bill for the last year is due and I have received notice that unless the amount is paid by this coming Friday 15 the goods will be sold at warehouse auction on April 20. Should they not realize $125 (the amount of the bill) I will be held responsible and still lose all.

My friend Manya often brings me to her home (where I am today) because she feels I do not have proper care. It is the only way she can help me and I appreciate her kindness oh, so much, but I feel embarrassed that I can do nothing in return.

Dear friends, I have hesitated to burden you but the last moment has arrived. I tried to get a post at colleges, the USC [University of Southern California] and UCLA [University of California at Los Angeles] but they cannot consider me because I have no degree in the art of the Dance!! From whom could I get a degree in the form of an art I created myself, toured the world with phenomenal success and received the acclaim of the finest critics in the world? It is too ridiculous to think of, and how discouraging! What good has it done me to have slaved to bring beauty to millions if at my age and with my experience and achievement and knowledge I am deprived of passing on my work to the coming generation because of red tape.

I have not been able to teach privately because I have had no money to rent a Dance Studio and advertise.

Dear friends, please let me know at once if you can help me. I have no one else to turn to.

In any case I know I'll not lose your friendship for having written this letter to you. Although we see each other so seldom I think of you very often and love you dearly.

I promise to return the money as soon as I am able. It sounds funny to say that, considering my present position, but believe me, I will and luck may come my way again, if I live.

Devotedly, Maud Allan.

Whether she sent the letter is unknown, but amongst her papers is an empty envelope stamped April 21, 1949, bearing the return address of Robert Gifford. As with so much of Maud's autobiographical material, this draft letter is a blend of fact, falsehood, and fantasy. It was a sad truth that she had indeed sunk "from affluence" in to "a small ugly room." It was also undoubtedly true that academic institutions would not see fit to employ her as a dance instructor. On the other hand, she was clearly fantasizing in pretending she had funds in England. Nor did she instruct her "London lawyer" to dispose of some of her possessions at this time: all were sold shortly before her death.

Distressful as her last years were, they had their memorable moments. One day, for example, two or three years after the Second World War was over, Manya Cherniavsky took her to a lavish reception given annually by one of the leading artists' agents in Los Angeles. Among the guests was Artur Rubinstein. Recognizing Maud from afar, Rubinstein approached her, bowed low, took her right hand and, raising it to his lips, kissed it with all his stylish grace, before the two former Berlin students plunged into animated reminiscences.[16] At another social gathering Henry Duffy, a local impresario, was introduced to Maud. Duffy looked at the seated figure for some seconds and then, turning to the person who had introduced him, asked, "You mean *the* Maud Allan?" Thereupon, as if stunned, he dropped to his knees and kissed her hand. Rising, he told her that as a young man he had seen her dance in Chicago in 1910 and had never forgotten the experience.

On another occasion in the mid-1940s, Manya Cherniavsky and Maud attended a concert at the Hollywood Bowl. Adjacent to their box sat Charlie Chaplin and Leopold Stokowski. During the intermission Chaplin recognized and politely greeted Maud; but Stokowski sat silent, evidently failing to recognize let alone to remember having conducted for her. Maud was hurt. With ice-cold politeness she said, "Good evening, Stoki." Stokowski scrutinized her and apologized for still failing to recognize her. Maud reminded him of the concert in Cincinnati on February 12, 1910, whereupon Stokowski exclaimed, "My God, another world!" Maud replied, "And a good one it was, too."

A somewhat less successful encounter occurred when Maud attended an evening's entertainment at Freemont High School in Los Angeles. On the program was a "Greek pantomime" in which groups of students would hold a pose for several minutes. This particular production – a variation on the living pictures entertainment – was the pet project of the school's music teacher, the elderly Miss Ida Bach. Flustered with the excitement of the evening and with the prospect of meeting Maud, an idol of her youth, Miss Bach blurted out, "Oh, Miss Allan, I remember seeing you when I was a little girl." Maud froze, for to judge by Miss Bach's looks, she was close to or beyond mandatory retirement. The evening proved a fiasco.

Irving Ross was a teacher at Freemont High and a fine amateur pianist. It was he who had taken Maud to the evening's entertainment at Miss Bach's request. Ross recalls that once, while he was playing a Chopin waltz, Maud interrupted him and with great charm, tact, and musical sensitivity suggested a distinctive rhythm and phrasing. She illustrated her interpretation, not by sitting at the piano, but with the mere movement of her hands. Ross insists that she was able to convey more of her intent than any pianist could have done by the orthodox approach of playing the passage in question. Despite their shared love of music, she never played the piano in his presence.[17]

Scribbled in her *Jottings* is the name Walter Wanger, who from 1934 to the early 1960s was a leading Hollywood film producer. (It is likely that Maud met him in the mid-1930s, when she was attempting to land an assignment in Hollywood.) While the nature of her contact with Walter Wanger is unknown, the ultimate result may be seen in *Salome, Where She Danced*, a movie released in 1951, starring Yvonne de Carlo. It is not amongst Walter Wanger's more successful productions, and is certainly closer to Maud Allan's life and career than to the biblical story that has inspired at least six film treatments.[18]

Although the plot of this movie, essentially a vehicle for promoting Yvonne de Carlo's dancing, is confused and sketchy, it does relate to Maud Allan's early career as the Salome Dancer. Set in the late nineteenth century, it opens with the sensational success in Vienna of an American dancer's portrayal of the biblical Salome's dance. High-ranked military officers duel over the dancer. Apparently accused of treason by one of her disgruntled admirers, Salome leaves the country and heads for San Francisco, where once again she attracts hosts of admirers who, with a fervour of the Wild West, fight over her favours.

The most significant of these admirers is a rich, bearded, and politically powerful gentleman who, while attempting to gain Salome's attention, is seen issuing orders against the backdrop of the Cliff House, a ruin on Sutro Heights. (The model for this particular character is surely Adolph Sutro.)

To associate so explicitly the names of Mayor Sutro and Maud Allan with this film may seem questionable, but there remains one tantalizing piece of circumstantial evidence. The scriptwriter of this film was San Francisco-born Charles Lamont. In 1898, the year Charles Lamont was born, Theo was executed for the murder of Blanche Lamont. Although it has been impossible to document any family relationship between Blanche and Charles Lamont, the story of Theo and his victim would likely have been known to Charles. It is difficult to believe that any treatment of these events from the pen of a Lamont would be coincidental. *Salome, Where She Danced* was, it would seem, a private, expensive, and very bad joke.

Maud's personal grace and presence, which throughout her life attracted so much puzzlement from her more sophisticated friends and admirers, also had its influence in Hollywood, in a strangely indirect fashion. One day, sometime in 1936 or 1937, Myron Futterman, a dress manufacturer, contacted Manya. A patient of Manya's husband, Mr. Futterman was in his forties at the time. He had recently married his second wife, an aspiring Hollywood actress some twenty years his junior. (The marriage lasted only a few months.) Mr. Futterman explained to Manya that while he believed in his bride's potential as an actress – she had already appeared in a number of minor movies – she lacked the social and cultural prerequisites for a successful Hollywood career. Mr. Futterman therefore asked Manya to instruct his young wife in these niceties to which Manya had been introduced during her three years at King's House School, Highgate, and had honed by observing at close quarters the grace and elegance of her mentor, Maud Allan.

Manya readily accepted the assignment. For about a year, this student regularly spent hours with "Madame." (Like her brothers Jan and Mischel, Manya lost all track of time while teaching.) Manya instructed her student in social graces and theatrical techniques, from posture and elocution to singing. Occasionally, at the end of a session the student's admirer (and future husband) would call for her. He was soon to land the star role in *Brother Rat*, which launched an acting career that would lead him to the White House. Manya's student was Jane Wyman, the first Mrs. Ronald Reagan and one of Hollywood's *grandes dames*.

Two other incidents, which would defy belief were it not that Manya's tape-recorded recollections are so uncannily detailed, occurred in 1948. Manya and Maud attended a musical soirée in San Francisco to celebrate the birthday of "Singapore Joe" Fisher, a wealthy individual long active in San Francisco's musical and cultural life. After the music making, to which Manya, a fine cellist, contributed, an elderly man brought the conversation around to a torn and ragged photograph album. As he passed around this album, he explained that it contained the photographs of those, so he claimed, he had executed as official hangman at San Quentin Prison. The album included, of course, his four-teenth victim, Theodore Durrant.

Upon realizing what was afoot, Maud fled the company, to all appearances as cool and graceful as always. Presum-ably someone had invited the old man to this gathering for the express purpose of hurting Maud Allan.

During this same visit to San Francisco, Estelle Johnstone, an old acquaintance, invited Manya and Maud to dinner to meet an elderly lady who was very anxious (Estelle would not explain why) to meet Maud. With noticeable reluctance Maud agreed to accept the invitation. During dinner, this aged lady spoke of her young adulthood in San Francisco, and casually asked Maud if she did not have a brother. Maud very abruptly said she had no brother, whereupon Harriet, Estelle's sister, remarked that as a young woman this elderly lady had rented a room. Someone managed to cut short further comment from Harriet, but Maud went white.

The next day Manya learnt that this ancient lady had rented a room in the Durrant household and left because the police and detectives had visited the house so often follow-ing Theo's arrest. This was why she had been so interested to meet Maud Allan.

About two years before her death, Maud disclosed a wish to make her funeral arrangements, and asked that a sales representative from Forest Lawn Memorial Park visit her. The result was worthy of Evelyn Waugh. The representative came promptly enough and spent all afternoon closeted with her prospective client, but she left empty-handed, bitterly complaining that Maud had shown an insatiable interest in the business, but none in a contract.

Members of the Cherniavsky family recall Maud's similarly morbid behaviour when Perky, her beloved lap dog, died of old age. Maud demanded that Perky, who was as devoted to his mistress as he was suspicious of all other humans, be buried in the newly opened pet cemetery some way from Los Angeles. Maud travelled to the cemetery in the back of the Cherniavsky car, studiously contemplating the dog's body, which lay in a basket on her lap. At the cemetery, she insisted upon seeing the animal cremated, just as her parents reportedly had watched their son's body being incinerated more than fifty years earlier.[19]

Maud had few remaining friends; yet whenever any member of the Cherniavsky Trio visited his sisters in Los Angeles, he would spend time with Maud. The most frequent visitor of the three brothers was Jan, who lived in Vancouver. In a letter to her sister Mary Cherniavsky, dated February 25, 1954, Jan's wife, Elspeth, wrote that Jan had found Maud "still with traces of the Grande Dame, very aged, sitting and scarcely able to get out of her chair, in very decayed circumstances, reading her old critiques. Manya takes her some food once a week, which Maud cooks on a ring in her room. Maud gets other boarders to buy – and cook – other food for her."

About a year before her death, the storage firm, Swain's of London, advised that the bill for Maud's furniture, in their keeping since 1940, amounted to £356 and that they had a court order to auction off the items to settle the outstanding bill. Manya was able to postpone such drastic action pending a visit to England, scheduled for the summer of 1956. Maud by this time was falling into periods of vagueness and was never told of this final blow; during these lapses she would ramble on about death by hanging.

Finally, it became evident that she could no longer look after her most basic needs. Her friends banded together and, in order to spare her the horror of spending her last days in a public institution, pledged a monthly sum to maintain her in the Mission Convalescent Home, adjacent to and affiliated with the Los Angeles County Hospital.

It was here that Manya Cherniavsky and her husband, Lionel Correra, took me to visit Maud on December 31, 1955.[20] She was sitting up in bed, in a room she shared with five other residents, noticeably less well preserved than she. As we gathered around her, I was introduced as "Mischel's son." In the midst of desultory conversation – she was inordinately pleased that she had gained four pounds during the past two months and now weighed 114 pounds – she suddenly turned to me, her eyes sparkling. "You're a nice-looking young man," she said. "Why don't we run away together?" But she did not stay for an answer. Instead, she focussed her attention on Manya. "Now," she announced, "I'm going to show you how well I can walk!" Throwing back her bedclothes, thereby exposing the emaciated legs that in days gone by had carried her so gracefully to triumph, she carefully turned and put her feet on the most modest of bedmats. Holding herself upright she managed a few steps before settling with as much grace and dignity as she could muster, into a wheelchair that like the taciturn butler of West Wing, stood waiting by her bedside.

"Come into the garden, Maud," I murmured, as I carefully wheeled her into the bright sunlight. Hearing this invitation, a gentle shock of mild surprise animated her still luminous eyes, and she smiled that ineffable smile that had, so often and for so long, enchanted her public, her admirers, her friends, and her victims.[21]

I then asked, with posterity in mind, if she would pose for a group photograph. She glowed with pleasure, and even suggested she stand up for one pose – an idea that on second thoughts she did not pursue. Instead, she sat upright, as her mother had instructed in letters written sixty years earlier; holding her head high, she struck the pose of an old trouper. A few minutes later we bade her farewell.

In the summer of 1956, Manya and Lionel spent a few days in London, where Leo met them. Manya and Leo went to Swain's storage warehouse, where, after admiring a magnificent piano, a dining room suite (which sold for more than the storage debt), and a few other pieces of fine furniture, they came across a number of sea trunks. Having neither the time nor the inclination to rummage through trunks filled with ribbons, dress material, photographs, a pair of fencing swords (marked "Theo's"), and masses of neatly beribboned letters, they arranged for their disposal. Inside one of the trunks Leo found a neatly tied packet of "Letters from Leo," which he subsequently burned. He preserved the packets marked "Letters from Theo" and "Letters from Mamma," although, as already noted, he burnt a number of the letters that he considered too personal for public scrutiny.[22] Little did they realize that the contents would have been of sociological and cultural interest. For Maud Allan was central to the late Edwardian scene and in contact with the leading musicians and artists both before and after that era. (Her Berlin diaries, other family letters, and most personal memorabilia, including two *Salome* costumes, had gone with her to Los Angeles, where they were found in one of her three remaining trunks.)

She held on through the summer and then gradually grew weaker. But she showed no fear and expressed no regrets, confident that she would be rejoining her mother and her beloved Theo. "Rest, my darling," she had written in her diary at the time of Theo's execution in January 1898, "I believe in a *Wiedersehen*. We *shall* meet again in the Happy Land of our Heavenly Father."

When she died in her eighty-fourth year on October 7, 1956, her death was reported in the *New York Times*, the *Times* of London, some California papers, and a number of dance publications. Not surprisingly, the obituaries were brief and inaccurate; all reported she was aged 73. And yet, for at least one youthful admirer of her triumphant days in London, she was vividly alive. Shortly after I had visited her, I happened to meet Sir Herbert Read, the distinguished English critic, poet, and art educator. When I asked if the name Maud Allan meant anything to him, he replied, "Why, of course, she was the Marilyn Monroe of my youth."

Then I sketched the true story (as I knew it then) of this artist, this dancer by default, this symbol of Edwardian society, and, perhaps above all, extraordinary member of the "great republic of human nature."

Postscript – The property on which her beloved West Wing stood before being demolished in 1948 is now an untended, fenced-off area in London's Regent's Park. On one side is a City of London waste disposal and incinerator operation; on the other is a tennis and golf school.

The original Durrant home in San Francisco, a rowhouse at 425 Fair Oak Street, is an empty lot – the only one on that well preserved street.[23] Her parents' bungalow in Los Angeles was levelled in the early 1950s to make way for the expansion of an adjacent nursing home.

During the summer of 1987, the house that Maud's childhood friend Alice Lonnon had built on Mount Palomar, San Diego County, in the early 1920s was destroyed in a flash forest fire.

Nothing beside remains, save this *living record* of her memory.

*N*otes

1. Manya Cherniavsky recalled Maud telling her that in one of the visions, Isabella Durrant stood over her saying, "I am always at your side, guiding you."
2. According to Manya Cherniavsky, who was visiting London with her husband a few months later, her brother Mischel

became Verna's unwilling confidant throughout this particular crisis. Mischel chose not to reminisce about Verna – or perhaps, as he was then eighty-eight, she had passed from his generally alert memory.

3. Although it has been impossible to establish her family background, it is probable that her father was a beneficiary, direct or indirect, of the $600,000 estate of William A. Aldrich, who died in Piedmont, near San Francisco, in 1892. The bulk of this estate was left in trust for William A. Aldrich's two sons and two daughters. At the time of his father's death, one of the sons, George, was confined to the Napa Insane Asylum; on December 28, 1895, the *San Francisco Chronicle* reported that the other son, William, had taken action against the trustees, charging that "fraudulent representations were made to the deceased regarding the legality of the Trust." He asked "to have one fourth of the estate distributed to himself." The court ruling is unknown.

4. To give some sense of the value of the pound sterling at the time, Verna reports paying her two maids £1 a week each. The leasehold on West Wing, amounting to £595 a year, excluding taxes, was therefore substantial.

5. The music critic for the *New York Times* in 1907, when Strauss's *Salome* caused such a "social" uproar, was Richard Aldrich, at the start of a distinguished career.

6. Until the mid-1930s Holford House (except for West Wing) was, for some years, a training college for the Baptist Ministry. After the college moved to Oxford, these quarters remained empty. The college dining room, where debates were held, adjoined Maud's Music Room.

7. On December 8, 1937, Verna wrote to Maud:

> Darling, I am so humiliated you have not written to Robin – I can't think why you haven't – you could spend money cabling when you wanted to – the least you could have done was to write to her immediately. She gets nothing out of it – not even interest. Has done it just to help us, and after all you're not a close friend of hers. I am so ashamed, whenever I see Robin she asks if I have heard from you. I told her I had and that you were writing to her. If you haven't by now, don't let one hour elapse before you do. But surely you have! I just can't bear the thought that you haven't.

8. Manya recreated the following scene. As she and Maud were on their way to a luncheon with Marguerite, one of the potential sponsors, she said to Maud: "Now whatever money Marguerite offers for this project, don't ask for a penny more. She's a fine woman and don't spoil my friendship with her."

Maud raised no objection.

Summarizing the promising discussion at the end of the luncheon, Marguerite explained: "I feel this way. I would like to help you both – in my own way and without my husband's knowledge. [In other words, there was a limit to what she could fund.] To start, would $1,500 be enough?"

"So far as I am concerned, that would be most generous," Manya dutifully responded.

Turning to Maud, Marguerite said: "For your dancing lessons, you will need more room, won't you, Maud?"

"Yes, that's true," Maud agreed, "but I'll also need wall-size mirrors, of course."

"That would cost quite a lot, Maud," Marguerite replied in a tone indicating that at so early a stage she would be unwilling to cover such a large expense.

Deaf to the hint, Maud, rather than pleading her case, demanded high-quality wall-size mirrors, acknowledging the cost would be in the thousands of dollars.

"In that case," an obviously offended Marguerite remarked, "I'll have to consult my husband. I had hoped to do this on my own, for my own pleasure, but . . . "

Manya looked at Maud ("I could have slapped her face") and Marguerite looked at Manya, as if saying "She's impossible!" A painful silence reigned as the three women finished their coffee.

"I'll call you, Manya," Marguerite said, as her guests rose to leave.

The next day Marguerite called Manya. "If you want to do this on your own, go ahead," she said impatiently. "I wash my hands of the whole affair."

9. Mrs. Millard told Manya that Frank Lloyd Wright (who had earlier designed a home for her in Highland Park, Illinois) came in to see her one day as the house was nearing completion. As he bounded up the stairs, he hit his head on a low ceiling. Rubbing his head and embarrassed, he said, "That's

exactly what I wanted to see you about!" In his autobiography Wright pays warm tribute to Alice Millard's early and lasting confidence in him.

10. The *Los Angeles Times* of January 28, 1938, reported that "Mrs. Millard incurred a fractured shoulder and concussion and Miss Allan suffered several fractured ribs and leg injuries." In a letter of March 12, 1939, Verna asked Maud:

> Has your leg healed alright and is your back strong now? One of my friends' husband is a very fine doctor – we discussed your injury and he said your back would get strong and alright again, but that it takes time. I think you are wonderfully brave – I really don't see how you go through everything so finely – but keep your courage up and don't go down to the depths.

11. The trio had first met the future maharajah and his elder brother during their 1912 tour of India. (Mischel casually mentioned seeing erotic pictures on the lids of cigarette boxes when the trio visited the Maharajah's Palace at Cooch Behar. Mischel was sixteen years old in 1912 and quite proper.) In London the contact developed into a friendship. The maharajah and his family had become highly westernized: both sons had been educated at Eton; they mixed with Edwardian society in London and entertained a stream of Western guests at the palace in Cooch Behar.

The elder brother (who was maharajah in 1912, the time of the trio's visit) fell in love with Edna May, an English actress. When opposition to Westernization kept him from marrying her, he drank himself to death with champagne. He died in August 1913. His newly married brother succeeded him and travelled from England to India on the same boat as the trio. In his letters to his wife, the tour director mentioned that as soon as the ship had crossed the Suez Canal, British government officials and Army officers on board deliberately ignored the maharajah and his entourage.

12. Only after the typescript had been discovered was Mischel asked whether Maud was present at this visit and if she had danced at that time. His answer to both questions was a categorical yes. He added, without prompting, that she had done so at the maharajah's specific suggestion. He did not indicate how elaborate the "dancing" was. (Two or three days

after this exchange he fell into a coma and within a week died in his sleep, aged eighty-eight.) When asked about the incident, his brother Jan, at the age of ninety-three, said Maud had indeed danced "a few steps."

13. All we do know of Maud's activities is that during these years she contributed her reminiscences of the Palace Theatre, the scene of her triumph in 1908, to a BBC program celebrating that theatre's history.

The Reverend A.J. Stuart Thomson, who was a student at Regent's Park Baptist College from 1933 to 1936, writes:

> She introduced Oske-Non-Ton, a "Red Indian Chief," complete with his Chief's dress and wigwam, to give a recital before entertainment and other agents, plus especially invited guests. The students of Regent's Park Baptist College were asked to entertain the guests. I had to look after Lady Fitzgerald. Later, Oske-Non-Ton took the lead at the Albert Hall [London] in a production of *Hiawatha*.
>
> Another project was a ladies' fashion show, which was filmed. The imposing porch and grounds [of West Wing] proved an ideal setting.
>
> Miss Allan was highly respected by the students, and, I may add, so was her chauffeur and companion, Miss Aldrich. I understand that after we left, Miss Allan felt that Holford House was very quiet, because she missed the students who held debates and took their meals in quarters adjoining West Wing.

14. This was a pre-fab, Tudor-look do-it-yourself kit, offering two alternative floor plans, two or three bedrooms, kitchen and living room. It cost, "with carriage paid in England and Wales . . . £199/15/10." Nesta Macdonald, who kindly researched this material, comments: "It is unbelievable that anyone could contemplate putting this pseudo–Anne Hathaway style cottage down beside West Wing or anywhere on Crown property. The most amazing thing is that the civil servants countenanced it and made no invidious comments."

15. Ruth St. Denis, whose influence on modern dance has been strong, and who was performing in Vienna when Maud introduced *The Vision of Salome* there in December 1906, was working as a riveter in the same plant.

16. It is very likely that Rubinstein's path crossed Maud's in Paris in 1907, when Maud was dancing *The Vision of Salome* there. Rubinstein was in Paris under the management of Georges Austruc, who was also presenting Strauss's *Salome*, which Rubinstein helped rehearse. He also performed – for a substantial fee – a piano version of the opera at private parties. It is highly probable that he was aware of Maud's encouraging critical success and would have contacted her. (*My Early Years*, New York: Knopf, 1973, pp. 215–18.)

17. For the more than forty years they knew her, none of the Cherniavsky family, save perhaps Leo, ever heard Maud play the piano. During their tour with her, Jan Cherniavsky recalled inviting her several times to play the piano with or for the trio, but she refused.

Etienne Amyot recalled Verna telling him that Maud played the piano in West Wing, but only in absolute solitude.

18. The movie treatments of the Salome story include:

(i) *Salome* (1918), starring Theda Bara.

(ii) *Salome* (1924), with Mme. Nazimova, "after the Aubrey Beardsley drawings in the first edition of the Oscar Wilde play on which the picture is based."

(iii) *Salome of the Tenements* (1924), with Godfrey Tearle, adapted from a novel by Anzie Yezlerska.

(iv) *Salome, Where She Danced* (1945), starring Yvonne de Carlo and Walter Slezak.

(v) *Salome* (1953), starring Rita Hayworth, Stewart Granger, Charles Laughton, Judith Anderson.

(vi) *Salome's Last Dance* (1988), directed by Ken Russell and starring Glenda Jackson.

19. Maud Allan's obsession with death was so extreme that when the two-year-old daughter of close friends died in 1932, she asked to spend a few minutes alone with the body. Subsequently it was found that the child's hair had been disarranged.

20. This account is based on an extant letter I wrote to my parents on January 3, 1956.

21. In a personal letter Irving Ross recently wrote: "I recall a conversation with Maud when she happened to smile beautifully. I said to her 'Maud, you have a lovely smile, but when you smile your eyes *don't* smile.' She looked reflective, and replied, 'Yes, that's what they tell me.' "

22. In a personal communication of January 12, 1983, the late Doris Langley Moore recalled: "The last time I saw Leo was in 1956. He said that he was Maud's executor and had destroyed a quantity of letters from her mother showing that Maud knew her brother was guilty though she always maintained his innocence when the matter could be mentioned at all. (It never was, by the time I met her.)"

23. At the farther end of the block stands the Episcopalian Church of the Holy Innocents, built in the late 1880s. When told of this in the summer of 1985, Manya laughed long and loud – and very probably for the last time in her life. She was hospitalized a few weeks later and died before the year's end.

"Maud was the least innocent person I ever knew," Manya said, as she explained her paroxysm of laughter. The suggestion that Maud and her brother may have regularly passed by that church on their way to school merely added to Manya's merriment.

Bibliography

Aldrich, Verna. "Two Years in the Life of a Great Dancer." Unpublished typescript, c. 1935.

Allan, Maud. *My Life and Dancing*. London: Everett & Co., 1908.

Asquith, Lady Cynthia. *Diaries, 1915–18*. London: Hutchinson & Co., 1943.

Bade, Peter. *La Femme Fatale*. New York: Mayflower Books, 1973.

Beecham, Sir Thomas. *A Mingled Chime*. New York: Putnam, 1943.

Boutelle, Grace Hodson. "Maud Allan and Her Dances." in *Pall Mall* magazine, 1909.

Busoni, Ferruccio. *Letters to His Wife*. London: Arnold & Co., 1938.

Chimenes, Myriam. "Les Vicissitudes de *Khamma*," in *Cahiers Debussy*, Nouvelle Série No. 2, 1978.

Cohen-Stratyner, Barbara Naomi. *Biographical Dictionary of Dance*. New York: Schirmer Books, 1982.

Colonna, Victoria, Duchess of Sermonetta. *The Sunset of a Golden Age*. London: Hutchinson, 1928.

Dent, Ivor. *Busoni*. London: Oxford University Press, 1936.

Devi, Goyatri, and Santha Ramer Rav. *A Princess Remembers*. New York: Lippincott, 1976.

Dijkstra, Bram. *Idols of Perversity: Fantasies of Feminine Evil in Fin-de-siècle Culture*. New York: Oxford University Press, 1986.

Duncan, Isadora. *My Life*. London: Victor Gollancz, 1930.

Durrant, Theo. [pseud.] *The Marble Forest*. New York: Alfred Knopf Inc., 1951.

Ensor, B.C.K. *England, 1870–1914. Oxford History of England*. Oxford: Oxford University Press, 1936.

Flitch, J. Crawford. *Modern Dancing and Dancers*. London: Grant Richards, 1912.

Godfrey, Sir Daniel Eyers. *Memories and Music: 35 Years of Conducting*. London: Hutchinson, 1924.

Hall, Elsie. *The Good Die Young*. Capetown: Angus & Co., 1960.

Hardinge, Lord. *My Indian Years*. London: John Murry, 1948.

Howe, Russell. *Mata Hari: The True Story*. New York: Dodd, Mead & Co., 1986.

Illustriertes Konversation Lexicon der Frau. 2 vols. Berlin: Martin Oldenburg, 1900.

Kettle, Michael. *Salome's Last Veil*. London: Cassell, 1977.

Kunel, Maurice. "Marcel Remy Critique et Conteur liégeois," in *La Vie Wallone*: Revue Mensuel Illustrée, 1923.

Langley-Moore, Doris. "Autobiography." Unpublished manuscript.

Lauder, Sir Harry. *Roamin' in the Gloamin'*. London: Hutchinson & Co., 1928.

Legg, L.G.W., ed. *Dictionary of National Biography, 1931–1940*. Oxford: Oxford University Press, 1949.

Lesure, François, ed. Debussy: *Lettres 1884–1918*. Paris: Hermann, 1980.

Lockspeiser, Edward. *Claude Debussy: His Life and Mind*. Cambridge: Cambridge University Press, 1978.

Mann, William. *Richard Strauss: A Critical Study of the Operas*. London: Cassell, 1964.

Marvell, Roger. *Ellen Terry*. London: Heinemann, 1964.

Maud Allan and Her Art. London: Gale & Polden, 1908.

Maudie. c. 1910. Republished by W.H. Allen & Co., London, 1985.

McDearmon, Lacey. "Maud Allan: The Public Records," in *Dance Chronicle 2*, No. 2. Marcel Dekker Inc., 1978.

Morella, Joe, and Edward Epstein. *Jane Wyman: A Biography*. New York: Delacourt, 1985.

Morgan-Powell, S. *Memories That Live*. Toronto: Macmillan, 1928.

Nesbitt, Edith. *Salome and the Head: A Modern Melodrama*. London: Alston Rivers, 1909. [Republished as *The House with No Address*. London: George Newnes, 1914.]

New York Times film reviews, 1913–1974, 11 vols. New York: Random House, 1970.

Niehaus, Max. *Isadora Duncan: Leben, Werk und Wirkung*. Wilhemshafen: Heinrich Shofens, 1979.

Orledge, Robert. *Debussy and the Theatre*. Cambridge: Cambridge University Press, 1979.

Padgette, Paul, ed. *The Dance Writings of Carl van Vechten*. New York: Dance Horizons, 1974 [Reprinted 1980.]

Pemberton-Billing, Noel. *Defence Against the Night Bomber*. London: Hale, 1941.

Ponsonby, Sir Frederick (Lord Sysonby). *Recollections of Three Reigns*. London: Eyre & Spottiswoode, 1951.

Read, Donald. *Edwardian England*. London: Harrap, 1972.

Rubinstein, Artur. *My Early Years*. New York: Knopf, 1973.

Schnabel, Artur. *My Life and Music*. London: Longmans, 1961.

Simmons, E. Romayne, and D. Holland. "Salome and the King," in *Dance Magazine*. November 1967.

Slonimsky, Nicholas, ed. *Baker's Dictionary of Musicians*, 7th edn. New York: Schirmer Books, 1970.

Stevenson, John. *British Society 1914–1945*. London: Penguin, 1984.

Stevenson, Robert Louis, *Works*, Tusitala edn. London: Heinemann, 1923.

Stewart, Robert and M.F.. *Adolph Sutro: A Biography*. San Francisco: Howell North, 1963.

Stucke-Schmidt, H.H. *Ferruccio Busoni*. London: Colder and Boyes, 1970.

Szigeti, Joseph. *With Strings Attached: Reminiscences and Reflections*. New York: Knopf, 1967.

Terry, Ellen. *Memoirs*. Westport, Connecticut: Greenwood Press, 1970.

Terry, Walter. *Miss Ruth: The More Living Life of Ruth St. Denis*, New York: Dodd, Mead & Co., 1984.

Thiemen, Ulrich, ed. *Allgemeines Lexikon der Bildenden Künstler*. Leipzig: E.A. Seemann, 1907–50.

Thompson, Paul. *The Edwardians*. London: Wiedenfeld & Nicolson, 1975.

Wilde, Oscar. *Salome*. London: Lane, 1912.

Wright, Frank Lloyd. *An Autobiography*. New York: Horizon Press, 1977.

Index